Love Unrehearsed

ALSO BY TINA REBER

Love Unscripted

Love Unrehearsed

THE LOVE SERIES, BOOK 2

Tina Reber

ATRIA PAPERBACK

New York • London • Toronto • Sydney • New Delhi

ATRIA PAPERBACK
A Division of Simon & Schuster, Inc.
1230 Avenue of the Americas
New York, NY 10020

First Atria Paperback edition January 2013

ATRIA PAPERBACK and colophon are trademarks of Simon & Schuster, Inc.

For information about special discounts for bulk purchases, please contact Simon & Schuster Special Sales at 1-866-506-1949 or business@simonandschuster.com.

The Simon & Schuster Speakers Bureau can bring authors to your live event.For more information or to book an event, contact the Simon & Schuster Speakers Bureau at 1-866-248-3049 or visit our website at www.simonspeakers.com.

Manufactured in the United States of America

10 9 8 7 6 5 4 3 2 1

Library of Congress Cataloging-in-Publication Data

Reber, Tina.
    Love unrehearsed : the love series, book 2 / Tina Reber. — 1st Atria paperback ed.
        p. cm.
1. Women—Rhode Island—Fiction. 2. Motion picture actors and actresses—Fiction. 3. Love stories. I. Title.
    PS3618.E35L66 2012
    813'.6—dc23

                                        2012037232

ISBN 978-1-4767-1897-2
ISBN 978-1-4767-1898-9 (ebook)

Mom,
This one is for you.
You were right.
There's not a day that goes by
that I don't miss you.
Thanks for all the wisdom.

Love
Unrehearsed

6:49 A.M.

―――――

H E'S MINE!" LAUREN Delaney screamed as she pushed through the crowd, violently shoving the innocent bystanders that separated us out of her way.

Her famous face, painted to perfection by a team of high-priced Hollywood makeup artists, was psychotically twisted like a woman possessed by the devil.

Instant terror crept through my veins and spread throughout my entire body just from the sight of her. My muscles locked down, instinctively preparing for an altercation that was long overdue.

Despite her hellish demeanor, the conniving bitch still managed to look glamorous in her shimmery silver gown and stilettos as she charged straight at me. The blockbuster-hit starlet obviously had no intentions to fight fair tonight. The crowd parted and it took a fraction of a second after that for me to notice the bright lights gleam off a long-bladed knife clenched in her fist.

My mind ordered my body to run.

A girl-fueled screaming match I could handle, although the verbal bitch-slapping I secretly desired to unleash on her would be best delivered in a more private setting. I could even deal with some hair pulling and feeble punches, if she left me no choice but to defend myself. Lord knows I wanted to rip her to shreds and dance on her grave for all the problems she had caused. But at this moment, I was in no way prepared to fend off a knife attack.

Thousands of flashes blinded me as the photographers swarmed like angry bees, stinging my eyes with each click. As I raised my hands to shield my face from the relentless paparazzi, Lauren plowed into my chest, knocking the air from my lungs and my feet out from under me. The back of my head slammed onto the red carpet, sending an instant message of overwhelming pain through my skull. Speckles of white blended in with a sea of crimson as I tried to refocus through the blur.

"Get off of me!" I screamed as she straddled me. I caught her by the wrist as she raised the blade, straining with her to keep from being stabbed.

"You really think you belong with him?" Lauren taunted as she pressed the blade closer to my face. Planted on top of me, she definitely had the upper hand and the advantage of leverage. The sting from the cold steel made me wince when the sharp tip scraped over my cheek.

"Are you prepared to die for him, bitch?"

Little did she know that when I thought I had lost Ryan, a vital part of me did die for him that day. But it was the risk that I took to become involved with a famous celebrity, knowing that there was the possibility of my heart being returned to me in pieces. Thankfully, the miracle of my reunion with Ryan breathed new life into me, and my fractured heart and soul were well on their way to full recovery. I knew I could survive anything now.

As I struggled with her, darkness loomed around the edges of my thoughts, sending a chill through my veins. Foreboding concrete block walls suddenly formed and surrounded us, filling me with dread as they encased us. Fear of impending death swelled inside me as we were being entombed.

I tried to scream but Lauren's fingers tightened around my windpipe, cutting off the flow of precious air.

A vision of my father, resembling a faint memory, ghosted and then solidified into view. His fury was palpable; he appeared ready to go on a murderous rampage. His angry fists slugged into the hazy figure of a lesser man.

His bloodied hands wrapped tightly around a young man's throat, mimicking the choke hold Lauren had on me. The two men continued to struggle, knocking things over in their wake. A large metal object flew from the wall and crashed heavy to the floor, causing a scream to tear from my throat as it missed my head by inches. My tears burned as they dripped uncontrollably from the corners of my eyes.

I strained through the haze to see the young man's face, but no matter how hard I tried to focus, his features remained obscured by long, straggly, jet-black hair.

Suddenly, for no explainable reason, I didn't care about myself anymore. Or my father. Or Lauren. I wanted to help the young man. I needed to help him, defend him. I had to stop my dad from killing him.

The guy looked right at me and spoke in an echoed rush as my dad continued to strangle him. "I love you, baby girl. I would *never* hurt you."

A tiny voice inside me knew that he spoke the truth. Still, my body shook, watching his white teeth turn an ominous red when he smiled at me.

"You will never touch her again!" my dad shouted.

A bloodied tear fell down the young man's cheek. And then another. I wanted to go to him and wrap my arms around him because that's what you do when people are sad. Big teddy-bear hugs always make the tears stop.

Lauren's clenched hand shook my neck, instantly reclaiming my attention. With a snarl, she raised the blade high in the air.

As I watched the blade come down, reluctantly resigned to letting Death take me and the darkness claim me, one last word echoed through the air.

"Cut."

CHAPTER 1

Eye-Opening

WHAT THE HELL?" Ryan's head flew off his pillow, roused from his deep sleep when I screamed.

I sat up and kicked the blankets away with my feet, panicking to untangle myself as I rubbed the phantom pain stabbing fire into my chest. *Holy shit. Holy shit. Damn, that felt so real. Okay, calm down. It was just a dream. Just a dream.*

Ryan leaned up on the mound of hotel pillows. I could see him scanning the room, looking for some sort of danger. "Tar, are you all right?" His hand grasped my thigh as he shifted his body closer. "Taryn, what happened?"

I wanted to answer him but I was momentarily stunned and completely incapable of coherent speech, still caught in a freaked-out haze between nightmare and reality. I tried to say something, I really did, but all that came from my mouth were raspy, stuttered breaths.

Fortunately it didn't take me long to realize where I was, for it had been less than twenty-four hours ago when I boarded a plane and departed Providence, Rhode Island. Now I was shaken and panting for air in a luxurious hotel suite in Los Angeles, ripped from sleep by my own ridiculous thoughts.

Ryan tugged my chin; his voice was frantically curt. "Look at me." His hand brushed my long hair out of my eyes. "Taryn, are you okay? Tar? Answer me."

I grasped his arm and managed a weak nod. "Yeah, I'm okay. I'm . . . I'm so sorry I woke you."

"Don't worry about me," he insisted, curling up closer.

If his throbbing pulse in my hand was any indication, I'd say I had scared the shit out of him, too.

He smoothed my hair back, wrapping a few strands behind my ear. "What happened? You have a nightmare?"

I nodded, trying to save myself from having to explain.

"Jeez, baby." Ryan sighed. "Come here. Try to relax." He coaxed me back down to his chest and tugged the sheet and blankets over us again.

His skin was warm and the hand rubbing my back was so comforting that I felt my erratic breathing starting to calm.

"It's okay. I've got you." He kissed the top of my head, resting his lips there as he hugged me.

There, in his arms, I felt completely safe. But out there in the public eye, things were out of his control. I had learned early on in this relationship that the terror factor grew exponentially when you're a celebrity. And *dating* a famous celebrity was no different—actually it was worse when delusional fans became obsessively jealous, insanely possessive, and wanted you out of the way. Even normal, sane people lost their minds when it came to celebrities. Combine that with a world full of crazy people and the threats became very real.

I was thankful that Ryan was insistent about sending Mike into LAX yesterday to escort us safely out of the airport, or else the paparazzi would have eaten me alive. Ryan's public proposal painted a new, fat target on my back. It was one thing to be the local "fling" he had while on location; it was completely another once rumors started circulating that he actually put a ring on my finger.

How the hell they recognized me among all the other people hurrying through the airport was mind-boggling. Trying to get through the gauntlet of paparazzi in LAX was akin to sidestepping land mines. While I was very grateful for Mike's protection, I still think the photographers only noticed me because they recognized Ryan's bodyguard first.

Heck, every public picture taken of Ryan lately had Mike in it somewhere—holding back fans, watching the invisible perimeter around Ryan with the expertise of a trained hunter. Between his gorgeous body and killer smile, Mike Murphy was becoming as famous as Ryan Christensen.

"You want to tell me what the hell scared you awake like that?"

Aw shit. I shrugged, not willing to ruin my first morning finally back in his arms by getting into some stupid nonsense. "It was just . . . I don't even remember it anymore. I'll be all right."

Ryan huffed softly as I waited for him to call me out on my little lie. "Did you dream about her again?"

I tensed, not exactly sure which "her" he was referring to.

When I didn't respond, he tightened his arms. "She's in jail, Taryn. She can't hurt us anymore."

Well, at least he had the psycho-bitch part right. Shame he picked the wrong one. Angelica, our incarcerated stalker, wasn't the one who had haunted my thoughts but I wasn't about to set him straight.

"I know. It was just a stupid dream."

"Why don't you tell me about it? You'll feel better if you get it out."

Part of me wanted to share, but what the heck would I tell him? *I dreamt about your über-famous, crazy-bitch ex-girlfriend trying to kill me? Oh, and if that isn't bad enough, sometimes when I dream about my dead father, he's bloody and choking the life out of some teenager with pitch-black hair?* Some things are better left unsaid.

Ryan let out a lengthy yawn and stretched his legs, poking me in the rear end with the one part of his anatomy that was already wide awake. His two-day-old beard felt wonderful, scratching my back when he rubbed up on me. With a kiss on my shoulder, he said, "All right. I won't ask anymore. You talk about it only if you want to. What time is it?"

I glanced at the clock on the bedside table. "It's almost seven."

Cool air brushed my naked body as he rolled out from underneath the warm covers.

I tried to banish the last remnants of my nightmare from my memory, but certain parts were playing over and over again like a bad video stuck on repeat. It wasn't the first time I dreamed about the boy with black hair and bloody red teeth. He had made repeat appearances in my dreams for as long as I could remember, always rehashing the same scene where my father is trying to kill him.

The part where Lauren Delaney factored in was a new and very unwelcome addition to the nightmare.

Bitch.

How pleased she must have been with herself when she nearly succeeded in breaking up my relationship with Ryan. Thankfully, she failed. My disgust for her intensified. I couldn't let her get to me like this, not even in my dreams.

I shook my head as if it would help clear away the horrible visions. I had to own up to the fact that it was only my tormented thoughts haunting me; it's not like Lauren ever physically assaulted me in real life. No, her assault was much stealthier, leaving a trail of false evidence to lead me to believe she and Ryan had rekindled their previous relationship. My heart still ached thinking that just five short days ago I truly believed Ryan's parents had shown up to move him out of my apartment.

I glanced at my new diamond engagement ring—Ryan's promise of a future and total commitment to me. His intention of "*Forever*" was etched inside the band.

I vowed to myself that I'd do everything within my power to prove her and everyone else wrong. Ryan Christensen was the best thing that had ever happened to me. His love was like an invisible blanket that I had the privilege of wearing every day. But if our relationship was going to survive the test of time, I had to start handling things differently.

My eyes followed Ryan in the dim light as he shuffled across the carpeting. His muscular arm flexed, accentuating his biceps, when he used his hand to comb his tawny, disheveled hair back. My eyes drifted from his yawning mouth, down the contours of his hard, naked body, to his other part that was still semi-erect.

All of the pictures ever taken of this man and all the posters with his likeness on them could never do the real thing justice. All six feet, two inches of his cut, buff, and tight movie star body was one hell of a mental and visual distraction.

I never knew I could love a man so much and have it returned to me in spades. Even when things were at their worst, he didn't give up on me. That alone said it all. A small smile formed on my lips as I thought about eating him for breakfast.

"What?" he asked with a sleepy smirk. Ryan crawled back into bed, snuggling around me.

I secretly hoped that after my rude awakening he'd be able to fall back asleep, considering that it was well after midnight when his family and our friends finally left our suite last night. Ryan had arranged for Marie and Gary and Pete and Tammy to come to L.A. with me, another secret surprise that I didn't know about. I gave Marie a long lecture on the plane about how much I hate secrets, no matter how much he wanted me to be surprised. Over these last few weeks, she and Ryan had become thicker than thieves.

I spotted the opened bottle of champagne left out on the nightstand. My mind instantly recalled how he had tortured my breasts with the edge of the ice-cold bottle, making them painfully alert. How I got even with him, hiding a piece of ice from the bucket in my mouth and then torturing his nipples with the same attention.

"I'm all sticky," Ryan muttered softly.

"I was just thinking about that. Sticky, but oh so worth it."

He growled in my ear. "I do believe we'll have to do that again. Maybe try extra-sticky honey next time?"

"Or melted chocolate."

He swept my hair to the side and started kissing and biting my neck. "Definitely. Oh, there are so many things I can drizzle and lick off your body. The possibilities are endless."

His teasing tickle caused a bone-jolting shiver to blast through my body.

His eyes quickly leveled on mine, then he grimaced at me. "You know I'd never let anything happen to you. You know that, right?"

He must have misread my reaction. I knew he meant well but some things were out of his power—that is, unless some guy was trying to talk to me. Then the protective, jealous boyfriend reared its head and jumped right into action. "I know."

Ryan squeezed my arm. "Okay. Maybe we should get in the shower. I want to have breakfast with everyone before I have to leave." He buried his face in my neck. "Fuck, this is going to be a long day."

The thought of having to move from this entangled position made me groan. I nuzzled in deeper, holding his head to my shoulder. "I'm too comfortable. Can't we just stay stuck to each other instead?"

Ryan growled, palming my ass. "Oh, that is *so* tempting."

I let out a small sigh, knowing that the incredibly famous Ryan Christensen had an insane schedule ahead of him, jam-packed with one appearance or interview after another promoting the premiere of his latest movie, *Reparation*. He'd only been in L.A. one day more than me and he'd already been on several magazine shoots and a photo call.

My pulse skipped, thinking that in a few short days we'd be on numerous planes destined for places like London and Paris—cities I'd never been to before. But as enticing as touring Europe sounded, I was perfectly content wrapped in his arms and going nowhere.

"Call in sick," I whispered. "You lie and I'll swear to it."

His chest shook with laughter. "David, cancel everything. My gorgeous fiancée is glued to my body and I have absolutely no desire to put on pants—ever."

I couldn't help but laugh with him.

Ryan coiled a long strand of my hair around his finger. "Believe me, if my schedule wasn't so tight, we'd be naked for days, weeks even."

I dug my fingertips into his tight rear end, lost in the sensations of his warmth, his strength. "Then maybe we'll have to block off a month or two of downtime? I think after all of the stress we deserve it."

Ryan pressed me back into my pillow. "Let's make that a priority." His glorious smile suddenly faded, turning from light and playful to serious. "You are the most important thing to me, Taryn. I hope you know that." His thumb stroked my cheek repeatedly. His eyes grew tender, then repentant. "I know the last few weeks have been rough."

Rough? That was putting it mildly. Testing my will to survive massive heartache would be more accurate. I moved my left arm out from between us, rotating my wrist. It was starting to ache from being bent awkwardly underneath him. Sometimes it still felt like I was wearing a cast, even though it had been off for almost two weeks.

Ryan grimaced. "Does it still hurt?"

I shrugged. "It gets sore. Stiff, sometimes."

His eyes narrowed as he worked on some other thought. His hand softly stroked down my stomach. "Have you . . . have you seen the OB doctor since . . . ?"

I nodded. "Last week. Marie went with me."

Ryan's jaw tightened and flexed. He appeared upset about it.

"What?"

"Why didn't you tell me?"

I couldn't believe he was asking me this—with a clipped tone to boot. Last week he was wrapping filming on *Thousand Miles* and apparently still contemplating his feelings for me because we sure as hell weren't having heartfelt conversations.

He nudged me for a response.

I met his eyes. "What kind of answer are you looking for?" I asked softly. "We were barely speaking to each other last week, Ryan. I didn't think you cared anymore. I was waiting for you to tell me we were over."

He grasped my left hand, kissing my fingers around my sparkly new engagement ring. "Oh, sweetheart . . . I'm sorry. I know I really fucked up. Things were just . . . and I was mad. *Shit.*"

I brushed my hand on his cheek. "We both did."

Ryan frowned, leaning his face into my hand. "Please tell me now. What did the doctor have to say?"

"She said everything is back to normal. She renewed my birth control. I go back in a year unless I have issues."

Apparently he was holding his breath because it all came out of him at once. "Okay. Good." He scrubbed his forehead with his hand, pushing his bangs up. "Man, I don't even know how to go about making this up to you. I know I hurt you. Believe me, I know. But I'm going to spend the rest of my life making it up to you. I promise."

I swallowed hard, knowing my actions and knee-jerk reactions were what caused us to almost break up. "It's my fault. I'm sorry for losing faith in you."

His shoulder rose and fell as he gazed at me. "I think we both learned a hard lesson—one that we can hopefully move on from and be stronger from."

I nodded, done with the heaviness. "I like the idea of going away somewhere. Just the two of us."

That perked him up and with that, his tense face softened. "Let's take a look at my calendar and schedule some vacations. We can go anywhere you want, baby. Anywhere."

With a tilt of his head, his lips found mine. So tender, so loving. We lay there for a long time, naked bodies entwined, eyes gazing into one another, sharing whispered "I love yous."

God he was beautiful, all naked with his broad shoulders and muscular arms wrapped around me. His hair messed from peaceful sleep.

As much as I try to never think about it, I couldn't help but feel a bit smug, knowing most of his fans would willingly give up a limb, a family member, and a kidney to see him this exposed. *Sorry, ladies. Hate to break it to ya, but he's all mine.*

Hungry for him, I trailed open-mouth kisses down his hard body, barraging him with a mixture of sensations; scoring fingernails over his pecs, soft bites over the muscular swells of his stomach, the soothing wetness of my roaming tongue.

Ryan's eyes scrunched together and he melted back into the pillows when I slipped my wet lips and tongue around the length of him. Our time together was limited so I was going to make every second count.

"Oh, *Tar*," he whispered, tensing from the onslaught. His fingers coiled in my hair, tugging, pressing, guiding me up and down as I pleasured him. Damn, that was such a turn-on for me. I raked my hand up his chest and swallowed him deeper, drawing out surrendering moans from his throat, watching him watch me.

I had just begun to get creative with my hand and mouth when the shrill of his cell phone rudely interrupted our moment.

"Grrr . . . what?" he growled, refocusing his attention to the nightstand. "Who the hell is bothering me *now?*"

I laughed to myself, immediately thinking of the one person who has a knack for calling at the worst possible times. She must have a sixth sense for knowing the exact moment when her son is about to get laid.

"Ignore it," I murmured, taking him as deep as I could go without choking. I wanted him to relax and forget about his constantly ringing cell phone, his hellacious schedule, and gauging by his purrs and the fact that he just moaned "*oh God*" again, hopefully in a few more minutes he'd forget how to spell his own name. I hoped that the caller would give up soon; the continuous ringing was annoying.

Two minutes later, his phone chimed again. "You've got to be kidding me," Ryan groaned. He twisted to grab his phone but it was several inches out of his reach.

"Mmm-mmm." I held him firm, pinning his hips back down.

"Just let me turn it off."

"No. You'll check messages. Leave it."

"No, I woh—oh, fuh . . . ," he hissed, sucking in a breath between his teeth. "Damn that feels good. Mmm . . ."

Yeah, I knew you'd like that.

His hands immediately returned to touching me, finger-combing my long hair out of the way while I tried not to mentally count the number of times his phone rang.

Ryan tugged my chin, huskily growling, "Stop, baby. Stop. I don't want to come yet." The moment I looked up at him, his hand swept my neck and he pulled me up to his mouth. "Come here."

I wanted to drink him into every cell in my body. Take him to new places where pleasure and love were as necessary as oxygen. I sucked his top lip into my mouth, wanting, needing.

He moaned in my mouth and wrapped an arm around me. With one fast swoop, he effortlessly flipped me over, hovering on top of me.

Long fingers brushed fire up my thigh and slipped deep into me while he feasted like a starving babe on my breast. Desire to feel more than his slick fingers inside me had me tingling, but all those wonderful, erotic thoughts flew from my mind the moment his freaking cell phone rang again.

"Son of a . . ." He rolled away from me and slapped his hand down on the intrusion. In all honesty, at this point I was curious to know who the hell was being so damn persistent.

He looked at the display and scoffed, answering my questioning stare. "It was Marla. All four times. I'm turning it off now."

No sooner did he say those words than the landline telephone on the table in our suite shrilled loudly. That got one very angry, rock-hard, and unsated man out of his bed. Someone was about to get holy hell unleashed on them.

"What?" he said with venomous bite, letting whoever was calling know his exact feelings about being disturbed. "I *was* trying to sleep. *Now?* Why?" His jaw clenched. "This can't wait an hour? No. I just woke up. Fine. Give me ten minutes," he muttered. "I *said* ten minutes."

Ryan grabbed his clothing off the floor and cursed. I hadn't seen him this pissed in a long time. "Tar, you need to get up and get dressed."

"Why? What's going on?"

Ryan looked at me warily as he pulled his jeans up over his naked body.

I started to worry. "Hey. What's going on?"

His lips puckered with disgust. "Marla and David are on their way up."

I groaned to myself. Wouldn't be the first time his publicist and manager disrupted his life at an inopportune time. To say they were overbearing was an understatement. He jostled the clothing around in his open suitcase with frustration, sparking my next question.

"Why?"

He rubbed his forehead. "Photos were leaked," he mumbled.

A wave of fright pricked at my nerves. "What photos?"

I watched the back of his head sway. "People in the bar took shots of me proposing to you on Saturday," he muttered over his shoulder. "Pictures and videos are all over the Internet now."

I drew in a deep breath as his sudden anger about this blindsided me. Ryan was so riled he had trouble picking two T-shirts apart. *You proposed publicly. I figured a few bar patrons would capture pictures on their cells. What did you expect?*

"So? How bad is it?"

Ryan signed heavily before looking back at me with apologetic eyes. "Tar, you know how it is. Pictures were on some fan sites and Twitter that night already."

I stared at my feet, trying to understand. This was not bad news, or was it?

"Taryn." Ryan interrupted my thoughts, tossing my jeans over to me.

I let out another sigh as I shoved my right foot into the pants leg. "Why didn't you tell me about this being a problem sooner?"

"'Tar—you know why," Ryan muttered as he slipped a T-shirt over his head. "Let's not go there, okay, babe? Please?"

"But . . ."

He appeared resigned but tense. "But what? This is not stuff I want you worrying about, that's why."

I shook my head. "That's not . . . I'm just a bit confused. Yesterday when Mike collected us at the airport, he warned me that the paparazzi were going to swarm and I asked him if I should hide my ring. When he called you to ask, you said to tell me 'never fucking ever take your ring off.' So if it didn't matter for me to be seen with this ring and to have people know we're engaged, why does it matter today?"

Ryan narrowed his eyes. "And did you?"

I was momentarily stunned, knowing that that brusque tone wasn't really meant for me. "Did I what? Keep your ring on or get photographed wearing it?"

He shrugged. "Either. Both."

I supposed this was information he needed before being bombarded. "Yes, I kept your ring on, as it will *never* leave my finger, but no, I did not allow the repugnant thieves to make their living off of our happiness. I kept my hand tucked in my pocket."

He nodded once. "Yeah, well, keep that in mind," he said on his way to answer the door.

Marla Sullivan, Ryan's icy publicist, greeted me with a half smile, half snarl as she charged into the living room of our suite. Even though it was early in the morning, she was already dressed in a crisp designer business suit. Her short black hair was equally as tailored. An oversized black bag dangled from her red, pointy fingernails.

"Sit," she ordered.

Ryan glared at her for a moment and then pulled out a chair at the large dining table.

"*Weekly Reporter, CV Magazine* . . ." she announced in a scathing tone, dropping printed sheets of paper on the table in front of him.

"You're on all of them. I suppose this is why you've been avoiding my phone calls for the last four days."

Ryan barely glanced at them. He slumped back in his chair and started to rub his forehead, pushing the paper away with his other hand. "I've seen them already. So what."

I edged my body closer. That's when I saw for the very first time the grainy, dark pictures of Ryan standing on top of a very familiar round oak table and another dark picture of him kneeling in front of me. Candid shots from Saturday night when he proposed to me publicly in my pub were now plastered all over the tabloids. My heart sank in my chest from their blatant exploitation.

"'So what'? Ryan, you were standing on a table in the middle of a bar! What were you thinking?" She scolded him like he was a child.

Ryan rested his elbows on his knees while he bowed his head, refraining from giving her an answer.

"Well, this certainly counters the shots they got of her standing in the middle of the street in Miami two weeks ago," she said callously, nodding her pointy chin in my direction.

Leave it to Marla to remind me of the huge idiot I made of myself when I stood in the downpour staring at what I thought was Ryan cheating on me with his co-star, Lauren Delaney, when in fact they were still on location filming.

Ryan straightened and scoffed harshly at her comment. "Don't even go there," he warned through his teeth, giving her an angry glare.

It didn't matter that Kyle Trent, my former bodyguard, and Lauren Delaney, Ryan's co-star and former girlfriend, conspired together, forming an awkward alliance to insidiously destroy our relationship. The only thing that the press was concerned about was the photographic evidence of my mental breakdown from Ryan's supposed infidelity. CAUGHT CHEATING! all of the headlines announced.

And now, all of the headlines flashed ENGAGED!

Two weeks of ups and downs and aggravating media scrutiny—*Ryan and Lauren are together, Taryn catches Ryan cheating, Ryan and*

Taryn call it quits, Ryan's secret flight to Seaport, Rhode Island—were now topped off with new photographic evidence that he actually climbed on top of a table.

"Ryan, we've had these discussions. Do you want to destroy your career?" She waved her hand in my direction. It was apparent that she meant *I* was the one destroying his career.

"No! Of course not!" he bellowed.

Marla huffed and poked her finger on one of the papers. "Well, I told you to keep this inane decision of yours private. So much for that."

I gasped in shock. *Inane?* Is she really standing there lecturing my fiancé and implying with the tact of a wrecking ball that his decision to propose to me was stupid and asinine?

"Do you think you could have at least warned me first that you actually went through with it?" She slapped one of the sheets down on the table in front of him. "I come back from Monterey to be completely blindsided by this, too?"

I rolled my eyes at her comment and her overdramatic little meltdown. Her shiny, black patent leather high heels captured my attention. I surmised that her shoes must match the color of her heart today.

"I got caught up in the moment. It's my business," Ryan grumbled, taking the submissive position to this domineering bitch. It was the first time I saw him bow down to anyone. This was not the "fuck you, no bullshit" posture he took with the rest of the world. This woman was making him fold like a house of cards in the wind. I pressed my lips into a hard line, holding my tongue.

"Caught up in the moment?" Marla questioned incredulously. "Is that your *excuse?*"

Ryan shot her a dirty look and sprang up from his chair when there was another knock at the door. "David," he said flatly, his eyes refusing to look up when his manager came into our suite. David Ardazzio slowly shook his head at Ryan, showing his displeasure at being summoned.

My heart rate picked up as I processed David's overall demeanor. Now both of Ryan's "handlers" were here to gang up on him. The Witch and the little Slime Ball, here to tag-team him and beat him further into submission.

I'll be damned before I let them make him feel like crap for proposing to me. I felt my hands curl into tight fists, bracing for what appeared to be a pending battle.

"David," Marla greeted Ryan's manager. "Well," she huffed, annoyed, "let's talk about damage control." She uncrossed her bony arms and picked up a few of the printouts, tossing them in David's direction. "There are two videos of him singing on YouTube as well."

"I know," David admitted. "You really know how to stir up a media shitstorm, my friend," he chuckled lightly as he feigned looking at the photos. I'm sure by this point he was intimately familiar with them.

Ryan was too busy stewing and staring at the floor to respond. It took a split second after that for David to redirect his glare at me. This was not the first time Ryan's manager had issues with me and it was starting to become apparent that we all might never get along. This was so *not* good.

"I don't know why you're making such a big deal about this," Ryan bit out before casting his glance my way.

"I don't, either," I added, giving him my support. If this was how they handled happy news, I'd hate to see how they handled a majorly bad shitstorm.

David sort of shrugged it off. "It's not really, Taryn. What you have to understand is that Ryan's career is potentially riding on how well *Reparation* premieres. This is his first major motion picture lead role outside of the *Seaside* franchise, and the critics, the major studios—everyone is waiting to see if he can carry a film on his own. This premiere is big, and it's all about image control, that's all. This is nothing new, Ryan."

Image control?

I glanced back at one of the printouts. "I'm sorry, but I still don't understand. What does our engagement have to do with any of that?"

Marla's head jerked in my direction. "Well I'm sure you'll start to care when he's offered subpar roles and the money isn't there anymore."

I could have done without her "isn't it obvious or are you too stupid to realize it" glare.

Ryan's fist hit the table. "Do *not* talk to her like that," he warned, pointing his finger at her.

"*Marla*—" David said, attempting to quell her temper.

"I couldn't care less how much money he has. Despite what you think, my feelings for him aren't tied to his fame or his fortune. Are you trying to say he won't get offers and people will stop coming to see his movies because we're engaged?"

I noticed Ryan's lips twitch with that.

"No, no." David tried to dismiss my assumption, halting me with his hand. "Aaron and I have been—"

Marla interrupted. "Ryan's career is only beginning to blossom. His future prospects all stem from the decisions he makes now. Do you want to see him fail?"

My spine stiffened further. "Of course not!"

"Jesus Christ," Ryan groaned, but she ignored him.

Marla continued to address me. "Then you'll both need to accept that the public's perception of his status and behavior greatly affects his marketing viability. He needs to remain low-key and professional at all times—without scandal or opportunistic individuals taking advantage of his good fortune."

Her last words felt like a slap. "Are you insinuating that I'm one of them?"

Ryan sat up, arching into defense mode, but stopped when it looked like Marla was going to apologize. For a moment, I thought she would attempt to be civil.

"In this business, negative impressions can linger for years, in some cases having irreparable consequences on an actor's career. Ryan is here to do press for his movie, not to be inundated with questions about his ridiculous display. His moment of indiscretion is now hugely overshadowing the premiere of *Reparation*. You forget that he is being paid by very influential people to promote the movie, not to explain why he climbed on a table," Marla informed us harshly.

She turned her glare on Ryan. "How many times do I have to remind you that you do not want this kind of press?"

"I know what my responsibilities are!" Ryan snapped angrily.

"Then you should have controlled yourself and realized that standing up on a table in the middle of a crowded bar was a bad idea!" she zinged him back.

Ryan stretched his fingers as if he desired to choke her. "Do you *really* want to keep pushing me on this? I get the point."

"Well, someone's got to keep on top of your behav—"

Gaaaaahhhh!

"Enough! Just stop it!" I broke in. "I don't care who you are. You will not take one of our most precious memories and turn it into something he should feel guilty for doing. I will *not* allow it."

I stood behind Ryan and rested my hands on his shoulders, actually fearing that if I let go of him, table, chairs, and bodies would go flying. "So he stood on a table and asked me to marry him. So what? You're making it sound like he was high on dope and clubbing baby seals when he did it. Surely this, this *disclosure*, can be turned into something positive."

Marla stared blankly at me, apparently surprised that I had the guts to speak again.

She turned her attention back to him. "Ryan, perhaps it would be better if David and I continued this meeting with you privately to discuss our action plan. I'm sure your Taryn has other things she needs to attend to."

"Excuse me?" I glared at her, completely astonished that she would even think to remove me from the discussion. This bitch had some nerve.

Ryan pulled out the chair next to him, startling me. "I don't think so. Anything you have to say to me you can say in front of my fiancée, too. This affects her life just as much as it does mine. *I'll* decide what doesn't require her involvement, not you. Got it?"

Marla stared at him blankly.

"Got it?" he said with punctuated force.

Marla breathed out her unhappiness and righted herself in the chair. "Of course."

Relieved, I took a seat and patted his thigh in private to thank him. He covered my diamond-clad hand with his own.

"Now then . . . we will inform all of the interviewers at the press junket today that questions about your personal life are off-limits. Someone will be present at all times to ensure that those questions are averted so as not to detract from the *Reparation* and future *Seaside* premieres. We'll put the same stipulations on all of your appearances throughout the junket as well."

Ryan looked like someone had strapped him in the electric chair and stood by with a heartless hand itching to flip the switch. I could tell his thoughts were mulling over the best ways to escape. I rubbed my fingertips over his back, trying to ease his tension.

"You will have to handle yourself appropriately during your appearance on Jimmy Collins tonight and with Nigel Allen on *Night Life* tomorrow. You should know by now how to avoid those types of questions," Marla said. "But just in case I'm wrong . . ."

While she was on her soapbox, I picked up one of the tabloid magazine prints, eyeing the supposedly scandalous front cover.

"We'll handle your discussion topics at the pre-interviews . . . ," she continued to drone.

I tried to listen intently to her aggravating words, but my mind was suddenly very preoccupied, thinking of ways to choke the ever-loving shit out of her so she'd shut the hell up.

To me, the tabloid cover didn't look bad at all, compared to some of the other reports that were previously printed about Ryan and me. Even the story byline wasn't too hateful. Eyewitnesses had reported that "Ryan sang a beautiful song while playing his guitar before professing his love for local business owner Taryn Mitchell." What's so scandalous about that?

It was times like these I wished some of those inhuman special powers portrayed on film could actually happen, like being able to cut off the flow of oxygen to her lungs with my mind, or hurling her across the room just by imagining it. Evil thoughts, I know, but this woman brought them out in me. Especially when she was smacking her lips together, lecturing my future husband on the proper behaviors of A-list celebrities and dictating the cryptic responses he should give today to avoid talking about our relationship in public.

Ryan and I both jumped slightly when there was another knock on our hotel door. I was thankful for any diversion that veered my mind off strangling the shit out of her.

Through the peephole, I instantly recognized the young, long-haired blonde standing outside our room, having seen her glowing face and friendly smile the last two days when we had numerous chats over our computers. She had a large messenger bag slung over her shoulder and a thick manila envelope pressed to her chest.

"Hey. Come on in," I said warmly through the opened door. With all the reprimanding that was happening in our room, I had forgotten that Trish, Marla's assistant, was coming to help me get dressed properly for the premiere.

The second Trish stepped into the room it seemed like the air changed and it was easier to breathe in here.

"It's nice to finally meet you in person."

"You, too." Trish bounced excitedly and hugged me like we were reunited college friends. "Even though I sort of feel like I know you already." I noticed Trish's eyes glance past me into the room where her boss sat, still lecturing Ryan. "How's it going so far?"

I shrugged. What could I tell her? That I thought her boss was a royal bitch whom I wanted to toss off the roof of this hotel?

"Did she say anything about doing a press release on your engagement?" she whispered.

"What is your problem? Why are you being like this?" Ryan asked Marla harshly, trying to keep his voice down.

I shook my head at Trish. "No. Not a word."

Marla made her signature throaty scoff, the one that sounds like a cat starting to choke up a hairball. "You're starting to fly on a whim while the rest of us are left to clean up the mess."

"What mess?" Ryan asked. "I got engaged. Big deal. I'm not the first actor to do this. I just don't understand why you hate her so much."

Trish frowned as Marla made no attempt to hush her reply. "Ryan, I don't hate her. And I certainly won't *hate* the next girl, either. You're young. You have the world at your disposal. It's my job to guide the perception that the world has of you, so those doors continue to open for you."

Ryan raised his voice. "I'm telling you right now, there won't be another one. Get that straight."

Trish and I walked back into the dining room. She carefully placed the stuffed package on the table next to Marla's arm, almost bowing as she set it down.

"Are these the new press packets?"

"Yes. I just came from the printer," Trish said mildly.

Marla opened the envelope, taking her good old time scrutinizing the contents. She was just starting to complain about a mistake she found when Ryan interrupted.

"Are we done?"

I blinked in Ryan's direction. Gone was the normal, even-tempered man I loved. In his place was a seething time bomb ready to explode. My heart pinched with fright hearing the menace in his tone.

Marla pretended not to hear him. How could she not?

"David, we need to schedule a meeting with Len Bainbridge. We've already received offers for exclusives on this. Celeste Crawfield left me ten voice mails; *Glam* wants first dibs for a cover story. Huge offers are starting to pour in and we both know how messy engagement- and wedding-generated earnings can be. Len should start drafting a prenup immediately for Ryan before his fortune is compromised and—"

Ryan stood up; his chair crashed to the floor, jolting everyone's attention. "That's it. We're done here. Get out. *Everyone.*" He grabbed the papers on the table and flung them at her. "And take this bullshit with you."

She sighed like an unhappy, controlling mother. "You know things need to be formed legally, Ryan."

"I don't care!" Ryan yelled. "It's none of your goddamned business!"

David was indifferent to Ryan's order, taking the time to adjust his sleeves and peer at his watch. Apparently movie star temper tantrums were old hat. "I'll call the lawyers and get things rolling. Your car will be here at nine and—"

"I said get out! *Out!*" Ryan shouted at him, the veins in his neck cording from the strain. He nodded his chin at the door. I had never seen him this angry. If he'd yelled like that at me, I'd be running for the elevator.

Five seconds later, our bedroom door slammed shut.

I found Ryan leaning with both palms flat on the glass window, his head hanging between his arms, panting as if he'd just been released from a caged death match. I feared that even whispering his name might cause him to detonate.

I sat on the edge of our crumpled bed in silence, giving him ample time and space to calm himself while I mulled over how the news of our happiness had just turned into a twenty-minute patronizing lecture.

What should have been hugs and champagne and congratulations with smiles and pats on the back was the exact opposite—anger and heartless animosity mixed with ugly accusations and assumptions from the team he had managing his life.

Pressed against the glass like that, I wondered if Ryan was regretting his actions now.

I feared sooner or later, one of us would.

Not willing to take such chances, I stepped to his side. Ryan looked at me warily before clutching me to his chest.

Now was not the time for regret.

CHAPTER 2

Deviation

RYAN HAD JUST started eating his omelet when his little weasel manager, David Ardazzio, walked into the hotel restaurant to collect him. The hand that was tenderly stroking my thigh in private under the table suddenly stilled and tightened.

David, of course, had to adjust his wristwatch; his way of saying "it's time to go" without appearing like a dickhead, I suppose. My eyes narrowed, giving him my own silent message in return, one that boldly said, "Mess with my man anymore today and I will dig my fork into your chest to find out if there really is a heart in there." Hah! My first twenty-four hours in L.A. and I was already becoming cynical and hostile.

Considering I had just spent the better part of the last forty minutes trying to get Ryan to lose the murderous scowl on his face—five of said minutes were spent just holding him in the shower so we could apologize for loving each other—my hostility was justified. I'd like to think that precious water supply could have been used for much better purposes, like to wash off the sweat from our interrupted wake-up sex or even better, initiate a second session of incredibly hot shower sex after incredibly hot wake-up sex.

But no, sadly, we used the water to bathe, mask our disappointments, and attempt to exorcise unwanted demons from our thoughts.

The only reason Ryan was appearing somewhat lively and animated now was that his mother was sitting across the table from us, all shiny and happily oblivious. We both knew that all it would take was one slip and she would press for details. Lord knows neither of us was in the mood to be interrogated by Mom.

Ryan had enough on his plate. His day was packed with one-on-one interviews, a photo call, an open-panel Q&A with the press, and at the end a TV appearance on *The Jimmy Collins Show*. Taping was scheduled for 5 P.M.

"Ready to go, Ry?" Mike Murphy, Ryan's personal bodyguard, asked as he slowly rose from the large dining table. Mike took extra care wiping his lips on his linen napkin and then ran his hand through his short, dark brown hair, stalling while Ryan quickly shoveled more breakfast into his mouth.

I was so relieved that Mike had stuck with Ryan all these months. He was the only person within Ryan's entourage that I truly trusted. He was there with us in the hospital when I lost the baby. He shielded us diligently when we dealt with our psycho-fan stalker and was by our sides so many other times that I lost count.

Ryan considered Mike to be one of his best friends and I regarded him as our own personal savior.

I glanced across the table and noticed Marie trying not to be conspicuous with her gaze, but I knew better. She and I had been best friends for so long; I knew the look she wore when she was stripping a man naked in her brain. And right now she had the former marine flat on his back on top of this table begging for her mercy. Can't say I blame her. Mike was thirty-two, very single, six foot three with an incredibly buff body, and to say he was merely good-looking would be insulting.

"Gotta go, babe," Ryan said in my ear before he kissed me quickly, snapping me out of my internal speculations. He patted his jeans pocket. "You need anything, just call me. I have my phone set on vibrate. Mike gave you all of the security details for the show tonight and you have our credit card and stuff if you need it. Have fun shopping. Whatever you ladies want, get. All right?"

"Got it."

He gave me a hard, stern stare. "I mean it."

That was his way of reminding me to get over my issues with spending his money.

"I know you do. I understand."

"Good."

He leaned in to give me another kiss.

"Get something sexy to wear for me," he growled on my lips. "A few somethings, okay?"

I was glad to know thoughts of me in lacy undergarments were helping him step out of his funk. "You bet. Slutty towels in every color just for you." Just as the words left my lips, I noticed one of the waitstaff take our picture on a cell phone.

Ryan tipped my chin and gave me a renewed smile, grinning at our private joke, oblivious to the girl stealing a piece of our moment. "That's my girl. I'll see you later."

While everyone finished their breakfasts and chitchatted, I found myself getting lost in my thoughts again from the void left behind by Ryan's empty chair.

I pushed a piece of pineapple around on my plate, still feeling the tingle he left on my lips, wishing he didn't have to rush so much, and hating that no private moment in public was sacred.

Marie and her husband, Gary, started sniping at each other again, pulling my attention to their hushed argument. They'd been fighting a lot lately, even getting into a heated argument on Sunday at our impromptu engagement party held at their house. Gary had been so mad, he ended up getting in his car and leaving, causing everyone there to feel as though we were intruding. Every time I asked Marie what was going on she'd casually dismiss it, simply stating that he was being an ass again.

So I didn't probe. Instead I drifted off into my own dilemmas, thinking how my mental breakdown over the last few weeks was such a ridiculous waste of energy. Had I known then what I knew now, all of the extra anguish and heartache swirling around the edges of my thoughts could have been avoided.

I glanced over at my other girlfriend, Tammy, who was buttering a piece of toast while her soon-to-be husband, my longtime friend Pete, talked and laughed heartily with Ryan's brother and sister-in-law, Nick and Janelle. Ryan had arranged for everyone important in our lives to be here. Another reason I loved him dearly.

As I took in the faces of my most cherished support crew, a sad thought occurred to me.

While two weeks ago in Miami I had carried on uncontrollably like an immature little girl, crying and insisting that Ryan had cheated on me with Lauren Delaney, all of the people sitting at this table had known that he was going to propose.

How long had they all known his intentions? Weeks? Months?

Suddenly I felt like a huge ass all over again, quite embarrassed by my completely irrational behavior when my friends had to break my bedroom door down to get to me. I had been physically and emotionally broken, locking myself away from the world while thoughts of Ryan being unfaithful tore me to shreds. No wonder Marie slapped me across the face when I became somewhat hysterical. I must have looked like a blithering idiot to all of them.

But I couldn't stop the flood once it started. It drowned me.

I stared at the blank whiteness of the tablecloth. *How close I came to ruining this relationship—ending it, actually. Well, no more of that. Ryan has been nothing but faithful and trustworthy. He adores me and I want him more than I want my next breath.*

"Taryn?"

Fingers touched my shoulder, startling me. Trish was standing behind me; her golden hair was pulled back by the sunglasses that rested on top of her head.

"Are you ladies ready?" Trish asked.

With a smile, I nodded and grabbed my purse. A large, chauffeured Suburban pulled up to the front doors and all of the ladies climbed in. Twenty minutes later, we arrived at the "hall of many dresses." Well anyway, that's what Marie called it. She was right.

"Oh, what a day," Trish sighed, eyeing a shimmery, burgundy-colored Prada gown. I had separated myself from everyone else to follow her through the rows.

"Bet you're glad to be out here instead of in the office," I commented, figuring she was enjoying shopping more than working.

"You have no idea." Trish exhaled with relief. "Especially since *she* is on the warpath today."

I frowned slightly, pitying all of those poor people who had to deal with Marla on a regular basis.

"I still don't understand why she's so angry about things," I muttered.

"I do," Trish said, fumbling for her BlackBerry, which had just beeped. "She found out from the sleazy tabloids that her number-one client got engaged. Be glad that you missed that. She went absolutely ballistic."

"I already know she despises me," I grumbled quietly. "And that little-known fact adds a ton of stress on Ryan."

"Don't feel special. She hates everyone," Trish said matter-of-factly, as her thumbs pushed a few buttons on her cell. "I've been with her for seven years and she still doesn't like me."

I flipped the tag over on a cream-colored dress. "Well, I didn't like the way she talked to him this morning. She yelled at him like he was a child and I sort of wanted to punch her."

"I wish you would have," Trish said under her breath.

"Hate her that much, too?" I asked jokingly, following her around to the next rack of dresses.

Trish snickered uncomfortably. "Some days are worse than others. Unfortunately in this town, it's hard to catch a break, no matter how skilled you are. That's why so many actors are waiters. And PR? If you're not with an established firm, you starve. Since I like to eat, I've learned to shut my mouth and do as I'm told."

This morning's badgering continued to plague me. "Trish, really, is it *that* bad that people know about our engagement?"

She paused. "Well . . . it *is* his personal business that's out there now." She moved a little closer. "Did he really stand on a table when he proposed?"

I sheepishly smirked and nodded to confirm.

Trish's grin widened. "Can I see the ring?" she asked excitedly, requesting my hand. "Wow, it's gorgeous! So that's what half a million looks like. I'm so glad he went with William Goldberg. His rings are absolutely breathtaking. I love the huge trillions on the sides." She laughed lightly while inspecting my ring. "This was definitely, *definitely* worth the trouble! Flawless . . ."

I didn't understand; my brain seized when she let it slip how much Ryan spent on my ring. I shook my head, trying to prevent the high-pitched ringing and the urge to pass out from taking over. "Um . . . ahh. What do you mean? What trouble?"

"Sneaking Ryan around to meet jewelry designers?" she said tentatively. "I spent hours coordinating that. No offense, Taryn, but I was relieved when you couldn't make it to the Academy Awards. I was freaking out trying to arrange a meeting without you knowing about it."

My mind traveled back to the end of February, when I was recovering after being hit by a car and missed my first opportunity to be with him at the Oscars. I glanced at my hand, grateful to her in so many ways.

"Well, from the bottom of my heart, thank you for all of your hard work. I truly appreciate it."

Just then something else dawned on me. "Wait . . . if you helped him get my ring then why is Marla so mad? I mean she obviously knew . . ."

Trish looked guilty. "She knew he bought a ring but Marla, being the evil bitch that she is, tried to ta—you know what? It doesn't matter."

I should have figured as much. "She tried to talk him out of it," I muttered, finishing her sentence. "I'm bad for his career."

Trish looked baffled. "Why would you think that?"

I'm surprised she had to ask. After all, it was her boss that did everything except say those exact words out loud. Marla's actions and comments certainly got that message across. "What about the fans? Are they going to turn on him like that if he's not single anymore?"

Trish laughed quietly at my apparently silly question. "His fans are not going to turn on him unless he starts making shitty films. I can't believe she's telling him to avoid it with Jimmy Collins tonight, though. Bad, bad, bad . . . ," she muttered, shaking her head.

I stared at her, questioning why she felt that way, especially since she was working so hard to impress the evil bitch.

Trish pursed her lips, then smiled at a little black dress. "What do you think of this one for your friend Marie? I think this would look fabulous on her. All of the gowns that we preselected for you are in the dressing area. You'll have to try them on. And now that you two are officially engaged, we need to get you lined up for all your appearance dresses. First rule of fashion, always know who designed your dress. It's the first question anyone asks."

I barely looked at the dress she held up. "Trish, talk to me. What should he do?"

"Nothing. Everything will go on the account and—"

"No, not about the dresses. The interview tonight. You seem to think he should handle it differently. Ryan thought she was going to tell him to admit our engagement. If it was up to you, what would you tell him?"

Trish recoiled. "Taryn, I can't tell you that! Besides, if she ever finds out that I advised you, she'll fire me on the spot. I can't."

I followed her around a circular rack of dresses, searching for a new angle. I wanted to hear her opinion now more than anything. "Okay. Well, what if I hired you to represent me—then would you advise me?"

She turned and looked at me, completely shocked. "You don't understand. I don't have any clients—Marla does. I have a tiny shithole apartment that I can barely afford, a crappy car, and college loans I'll still be paying when I die an old lady."

"Trish?" I encouraged. "I swear, no one will ever know. Our secret."

Trish took a deep breath. "Ahh," she groaned, glancing around the store. "If she ever finds out that I talked to you, I swear I'm coming to live with you and Ryan when I'm homeless.

"The story is already out there," she continued, "backed up with *picture* evidence. All those women, those fans, are clinging to the idea of romance with him and seeing him standing on a table and then down on one knee to propose to you—well that's romantic as all hell. He needs to remain honest."

I nodded in agreement.

"But it's his business. It's *his* choice and, well . . . yours, whether you want to keep your private life private or not."

"Taaaar?" I heard Marie call out my name from the dressing room.

Trish's panic was evident. "Shit, if Marla finds out I said *anything . . .*"

"I won't say anything—I swear—but I wish Ryan would get a second opinion before he goes onstage tonight. He believes everything that Marla tells him."

Trish's eyes flashed to the door when a few new customers walked in. "She already called Jimmy Collins's producer."

I thought about Ryan being in front of the cameras tonight delivering canned, lame answers. "If I get him alone, will you talk to him? You could really make a big difference in his career."

Trish looked shocked. She kept shaking her head. "Taryn, no! I can't!"

"He's going to look like an idiot," I muttered.

"Taryn, did you try on any of your dresses yet?" Ryan's mother, Ellen, asked.

I motioned my answer; I had yet to even look at them. Ellen held up a midnight blue dress, but I was so preoccupied mentally that I only pretended to admire it.

"Come on." Ellen pulled me along by the arm, hailing the stylist with her other hand. "We have to get you focused because we're running short on time."

* * *

I TRIED to put Marla's condescending tirade out of my mind and enjoy the rest of the day, but the moment I saw her following Ryan when he came into the dressing room backstage at *The Jimmy Collins Show* my overwhelming hatred for the woman came rushing back. And despite Ryan's outward appearance, I knew that just below the surface he was still somewhat forlorn.

I tried to be cheery enough for the both of us; after all, I was excited just being backstage like this, and it helped a lot that his father and Pete were here to lift his spirits. The men were talking about the Stanley Cup playoffs, joking that they were going to relocate their dinner plates by the first television they found in the restaurant tonight. I was thankful that Ryan's brother kept his sarcastic, hurtful comments to himself this time. Ryan had enough on his mind; he didn't need to be pushed over the edge tonight.

Marla was hovering around Ryan. She acted like he was *her* property, and she was on the defensive, blocking anyone who attempted to come close to him. She rudely interrupted the conversation he was trying to have with his family and I felt my anger flare. It was even more infuriating when she wouldn't make eye contact with me. How petty and childish.

Sadness swirled back in me as she schooled him on the appropriate responses he should give during the interview to deflect any surprise questions Jimmy Collins might spring on him. Marla's black heart didn't change colors.

I stewed privately, twisting the diamonds on my finger to keep my hands busy while I paced behind the large black leather couch.

Ryan's mother looked at me with concern in her eyes. "Taryn, would you like to sit?" Ellen asked, patting the space next to her on the couch. "Please. Come."

I shook my head slightly, watching my fiancé intently. "That's okay, Mom," I said softly. "Thanks, but I'm fine."

Trish slipped into the room through the closed door. Her eyes darted around, quickly assessing the tension in the room. I hoped she could read my body language to see how upset I was. We all heard Marla clearly when she told Ryan to "try not to screw this up."

My fingers clenched into the back of the couch to keep from lunging at her. Ellen let out a maternal tsk and an audible huff, glaring eye daggers at Marla.

Trish quickly intervened. "Marla, excuse me. An assistant just told me that the stage director is looking for you."

"Now?" Marla questioned. She looked at her watch and collected her bag. "Stay with him," she ordered.

Ryan was sitting in the swivel chair, rubbing his forehead.

Trish appeared conflicted as she sidled up to his chair. "Ryan? Can we talk for a minute?"

Ryan followed her to the back corner of the room.

"So, are you ready? Are you all right with the format?"

He shrugged. "I guess so."

"Trish, just tell him," I pleaded, gazing nervously back at the door. I knew we only had ten minutes, if that, to get Ryan prepped.

"Tell me what?" Ryan asked, confused.

Trish cleared her throat. "You know Collins is going to ask about the proposal regardless."

Ryan sighed. "I know. He wants the exclusive."

"I was just wondering . . . if Marla wasn't advising you, how would you handle it?"

Ryan shrugged. "I don't know. Why?"

Trish took a deep breath. "I think the advice Marla gave you might be a mistake."

Ryan looked at me, questioning why we were doing this to him right before he was due to walk out onstage.

"It's your personal business, Ryan, but look at it this way—if you deny that you're engaged, now that there are pictures and videos, your credibility is going to be *worthless*." Trish reflexively glanced over her shoulder again to make sure Marla was still nowhere to be seen.

"When Collins brings it up, I think you should admit to it. Don't embellish the story with personal information; just be honest and somewhat open. Your fans are going to cling to you if you expose your sensitive, romantic side," she continued.

"I'm worried about the extra media attention on Taryn," Ryan said, looking worried and guilty at the same time.

"Don't worry about me," I said adamantly. Ryan shot me a look, wordlessly telling me that it was impossible for him to do that.

"If you don't fess up to it now, the media is going to keep pursuing the story and it's going to get worse. Hiding it will only sensationalize it and Collins already knows that Taryn is in the building."

Ryan nodded. "Tomorrow's press conference?"

"Covered, just like today. Still Q-and-A only on the film," she quickly replied.

"But I've spent the entire day avoiding the subject," Ryan stressed.

"I know, but Jimmy is going to put you on the spot out there in front of a live studio audience regardless, so you need to be ready for it. This is a huge story, Ryan, and you know he wants it! Collins is renegotiating his contract with the network and he's looking for the ratings boost. If he gets you to admit it—"

Ryan's eyes widened. "What? Marla never told me that."

Trish searched through her bag and retrieved a sheet of paper, which she immediately handed to Ryan. "Just having you on the show tonight in light of everything is upping his points. See? You're going to have to respond to it one way or another."

He held back a curse. "How do I handle *Night Life* tomorrow then?"

"Same way," Trish advised, stuffing the paper evidence back in her bag. "If you open up to Jimmy now, Nigel Allen is going to press even harder for new details tomorrow. His ratings are going to jump just because you acknowledged the engagement tonight—if you choose to do that. But if you do, then you'll have both Collins and Allen in your pocket for further PR. But let's not worry about that now. You've got to concentrate on handling *this* appearance."

Ryan glanced over to the doorway that led out to the main hallway. "Marla doesn't know about this, does she?" He motioned with his finger, swaying it between the two of us.

"No," I answered. "Trish is sticking her neck out to protect your reputation."

"I'll probably get fired tonight," she huffed. "But anyway, you need to turn scandal into opportunity, Ryan. Treat it with honesty. Jimmy said that if he gets you to talk about your engagement, he's going to try and contrast the romance in the movie back against your admission to keep it moving. I was there when Marla talked to him and his producer just before you came in for your pre-interview."

Ryan blew out a big lungful of air through his pursed lips.

"It's a good segue from your personal business back to the film," Trish advised. "If you choose to talk about it, keep the details on the surface and take your time so you don't blurt out anything too personal."

"Tricia!" Marla barked harshly from the open doorway. Her high heels were clicking forcefully in our direction.

Ryan strolled away, deep in thought when Marla reached us. I thought about going with him just so I wouldn't have to be that close to Marla, but I could not let Trish take the heat alone. After what she just did for us, I was not going to abandon her.

Trish was prepared, calmly deflecting Marla's anger at being called away for nothing with quick answers. I looked away so she wouldn't notice my smirk.

Ryan purposefully walked over to me and gathered my hand in his, pulling me away from Marla. "How are you doing?" he whispered privately.

I gave him my best "doing okay" nod and wink, even though my eyes slid back to see where Marla was. I think he caught my glance because he sighed heavily.

"How are you?" I asked.

"Excuse me, sir, we're ready to seat your guests," a crew member said to Ryan.

"I'll see you later," Ryan whispered, grasping my fingertips to pull me in for a soft kiss.

"Okay, hon. Good luck!" I watched his retreating back as a production assistant led him away.

Our group was ushered out into the hallway so we could take our seats in the studio audience. We had our own section off to the left side of the stage; I sat in the seat next to Ryan's mom. Janelle, Ryan's sister-in-law, sat next to me. Ryan's father, Bill, kept fidgeting in his chair, anxiously waiting like the rest of us for Ryan to make his appearance onstage. Ryan was in the primary guest spot for the show, so he would be up first.

Janelle leaned over. "Are you okay?"

I was staring at one of the TV monitors, twisting my ring. My feet were bouncing up and down on the floor.

I shrugged. "Just nervous, I guess."

"Why?" she questioned me strangely.

I leaned closer. "Photos of his proposal were leaked."

Janelle scoffed. "Ah, so what." And then I think it dawned on her. "Oh, he's going to get asked about it now, isn't he?" she said, appearing happy about it.

I nodded a few times, unwilling to tear my eyes away from the stage.

I held my breath as the camera returned to the host, Jimmy Collins, now seated at his desk after his monologue. His fingers picked at a magazine that lay facedown in front of him.

"Unless you've been living on the dark side of the moon, you know our first guest tonight had his breakout role playing time-traveling hit man Charles Conroy in the hit movie *Seaside*. He's here tonight to tell us about his latest film, *Reparation*, which opens in theaters nationwide this Friday. Here he is on the cover of *Entertainment Week*. Please help me welcome Ryan Christensen!"

Music blared out of the studio sound system as I watched Ryan come out from around the corner. The entire audience sprang from their chairs. Women all around us went absolutely crazy, jumping up and down and shrieking for him. Their screams were ear-piercing.

Ryan waved and smiled, scratching his forehead before being greeted by Jimmy Collins. He looked nervous and totally overwhelmed by their reception.

Ryan leaned forward when he sat down, almost resting his head between his knees from the shock of the audience's continued excitement. I could tell by the expression on his face that he was once again blown away by their devotion. I was glad to see he was still so humbled by it. Janelle leaned closer, excitedly nudging me with her elbow as she clapped for her brother-in-law.

"Your fans come out in masses! Thanks for stopping by here tonight. How have you been?" Jimmy asked Ryan, trying to proceed with the interview. The studio audience finally simmered down just barely enough for us to hear them speak to each other.

"Good! Real good, thanks!" Ryan replied. "Thanks for having me."

"You know, you're not the only one who can make women scream like that," Jimmy teased. "Now if I could just get the women to stop screaming obscenities at me, I'd have this thing set!"

The crowd laughed at his joke.

Ryan snickered uncomfortably and took a sip from the cup they had sitting there for him. "Sometimes they scream obscenities at me, too," he admitted.

"I heard you had quite a reception by one of the fans when you arrived here," Jimmy prompted.

"Yeah, I had just gotten out of the car and I was signing a few pictures and whatnot and I looked up and this girl lifted her shirt and flashed her ... at me." Ryan motioned, appearing both excited and appalled at the same time.

I gasped slightly at hearing the news that some girl showed her breasts to my fiancé.

"Did she want you to sign them?" Jimmy repeated Ryan's motion.

"I honestly don't know if she said anything at all. She was jumping up and down and screaming." He laughed. "It was hard to hold a conversation with things, um, bouncing like that."

Jimmy laughed and continued on. "That's funny! So how are things? I think the last time you were here was about six months ago and we were talking about *Seaside*."

The women in the audience went berserk from hearing that word.

Ryan looked out at the audience, shaking his head in amazement at their devotion.

"And I can see that the fan reaction has tripled since then. Wow!" Jimmy rubbed his ear. "It's like pressing a hot button. Anytime I want to get my wife in the mood, I just burst into the bedroom and yell '*Seaside*' and she instantly starts tearing her clothes off."

Ryan laughed uncomfortably. "Glad to hear it works for you."

"Of course it helps when I'm wearing my 'Charles' mask. I mean you and I are built so much alike that she can hardly tell the difference," Jimmy joked, noticeably rolling his eyes to get a laugh out of the crowd.

"So how's life been treating you?" Jimmy asked.

"Things are great. Really great! I just came from Miami, where I've been shooting a movie called *Thousand Miles*. It's a bit of a thriller."

That's it, honey, pitch your movies. Keep the tempo going.

"And in like another two weeks I'll be back on set in Vancouver for my next project," Ryan said, nervously scratching his neck.

"And what's that?" Jimmy asked.

"It's a film called *Slipknot*. Jonathan Follweiler is directing it. This will be my first time working on a project with him, which is very exciting. And I get to do a little rock climbing, which I'm *really* looking forward to trying. It's something that I've never done before. A little danger."

"I hear you've been practicing for it, though. Climbing on tables and stuff?" Jimmy goaded Ryan with his comment, raising his eyebrows and tapping the note cards he held in his hand on the desk to get a rise out of the audience.

Laughter exploded all around us. I watched to see if Ryan's expression would change, and sure enough, he flushed with embarrassment.

Jimmy quickly fired off his next question. "Now is the second *Seaside* finished or are you still working on that, too?"

Ryan fidgeted, adjusted his posture in the chair. "No, we're finished. We wrapped in December."

As if on cue, the audience screamed again.

"And where did you film that?"

"We filmed this one in a little town called Seaport in Rhode Island. It's a beautiful place right on the coast."

My breath hitched.

"And . . . what did you do while you were there? Meet anyone special?" Jimmy asked with the inflection of a nosey mother.

Ryan's mouth opened and closed a few times; he appeared at a loss for words as he nervously scratched his forehead and squirmed in his chair.

Like a flash, in fast-forward I envisioned Ryan saying nine different answers, one right after the other. My hopes rested on the one where he points at me and tells the world that he's madly in love.

"We met a lot of nice people there," he admitted slyly, smiling out at the audience when they screamed their excitement again. Ryan glanced over in my direction and, for a brief moment, I think our eyes met. "Everyone was great to us."

I smiled proudly at my future husband.

"So, Ryan, you know everyone wants to know so I'm just going to ask. There are all these rumors flying around and pictures of you climbing on tables. So please—put these poor women out of their misery already and tell us. Are you an engaged man now?"

My fingers reflexively clenched the armrest as I held every bit of oxygen in my lungs, waiting . . . anticipating. Jimmy had defied the interview agreements and put Ryan on the spot.

Ryan smirked, looking bashful and guilty, and for a moment I thought he was just going to blurt it out, as if the news he held so privately would just gush from his lips.

As quickly as it came, I saw the exact moment when it left.

"When aren't I engaged?" Ryan bantered, trying to be funny. "Let's just say I'm very, *very* happy and in a very good place in my life."

The audience responded with a few outbursts and claps, but that was that—a fleeting moment—gone. Not one mention about his personal life or the woman he pledged his undying love to from the top of a barroom table in front of his parents, my friends, and a crowd of strangers.

Physical disappointment pricked like a thousand needles into my arms, my chest, finally forcing my reluctant lungs to exhale.

Why didn't he just . . . ?

Janelle looked at me with apologetic eyes, apparently feeling sorry for me. I slid my eyes away, refraining from engaging her pity.

After all this time, after all the reports and press, after the printed speculation of our engagement, I was still a part of his life to be publicly disavowed.

CHAPTER 3

Atonement

W ow," RYAN BREATHED out, setting his dark gray suit coat down over the chair when I came out of the bedroom.

"What?" I asked reflexively. I wasn't sure if he liked what he saw or not, considering I had just spent the last two hours being painted, brushed, curled, and sprayed. I felt like an overdone walking makeup ad.

I smoothed my hands across the bodice of my strapless gown to assure that everything was in place. The wardrobe stylist had selected a black satin and chiffon sheath, overlaid with fine silver lace by Versace. It had a high slit to show a little thigh and flowed like water over my curves. A teardrop diamond pendant and matching earrings finished off the look.

"You are absolutely stunning," he continued breathlessly, pacing each word as if to give it proper emphasis. His swagger and smoldering eyes told me that I wasn't the only one having naughty thoughts about stripping each other bare. He was absolutely beautiful dressed up. My desire to rend the shirt right off his back and roll my tongue around on his muscular chest had me hungry and blushing.

"What do you think?" He seemed unsure of his attire, tugging at his vest to straighten it. "Does this look okay?"

It wasn't the first time I had seen him in a suit, but tonight in a three-piece, custom-tailored, charcoal-gray Armani he looked devastatingly handsome. I nodded emphatically, distracted by thoughts of him wearing nothing but that white dress shirt at some point in the very near future. *Opened instead of buttoned to display every hard line of his chest and abs.* I straightened the knot of his black-patterned necktie and smiled. "I think you look like a gorgeous movie star."

Ryan cradled my face in his hands and smiled gently, kissing me softly as he always does. His blue eyes, framed by those gorgeous long lashes, locked on to mine. "I love you," he whispered.

I kissed him and returned his sentiment, but deep inside I privately ached. All day I had tried to get over my sullen mood, and even though I loved him with every fiber of my soul, I couldn't help but feel disappointed by him. Okay—honestly, I was feeling very disappointed by him.

"Hey." He gently grasped my arm when I turned to walk away. "What's wrong?"

I didn't want to get into a discussion about my dejected feelings before his premiere. He didn't need to deal with that right now. Mom always used to say to "sleep on things for a night" before acting rash. Maybe with time I'd see things in a different light. I had spent most of last night praying for an epiphany.

"Nothing is wrong." I tried to dismiss his keen observation by putting on a forced grin to shake off his speculation.

"Bullshit," he returned with a sharp laugh as he followed me into the bathroom. "You don't think I can tell when you're upset, Tar? Give me some credit."

Ryan trapped me at the bathroom sink; his chest pressed into my back. I could feel the warmth of his breath heating my ear. "I know you better than you think I do."

I swallowed hard, loving that he cared to know my feelings but hesitant to share them before I had sorted those feelings out.

"You've been this way since dinner last night, and every time I've asked, you've avoided telling me. So please don't tell me you're *fine* anymore. What's going on?"

He kissed my bare shoulder tenderly.

I opted for saving him from my bruised emotions. "It's not important. We can talk later. You have enough to deal with right now."

His arms crossed over my abdomen, pulling me closer. "No. I'm not waiting that long. We made a promise to each other, remember? More open and honest? I want to know what's bothering you, and I want to know what it is right now."

I looked at him through our reflection in the large mirror, stalling.

"Right now," he ordered, his voice taking on a new, direct tone.

My will cracked. "I thought you were going to say something on the show last night, that's all." I casually added a shrug, trying to lessen the impact.

"About what?"

My apprehension to go down this road made me fidget. "About being engaged. I just thought . . . since you didn't say anything on Jimmy Collins that you might say something on *Night Life*, but you didn't. I'm trying not to be one of those needy girls, Ryan, but I just don't understand why you've avoided confirming it when they asked."

I hoped his reasons weren't any of the ones on my speculated list.

It took all of ten seconds for him to break eye contact and make a few of his standard throaty noises before his hands freed me. Next came his "stare at the floor and rub the forehead" maneuver.

I turned my eyes back to the sink counter. This repeat pattern of having to walk on damn eggshells around men was getting so freaking old. "See, this is why I didn't want to say anything. I know you have your reasons, Ryan. It's just . . . I thought I was your fiancée, but I can't help but feel as though I'm some dirty little secret."

Ryan closed the lid on the toilet and sat down. "You're not a dirty secret, Taryn. Nor have you ever been."

"Are you ashamed of me?"

He paled as if I'd just smacked him. "Of course not! Why would you even say that?"

"You denied being engaged to me on television and during every interview. I don't understand why, beyond Marla telling you not to, so what else am I to think? I'm sorry, but I can't help feeling the way I do."

"What the hell do you want me to do?" he grumbled, letting his hands slap down on his thighs.

I held his gaze, worried that he might think I was even remotely interested in having this turn into an argument. "I love you—with all of my heart. I want to be your wife, your partner. I want to be by your side through all of your adventures. But I don't know what I'm supposed to do or what role I'm supposed to play. Help me to understand, Ryan. Help *me* to be a part of all of this."

Ryan exhaled with new frustration. "Tar, you see how things are—the paparazzi, the fucking tabloids. They take *everything* from me. Everything I hold sacred. Why can't our private life stay private, you know? If I give them that, then what do I have left? Nothing."

Massive confusion tore through my mind, followed closely by my anger. "Maybe I should just stay here then. That way I can stay a private matter," I muttered to the tiled floor.

"No. Fuck that."

I studied the design in the lace of my dress for a moment before begging his eyes for some clarity. "Just answer one question. Why did you do it? If you don't want to acknowledge that we're engaged, if it's supposed to be some well-guarded secret, why did you make your proposal public?"

"You don't understand." With a short huff, Ryan stood and stepped around me to head toward the door.

Wonderful. Just like every other guy I've ever been with. Bail when the topic gets a little uncomfortable. That's it. Walk away. "You're right. I don't."

Ryan stopped on the threshold and gripped the door frame with both hands, completely surprising me. His head hung low for a moment. "I didn't say anything on Jimmy Collins because all that asshole wanted was a confession to up his ratings."

He turned around and then paced the length of the bath, from the cavernous sandstone-tiled shower to the doorway and back again. "The intimate details of our personal life are *not* for public discussion,

Tar. Nor am I going to allow it to be used to make other people rich. That's *our* life—our business."

I drew in a quick breath when he moved to stand directly in front of me.

"I make movies. That's what I do for a living. If I go on a talk show, it's to talk about my job, drum up more hype for the movie. Not to spill secrets about our personal life."

"But there's so much of your life that's public. I always thought it was happy news when people got engaged."

His hard glare softened as he took my left hand in his. "It *is* happy news. You're my everything, Taryn, not my secret." Ryan's right hand drifted down my cheek, touching much more than just skin. "I just don't want to share what is most sacred to me with the entire world on a talk show. You're my world, babe. Mine. Not theirs. They can have me, but they can't have you, too."

His brow creased, frowning as though he was torn. "I was going to sing a different song to you when I proposed. I had it all planned. Everything was supposed to be private. But then everything got so screwed up and I ran out of time." He rubbed his hand over his head. "Hell, everyone thought I'd been unfaithful to you, Taryn. Even you. At that time, considering . . . well, I felt a grand gesture was necessary."

I took a deep breath, strewn with personal regret, knowing I was one of those who doubted.

Ryan dipped his head to recapture my eyes. "I was mad and hurt and then I thought . . ." His hand cradled my cheek. "God, I was so scared of losing you."

Repentant tears pooled in my eyes as memories of that planted love letter and disastrous trip to Florida flooded back into my thoughts. "I thought I had lost you."

His head swayed, forming a silent no.

I wiped the moisture from under my eye. "That song, the one you sang to me, I loved it. It was beautiful. Perfect. I'd really love to hear it again sometime."

He smiled. "I wrote that song on the airplane. I wanted you to know how serious I am about us. How much I want you in my life, Taryn. I meant it when I said forever. That's why. You are *it* for me. But the *me* that knelt in front of you that night and the *me* that is standing in front of you right now is not the same *me* that's out there in the spotlight." He thumped his hand over his heart. "They only get the outside, not the inside. That's for you."

God, the way he looked directly into my soul, I knew he was sincere. I rested my hand on his heart. "You know I love you, Ryan. All sides of you. Sometimes I—"

"Sweetheart, we've been through so much together." His voice cracked. His thumb brushed over my lower abdomen. "There are things that I just don't want to openly talk about, especially on national television. You bring me peace. That's mine to cherish, not theirs."

"And I hope you know that I'm trying to understand how all this works. That's why I didn't even want to start this conversation. I was trying to sort it out on my own. I guess I just don't understand Marla's reasoning sometimes."

"I don't understand sometimes, either, but I'm trying to trust what she says I should do. She has her reasons for protecting me—I mean us. She didn't want me to sensationalize it on national television, although the story is out there already." He shrugged.

Ryan tucked a stray strand of hair behind my ear. "Besides, in less than an hour, millions will know. As much as I want to protect you from the total craziness that is my life, I know I can't do that forever. So everything changes tonight, but it changes on my terms." He gently smiled at me, rubbing his thumb over my lips.

I breathed a sigh of relief but it didn't seem to last long. Twenty minutes later I watched as he roamed around our bedroom, obviously on a frantic hunt.

"You put your watch in the bag inside your suitcase." I pointed, knowing what he was looking for.

"How did you . . . ? Thanks. I don't know what I'd do without you," he mumbled.

I thought about saying something witty back to him but I refrained. He had been in his own private foul mood ever since lunch, when Trish called his attention to all the slams that he received from the press this morning. Ryan emphatically stated that he didn't care about the negative comments, but it was obvious that he did.

Instead of sitting and relaxing, Ryan paced. The more he paced and the closer it came time for us to leave, the more agitated he seemed to become. He picked his suit jacket up and then immediately set it back down, only to pick it right back up again. Then he patted his pockets, checking that he had his cell phone for the umpteenth time.

I was putting my lipstick in my small evening bag when Ryan breathed out forcefully.

"Is it hot in here?" He started pulling the collar of his shirt away from his neck and I noticed he looked a little pale.

I shook my head. I actually thought the room was cold.

He wiped some moisture from his brow. "I'm freaking sweating."

I was starting to think that it was more than the temperature that was making him sweat. "Are you feeling sick?"

"A little. I sort of feel lightheaded, actually. Man it's hot in here." His breathing became labored and he was turning white.

Oh, no. Not now.

I did the first thing I could think of—I got him air.

Ryan was leaning on the wall absorbing the full blast of the air-conditioning vent when our family and friends convened in our suite.

Ellen peeked around one of our bedroom's double doors. "What's wrong with Ryan?"

I tried to prevent her from hovering by blocking her entry. "He's feeling a little queasy," I lied. "He'll be all right. He just needs a minute."

I had seen Ryan like this before and I knew exactly what was happening. Although he wouldn't admit it to anyone, he was quietly freaking out. I was also wise enough to know what it was that brought it on.

"He'll be down when he's ready," I said to David when he poked his nose around the door. I didn't mean to get snippy with him, but Ryan didn't need anyone snapping their fingers at him right now. It's not like anxiety attacks have an exact timetable. I was glad when Mike took over and cleared everyone out of our suite.

I rubbed Ryan's back and shoulders. The first time I'd seen him like this was when the street and sidewalks outside my pub were crowded with fans.

"You okay?"

Ryan's head dipped, slowly swaying his assent; he was breathing heavily.

My heart ached for him, knowing his private suffering. "Mike will be by your side the entire time. You know he won't let anything happen to you."

"I know," he whispered, trying to measure his breathing. "But things are different now."

"You've done this countless times before. You're going to be just fine. Your fans adore you."

"It's not me that I'm worried about." He shook out his hands. "You have *no* idea. No idea. You don't know how easy it is for someone in the crowd to just stick out a knife or a needle or a . . . or a gun . . . God, if something ever happened to you—"

I knew he was deep in the panic stage now. "Hey, come on. Just breathe with me." I wrapped my arms around his waist and paced each breath—slowly in, slowly out—hoping that this would calm him like it did the last time. "No one is going to hurt us."

He cinched his hands around my arms, almost too hard, and glared down at me. "We share the world with lunatics, Taryn. You've seen how far some of my fans are willing to go, *so don't tell me there is no threat!* Angelica was just one of hundreds." I gasped a little. I think he realized how hard he was gripping me. His hands eased slightly. "I want you to stick tight to the event security tonight. If they tell you to move or go you listen, okay? No questions. You follow their orders. Do you understand?"

"Yes."

"I'm not kidding, Tar. You've never experienced this. It's going to be a shock. You've never seen crowds like this. If shit goes down, security is going to block me from getting to you." Something new, something frighteningly alarming, coated his expression. This was beyond panic. His possessive grasp tightened again. "They will be in my way and I won't be able to protect you myself and Mike will be—"

I pressed into him tighter as my own body trembled. "Ryan, please. You're sort of scaring me. I get it."

He sighed heavily into my hair. "I'm going to demand extra security from now on. Make sure you're well protected."

"Honey, you need to calm down. You're shaking. Didn't you take your medicine today?"

He sat down in one of the chairs. "No. Can you get me one? Hopefully that will . . . will do the trick."

I dug through his bag for his anxiety medicine. No one knew that the famous Ryan Christensen suffered from agoraphobia. Large crowds totally freaked him out. "You know you have to take these every day. You're not supposed to skip."

He finished the glass of water while I hoped we had enough time to let the medicine kick in. Usually, he was good within a half hour. A gentle knock on our door startled us both.

Mike was waiting. He had changed out of his casual attire from this morning and was looking downright sexy dressed up in a black suit, white shirt, and sharp cobalt-blue tie. I had appreciated his good looks before, but dressed to the nines, he was freaking gorgeous.

He looked at Ryan with brotherly reverence and understanding, truly concerned and full of caring. "Are you okay, man? Your team is pushing to leave but just tell me if you need more time. I'll call downstairs and tell them to wait."

Ryan was mostly pulled together but still agitated. His masked anxiety lay just below the surface, ready to flare at a moment's notice. "I'm ready. Let's do this." He glared at Mike. "I want extra security on Taryn tonight. No less than two near her anytime she's not with me. No slipups. You got me?"

Mike nodded and said, "It's already done, Ry. We have four on standby at the venue for your family."

The moment we stepped off the elevators, David swooped in on us. "Ryan, I need to talk to you a sec," he said with urgency, abruptly leading Ryan away by the shoulder. I held on to him as long as I could until our fingers unwillingly unlaced. He didn't even bother to ask Ryan how he was doing.

Several black sedans were lined up to take us to the *Reparation* premiere. Marla hurried to speak to one of the drivers—a heavyset man with a beard. David's hand was on Ryan's back, guiding him into the first sedan in line. David glanced once in my direction, then gave what appeared to be a stealthy nod to Marla.

I presumed Ryan would come back to collect me once his side meeting with David was over. The burly driver blocked me as I tried to see what was taking so long.

"Excuse me. I'm supposed to be with—" I pointed in Ryan's direction.

"Ma'am, you are in this car," the driver informed.

"But I'm his—"

"This way, please." He ushered me to the open car door.

Ellen appeared just as confused as I was. "Taryn, aren't you supposed to be with Ryan?"

Janelle moved her feet to make room for me.

I didn't know if I wanted to argue or yell for Ryan; instead I took the instruction at face value, collected my dress, and slid next to her on the car seat. It also appeared that I had no choice in the matter; not only was I physically blocked from getting to him, but Ryan's car was already rolling away from the curb without me.

This was not what I had expected, to be arriving at my fiancé's premiere in a different car, especially since he had just had a panic attack. I stared out the window, secretly hoping that Ryan was bothered by this arrangement, praying that he was at least thinking about it. But what if he wasn't? I had just assumed that I would ride in the same car. I racked my brain trying to remember if we talked about the arrangements or not, feeling like I should know these things.

Maybe he's required to be by himself when we arrive? After all, he is the celebrity, not me. But his mom said . . .

I thought about calling him but I figured I would be with him if I was supposed to be with him. Ryan would have seen to it.

But . . . he didn't.

I felt myself morphing from perplexed to upset, rapidly.

Is this a glimpse at our future? At *my* future? Keep the bartender wife life separate from the glamorous movie star life? That thought brought out my anger again. *Taryn, the dirty little secret.*

I started to hear Marla's voice in my head, advising Ryan that maybe it would be better if Taryn stayed home from now on. Her slimy forked tongue whispering into his ear that I'd probably be bored or he wouldn't have time to tend to his duties and to me at the same time. Would Ryan agree with her?

I huffed to myself, disgusted now that a team of stylists was hired to primp me like some poseur wannabe. I wondered how long I would be deemed bad for his public image.

I wished the driver had placed me in the other car with Marie and Tammy. Marie would have surely, in no uncertain terms, explained to me her interpretation of how things work in Hollywood while Pete would undoubtedly try to convince me that Ryan didn't mean to hurt my feelings.

Regardless, this scenario might be excusable once but this shit was so not happening a second time. *Not now while I have this enormous diamond ring on my hand. I don't care what my future husband does for a living. The wife I intend to be would be by his side, not tucked away like an afterthought.* I started to rehearse my "why I'm so pissed off" speech in my head when my cell phone rang.

"Tar, why are you with my parents?"

I swallowed my anger and sighed. "Because I was told to get in this car, Ryan. I just assumed you didn't want me with you."

Ryan cursed and told me to hang tight, whatever that meant.

I could see the packed crowd lined up behind metal barricades as our car started to slow, but instead of stopping at the theater our car kept driving down Hollywood Boulevard. We continued on for several blocks, eventually turning onto a narrow road between two buildings.

Bill and Ellen nervously looked out all of the windows when our car came to a stop. Our driver got out and quickly hustled to open my door.

I watched David climb out of Ryan's car, pausing to adjust his wristwatch. Ryan didn't wait for Mike to get his door. He hurried over to me.

"Tar, I'm sorry. Come with me, baby." Ryan led me by the hand.

Marla scurried in her designer heels from her car. "Would someone please tell me what we are doing here?" she asked frantically. "We have a tight schedule. You have to be on the carpet in five minutes. We don't have time for deviations."

Ryan stepped in front of me and turned to her. "If you—*ever*— pull a stunt like this on me again . . . ," he growled loudly.

Marla, of course, played up her confusion, pressing her hand to her chest. "What do you mean 'stunt'? What are you talking about, Ryan? No, No! I need everyone to get back in their cars—right now!" she ordered, clapping her hands several times to get their attention. Pete narrowed his eyes on me, wondering like the rest of them what was going on.

"You know *exactly* what I'm talking about," Ryan accused.

"No, I'm afraid that I don't."

"Don't give me that shit!" he yelled. "*You and David* . . . I'll fucking cut you both loose if you *ever* do something like this again."

"Hey, wait," David quickly interjected. "I told you I didn't have anything to do with car arrangements."

Ryan glared at him.

I scoffed internally at David's comment. He was such a lying scumbag.

"Ryan, please. I don't understand," Marla interrupted. "Why you are so upset?"

Between the eyelash-fluttering and her fake surprised tone, it was obvious that she was attempting to cover up her lies, too.

Ryan locked his teeth. He was seething. "I told you I was only going to wait until premiere night, but that was it. We discussed this today, Marla! So, explain to me why the fuck my fiancée was placed in a different car."

Marla's eyes shot over to me. I, too, was waiting for her explanation, relieved by the fact that he wasn't just mad about it—he was furious.

"Is this why you are so angry? How ridiculous," she muttered. "Ryan, this isn't your first premiere. You know what's involved when we arrive. Come on now. Let's all get back into our cars. You don't want to be late." She attempted to reach for Ryan's arm but he jerked it away.

"I'm not going *anywhere* until I get an answer," Ryan said defiantly.

She sighed, apparently bothered by his insolence. "I don't know what kind of answer you are looking for. This is about promoting your public persona and your film, not about parading your personal life. You know the chaos that ensues from your arrival. You simply cannot attend to her and your fans at the same time," she continued. "It's impossible."

"Oh, so now I have no say in the matter? Is that how this works now?"

"Well, what you want and what's best for your career can be two different things, Ryan. That's why you have us. To guide you."

I felt Ryan's hand squeeze mine tighter as he glared at her. "I know what you're trying to do and I'm telling you this shit stops *now*."

"Ryan, you're overreacting," Marla chided.

Ryan glared at her. "*Overreacting?*"

"Son, what's going on?" Bill asked, stepping into the middle of it.

"Nothing, Dad. Don't worry about it," Ryan said curtly, waving his father off.

"Yes. Overreacting. You have a duty to the studio and the producers and dragging her down the carpet is not the best time for a debut. The press will want to interview her, Ryan. And what is she going to say?"

God, this woman really irked me. "I think I can handle myself."

Marla blinked at my momentary interruption and then proceeded to ramble again. "She hasn't been through any media training. She won't know how to respond to questions properly. We can't risk making mistakes now. You do your interviews and then appropriate arrangements for photo opportunities will be m—"

"No!" Ryan said with utter finality. "I am not hiding this anymore. She arrives with me—tonight. End of discussion."

I felt like the child that should have stayed home with the babysitter.

Marla huffed, pinching the bridge of her nose. "If you would just listen to me for one minute. This is her first premiere. Let her get the feel for it and then maybe next time . . ."

I had just about all I could take seeing Ryan under such stress. I had to shove my own wants and needs to the side. "Ryan, it's all right. I'll ride with your parents and I'll stay out of the way and I won't speak to anyone. No photographs, no interviews, nothing. I promise. Just . . . let's go. You won't be late because of me."

"No!" Ryan growled again. He didn't budge when I tugged his hand. "Hang on, honey. This is *bullshit*. Cal and Kelly arrived together when we did the L.A. *Seaside* premiere, and here I am in a goddamned alleyway having an argument about wanting to arrive at *my* premiere with *my* fiancée."

"Ryan, calm down, buddy." David tried to smooth it over. "If you want her in the car—"

"Your public image is my responsibility, Ryan. Mine!" Marla said. "You've barely dated this girl, foolishly got her pregnant once already, and now you're engaged? Do you have any idea what kind of reckless image that sends? And how long do you suppose this one will last until it winds up being a court battle? One misstep, one misquote—that's all it takes to ruin things for you. We've had countless discussions about dating, asset protection protocol, and keeping your private life low-key and off the press's radar so the focus stays on your new career, but that doesn't seem to register with you. I've been trying to protect your professional image." Marla huffed. "If you, for once, would just do what you're told to do instead of running off like a lovesick teenager, life would be so much easier."

My stomach twisted and roiled and I wanted to throw up. The impulse to sprint down the alley and head for the airport came on right after that. My worst fears of being deemed bad for him were just confirmed. I felt like I was shattering inside. How can our love for each other possibly survive through all these constant bombardments, accusations, and heartaches?

Ryan eyed her with contempt. "What? Is that what you think of me? Oh ho," he grumbled. "We are so done."

"Calm down, Ryan," David said again, patting him on the shoulder to coax him away.

Ryan rolled his shoulder away with force. I could see the rage coat his face, pulling his lips, his nose, into a snarl. For a moment I worried that he was going to take a swing at David.

"No! Fuck that. I've had *enough*!" he shouted. "I'm done listening to you, Marla. Taryn is upset. I'm stressed-out. The press is making me out to be an asshole for not saying anything about the engagement—all because I've been listening to you and your bullshit.

From now on, we do this my way. And I'm only dealing with Trish. At least I know she cares about what I want. I should have listened to her advice instead of following yours."

Shit. I couldn't help but squeeze my eyes from Ryan's gaffe.

Marla couldn't hide her surprise, masking it quickly when she became fixated on her own manicure. "I'm afraid that's not possible."

Ryan rubbed his forehead before turning back to address her. "Okay, then I'll tell you what . . . let me make life easier for you, Marla. I'll get another publicist. It's as simple as that."

"Don't threaten, Ryan. It's so unbecoming. You are losing focus on what your job is."

Ryan scoffed. "That's it. We're done." He started to walk away, towing me by the hand, but then stopped abruptly and turned one last time, squaring his shoulders. "Marla . . . you're fired."

I gasped from the surprise. So did Marla.

"Ryan, don't be like this," she continued, trotting behind us as Ryan picked up our pace. "David?" she called out, looking for help.

"Ryan, you don't want to do that. Not in the middle of a press tour," David rebuked. "Come on, pal. You need to relax. Come with me. Let's take a walk and cool down. Nobody's getting fired."

Ryan pushed David's hand away. Mike immediately stepped in, making a hole between Ryan and his manager.

"I don't believe this! Who calls the shots around here—me or you? Or am I just your pawn? I meant what I said. She's fired. And *you* . . ." Ryan pointed at David's face. "Shit changes—*now*—or you're next. You're on my payroll, remember? You work for me. Don't you ever forget that."

David was treading lightly. "You're under contract with her firm, Ryan."

"Then do your goddamned job and get me out of it."

A few cars came screeching to a halt at the end of the road. Paparazzi sprinted from their open doors.

Ryan cursed under his breath. "Taryn, let's go. Dad, take Mom back to the car—now," he barked. I rushed toward the open car door with Ryan's hand on the small of my back.

"Ryan," Marla breathed out condescendingly.

"Go home, Marla," he instructed as he held my door. "You don't work for me anymore."

Paparazzi swarmed our car on both sides, taking picture after picture. We both shielded our faces, blocking their intruding flashes as best we could.

"Let's go! Drive!" Ryan ordered. Paparazzi continued to run alongside our car as we slowly rolled away; they shouted out our names, hoping we'd actually look at them. My heart was racing frantically. This was like a scene right out of a bad thriller movie with zombies and high-speed car chases. It was a relief when we were back out on the street.

With traffic, it took almost twenty minutes to drive back to Grauman's Chinese Theatre. Ryan squeezed and kissed my hand as I tried to get him to calm down and focus, thanking him for loving me and apologizing in between. My poor man was spun up and in worse shape than I was and it was time for him to put his game face on. Our car was pulling up to the curb.

This is it. Go time. I have never been this nervous in all my life.

Ryan let out a long, laborious breath, locking his eyes on mine. "Remember what I said. Eyes and ears open. Ready?"

As soon as Ryan's foot hit the sidewalk, fans started screaming. I froze from the shock of hearing the deafening volume coming from the crowd. Ryan waved quickly, fastened the button on his jacket, and then turned back to my open door to give me his hand.

Holy shit.

There are no words, no preparations that could ever be instructed, for what I was experiencing at that very moment.

Thousands of people, like a thrashing sea of undulating bodies, were screaming, packed in tightly behind the barricades that barely held them back. Many of them were waving posters, books, and pictures for Ryan to sign, shrieking at the top of their lungs to get his attention.

The words "frantic mob" and "oh my God, I'm going to die" quickly came to mind.

No wonder Ryan panicked earlier. Having so many people in such close proximity, shrieking for your attention, was ten steps beyond terrifying. I feared that at any moment the dam could give way, allowing the horde to breach our small plot of land and stampede us to death. I started to shake. My first survival instinct clicked in and I found myself desperately searching the rolling red carpet for all possible exits.

There were so many others inside the confines of the barriers, wandering, looking, it was confusing and overwhelming. Huge movie posters for *Reparation* were standing like statues, towering overhead.

A few people were speaking into Ryan's ear already, instructing him where to go and leading him forward. Hand in hand, we took our first steps, forever protected by our faithful bodyguard, Mike Murphy.

Photographers lined the other barriers, pushing, flashing, and yelling for us. Not only did they have expensive cameras, but I noticed there were quite a few with laptops as well, beaming the first pictures of us instantly to their tabloid and press feeds.

Trish hurried to Ryan's side. "I just received a call from Marla . . . she said I'm supposed to leave? I . . . I don't understand." Her eyes toggled back and forth between Ryan's face and questioning the cell she held in her hand.

"Marla and I are done," Ryan informed her quickly.

"What? Um . . . I . . . ," she stammered.

Ryan signed a few more autographs in between smiling, posing, and greeting his fans.

"You want a job?" he asked her privately, seizing my hand in his.

"Mr. Christensen, this way please," some man in a suit instructed, ushering us to follow him.

"Trish, I need a publicist—now," Ryan said, maintaining his focus amid all the chaos that surrounded us.

Trish's mouth opened but no words followed. Much to my relief, it only took her several seconds to finally nod and switch to full-on business mode, handling Ryan's appearance skillfully.

Ryan held me at his side, always within inches of him, even when he stopped to greet more adoring fans.

"Ryan, we have *Access Hollywood* and the ReelzChannel up first," Trish informed. "Taryn, you stay back here. Focus on Ryan as he speaks because you will be on camera. I need extra security right here." She pulled Ryan along by the elbow to keep him moving.

I stood off to the side, proudly beaming at my fiancé as he gave brief interviews. His smile, charm, and humbled enthusiasm never faltered even when Trish guided him from microphone to microphone.

Time and time again each reporter asked when we were getting married, to which he happily and repeatedly replied, "I don't know. We just got engaged. We haven't discussed it yet."

Just like that, with three simple sentences, our engagement became officially confirmed news.

After congratulating us on our pending nuptials, the *Entertainment Tonight* interviewer asked for my thoughts about the film. The intimidating microphone tilted in my direction and somehow my mouth turned into the Sahara and all of the saliva inconveniently disappeared from my mouth. I felt Ryan reassuringly squeeze my hand.

"I haven't had an opportunity to see it yet. Tonight will be my first screening," I answered with a smile, relieved that I didn't sound like an idiot.

"And I'm just looking forward to seeing her reaction." Ryan beamed proudly at me.

Fortunately that was the only question she asked before we had to move on to the next microphone.

As we walked the gauntlet of reporters, it became blatantly obvious why Ryan had freaked out earlier. Stand, pose, smile, turn, look, interview, sign this—all accompanied by excited screams and shrieks from thousands of enamored fans.

Seeing Ryan interact with his fans was both fascinating and scary. I feared for his safety as one after another reached for him. A moment of reprieve couldn't have come sooner. I was escorted by two hulking bodyguards over to Ryan's family, where I waited while he conducted more interviews and posed for photographers. The VIP area, where I tried to look like I belonged while a few very well-known celebrities passed through, seemed to be a safe place. It was also the place where I was able to catch up with some other familiar faces, namely Cal Reynolds and his wife, Kelly Gael. I was so happy to see that they came out to support Ryan's premiere.

While we were talking, a well-dressed woman with stick-straight, shoulder-length brown hair approached me. She looked to be in her forties, very fit, but true age was deceiving in L.A. As I took in the sight of her, I noticed that she had the most fetching smile and the rosiest cheeks I had ever seen.

"Excuse me. Hi! You must be Taryn?" she asked.

"Yes! Hello!" I returned her cheery greeting.

She held out her hand. "I'm Anna—Anna Garrett. I'm one of the film's executive producers. A bit overwhelming, isn't it?"

"Yes. Yes it is!" I said, glancing around. "And spectacular and amazing as well."

"I've heard so much about you; it's nice to finally meet you. Oh, I believe you've already met my husband?" she said in a very distinct British accent. One tiny tinge of panic crept up my throat as I hoped not to get falsely accused of anything. She tugged on a man's suit coat and the moment he turned around I immediately recognized him. He was the only film director I knew personally.

"Oh, yes! Yes of course. Mr. Follweiler. It's so nice to see you again!"

"Taryn my dear!" Jonathan Follweiler smiled, hugging me awkwardly. His rough gray beard pricked my cheek. "Oh, it's good to see you, too! How have you been? Well, I hope?"

I nodded quickly.

"You look absolutely radiant," he complimented, admiring me sincerely.

"You look quite dashing yourself, sir," I replied. His sapphire hankie and necktie suited him well.

"'Sir'? No, no, Taryn, please call me Jonathan. So how's our boy doing these days?" he asked, craning his neck in Ryan's direction.

"He's great." It was the most benign answer I could give, considering the earlier circumstances. "And he's anxious to get back to work." *And away from this insanity.*

"Good! So am I," he admitted on the sly. "Are you coming to Vancouver with Ryan?"

"Yes. As soon as we come back from the European press junket," I said.

Jonathan smiled warmly. "That's wonderful news. Then you and Anna can keep each other company."

I felt a hand touch my shoulder. It was Trish. "Excuse me. Sorry to interrupt. Taryn, we're ready for your photo op with Ryan," she said.

"Right. No worries," Anna said with a wink. "We can catch up later."

"I look forward to seeing you at the after-party," I said, reaching to give them both a hug goodbye. It was almost pure elation to finally feel accepted by some of the influential people in my new life—in our new life.

Ryan smiled and seemed relieved to see me again, but as soon as I was next to him, his brow furrowed and he appeared wary. "You ready for this?"

I gave him a reassuring smile and a quick nod. "I'm ready."

Ryan led me by the hand to stand in front of a huge wall emblazoned with the *Reparation* movie logo. He quickly stepped behind me, standing on my right side instead of my left.

"Okay," I giggled nervously, confused as to why he repositioned himself.

Ryan placed his lips right next to my ear. "Put your hand on my chest." He laughed lightly to make it look like we were sharing a private joke. "I want *everyone* to see your ring," he said emphatically, gazing into my eyes with a certain tenderness that was mesmerizing. "It's time to go big or go home. I want everyone to know you're mine, Taryn."

We smiled and posed while the press took our picture a million times. The photographers were yelling our names so often that I didn't know which camera I was supposed to look at.

Ryan's grin was infectious. "Did I tell you how exceptionally beautiful you look tonight?"

As I gazed up into his eyes, personal vanity was low on my emotion chart. Instead, I said what I truly felt. "I am *so* proud of you."

My smile broadened as he rested his forehead on mine.

"I love you," he whispered, his fingertips gently holding my raised chin. "Never doubt that." And then, in front of hundreds of cameras—softly, adoringly—he kissed me.

CHAPTER 4

Party

O NCE RYAN'S PUBLIC appearance outside was over, we made our way into the plush theater for the screening of *Reparation*. Gone were the feelings of doubt, replaced by new confidence about my role as his fiancée.

I tried to concentrate on the film but it was difficult, knowing that Ryan was mostly watching my reactions instead of the screen. He had already seen the film during private screenings when he had to do voice-overs and I knew he didn't like watching his own movies. He said it was the narcissistic aspect of it that bothered him.

Ryan whispered with disbelief into my ear. "Are you *crying?*"

"Shh." I elbowed him gently and wiped the moisture from my cheek. I couldn't help it; Ryan's character had just saved a bullied teenage girl from committing suicide when she tried to hang herself in the school cafeteria. To say it was heart-wrenching was an under-statement.

Ryan was overly concerned by my emotional reaction, laughing uncomfortably and nudging me as if to break the hold the film had on my attention. When I didn't give in to his provoking, he looked past me and sighed when he saw that his mother was crying, too.

I took his hand in mine and brought it to my lips. I didn't know how else to tell him how awestruck I was.

"Oh my God!" Marie breathed out, turning around to face us when the movie was over. Both she and Tammy were wiping their fingers under their eyes from the tear-jerker ending. The credits were rolling when I grabbed Ryan's lapel to pull him in for a quick kiss. I nuzzled up against him, wiping my tears away, trying to regain my touch with reality after that emotional roller-coaster ride. My future husband was absolutely remarkable. I had never felt so much pride for a man before this moment.

Less than an hour later, we arrived at the hotel where my first lavish after-party was being held.

Before our car came to a complete stop, Ryan focused on me, whispering last-minute instructions. "Stay with me, okay? Do not let go of my hand. And do not look at the paparazzi or say anything to them. Just follow my lead."

My pulse was thrumming at a dizzying pace. Paparazzi landed on our car from all sides, yelling, shouting, lighting up the nighttime sky with thousands of bright flashes. I anticipated that Mike would immediately open my door but instead he halted, yelling at the paparazzi to back up. Moving Ryan from place to place was a daunting task, to say the least. The three or four annoying paparazzi who hounded him while he was in Rhode Island with me were nothing compared to the fifty or more that swarmed us now. A few cameramen were shoving in closer, constricting around us like hungry vipers at feeding time, while brawny event security guards helped Mike move us along. I felt Ryan's hand tense as he speed-walked us toward the entrance.

Ryan's agent, Aaron Lyons, immediately collected us when we entered the lavish ballroom, giving me a warm hug and an adoring kiss on the cheek. Another welcomed relief. At least his agent wanted to be friendly and play nice.

Aaron knew exactly how to work a room full of Hollywood money and power, introducing us to everyone important and steering us away from those deemed unworthy of our precious time. Aaron treated me with kindness, continuously referring to me as "Ryan's fiancée, the lovely Ms. Taryn Mitchell."

We chatted with producers, studio executives, screenwriters, scriptwriters, cinematographers, sound editors, and every girlfriend, wife, husband, and partner who came with them. Business cards were flashed and I gladly took them when offered. This was high-profile networking—Hollywood-style. A far cry from the demands of owning a simple stand-alone business, but nothing I couldn't handle.

I at least had enough business sense to know that regardless of the particular industry, business is business—and it comes with a predefined set of rules. Most of the time, the power to make you or break you depends on your ability to make a good first impression.

This was Ryan's world and if I had any hopes of surviving in it, I had to start paying attention to how the game was played. So I started with the basics. Easy to do, since the majority of the room was male. And at the core, men are easily swayed by good ol' fashioned charm.

I laced in there another no-brainer that was as comfortable to me as breathing—the first rule of business. You want to know how something works, you follow the money. You find out how it's made and who controls it. And then you speak the language.

Ryan and I were in mid-conversation with his *Reparation* co-star and onscreen love interest, Jenna Rayford, and Jonathan Follweiler and his wife, Anna, when out of nowhere Marla approached and barged into our circle, wearing that fake smile she so insidiously presents to the rest of the unknowing world.

"Jonathan!" she said warmly, giving him an air kiss. "So good to see you again."

Ryan took a swig of beer from the bottle in his hand and looked away, making that little sucking sound through his teeth that he always does when he's irritated. I squeezed his hand gently and contemplated our exit strategy. It didn't take me long to come up with one.

"I'd like to talk with Kelly and Cal before they leave," I said privately in his ear, spotting them sitting at a table. "Come with me?"

Ryan didn't hesitate. We politely excused ourselves.

"Oh Ryan?" Marla called out, hurrying behind us. "I was wondering if we might speak."

Damn, we weren't quick enough.

Ryan stopped and groaned. "What?" he said sharply. "What do you want?"

"Oh, come now. Surely you're not still sour with me? What happened earlier is in the past. I know you didn't mean to say those awful things and I want you to know that I forgive you."

Ryan scoffed. "You really are a piece of work, Marla. I can't believe I've been so blind to you for all these years. Just so there's no confusion, I meant what I said earlier. You are no longer my publicist."

I was proud of him for sticking to his guns.

Marla's head wiggled on her neck as she collected herself. I could clearly, as if looking through a piece of glass, see her coat the tip of her next sentence with poison.

"Let me remind you—if you choose to sever our relationship, you sever your interactions with my entire organization as well."

"Fine," Ryan said, unruffled. "I'm sure you'll send me a bill."

Marla's lips twitched. "*Tricia*," she bellowed towards the bar where Trish was hiding, secretly observing. Marla impatiently snapped her fingers. God, I hated that. I wanted to snap her bony fingers like twigs.

"Tricia," she said with a forced grin, "Mr. Christensen has foolishly decided to terminate his contract with Brown and Sullivan. I can't help but feel as though you had something to do with this."

Trish instantly appeared mortified and shook her head in denial.

"Well, in any case, it doesn't much matter anymore. I gave you specific instructions earlier and you chose to defy them. I cannot have my employees thinking they can undermine my decisions."

"Marla, I thought you would want me to—" Trish tried to explain.

Marla cut her off with a flutter of her hand. "As I said dear, it doesn't matter. Your employment with Brown and Sullivan is hereby terminated, effective immediately. You can contact HR to arrange picking up your personal things on Monday. Give me your security badge." Marla held out her hand.

I felt the shock hit my chest and creep up my throat. The very last thing I wanted to happen was playing out in front of me. I wasn't sure if Ryan was completely serious when he offered her a job.

"You're firing me?" Trish asked. Shock and anguish made her lip quiver.

Marla smirked. "You are quick," she said condescendingly. "Perhaps you won't be so underhanded in your next job."

Trish's hand trembled as she dug in her clutch purse. I wanted to hug her and scream a few obscenities at Marla for being such a royal bitch. Man, she was cold.

Ryan rubbed his forehead. "Look, if you're pissed-off at me—fine—but don't take it out on her."

Marla crossed her arms and planted a high-heel-clad foot. "I don't see how any of this concerns you." She snapped her fingers for Trish to speed it up. "She disobeyed my orders."

"And I overrode them!" Ryan stressed. "I asked her to stay."

"And here I thought you could survive without my services," Marla snidely returned, flitting her eyes. Trish handed a card attached to a chain to Marla and sniffed back some tears.

My emotions swirled furiously. Anger, denial, hatred, and guilt raced through my thoughts, each trying to dominate. Ryan was speechless, searching for a good comeback that failed to surface.

I had to do something.

"Um, Ryan? I believe Trish is now a free agent," I stated. "And she is more than qualified to handle your PR." I gave him one of our private signals, darting my eyes at Marla briefly and scratching my chin, conveying the message that he should tell her to go to hell. His eyes brightened and he nodded.

"Yes . . . yes she is," Ryan confirmed.

"And you just so happen to be looking for new representation." *That's right, honey. Tell her off.* Marla could shove it deep where the sun doesn't shine. We might not be able to save Trish completely, but

I was going to make damn sure she at least walked away with her dignity.

"We're done here, right?" he asked Marla, dismissing her as if she were no longer of importance.

It was extremely enjoyable to watch Marla's face crumble in defeat. How I wished I could have videotaped it so we could watch it over and over again for laughs.

Ryan clutched my hand in his and glanced at his empty beer bottle. "What do you say, ladies—time to discuss Trish's new salary over a few shots of tequila? That is if you want to work for me."

Trish grinned from ear to ear. "Hell yeah!" she said enthusiastically.

"You can't do that," Marla said with failed authority.

Ryan smirked at her. "Watch me."

AFTER TWO hours of schmoozing with people I didn't know, I felt awful for not paying any attention to my friends. I searched the room for them, only to notice that one of my friends was sitting at an empty table.

"Hey, why are you sitting here all by yourself?" I asked Pete. I sat down in the chair next to him.

Pete looked confused. "I'm not alone. Gary just went to the men's room."

"Oh. Where are the girls?" I looked around for Marie and Tammy.

Pete pointed to a far corner. "They're over there yappin'. Gary is really pissed that Marie keeps touching that guy in the black shirt. You might want to say something to her before it gets ugly. He's kind of drunk."

I looked over and saw my two best friends laughing heartily with a group of people. I didn't know who the guy was, but he had short-cropped brown hair and looked like a male model from this distance.

I hadn't been able to spend much time with my friends since we arrived, but I did notice Gary sitting at this table, scowling all night.

"I'll take care of it—in a minute." I craned my neck to get a better view. "That's Marcia Gay Harden on Tammy's left. She played the principal, remember?"

Pete nodded but I could tell that he really didn't care. He wasn't impressed by celebrities unless they were wearing football or baseball uniforms. He actually looked tired and ready for bed. I could relate.

"Where's Ryan?"

I nodded in his general direction. "Over there. He's talking to Edward Zwick." Pete looked lost. "The director?"

"Ooh, he's talking to the director," Pete said in a teasing tone, like the simple fact that my fiancé was holding court with the who's-who of Hollywood was no biggie. Pete's face turned serious. "Are you sure you're up for all of this?" His eyes bore into mine, trying to read me.

I chewed on my lip as I pondered his question. The room was so full of wealth and pretentiousness, we were both feeling out of place.

"I know what you're trying to say, but all of this really isn't *Ryan*, either. He's uncomfortable with this, too, you know."

Pete nodded, mostly agreeing with me.

"Besides, maybe all of this is who I'm supposed to be. I've just been going through the motions for so long now, running the bar out of—out of guilt." I huffed. "If my dad were still alive, I'd probably be sitting behind some desk in Manhattan being completely miserable instead of being here."

"Yeah," Pete concurred. "Probably. Although you could have had your own fame, you know."

A tiny "gah" sound squeaked out. "Yeah right."

"Don't give me that shit, Taryn. You know damn well I speak the truth. But instead of trying to model, you let those idiots in school make you feel unworthy."

Memories of being singled out and bullied, enduring relentless taunting because I had bigger boobs than most and had a chubby boy for a best friend, weren't things I wanted to think about right now. Even Marie and Melanie questioned why I stuck around with Pete so much back then. But none of their opinions mattered more than what Pete had mattered to me. He was the only person who came to my rescue when Emily Howard pushed me down on the playground on the first day of school, and for years he was the brother I'd never had.

By the time we reached high school, Pete slimmed down, grew taller, and joined the wrestling team, but one thing remained the same—he always had my back. He was and still is my best friend.

Pete waved a finger around. "Over two dozen heads turned when you walked over here. I'm surprised you didn't trip over a few drooling tongues along the way. I was afraid I'd have to kick some ass to fend them off."

"Shut up."

"No, you shut up!" Pete seemed amused. "I think that's what I love the most about you, kid. You're the most self-deprecating person I know, even though you have absolutely no reason to be."

I winced. How absurd. "Everyone's just curious to see who was able to capture Ryan's attention, that's all."

"See? You can't even take a compliment about not being able to take compliments. You've always been an enigma, Ms. Mitchell. A complete contradiction."

I bristled with fake horror. "Did you just call me an enema?"

"Yep. You're a total pain in my ass."

I laughed at our banter. We had always had this easy friendship, even lasting while he was madly in love with Melanie, the sister of my ex, Thomas. Throughout the years I often pretended Pete and I were really brother and sister, separated by a tragic mix-up in the hospital. He was always there for me no matter what, watching over me like a brother should.

Something caught his eye. "Ryan is a good man . . . a *real* good man, Taryn. I'm glad everything worked out. You finally picked one that doesn't trigger my urge to bash his head in."

I smirked at his lording. "Thanks." It warmed my heart to know that Pete and Ryan had a lot of respect for each other.

The niggling memory of just seven days ago, when I thought Ryan's parents had come to move him out of the apartment, crept back into my thoughts. "I just wish one of you would have told me what was going on."

Pete's attention averted to his drink but it was time we had this talk. "I almost did. I came close to spilling the beans a few times. I couldn't stand seeing you in so much pain. Just know . . . it killed me."

"So why didn't you?"

He swirled the ice in his glass, hesitating. "Truth? Because I wasn't sure. I didn't know if Ryan would actually do it or not. I mean, he told us he was going to. Hell, he even asked us all for our blessing. But then you two were touch-and-go there for a few days and . . ."

He straightened up and looked me in the eyes. "If we would have told you he was going to propose and then he didn't . . . God . . . I just couldn't do that to you, Taryn."

I rubbed my hand gently, briefly over his shoulder, trying to alleviate his obvious remorse. "I understand. I . . . I just feel like such an idiot, carrying on the way I did. Seeing him kiss Lauren in that restaurant and that freakin' note . . . it was so convincing. I know I should have never doubted him, but standing there watching it, it was like reliving the Thomas nightmare all over again. Only this time, it hurt a million times worse."

Pete's lips curled into a familiar, sympathetic smile.

"I know what you're going to say next," I interjected, reading the rest of Pete's expression. "I have to put that all behind me now and never allow myself to get that low again."

"Yep," he confirmed with a smirk. "But what you also have to keep in mind is that this time around, you're with a guy who's totally in love with you."

I didn't need to be an interpreter to catch Pete's allusion. Despite his contrary actions and Pete's opinion, Thomas did love me. He even said it to me out loud once. He just didn't know how to show it all the time.

Pete glanced over in Ryan's direction. "I mean, just look at him. He's got all sorts of women hovering around him but he never acknowledges them—ever. He's been like that since the first day he walked into your pub. Like you are the only woman on the planet. And the funny thing is, no matter where you are in the room, Ryan knows exactly where you are. He may be talking to somebody rich and famous but he's *always* got one eye trained on you. That poor bastard. He's such a goner."

I rolled my eyes at his teasing.

"Speaking of goners . . . before I forget, Tammy has been bugging me. You know we still have a little problem with the wedding and who you're going to be partnered with. I didn't want to ask my cousin in case you wanted Ryan but . . . do you want me to ask Ryan?"

"Ask me what?"

My head jerked, surprised by his voice. Ryan reached out and gently caressed my cheek in his hand, silently mouthing "hi" to me. In that moment, everything else ceased to exist. His love for me was overwhelming and in that instant something new, something profoundly deep tied us even stronger. I felt it as sure as I felt my own heartbeat. I gathered his warm hand quickly and gave it a kiss.

"Oh hey," Pete said, giving me the "see what I mean" lopsided look I know so well.

Ryan straddled the chair next to me, pressing his body close to mine. My mind quickly veered to thinking about how much I'd like to just snuggle up in his arms and end this tiring day. I was starting to feel like Pete looked—exhausted. Ryan softly kissed the exposed skin on my shoulder and oh so seductively drifted the tip of his nose on my neck. *Freaking tease.*

Pete cleared his throat. "Ryan, I was wondering how you'd feel about being Taryn's partner in our wedding. I'd be honored if you were one of my groomsmen."

Ryan perked up a bit. "Really? Wow. Sure, I guess. Um . . . wait. I don't know," he said. That's when he parked his forehead on my shoulder.

"I thought you were clear for the first weekend of September?" I reached for my phone to check his calendar, swearing that I had blocked it off, but other thoughts quickly dawned on me.

"I am, I think," he muttered. "That's not it. Pete, I'm honored that you asked but I don't know if that's such a good idea. You know I tend to cause a stir wherever I go. I don't want to ruin your wedding day. That's your day."

I set my evening bag back down on the table and sighed, imagining the pandemonium that would ensue from Ryan and me being seen in a church together. This morning's tabloid gossip reported that Ryan proposed because I'm supposedly pregnant. "Yeah, he's right. You don't want the paparazzi at your wedding."

"Ah, screw them. I want you there," Pete retorted emphatically, poking the white tablecloth with his finger to emphasize his point.

The more I considered it, the more I envisioned Tammy's wedding being ruined by party-crashers and hundreds of photographers all vying for a clear shot of Ryan in a tux. "No. It's not a good idea," I said remorsefully. "Just ask your cousin."

Ryan cleared his throat. "Um, I don't recall saying *no*," he corrected me. "Can I get back to you on that, Pete?"

I didn't understand why Ryan would need time to think about it. After the big deal that was made out of our proposal photos, I could only imagine the crap that would be printed from us being seen walking in and out of a church.

What's going to happen when Ryan and I get married? My mind filled with visions of helicopters flying overhead, security everywhere wearing hidden communication earpieces like the damn Secret Service—checking to make sure that the poor caterers weren't paparazzi spies.

Just as my mind started to drift further into those ghastly images, my slightly inebriated fiancé bit his teeth gently but firmly into the nape of my neck.

A heated tickle shivered through me as he whispered "dance with me" into my ear.

Ryan led me by the hand, weaving us through the bodies that slowly swayed on the dance floor. The tacky mirror ball that twirled over the center of the floor cast sparkles of twinkling light through the darkness, swirling me further into this amazingly enchanted evening.

I caressed the nape of his neck as he wrapped me securely in his arms, resting his cheek on my temple. It was nice to share a moment of peace in this very stressful day.

Ryan gently smiled. "Are you having fun?"

I beamed back at him and nodded. "Yes. Very much so. Thank you for yet another amazing night."

His deep voice lowered. "Thank you for sharing it with me. You really impressed me tonight, schmoozing with Universal's moneymen like that. You really know your shit about finances."

I shrugged. "I know enough to be dangerous. I just want to learn as much as I can about this business, that's all."

"Learn? By the look on Jeff Westfield's face when you started telling him all that shit about P/E ratios and ways he can diversify his whatever, I'd say you were the teacher, sweetheart."

Doubtful. Although I was trying to impress, I didn't want to be thought of as nothing more than arm candy with boobs.

"You don't think? He just offered you *a job.* At Universal."

"A comment like 'if you're ever in L.A. and need anything, come see me' hardly constitutes a job offer, Ryan. He was just being nice."

Ryan didn't agree. "For someone who can read people well, you're *way* off on this one."

"I can read you," I said smugly.

"Oh yeah? Can you tell what I'm thinking now?" That smirk of his contained many innuendos.

Our mutual smiles led to a kiss—one that was almost impolite considering we were among several hundred people. His lips parted and his tongue reached for mine and I couldn't help but drink him in. The tastes of whiskey and beer blended with champagne and chocolate, creating a flavor that was all our own.

"God, the things I want to do to you right now," he breathed out on my lips. "What do you say we get out of here? I need to lay you down on a bed."

"Oh really?" I teased, somewhat breathless.

"Uh huh." Ryan nodded devilishly. His eyes narrowed on me. "What, aren't you in the mood?"

"No, no, I am. Absolutely," I quickly replied. "But . . ."

"But what?"

"I'm just curious. So what is it *exactly* that you want to do to me? It's just . . . I want to know what's in store for me before I agree to leave this wonderful party."

Ryan smirked, his hand resting on the small of my back, guiding our hips. "I thought we'd play it by ear. See what pops up when we get there. But I can definitely tell you that I have something *huge* that I want to give ya."

I made a face at him, biting my lip thinking about it. "Er . . . I don't know. I was hoping for more details than that. I think you'll have to come up with a better script."

He folded our hands to his chest and swayed us to the beat.

"How about we play 'bad cop—hooker'? I'd like to see you restrained."

With full intent to tease, I sneered at his suggestion. "I've seen that movie already. Maybe you should hire a scriptwriter. I think I met a few of those tonight. Let me go find one . . ."

Ryan pulled me back to his chest roughly, never releasing his hold on my hand.

"I thought that this might be a co, co, llab . . . collab-bora-tive effort. Shit."

"*Great* . . . sloppy five-minute drunken sex," I whined, messing with him further.

Ryan gave me a playful leer and tightened his grip on my body. "Believe me, woman, I'm far from drunk. I'm going to take my good ol' time with you," he whispered, his lips brushing my ear. "Use the sheets to tie your little smart ass to the bed. Punish you for doubting me. See how long you can ride my tongue before you scream."

His erotic words tugged on that sweet spot deep within my core. I could definitely go for one of his tongue lashings.

I ran a hand over his hard chest, down his flat stomach, imagining my fingernails turning into claws, effortlessly shredding the white dress shirt that separated me from his skin. I whispered into his ear, "I'm betting that you pass out as soon as your head hits the pillow."

He took the back of my neck in a possessive grasp as he raked his top teeth over his lip. "That's a bet you're sure to lose, my love, because I am definitely, *definitely* up for the challenge."

I squeezed my fingers into his buttocks, coaxing his hips to grind in a bit harder as if he were already naked and between my legs. I didn't care that we were in a room full of people.

The music swirled and the lights danced around us, sending my blood into hyperdrive. Ryan's finger drifted, seductively snaking down my neck, over the hollow of my throat, down to the crest of my cleavage. I envisioned his tongue snaking the same path.

He sighed, almost saddened, resigned. "The hardest part is knowing that underneath this *incredibly* sexy dress is a totally hot lace bustier and sheer panties that you put on when you thought I wasn't looking. But I have to confess . . . I was *so* looking."

I nudged him lightly. "That was supposed to be a surprise!"

All playfulness was gone, replaced by determination and hunger. His lips came down on mine, taking ownership of my mouth, of my senses. One touch of his tongue was all I needed to open and let him in.

"Don't be mad," he murmured, reminding me that he still possessed total control of my body. "I'm an actor, remember? I can play *surprised*."

My mind drifted, picturing his long, hard body holding me fast to the bed. He wants to pretend to be surprised? I'll give him surprised.

"You're obviously not a very good Peeping Tom, since you failed to mention that I'm wearing your favorite item."

He glanced down at the floor. "The stilettos?"

I shook my head.

As if I'd just told him Santa Claus was truly real, his eyes opened wide, all glistening and hopeful. His hand flew to my thigh, seeking confirmation. A deep, feral groan rolled up this throat when he found the top band of my nylons.

I bit his earlobe tenderly. "I'd much rather you played evil doctor with me."

That was apparently all he could take.

"I am going to fuck you in those shoes. That and the nylons. When we get back to the room, they stay on." Ryan grabbed my hand and quickly led us through the crowd. There was no stopping him. He was a man on a mission.

CHAPTER 5

Oui

THROUGH MY BLISSFULLY heavy eyes, I barely took in the sights of another opulent hotel suite, dimly lit from the soft glow of a table lamp. The last eleven days had blurred into one continuous streak of hurried travel, decadent meals, paparazzi chases, limo rides, blinding camera flashes, and screaming fans to the point that I was dizzy from it all.

Ryan's mouth tenderly caressed the base of my neck as he panted heavily from physical exertion. My lungs ached as if they were at risk of collapse from dragging in so many repeated shallow breaths.

His muscular back arched, allowing refreshing air to channel between our sweat-soaked bodies. His hips rolled and pushed in one more time, sending another ripple through me as his hands pinned my wrists to the bed. I felt the bristly brush of his stubbly chin rasp over my cheek as he lifted his eyes to meet mine.

"Welcome to Paris," he said softly, rolling the tip of his tongue up the length of my neck, tasting me before covering my lips with his own again.

Considering our plane from Heathrow landed just two and a half hours ago and we were driven straight from the airport to this magnificent hotel, I had barely seen Paris. The first order of business, after spending a few hours salaciously flirting on the airplane, was to strip each other bare and make mad passionate love in this pristine bed.

Responding to his little tease, knowing that he was totally proud of his abilities to ruin me, would have to wait. Most of the pillows had been pushed to the floor, the sheets were in complete disarray, and powerful aftershocks from my mind-blowing orgasm were still jolting my body.

I took the momentary reprieve of my lips to exhale out the one French word I knew. "Oui."

Even making that one little sound felt like a monumental feat.

Ryan's gaze was thoughtful and intense, silently telling me everything that words alone could not define nor express. Desire to devour him overwhelmed me and I grazed my teeth over his muscular biceps before tugging his hair so I could suck that tasty little lobe of his ear into my mouth. Ryan let out a growl of pleasure before reuniting our lips for more passion.

Anticipation for what was to come, knowing that he was far from finished with me, heightened the sensations even further. He was being a considerate lover, pausing to allow me some time to recover before unleashing the rest of his wickedness on me.

I tried to steady my breathing and my pounding pulse, feeling the sweat of our lovemaking bead up on my hairline. Hot, wet, and tangled; there wasn't an open part of us left to be connected. I caressed my hands up over his muscular back to his shoulders; my arms wrapped tighter as if my grip could somehow pull him deeper into my soul.

When I drifted my hands down his sides to appreciate his most incredible rear end, he clenched and pressed into me again—slowly— still feeling very formidable and unyielding inside. His pelvis tipped and brushed up on me again, grinding his hips deep with carnal drive into my core.

I tilted my head, giving him full access to my throat. If the world were to unfortunately end at this very moment, I'd go a very sated woman. I felt his teeth graze my skin, his primal urges to covet and devour surging to the forefront.

Ryan's body suddenly stilled and he swept a few errant hairs from in front of my eyes, locking his gaze on mine. His face was so serene and yet so serious. He swallowed, collecting his breath before he said, "Je t'aime. Je t'adore. Veux-tu m'épouser?"

Hearing the inflection in his voice as he seduced me with foreign words, and hands that knew every inch of my body, made my thighs quiver.

I threaded my fingers into his hair as he placed soft, sensual kisses on my face, the corners of my mouth, my neck. Willing my mouth to do anything other than kiss him while he fucked me like this was difficult.

"I didn't know . . . you knew . . . how . . . to speak French."

Ryan captured my lower lip between his, swirling me in dizzying passion with each kiss, each lick, each succulent suck from his hypnotic mouth. He rolled his hips deliberately, reminding me that he was still very much in the game.

"I don't, but there were a few things I wanted to learn to say to you while we're in Paris. Like this. Making love to you."

My breath hitched from the feelings he invoked. "You had this planned?"

His nose brushed next to mine. Instead of answering, he kissed me deeply. His tongue said yes.

"Tell me," I gasped away. "Tell me what you said." I tightened my interior muscles on one of his surges, drawing an erotic groan from his chest. He pressed my hair back with his hands, cradling my face.

Ryan's words came out in a sensual whisper. "*Je t'aime* means I love you."

His muscular thighs shifted as his feet found new footing on the bed. My thighs strained farther apart to accept him. I felt his length top out inside me, surging the most intense of pleasures. Filling me like no one else could. Marking me as his from the inside with everything he had. His hands slid my arms above my head and he twined our fingers together.

Somewhat breathlessly but with much conviction, he said, "*Je t'adore* means I adore you."

Ripples of emotion coursed through my chest as he gazed directly into my eyes, me feeling so completely loved by this man, in complete awe of his presence, his gentle ways, his undeniable claim that he staked in my heart. Tears of joy blurred my eyes and dripped to the pillow.

"I adore you, too. You are my forever, *mon amour.*"

Ryan's mouth sealed on top of mine; his hips curled and surged like the unrelenting tide. Pressure was building up inside me, aching for another release.

As if a moment of deep contemplation struck him, his hips completely stilled and he cleared his throat—several times.

"*Veux-tu m'épouser* means will you—" His thumbs tenderly brushed the wet streaks left behind from my weeping eyes, taking careful measure to soothe it all. "It means will you marry me."

Air stuttered down my throat as the magnitude of his words aligned with their meaning. New tears welled and spilled from the edges of my eyes while the burning sensation of intense emotions gathered up in my chest, my throat. I felt as if I could burst at the seams.

I reached up and gently caressed his face. His eyes shimmered like two watery blue pools, glistening as magnificently as the diamond engagement ring on my left hand.

He slammed into me, deep. "Marry me, Taryn. I want to hear you say *yes* again. Tell me you want me."

My lips quaked, trying to form the ability of speech. "I want you." I ran my fingertips down the sides of his neck. "I need you to breathe. Yes. Forever. Till death takes my last breath."

His lips locked on mine, tying his question and my answer into an unbreakable knot.

Ryan's strong hand gripped my hip. "Mon amour," he said in my mouth. "You are home for me. You'll always be my home, Taryn."

I wrapped my arms around his shoulders and buried my face in his neck, kissing every inch of him uncontrollably. What started out as a private challenge to make love in every country we visited turned into something profoundly deeper. This was solidifying a union, consummating a promise to each other far beyond the intimate boundaries of physical love.

I said the only words that seemed fitting, but somehow they felt so inadequate. "I love you so much."

His hips stirred with more vigor; the bed steadily bumped into the wall. The look of painful pleasure creased his eyes. "I love you more."

I smiled and dug my fingertips into his rear, holding on, wanting him to climb deeper inside my soul.

His arms wrapped underneath me, lifting me from the warmth of the bed into a warmer embrace. I straddled up over him; my thighs provided the lift as his hand guided my rear to rock back and forth.

He lay all the way back, helping me adjust my legs. "Take me," he breathed. "All of me."

His length pummeled inside me. My hands wrapped at the base of his skull, holding his face steady so he'd look me in the eyes.

I sealed my words on his lips. "Till the day I die. Yours. Forever."

Ryan's hand locked into my hair, holding my mouth to his. "Come with me, baby," he whispered his plea, grinding me down on his pubic bone and the tip of his thumb. He kept at it, at an unrelenting, punishing pace. I felt as though I were being ripped apart and slammed back together all at once.

My head fell to his shoulder as the rolling burn of sensations, the shock-wave overload, coursed through my body.

With a deep groan, his body trembled and convulsed. I felt his warm release pulse inside of me, binding us together forever.

WHILE RYAN was busy shaving in the bathroom, I called Marie. "He proposed to me again—in French."

"While making love to you?"

"Uh huh."

"Oh my God, Taryn. That's the most romantic thing I've ever heard. Holy shit. Wait until I tell Tammy."

I moved my cell to my other ear so she could yell excitedly into that one. "No! Please don't tell anyone, Marie. Not even Tammy. This is so private. I shouldn't even be telling . . . I'm just . . . blown away. It was so amazing. I've never . . ." Moisture gathered at the corner of my eye again from thinking about it. "Ah. We have to change the subject. Tell me something else. So how are things going there? How's our pub?"

"Screw that. I want to hear more about sex in foreign countries."

"Marie . . . ," I groaned.

"The bar is still in one piece, Tar. Busy, although you'll be glad to know that the influx of obsessive fangirls has died down. Oh, and the five-foot cooler is shot. I can't believe he proposed to you *again* in French! God, I really hate you right now. Ryan Freakin' Christensen, naked in Paris, whispering French I-love-yous in your ear while doing you. Grr. So not fair. Man, why couldn't I have been the one to open the pub that day?"

I snickered lightly. "It wouldn't have mattered. You're married, remember?"

Marie snorted but not with humor. "Yeah, well. Not for long."

I grabbed my backpack to get my laptop, wishing I would have kept my big mouth shut. "Oh, Marie, come on. Listen, you know I didn't call to brag. Did we, um . . . did we get the tax bill in the mail yet? And what did you say about the cooler not working?"

"You are so determined to be a buzzkill, aren't you?" She sighed loudly. "Tar, I truly am happy for you. I hope you believe me when I say that."

"I know."

"Good. Then tell me more about your trip. I'd much rather talk about that than what's happening here. Please tell me Ryan is walking around naked."

I dug through my bag for my power cord adapter, laughing at her enthusiasm. "Towel."

"Damn. You suck."

"Very well, so he says. I just wish we had more time in each city. Two or three days is nothing. I can't believe it. In less than thirty-six hours we'll be in Barcelona. Time is flying by so fast."

"Ooh. Maybe he'll fuck you in Spanish. Can you call me while it's happening? God, I want to hear that. He should put that in his next movie—"

"Marie!"

"What? Come on, Tar! If I can't live vicariously through you, I'm gonna have to kill myself. I need to join you on your world tour. Can't I carry your luggage or something? Toss rose petals when Ryan walks?"

"What's wrong with the cooler?"

Marie let out a huff. "Someone needs to get laid on top of it. Maybe that will fix it."

"Call Gary. I'm sure he'll be happy to help."

I heard the familiar noise of the cash register tape cycling, grinding like the decrepit old-timer that it was. *One more thing in the bar that needs to be replaced.*

"Yeah, right. He hasn't talked to me since we got back from L.A., and to be honest, I couldn't care less if he ever does. I'm sick of him."

"Why? What happened?" I heard Ryan drop something in the bathroom and it made me flinch. Sounded like the can of shaving cream hitting the tiled floor.

"Ah, remember that guy from the *Reparation* after-party who thought I was a casting agent? Nate—the hottie with the incredible ass?"

I drew a vivid picture in my mind. Tall, dark brown hair. Wide shoulders with a narrow waist. Total GQ material. "Yeah. So what? Is Gary mad because you were talking to some guy?"

"Yep. When we got back to our room we got into a huge fight. He completely flipped out on me, told me I was flirting like a whore and stuff. It got . . . it got pretty ugly."

I swallowed hard, picturing Gary's anger potential at its worst. *I'll kill him if he laid a hand on her.* "How ugly?"

A few beats of silence passed. "Marie, did he hit you?"

She sighed. "No, although for a moment I wasn't sure—he was *that* angry. He said he wasn't happy anymore and he . . . he said he wants a divorce."

I felt my heart clench and I gasped. "Oh my God! No! What did you say?"

I heard her take a deep breath. "I told him if that's what he wants, I'm gone. It's not like this hasn't been brewing for a while now."

Oh, shit. "Why didn't you tell me about this before?"

"What's to say? You know how he is. When I try to talk to him about what's bothering me he shuts down or ignores me. We got into a huge fight even before we left for L.A. after I found out that he spent *another* three thousand dollars out of our account to buy another crappy car to fix up. When I told him I was mad that he bought it without discussing it with me first, he reminded me of how much more money he earns, and then he had the audacity to tell me to shut the fuck up."

"You're kidding?"

"No, I'm not. He's been . . . I don't know. I think he's seeing someone else."

I felt like freaking out. "Are you kidding me?"

"I'm not sure but I have that gut feeling, you know? He's just being really weird, yelling at me all the time. About three weeks ago, he said he was going out drinking with his friend, Tony, but he never came home. He said he crashed at Tony's but I'm pretty sure that was a lie. He's never done that before and he got all pissed-off when I asked him about it. All I know is that I can't take it anymore. I hope you don't mind, but I've been staying in your apartment the last couple of nights."

Now I really felt like crap for telling her about Ryan's second proposal. I was so wrapped up in my own little world that I had no clue she was suffering.

"Marie, you're my best friend. Whatever you need."

"Thanks. Anyway, Pete looked at the cooler. Said the compressor is shot. When we got back, the floor was all wet. I called for prices on a new one."

I didn't care about the damn cooler. "Wait. So, what . . . are you leaving him?"

She huffed. "I don't know, but I can't live this way anymore, Taryn. He's miserable. He's making me miserable. He's been avoiding me more and more, barely speaking to me."

"Sweetie, I'm so sorry."

I heard her tears crack. "You mind if I stay with you for a while?"

Her heartbreak was breaking my heart. "No, of course I don't mind. You can stay with me as long as you want."

I cursed inwardly, furious that Gary would do this to her and even more angry with myself for strapping her with all of my responsibilities while she was all alone.

"Oh, some lady from United Fidelity Bank called for your dad. Said something about a letter and him owing late fees for a safe-deposit box rental? I have her number. But just so you know, we've stopped answering the telephone. I'm trying to screen through the messages, but there are too many."

I groaned. Dealing with my parents' estate, and the unrelenting press as well, was a never-ending battle. "I have to get back there."

"No, you need to enjoy the ride for once and take care of you and Ryan and let other people handle this."

"I hate that I'm not there for you."

"Tar, you are. You are. Please don't think that."

I leaned up against the wall next to the French doors leading out to the balcony, mesmerized by the breathtaking view of the Eiffel Tower glowing in the darkened sky. My mother had dreamed of seeing the tower her whole life but never did.

After I said goodbye and ended our call, I felt horrible for dumping everything on Marie so I could be absent and carefree, running around the globe when she needed me the most.

But in a big way, having someone to take care of the bar was a huge relief, giving me a much-needed break from a life that I didn't choose.

I knelt down to straighten up the mess Ryan made when he dumped his backpack on the floor. The section of the newspaper he was reading on the plane was crumpled in the pile.

Curious, I paged through it, stopping on an article about another famous actor. I remembered distinctly that this was the last page Ryan read because shortly thereafter he appeared to be irritated by something and crammed the newspaper roughly into his pack. Right after that he laced his fingers tightly with mine. I thought maybe *Reparation* had gotten a bad review, but there was nothing else in this section of the paper that had anything to do with anything in our lives.

As I perused the story, my breath caught. The article stated that the couple had ended their four-year relationship, citing that their busy careers took them in different directions, ultimately causing their demise.

I glanced over at Ryan as he snapped the elastic band of fresh black boxer briefs around his waist, allowing me another delectable view of his chiseled abs. Could this be the reason why he was upset earlier?

Four years. That's as far as they made it in their high-profile relationship. Four measly years. Perhaps in their eyes it was long enough. In my mind, ending a relationship after four years would mean a very deep scar would be left behind, bringing the kind of heartache and devastation that's sure to kill a huge piece of your soul.

I looked down at the cell phone still clutched in my hand. I couldn't even imagine only having four years with Ryan. And yet here I was, blissfully happy, while watching Marie's marriage fall apart.

CHAPTER 6

Tour

"GOD, PARIS IS beautiful." I hid behind the tiny split in the curtain, trying to get clear shots of the sun rising over the landscape with my camera. "I have a view of the Eiffel Tower from my room!" I said excitedly, doing a little happy dance with my butt again.

Ryan laughed. "You know all your shots are going to have the glass reflection on them. Turn the flash off and go out on the terrace," he mumbled around his toothbrush.

I toggled through the settings, trying to figure out how to use my new digital pocket camera. "Can't. Don't think your fans want to see me."

Ryan groaned and pressed his chest to my back, looking over my shoulder. "How many are out there?"

"Too many to count." I tugged the curtain shut.

"We can always come back. It's different when they don't know where I am. You have full access to my schedule. Anywhere you want to go—just put it on the calendar. It's your job to manage my personal life, future wife."

Oh really? That got me grinning. Then a sad thought struck me. "It's going to be awhile until you have time off to travel for fun."

Ryan placed a soft, lingering kiss on my neck. "I know. We'll figure something out. And we also need to start thinking about building a house. Time that we had a place of our own to call home, don't you think?"

Home. That word sent an instant wave of elation through my heart and a smile a mile wide across my face.

"Big log house with a big ol' bedroom," he mumbled with his lips pressed to my neck. "How does that sound?"

"I think it sounds perfect. We're definitely going to need a big ol' bedroom for this." I grabbed the newly formed erection pressing up against the crack of my butt. "We just had sex in the shower. You're insatiable."

His hands palmed my breasts and a playful growl rolled up his throat. "I can't help that you made me hard again. It's all your fault."

Like a cat stretching, I reached around his neck. "I bet if you went out there right now with that massive stiffy you'd stop a few hundred girls' hearts from beating."

Like a naughty kid up to no good, Ryan seemed amused by my inadvertent challenge. "Since I don't have enough time to properly bed you again, let's test that theory, shall we?"

I panicked. "You're not!"

"Don't worry." He threw on his jeans and grabbed a T-shirt, whacking my rear with his hand as he passed. "Only you are privy to viewing my naughty bits, my love. Give me the camera."

Barefoot, he slipped out the door and into the morning sun. I kept the door cracked and watched as he walked to the railing. I could hear the rising screams and shouts from the crowd below. It sounded like the squawks from ten thousand excited birds trying to take flight. Ryan leaned over and waved, and then started taking pictures of the crowd, of the landscape, and of me standing by the door.

"Tar, come out here."

I stepped out and joined him. It was weird waving at screaming girls like I was someone important. *Yeah, hi, we're people up here looking out at you people standing down there.* I certainly wasn't the reason why they were gathered outside of our hotel and screaming at the tops of their lungs. Fortunately, there were eight floors separating us.

Ryan looked over at me and raised his eyebrows. "Wanna give them a show?"

"No! Oh my God, they'll hate me for sure."

"Hey, I'm just offering a bona fide public kiss here. Candid shots with lots of tongue action. Worth millions by the way."

I choked at the absurdity of that notion. "Like someone would pay a million dollars for a picture of us kissing."

"Don't laugh. Wait until the wedding photo offers come in."

"What wedding photos?"

Ryan took a few more pictures, stopping to look at them on the viewer. "Ours. When we get married. You're going to be shocked when you see the dollar figures tossed at us. Stand over there so I can get the Eiffel Tower behind you."

I leaned back on the railing, reeling in shock at the mere idea already. "Are you serious?"

He peered over the camera. "Do I look like I'm kidding?"

The thought of so many zeros for wedding photos seemed preposterous. "Like millions?"

"Probably like several million. We'll see—that's if we decide to sell. Come on, smile!"

He then stood next to me, trying to take our picture together.

"Would you want to do that? Sell our photos?"

He adjusted the camera settings and shrugged. "Honestly? No. That's private. But then again, it's also money barely earned for the front cover and an article spread inside. We could always donate it to charity."

Very noble idea. That made the idea more palatable. "You'd consider it? Giving the money to charity?"

"Absolutely. There are plenty of them out there. Charities for needy kids. Sick kids." He turned the camera around on us again and clicked. "You know, we don't have to wait for our wedding if you want to do something humanitarian. Talk to Trish."

I thought about the shoe box of photos I had back in my apartment. "It's hard to imagine personal pictures having anything more than sentimental value. But if we can, I'd like to do something to help children."

"We did a few charity-type things when we filmed the two *Sea-sides*. Anyway, we can think about selling our wedding photos later." He pulled me to his chest. "I'm rather enjoying the engagement phase right now. A lot."

His grin was priceless.

"Are you going to kiss me in public?"

Ryan smiled devilishly. "You bet your sweet ass I am. I'm capturing the moment, too."

His lips were on mine so fast I barely had time to breathe. Amazing how every thought melted away into a blur of nothingness when he kissed me.

He backed me up until my body made contact with the glass door, taking pictures of us with my camera held out, giddy with our playfulness.

"How long until those paparazzi pictures of us hit the Internet?" I joked, stumbling back into our suite.

"Ahh, who cares. You need to quit worrying about things like that."

Easy for him to say. That kiss probably hung a new tabloid target around my neck.

RYAN'S PRESS interviews started promptly at 9 A.M., held at a different hotel in Paris.

We were whisked away in yet another chauffeured town car, allowing me to gaze in wonder at the sights. That's when it hit me—another moment of awe at how lucky I was.

I slipped my hand into Ryan's, wondering how I could ever thank him for such a gift.

David, Trish, and Ryan's agent, Aaron, were in the car in front of us. Mike stretched his arms out to shield us as we exited. The press, foreign paparazzi, and a small cluster of fans shouted for our attention, snapping photos of our arrival.

"How long are we going to be?" I asked Trish, secretly hoping to visit the opulent gift shop and maybe the boutique several doors down that had a really cool leather jacket displayed on a mannequin.

She looked at her watch. "About three hours."

I clutched Ryan's arm right before he got too involved in the commotion. I knew I wouldn't be allowed anywhere near these rooms once the interviews commenced. The suite was prepped for the cast's one-on-one interviews. The movie poster for *Reparation* was standing behind a high-backed chair.

"I'm going to do a little shopping, okay?"

Ryan instantly tensed. "No."

Suddenly I felt caged, recalling the hours of boredom I sat through when we did this back in London. Made me regret not staying back in our hotel suite. In my mind I was going with or without his blessing.

"I just want to get a few souvenirs, and maybe find something more stately to wear to dinner tonight. I really want to make a good first impression."

Ryan's hard glare softened. "They will love you no matter what you wear. We have the gift thing with Burberry after this, so don't bother. You'll have a rack of free clothes to pick from."

I didn't want to leave it to chance that elegant cocktail dresses would be among the freebies. It's amazing how companies just give you stuff when you're famous. Besides, I promised I'd get a cheesy gift for Marie in every city. I motioned to the door with my eyes, ready to see who'd win.

Ryan groaned. "I really wish you wouldn't."

It was obvious that the last thing he wanted to do right now was get into a battle of wills with me. He relented. "I guess I can't expect you to sit around doing nothing. See if you can find someone to go with you, okay? I think some of Jenna's friends are floating around here. Just don't go by yourself."

I brushed my fingers on his stomach, not wanting to impose on his co-star or her family. "You've got to quit worrying so much."

My comment sparked a glare and an unspoken "no fucking way."

His lips pressed into a hard line as he noted the time on his watch. "Don't get lost. Two hours and then you get your butt right back here."

I didn't wait for him to change his mind. With a quick kiss, I made my way to the elevator, excited about the possibilities.

Forty feet to freedom and perhaps a cab ride to the Louvre? An opportunity to actually touch the Eiffel Tower? Tomorrow morning, 10 A.M., we'll be on a plane to Barcelona and there is no time this evening to sightsee.

I was just putting on my sunglasses when I saw the paparazzi and a sizable crowd of women standing outside near the entryway. I stopped twenty feet from freedom.

Shoot. Will they recognize me? Will they even know who I am if I'm not trailing behind Ryan?

Screw it. Only one way to find out. I followed a few patrons who were leaving, and tried to escape unnoticed.

The rule of "try not to make eye contact with them" had been instructed numerous times. Although no cameras were raised, I saw one man elbow his comrade as he pushed away from the hotel wall.

I headed in the direction where I thought we had come from, hoping to find the window with the white mannequin and the waist-length leather jacket. One quick glance behind me confirmed that Creep One and Creep Two were following me. I glanced again as my pulse tripped into double time. *Shit.* I thought they were paparazzi, but oddly neither one of them had a visible camera. Not good. Fortunately the sidewalks were busy enough and it was broad daylight.

Store, store, store . . . where the heck are you, store? I had walked three blocks already. Distance is deceiving when you're being chauffeured.

Finally, at the end of the block I found the window I was looking for and sought out the solace waiting on the other side.

The two men stopped short, peering through the glass to confirm I was inside. Perhaps it was the display of women's panties that stopped them from entering? My heart was thrumming much too fast for my liking.

An extremely thin blonde with razor-sharp cheekbones approached me and started speaking in French. By the inflection of her voice I could tell she was asking if I needed help but at that moment I didn't know if I needed assistance with clothing or with creepy stalkers. I could always call for a taxi and head back to safety.

"Mademoiselle?"

My eyes were fixed on the window as I watched the two men trot across the busy street. At least they weren't standing directly outside the shop anymore. Hopefully they gave up. The clerk touched my arm lightly, breaking me from my surveillance.

"Oui. Oui. Um, parlez-vous anglais?"

"*Oui.* Yes. Can I help you?"

Now that the language barrier was bridged, it was time to get down to business.

I tried to check the street without being obvious, pretending to glance at clothing but more worried about the unknown men who had followed me. God, when did I turn into this paranoid mess? I spent my entire life not being frightened or having to look over my shoulder, worried that some asshole with a digital camera was going to catch me doing something embarrassing. And now I was on heightened alert of my every mannerism.

Even something so naturally innocent like scratching a boob or a butt cheek could be captured as the next photo to grace a gossip magazine cover. Suddenly the thrill of finding some new Parisian designer clothing was gone and replaced by fear and suspicion. My first time in Paris was quickly turning sour.

I wondered how different things would be if I were here with Thomas. No one would give a shit about me then.

I squeezed my eyes shut, picturing his ruggedness vividly.

My mental reprimand swooped right in behind that. *I can't believe I allowed that thought to cross my mind!* That was so not fair to Ryan. *Like he has any control over this*, the voice in my head berated. My situation was still within my control, knowing that there are concessions to be made when being involved with someone as famous as Ryan. The choice comes down to either dealing with the public attention or passing up true love for anonymity.

I decided to pass up the leather jacket instead; an easy choice at eighteen hundred euros. I really didn't need to spend that kind of money; not when I had to replace an expensive bar refrigerator. After all this time, I still couldn't bring myself to feel comfortable using Ryan's credit card. While most women would think nothing of spending his money—money that I didn't earn or that we had pooled together—I could not. It went totally against the grain for me. Maybe if he were here with me I'd feel differently. It would have been something we did together. A twenty-two-hundred-dollar jacket would feel like a gift. But alone, it just felt like I was abusing his generosity.

After about an hour of meandering through the surrounding shops, and with no signs of my two unwanted friends, I headed straight back to the hotel with my meager purchases. No sooner did I reach the first intersection than I spied the two men I was trying to avoid spring up from seats at the outdoor café across the street. *Shit.* I felt the cold sweat break out. They were able to cross in my direction; traffic was hindering me from crossing at my corner.

I stepped closer to a tall man who was dressed very Euro-chic; when he glanced down at me I smiled, hoping to attract a new, safer sort of friend. I practically jogged to keep up with his long strides, but

I was determined to stay next to him. The two assholes were a few paces behind me.

Just as I started to feel relieved that the hotel was in sight, a new panic swelled. The front of the hotel was surrounded by a mob-sized crowd. Police were cordoning off the sidewalks as more people continued to gather.

I squeezed my way through the tightly packed crowd, trying to avoid the two creeps following me. When I finally made it to the end of the line, a police officer stopped me, blocking my way to the front doors.

"No, I'm a guest of the hotel. My fiancé is inside." I tried to keep my voice down and dug into my purse. "My name is Taryn Mitchell. I am engaged to Ryan Christensen."

My admission was instantly refuted as if I had just told the biggest joke. "*Oui, mademoiselle*, as are all of these women as well!"

I was incensed at being the focus of his ridicule. I frantically searched my tiny purse, only to realize that I never got an ID badge for the event, nor did I have my passport.

"Unless you have proof of your stay, I cannot let you enter. Back away from the gates, *s'il vous plaît*."

I tried to plead one more time, as this situation was turning dire. Several officers gathered, obviously intrigued by my issue; however, I was quickly dismissed as some delusional fan.

The officer's tone became harsh. "Mademoiselle, back away. Now! I will not warn you again."

I tried calling Trish but the call immediately rolled to voice mail. I didn't have David's number and calling Ryan was out of the question. Panic and a low-battery light were causing my nerves to twitch. *Mike, please pick up. Why is no one answering their damn phones?*

More women were gathering. The crowd was getting unruly and my two hours were just about up. Women of all ages, shapes, and sizes were gathered, all jockeying for the best view and spot to get autographs. The closer I got to the door, the less friendly they became, behaving like starving animals protecting their hunting grounds.

I looked over my shoulder to see that the two creepy men were just a few feet away and narrowing. Where the hell could I go? They didn't appear to be paparazzi, so what the hell did they want? Would they dare try to accost me while here in this thick crowd? Perhaps hold me for ransom, knowing that someone as rich as Ryan could well afford to pay? One stick of a needle filled with a knockout drug and I could find myself being carried out of here only to wake up duct-taped in the trunk of a car. Screaming wouldn't solve anything in this loud crowd and the police would probably arrest me if I tried to rush past any of these wooden barricades.

I squeezed in between several girls, receiving hostile glances in the process. The creepy man with the bad comb-over hairstyle stared at me like a hungry tiger ready to pounce. His squat face was pockmarked and unshaven and was probably on the first page of France's Most Wanted List. His tall friend with the newsboy cap was eyeing the police, nervously glancing back and forth as if he were watching a tennis match. I needed to put as much distance between us as possible.

Terror clenched my stomach as I saw him raise the black item in his hand. Panicked, I froze. I couldn't look away. And then he aimed and started to take my picture. I shoved my sunglasses over my eyes and ducked, trying to get closer to the hotel entrance, hiding my face while contorting my body through the narrowest of human passages. Come hell or high water, I was getting back inside that door.

I called Ryan's cell, only to land in his voice mailbox. Finally someone answered my frustratingly slow international call. "Mike! Oh thank God! I'm out front of the hotel, but they won't let me back in."

No sooner did I get the words out when someone touched my shoulder. "Aren't you Taryn Mitchell?" some young woman asked in a thick French accent. I could see her getting very excited about the prospect. I didn't know what to do.

"You are, aren't you? Do you think I could get a photo with you?" she asked with much enthusiasm.

Several other women near her all turned their attention on me and I felt like the mouse that had just been spotted by the starving cats. "Mike! Please come get me. I'm getting—"

"May I have your autograph, *s'il vous plaît?*" Pens, paper, and cameras seemed to appear from out of nowhere.

I tried to back up to get some space between me and the rising commotion, but I accidentally stepped on someone's foot. I turned to apologize, but the girl was less than forgiving, making her angry point by spouting off and giving me a hard shove.

I muttered a curse and without thinking, I pushed her back, defending myself. I was tired of taking random shit from his fans. After almost a year of enduring snide comments, insults, and threats combined with all the other random bullshit from everyone else who felt I didn't belong with Ryan, something in me snapped.

That's when her friends got involved and the shoving match started. Three against one. The girl in the black jacket palmed my face, scraping my sunglasses off. I didn't know what was more important—defending myself or retrieving the glasses, which were a gift from Ryan.

Someone grabbed my hair and yanked me off balance. One more hard push and gravity and inertia took over. I lost my grip on my small shopping bag.

Blunt-force pain cracked into my side as I clipped the edge of a wooden barricade, knocking a good bit of air out of my lungs. I tried to slow my fall, clawing desperately at the waist of the large male form in front of me. I felt skin tear when my arm scraped over the holster holding his gun.

Next thing I knew I was flat on my stomach with wood tangled around my legs, surrounded by men yelling in words I didn't understand.

Someone grabbed the back of my jacket and pulled me forward.

I tried to haul myself up on my arms, only to have them fold underneath me as I was pressed flush with the street. A sharp, crushing pain that felt like two hundred pounds of mayhem made my spine crack. Someone's knee was holding me down. Cinders scraped my cheek like jagged shards of glass when I tried to stop this horrible misunderstanding.

Panic swelled inside me and I screamed for them to stop and listen to me. Instead, a hand knotted into my hair and slammed my face back to the pavement, stunning me into silence.

The coppery taste of blood flooded into my mouth as I was dragged from the ground and placed in the backseat of a car.

Never in a million years would I have guessed that by 11 A.M. I'd be in handcuffs.

CHAPTER 7

Bruised

I COULD TELL THAT my bottom lip had been split open. It stung like hell when I drifted my tongue over it, even though a rough scab had already formed to close the wound. The rancid coppery taste that lingered in the back of my mouth was enough to turn my stomach.

The front of my shirt was speckled with brown spots of dried blood.

My entire left cheek ached and I wished I could wipe my face.

The last time I'd felt nearly this battered was when I was side-swiped by an SUV, but my mortification level this time was off the charts. How lucky for me to feel this bad twice in one lifetime. I suppose I should be grateful that I didn't fracture the same wrist for the third time.

I stared in a daze at the stacks of paper and files piled on the inspector's desk, and tried to stifle the spins and the full body tremors, desperately wishing I could rewind the last few hours of my life. This wasn't just an "oopsy," this was a monumental fuckup.

I knew I needed to be calm. An attempted explanation that I was shoved unwillingly, instead of their assumption that I actually meant to incite a riot and attack and assault the officer, was also better delivered if I wasn't babbling through tears. Needless to say, being detained by the police in a foreign country was beyond terrifying.

The scant contents of my small purse were strewn about on the inspector's desk. He scrutinized my lip gloss as if it were a chemical weapon. *It's cherry-flavored, asshole.*

"I don't remember the name of my hotel," I repeated with re-

103

newed frustration. "Our travel arrangements were made by Ryan Christensen's agent. We were driven by a chauffeur to the hotel from the airport. I'm telling you I don't know." My last words cracked from my throat as the handcuffs pinched my wrists. "Please, just let me make one phone call so we can clear up my identity."

My request was ignored.

Tired of looking at his smug face, I glanced up the wall at the large, round clock, snuffling back my tear-induced runny nose. Ryan's interviews should be over by now. Surely his team ushered him on to the next item on his agenda—the open photo call. I could only imagine how angry he'd be with me once he discovered where I was.

My thoughts were swirling. Would this incident be a deal-breaker for Ryan? Too embarrassed by my getting arrested to want to continue a relationship with me? Heck, if standing on a table to propose to me was enough to incite panic in Marla, what the hell would me getting arrested in Paris do to him?

Once they throw me in a cell, would Ryan be forced to leave for Barcelona tomorrow without me? What choice would he have? I knew nothing about France's laws or how long I'd be sent to prison. If the lengthy forms the inspector was filling out were any indication, surely that's where I was headed next.

The inspector continued to toss his false accusations to the point of madness.

"I was *not* reaching for the officer's gun nor was I attacking him," I strained with urgency. "Why won't you believe me?"

My brain kept repeating, *five to ten for assaulting an officer.* God, I should have listened to Ryan. I should have stayed in the fucking hotel when he said no to my request. Waves of remorse were coursing in like the tide, pressing hard on my chest with each surge.

"You have no passport, no identification. You claim your information is at a hotel which you cannot name," the inspector continued to drone.

Damn, he was irritating. This was the first time I was ever out of the country. I didn't even think to grab my passport this morning when I changed purses. I almost left with nothing on me, deciding a credit card and lip gloss were my only necessities. I wanted to slap that accent right out of his mouth. I glanced at the antiquated computer sitting on his desk. "My name and signature are on my credit card. And if you don't believe me, just search my name on the Internet. That ought to give you enough photographic proof." My glare was definitely a challenge, hoping that a few hundred pictures of me and Ryan would be enough.

The slight smirk on his face indicated he really didn't care. His callous attitude morphed my sadness into anger.

"Remind me to never come back to Paris if this is the way you treat foreign visitors. Do I have the right to call an attorney, or is that against your laws, too?"

The bastard ignored me and kept writing.

"The paparazzi took plenty of pictures of your officer's knee in my back. That ought to do wonders for your tourist business once that hits the media."

Inspector Clueless tore his eyes away from his paperwork long enough to glare at me and snip something under his breath in French. I could tell by the slur in his tone that whatever he said, it wasn't meant to be pleasant.

My pinched shoulders were starting to ache worse than where I nailed my knee on the macadam. "What happened to the women who assaulted me and stole my shopping bags? Why aren't they in handcuffs?"

He was still glaring when his telephone rang. I made out the word *interrogé* in his reply.

"Well, it appears that someone has arrived to collect you," Inspector Jerkoff said.

My heart lodged in my throat, seeing that first glimpse of Ryan being led through the office doors by several men in dark suits, followed by Mike, Trish, David, and Aaron. I had heard his raised voice arguing and insisting to see me and I knew he was going to take one look at me and be livid. My head dipped in shame.

"Taryn? Are you all right?"

Ryan dropped down on his knee next to my chair. His eyes were wide as he took my chin in his fingers, trying to be gentle in his angered state. "Sweetheart, what the hell happened to you?"

Only sputters came out first. "I tried to tell them who I was, but they said I was resisting arrest. My passport . . . I forgot it in our suite."

I managed to tell Ryan how I was followed, surrounded by fans, shoved over a barricade by angry women, and then dog-piled and slammed by the police.

Shock, concern, and a whole lot of fury crossed Ryan's face as he assessed my injuries.

The inspector attempted to give his version of the circumstances but Ryan abruptly cut him off. He stepped right up to the edge of the inspector's desk.

"Four grown men against one woman? She's like a hundred and twenty pounds, for Christ's sake! You needed four men to fucking subdue her?"

"I understand you are upset—"

"No! You have no fucking clue how upset I am. She's sitting here bleeding! And what if she were pregnant? Did your men consider *that* while they were assaulting her?"

A very distinguished, slender man in a dark blue suit and tie placed a heedful hand on Ryan's shoulder. "Monsieur Christensen, please, allow me." The man pulled a wallet from his inside coat pocket and flashed his ID. "Gérard Bertrand, Personal Attaché to the Prime Minister. I am here on his direct orders regarding this matter and I have heard enough. Let me have the file and remove those handcuffs from her at once."

My breath stuttered with overwhelming relief. Ryan brought the freaking cavalry with him. I guess the prime minister fully expected us to attend dinner with his family tonight, after all.

So many people packed the small office, all speaking at once in a blur of French and English. The handcuffs were removed, much to my relief. Ryan continued to fuss over the blood on my chin. Trish's phone was fused to her ear.

I knew he was angry. "I'm so sorry," I pleaded desperately, hoping they both would find the grace to forgive me. As social errors go, this was way beyond using the wrong fork at dinner or mispronouncing a translated word.

"Shh. Everything is going to be okay," Ryan whispered, pressing my hair back from my cheek to wipe a new tear away.

A tall man with a thick mustache and wiry gray eyebrows approached. "Monsieur Christensen, Mademoiselle Mitchell. Please accept our most sincere apologies for this misunderstanding."

Ryan blocked the hand outstretched to me. His own hands balled into tight fists again. "*Misunderstanding?*" he growled at the audacity. "Look at her! You call this brutality a *misunderstanding?* How about I beat the shit out of one of your boys like this—"

Mike pressed a hand into the center of Ryan's chest.

The man tucked my file under his arm, unabashed. "I assure you, I will personally investigate this matter. You have my word."

"Your word means *nothing* to me," Ryan spit out angrily. "Your investigation can't possibly begin to right this wrong."

I stood and interrupted, wanting nothing more than to get Ryan and myself out of this potentially explosive situation. "Excuse me. Am I free to go?"

The man's eyes darted to mine and a faint smile crinkled his lips. "*Oui, mademoiselle.* You may depart. No charges will be filed."

I nodded, brushing my fingers over the numerous scrapes on my face as if that would hide them better. "Can someone please take me back to the hotel?" I was done being humiliated and scared out of my mind. The need to grab my passport, dark sunglasses, and an airplane ride out of hell was driving me toward the door.

Ryan covered me with his jacket and, with his hand pressed low on my spine, guided me outside and into the backseat of a waiting sedan.

Trish was busy, calling in favors and sending texts to God-knows-who to cover this up. I wanted to curl up into a ball and die.

David was obviously distressed. He glanced at this watch. "We need to get you back to the Hotel Britannique for your photo call, Ryan. There's still time. We can put this setback behind us and still stay on schedule."

"No," Ryan said flatly, pulling me tighter to his chest when I tried to squirm away. I presumed we'd end up in a fight once he got me alone.

"Listen, I know this has been traumatic," David continued. "The Burberry thing was just a filler. Everyone else is at the photo call waiting for y—"

"I said *no*," Ryan spat. I felt the tension in his grip on my shoulder. His lips were pressed to my forehead when he breathed, "We're going back to our hotel."

Despite Ryan's declaration, David was still trying to persuade him to continue on with his scheduled obligations when we entered our lavish suite. "Okay, so what do you want me to tell the producers when I have to explain why you weren't at the photo call? And the premiere is at six. Our car has to leave here by five thirty."

"I'll handle dealing with the studio execs," Aaron said. "Under the circumstances, it's unfortunate but they'll understand."

David was unrelenting. "But if we intend to cover this up *properly*, he should make it to all of his scheduled appearances. Being a no-show only confirms the suspicions. He needs to be there, Aaron. You know it as well as I do."

Ryan wasn't listening to anyone. He marched off to the bathroom.

Trish had every electronic device known to man fired up and was multitasking her ass off trying to counterattack all the negative press before it surfaced.

I sat on the sofa, wallowing deep in guilt for causing all of this, wishing I could disappear back into the quiet of my apartment. I just couldn't shake it no matter what I tried to do. The fear and mortification were swirling in my chest like an angry tornado, sucking up every other emotion in its wake.

I'd never been in *any* trouble with the law, not even as a kid, and having my first taste of it was terrifying. Hanging out with Marie and my other best friend, Thomas's sister Melanie, I came damn close a couple of times, but somehow, some way, we always came out in the clear.

Several times Thomas and I came close to getting busted, like the time the cops pulled us over when we were driving back from a keg party at North Bay beach. God, I shook all the way home from that near miss. Or the time we were interrupted by shore patrol having insane sex at two in the morning out near the bluff.

Despite that, nothing as bad as *this* had ever happened before. And the ramifications that would stem from this were too numerous to even begin to comprehend.

Ryan sat next to me, scrutinizing my injuries. My breath hissed uncontrollably from the sting when he rubbed a warm washcloth over my cheek.

His eyes were so repentant. "Sorry, honey. I'm trying to be gentle, but we have to clean these cuts."

As much as I loved him tending to me, I wanted to pull the cloth from his hand. I felt like I didn't deserve that gentle hand.

David ended a phone call. "Marcia Gay Harden's assistant is going to come up and stay with Taryn while you're at the premiere, Ryan. Jenna's people are all busy."

"I'm not going," Ryan said softly, wiping my lip with the utmost care.

All eyes landed on him—even mine.

David became overly animated in the midst of his talent-manager meltdown, ranting on and on about not believing what he had just heard.

"I said I'm not going," Ryan repeated. David started arguing but Ryan paid no attention to him. An eerie calm was over him. *The calm before the storm. perhaps?*

I felt Ryan's hand tremble lightly when he tipped my chin up. "I need to call the concierge and get some medicine for you," he said softly. "I got most of the dirt out of the cuts but I'll be able to do a better job once I get you in the shower."

I stilled his hand. "Ryan, please. I've ruined enough. You have to go."

His nostrils flared. "I'm not leaving you. Not like this."

I took the washcloth from him, ignoring the fact that the once-pure-white towel was now tinged pink. "It's only for a few hours." I tried to smile encouragingly, feeling as dirty and stained as the cloth in my hand.

His lip quivered ever so slightly as he shook his head. "I can't."

I locked eyes with David, wishing he wouldn't hover. I was about to do him a huge favor. "Can you please excuse us for a moment?"

I hoped David could read me enough to know that I was trying to do the right thing. Mike, bless his soul, cleared everyone out of our suite.

Ryan pulled his shirt off and tossed it to the floor. "Don't try to talk me into going."

His tone left no room for argument. I was resigned to the fact that I wasn't going anywhere tonight anyway, least of all a stately dinner with the prime minister of France and his family.

"The world is not going to come to an end if I miss the premiere."

So he thinks. Maybe not, but his fans would surely be outraged.

He cracked open a bottle of water, gaping at me. "What?"

"You have obligations," I hesitantly muttered.

"I don't give a *fuck*."

I shook my head to disagree. He was just reacting to his own emotional overload, which I caused. "This is your career, your movie. I won't let you ruin that. Not for me." I searched my bag for anything resembling an aspirin.

Ryan frowned. "I'm not going without you."

I stopped in front of him on my way to the bathroom. "Yes, you are." As I turned for the bathroom doorway, a stick of nasty pain shot into my ribs again.

One lift of my shirt and a sideways glance in the bathroom mirror confirmed my suspicions. I had a gigantic black and blue mark across my waist at least six inches long. It reminded me of the colors of the sky at dusk, wrapped in tender pain. *Well, at least it wasn't the right side like last time when the car struck me, but it sure looks the same.*

Ryan gasped. "What the *hell* is that?"

He startled me. I quickly dropped my shirt, tugging hard on the hem.

That's when he saw the gash on the back of my forearm for the first time as well. His long fingers circled my wrist.

A puffy red welt and scabby road rash decorated my arm.

"It's nothing." I pulled my arm away.

"The hell it is."

He shifted to face me and tried to lift my shirt but I held the hem, pulling it taut.

"Let. Me. Look," Ryan ordered, growling through his teeth. It was clear that he wasn't asking. It was obvious that his tolerance was all used up.

Tired of fighting it, I acquiesced. Ryan's eyes scrunched together as if he were in pain, too.

I didn't know what to say other than "I'm sorry." I pulled my shirt down as if it would hide my shame. "Please, go to your premiere. I've already done enough damage to your career for one day."

I turned the water on, planning on using the shower water to cleanse my wounds and mask more tears that I needed to shed before I drowned internally. After my shower, I'd pack. Overwhelming feelings of failure made me want to run and hide.

"No. Taking care of you comes first for me, sweetheart."

If he only knew how much I felt the same.

Ryan carefully pressed his body into mine, wrapping his arms around my shoulders in a tender embrace as if I were frail. "And I want you to stop saying you're sorry. You have nothing to be sorry about."

I shook my head and tried to tear away from him. God, he couldn't be more wrong.

"I should have listened to you and never ventured out on my own. And now . . . now I've humiliated us both. I don't even know how you can stand to be so nice to me right now."

Confusion blanketed his face. He freed one arm long enough to turn the shower off. The bathroom was turning into a sauna, steamed up tight with fog.

"Do you think if I had any other job, your first trip to Paris would have been different?"

I tried to push him away. "Ryan, don't . . ."

He lifted my chin, refusing to let me go. "Or would the paparazzi have been stalking you when you strolled the streets of a safe foreign city? Instead of being out there enjoying all the sites with you, as a couple, protecting you like a man should, you were left to fend for yourself, *again*. Do you think that makes me happy or feel worthy of you? Let me tell you, *it doesn't*. And now, seeing you injured like this . . ."

"Stop it, Ryan. Please. *None of this* is your fault. You had nothing to do with this. It was my stupid decision to go out. I didn't think it would be a big deal to go shopping on my own. I know better now. I won't make the same mistake twice."

His frustrated growl raised up a notch. "*Do not* put this on yourself, Taryn."

My mind raced. "How can I not? You're here trying to do your job. I was the one making headline news wrestling with the cops. It seems like every time I try to make it easier or find my place I end up making it ten times worse somehow."

I had to hold it together before I completely lost it. "I just want you to be happy, Ryan, without jeopardizing your career. The media is going to rip you . . . I can't stand it, knowing I caused you pain and humiliation today. You have no idea how sorry I am. I should have stayed out of the way."

I walked back into the bedroom and grabbed some of my clothes, shoving them back into my suitcase.

"What are you doing?"

"Packing."

"We don't leave until the morning."

I ambled around the room collecting my things, feeling soreness in my bruised knee. I knew if I stopped moving the tears would flow and I really didn't want to cry in front of him right now.

"You've spent enough time today worrying about me," I muttered ruefully. "Please just . . . You need to get ready for your premiere."

His face fell. "Babe, are you hurt somewhere else? You look like you're limping."

If I tell him, he'll blow off the premiere for sure. Well, not because of me, he won't. I tried to shove the pain aside. "No."

Ryan marched over to me, ripped my shoes from my hand, and hurled them across the room.

"Stop fucking packing! "What part of *I'm not going without you* didn't you understand? You expect me to what, just roll out of here without you so I can come back later to find that you've run off?"

I shook my head, adamantly denying his assumption. I doubted France had a big enough rock for me to crawl under.

"You think I don't know your MO by now? How you willingly martyr yourself for my greater good? Dammit, Taryn. You think all this shit means that much to me? I can't believe you'd think I'd just leave you here alone after all you've been through today." He threw a few of his own clothes into his open suitcase. "You wanna go? Fine. Let's go. We'll be on the next fucking plane home."

I set my jacket down. His newfound anger frightened me. "I wasn't going to leave." *Well, not that I would ever admit.* "It's just . . . I feel like shit for bringing this on you. I'm mad, and embarrassed, and frustrated."

The scab on my lower lip pulled, reminding me that I had matching bruises on the outside as well.

"I will *never, ever* put you in a position where you'd have to choose between me and your career, Ryan. *Never.* I'll never do that."

I gathered up my shoes from the floor. *Why he puts up with me, I'll never know.*

"What did you just say?"

I froze. I didn't think my internal grumblings were audible.

"Did you just say, 'put up with you'?"

I reluctantly nodded.

Ryan grabbed one of the ornate side chairs, forcefully pulling it closer to the bed. He propped his legs up, crossing them at the ankles. "Oh, I've gotta hear this shit. Please, go on. Enlighten me how I *put up* with you."

Common sense told me this wasn't going to end well so why bother starting. I should have kept my mouth shut.

"Well?" He was growing impatient. So was I.

My Christian Louboutin black pump ricocheted off the lid when I lobbed it at my suitcase. I was so riled I'd resorted to mistreating the thousand-dollar shoes that Ryan had purchased for me. "All I wanted to do was look at a jacket and even that turned into a disaster."

He looked around the room. "Did you buy it? I don't see any bags."

"No, I didn't."

"You went shopping and didn't buy anything?"

"I lost my shopping bags when I fell. I bought some gifts, but everything I bought disappeared in the melee."

Ryan sat up. "How much did you lose?"

I shook my head. "Doesn't matter."

"What do you mean it doesn't matter?"

"I used my credit card so it's my loss," I muttered contritely.

"Jesus Christ, Tar." He got up and stalked around the room. "Where's your purse?" he growled, shoving things around to look for it.

"What do you want it for?" I moved my coat to get it.

"Because *now* you've pissed me off." He grabbed the small bag from my hand and yanked on the zipper. Then he slipped my credit card out and examined it.

"This," he said, holding it up, "is mine now. It doesn't exist." He looked at the other card, which was our joint card, and shoved it back in its slot.

"Wait, stop—"

He grabbed his wallet out of his jeans pocket and confiscated my card. "I don't give a shit if you need it to put gas in your fucking car; you use *our* card from now on."

He was being ridiculous. I held out my hand. "Come on. Just give it back."

He shoved his wallet back in his pocket and glared at me. "Do you want to wear that ring?"

"What?" I looked at my hand.

"Do you want to be my *wife*, yes or no?"

Now he was scaring me. "Of course I want to be your wife, but th—"

"No buts. It's a yes-or-no question, Taryn."

I squared my shoulders. "Yes."

"Yes, what?"

Gah. "Yes, I want to be your wife."

"Good. Then get over your shit. Got me?"

"Ryan, you know I—"

"Got me?" he yelled louder. "I'm not playing this game anymore, Tar. All this bullshit provides for one hell of a lifestyle so deal with it. *I* provide. *I* take care of what's mine. And if you even so much as breathe on my wallet to get your card so help me God I will tie your ass up, lock you in a fucking room, and play Guns N' Roses on end-less loop."

I gasped. Now he was fighting dirty. "You wouldn't ..."

"Oh no? Try me."

"You can't take my cr—"

"Oh no? 'Welcome to the jungle, baby.' Over and over again. That what you want?"

I rubbed a fingertip over my cracked lip, cringing. "No."

"Good, now that we have that settled, why don't you tell me how this other bullshit got started."

"I woke up?"

He frowned at me.

I sat down on the edge of the bed. "There wasn't a huge crowd outside when I left the hotel."

"And?"

"And ... when I came back there were hundreds. The police wouldn't let me enter the hotel without proof of stay. I tried to get closer to the entrance and then I accidentally stepped on some girl's toe."

Ryan stared at my incredulously. "A toe. This"—he waved his hand up and down—"all started because you accidentally stepped on some girl's foot?"

I nodded again, hating how ridiculous this all sounded. "I tried to call you." I hoped my sheepish look was enough to indicate how remorseful I was. "I was trying to squeeze past them and it just happened. Some girls recognized me and asked for my autograph and then someone wanted to take pictures and then I stepped on someone's foot. I tried to apologize but another girl shoved me and I bumped the girl behind me and ... well, they shoved me and I shoved back."

This apparently amused him.

"It's not funny."

He wiped his hand over his lips. "I'm not laughing. But I'm glad you defended yourself."

I chose not to reply. Defending myself was my downfall.

"So are you going to explain how I put up with you or should we just throw more shoes around instead?"

I turned back to him and grumbled, "You threw the first shoe."

He was unruffled. "I did. And you're avoiding answering me."

"Okay, fine. You want to know? Your publicist, your manager— hard to hide the fact that they both despise me. The only one who's nice is Aaron and I suppose it's only to keep you happy. I know they all think I got pregnant on purpose."

I tossed the other black stiletto into my open suitcase, gentler this time. "Taryn, the evil little temptress, out to trap you and steal your millions." I took a deep breath.

"We both know how you got pregnant, sweetheart," he said softly. "It may have been an accident instead of something we planned for but it certainly wasn't intentional. And it was a risk we took together. Besides, if I didn't want to have kids with you someday I would have been wearing condoms from day one."

That stopped me dead in my tracks. "I've always wondered about that, actually."

His brow rose. "About?"

"The unprotected day-one part."

He laughed shyly as if he had his own private joke. His eyes locked on mine. "Tar, I knew that very first day I stumbled into your pub that you were the one. I think I fell in love with you when you were rubbing that shit on my cuts."

I gasped, shocked by his admission.

Another private thought wisped through him, causing a sly grin to form. "I started to have naughty fantasies about you being the mother of my kids when you were kicking my ass playing pool. By the time we finally hooked up, I honestly didn't care one way or the other if I knocked you up. Feeling your skin on mine was worth taking the risk. And if getting you pregnant meant that you were tied to me somehow permanently, even better."

I instantly softened at that. Melted, died, and floated to heaven, actually.

He held his arms open, welcoming me. I curled up in his lap and snuggled into his neck, never wanting to let go.

His nose drifted over mine. "You know I want kids, so I couldn't give two shits about what Marla or anyone else thinks. All I care about are the decisions *we* make as a couple."

I brushed my lips on his for a kiss, loving him even more than I thought was possible.

Ryan lounged back and I rested my head on his shoulder. "But," he said conspiratorially, "back to the Marla thing. I found out earlier today that on the day I proposed to you, Marla caught her husband screwing one of the bartenders from the Chateau in her shower."

My head popped off his bare chest. "No kidding?"

"I think that explains some things, don't you?"

I nodded. "Yeah, it does."

He combed my long hair back. "Trish wanted to tell you about the email she got this morning but I guess I spoiled all her fun now."

I envisioned Marla walking into her palatial estate, catching her husband's wet, naked ass in mid-thrust. Oh to have been a fly on the wall for that one. Still, part of me could relate all too well to that scenario and I actually pitied her.

"Bartender, huh? She probably thinks we're all sluts."

"Well, that's her problem, not ours, okay?"

I nodded. "Okay."

Ryan gently rubbed his hand up and down my back, lulling me into a stupor.

"I just wish David didn't hate me, too," I said.

Ryan huffed. "David sees you as a distraction."

The way he spoke, I could tell that wasn't all there was to it.

"And?"

"Annnd . . . I really don't care what he thinks."

"He's had it in for me ever since we had that dinner meeting with Follweiler."

"Yeah, he doesn't like you influencing my career decisions."

"Maybe I should keep my opinions to myself then."

Ryan stirred. "No way. Screw that. I want to know what you think. Your views aren't jaded like his are. Besides, I know what's temporary and what's permanent in my life."

He shifted me on his lap. "Anything else you want to get off your chest while we're on a roll?"

I scratched my puffy lip and muttered, "I was arrested today."

"No, you weren't, remember? No charges?"

"There will be photos of me getting taken into custody in every paper, Ryan."

"And you're expecting me to be mad at you about it?"

"Well, *yeah*. Not just mad, furious actually."

"I am mad. I'm freaking furious, but not at you. I'm pissed off that hordes of women prevented you from getting back into the hotel and that you were manhandled and treated like a criminal and injured. That's what I'm pissed about."

I bristled. "You don't need negative press."

Ryan shirked it off. "It is what it is. If it bleeds, it leads. This isn't a scandal, Tar. It will blow away eventually so spending a lot of energy on it is a waste. Okay?"

"Okay."

Ryan stood up with me in his arms. "Oh, you're a big lug," he said. He smiled and kissed me before setting me gently down on the bed. "Hungry? I take it they didn't feed you in the slammer."

I frowned at his lame joke, but he was too busy reading the room service menu to notice. "Starving, actually."

He glanced back at me. "Come to think of it, I *am* sort of mad at you, though. If you were so desperate to try bondage and handcuffs and shit, all you had to do was ask. I'd be more than happy to go there with you. We have yet to fully explore the depraved side of sex. Hell, we haven't even scratched the surface."

Leave it to him to find the humor in it all. Ryan ordered a late lunch and then called the front desk for antibiotic cream and ibuprofen. I was relieved that food was on its way.

I snuggled with a pillow on the bed. "You still need go to your premiere. You know that, right?"

Ryan grabbed his cell. "David, what's the stylist's name that's traveling with Jenna? No, the girl that does makeup. I need you to find her and send her up here."

After he ended the call, he climbed over the bed to me. I curled up to his chest.

"I know why you're bent . . . and I don't care what the papers will say. A week from now it will be forgotten and someone else will wear the target for a day."

What a relief. "Thank you. I'm glad we can talk things out like this."

He stared at me for the longest time. I could sense the sadness building. "When I think of the things that *could* have happened to you, worse than these scratches on your cheek—"

I stilled his lips with my fingers. "Shh. Stop."

His hand brushed down my side, pausing over my stomach. His eyes scrunched closed and he swallowed hard. "You will always be my first priority, Taryn. Always. Just knowing you were hurt today is killing me."

I gazed into his eyes. "I don't know what I ever did to deserve you. I love you so much. But . . . I am not going to add any more fuel to this situation by appearing battle-scarred in public. I won't . . ." Visions of thousands of cameras chasing down picture evidence of my wounds scorched my mind. "I will *not* embarrass you that way. I promise. I'll be here when you get back. No matter what time that is."

He frowned. "I don't think so. Since you insist that I go to the premiere and I absolutely refuse to leave you behind, I guess we have to compromise. I'll have a separate car take you so you won't be visible to the general public. I think you know how this works now."

I nodded.

"You can skip the more public appearances, but you *will* be with me every other moment tonight. And that, my love, is nonnegotiable."

CHAPTER 8

Recover

WE HAD BARELY parked our luggage in the foyer of our newly rented condo when Ryan began to peel his clothes off. He pulled his T-shirt up, revealing his muscular body and those glorious washboard abs.

My mouth watered, admiring the poetry in motion stalking me like a hungry predator, all chiseled and cut to perfection. No wonder women around the globe practically faint in his presence. He was breathtaking. And all mine.

With a playful smirk he tossed his shirt to the floor, driving me back into the depths of a dimly lit room. Six days had passed since the Paris debacle but the press was unrelenting. I knew his ego was also smarting since *Reparation* wasn't pulling in the box-office sales that his team had hoped for. Ryan, however, continued with the pretense of being unfazed by it all.

"Looks like a nice place," I said jokingly, unable to tear my eyes away from his heated stare. Everything beyond his smoldering blue eyes seemed to blend into a blur of neutral color.

I took a few steps backward, afraid to drop my guard, bumping into a decorative chair along the way. My backpack slipped off my shoulder and hit the floor.

He nodded once, not caring in the least what the place looked like. "Find the bedroom."

"Don't you want to unpack first?"

His gaze was dark and full of lust. "No. Sex first. You have five seconds to get naked or I will rip those clothes right off of you."

My pulse spiked. "Someone a bit anxious?"

He returned with a salacious smile. "You started this."

"Uh-uh. You were the one bragging. Think you can best your five orgasms? Not that I doubt your mad skills or anything."

"Oh, do I have plans for that mouth of yours." He continued his prowl, stripping his socks with each step. "Three seconds. Lose the clothes, Tar. Now. Or do you want me to leave red fingerprints on your ass?"

"You wouldn't . . ."

The devil in his glare said *oh hell yeah, I would.*

"Want to find out?" He prowled, closing the gap. His admonishing tone heated my skin. "You might like it."

I only managed to get one shoe off while removing my shirt, backing up with every step. My retreat was halted by the couch.

"That's a good place to start." Ryan grabbed the front of my jeans and yanked me forward.

"You're so adorable when you're flustered," he murmured, drifting his fingertips down my cheek, softly, reverently. "Let me be the first to welcome you to Vancouver." He opened my belt, slowly pulling each inch of the leather free from their loops. "We're gonna have to perform a cavity search, though. Make sure you didn't smuggle anything into Canada. I'm going to keep this item in case you need restraining."

He tucked my belt into the back pocket of his jeans.

My heated pulse jumped another degree.

Zipper down, his hands slid over my rear, fingers curving right into where I burned the most.

He had been toying with me the entire flight, innocently brushing fingertips over my chest, whispering in my ear all the things he was planning on doing to me. Torturing me into this frenzied state.

His mouth locked on mine, kissing me into oblivion. Nimble fingers unlatched my bra while I shoved his jeans down on his hips, clutching his arousal firmly.

"Enough foreplay. I need to be inside you—now," he groaned in my mouth.

I used my foot to push his jeans the rest of the way down to this ankles. "What are you waiting for? Take what's yours."

"Plan on it. Just making sure you're ready for me." He fell back on the cushions, deftly pulling my legs over his thighs so I was straddling him.

He gasped then groaned when he was fully seated inside. Sinking down on him was sheer bliss, like coming home. Cheek to cheek, his hands held my hips, rocking me back and forth as my knees gave us lift.

I sucked the curve of his top lip, lost in his kiss and skillful tongue.

His kiss drifted to my chin, my neck. I cradled his head in my hands when he took my breast into his mouth. I relished his hard tug, melting my entire existence into sensory overload.

In an instant, I was dipped backward, hissing when my skin came in contact with the cold wood of the coffee table.

He withdrew and replaced my sudden emptiness with his mouth and fingers. My back arched, moaning from his touch.

He bit his teeth into my thigh, driving his fingers into me with no mercy in sight.

The moment his tongue returned, I flew apart.

"That's one." I felt his smug smile turn into tender kisses on my skin. He pulled me flush to his chest, sucking my neck below my ear. "Five more to go."

Oh shit. I should have never challenged him.

"Stand up," he ordered. Ryan pressed his chest to my back, wrapped an arm across my chest, and, with a quick leg lift, pushed back inside me. His other hand snaked down to where we were joined. *Holy hell. Standing jackhammered sex.* He was on fire, taking me with him into the flame.

He bent me over the couch. Wet fingers started rubbing and pinching over my sensitive skin.

A few more moments of this and I'll be over the edge again. "Don't stop," I ordered breathlessly.

"I'm close," he growled. "Come with me."

Knowing I had this man wound so tight he was exploding was my undoing. This one hit harder than the first. On a curse and a gasp, I cried out from the surge of pleasure. He was slamming me so deep, prolonging my mind-blowing orgasm, dangling me on the precipice of pleasurable pain.

His hands dug into my flesh as he found his release, groaning with each pulse.

We ended up collapsed on the couch. Both of us panting and spent. His hand was so soothing, running from the back of my head and down my spine as I lay on top of him.

"This is a comfy couch," he snickered while tempering his breathing.

I grunted. So was his chest. "I'm ready for a nap."

"Oh, no. No sleeping. We're just taking a rest. We still have to test the shower and the bed and that dining table over there. And you still have four more orgasms to achieve."

I grinned so wide it hurt.

RYAN'S CELL rang again. It was still light out but I didn't care. I was mostly under the covers, naked and entwined around the love of my life, balancing on the edge of bliss and unconsciousness. My entire body felt as if my bones had disappeared somewhere between the fourth and fifth orgasm. He managed to take me to six.

He kissed my forehead. "Are we taking any calls yet?"

I managed a nod. "I'm done."

"For now," he added, kissing my hand that was still laced in his.

I wondered if he could feel my eyes roll on his chest.

He fished his cell out of his pants pocket. "That was my mother again. I'll call her later. I can't do mom convos after four hours of sex."

I quickly became acutely aware of how many muscles were needed to muster a tiny laugh.

As he was toggling through his texts, his phone chimed again. "Boy, we're popular."

I had turned my phone off earlier; I was surprised he actually answered his.

"Hi, Marie. No, it's okay. Wait. Slow down. I can't understand you." He sat up suddenly. "Yeah, she's right here. Hang on."

The second I heard her voice, the way she said my name, I knew something terrible had happened. "What's wrong?"

Marie sniffed. "Hey, listen. I don't mean to bother you but would you mind if I borrowed your car?"

Odd. "Yeah, sure. Take it if you need it. You know where the keys are. Did your car break down?"

I heard her faint, humorless chuckle. "No. I, uh, no longer have one."

Ryan was staring at me.

"Gary came here today. He took my car back, Tar."

I stared back at Ryan. "What do you mean Gary took your car back? Like repossessed it?"

Marie blew her nose and tried to talk through angry tears. "Yep. He said since it's in his name, it's his. Whatever. It was a piece of junk anyway."

"Why is he being such an ass?" Ryan asked.

I held up a finger for him to wait. "He can't just take your car, Marie. I don't care whose name is on it."

"That's marital property," Ryan added.

Desire to kick Gary in the balls was overwhelming. "You need to see an attorney . . . now."

"I know. I have some calls to make," she said sadly. "This was the final straw."

I wanted an answer to Ryan's question. "Marie, why is he being like this? I mean, he's becoming spitefully cruel."

She scoffed. "Tell me about it. Taryn, I saw him with her. I went over to his work to confront him and he was leaning in her damn car. And then I went over to my house to get some of my stuff and my key wouldn't work. He changed all of the locks on the house, Taryn! He said since I've never appreciated anything he's ever done for me that I can try going without."

Ryan nodded his chin at me, wanting to know what was going on.

I shook my head adamantly. "Marie, he cannot just lock you out of your own house."

Ryan's eyes opened wide with shock from hearing my side of the conversation.

"You know, I've been trying to figure it out. Ever since he went out that one night with his bachelor buddies in January, we've been fighting. Right after that he started getting mysterious phone calls and texts and shit. Telling me to mind my own business whenever I asked about them. He was never like that, Tar. Never."

"Did you flat out ask him why he's being like this?"

"Yeah, I did," she sighed. "But he never answers the direct question. He just throws it up in my face about how he's sick of me doing this shit to him, whatever that means. At first I thought it was because we weren't spending enough time together, but when I am home, he's out in the garage working on something, ignoring me," she scoffed. "He's dredging up shit that happened years ago."

"Oh man," I groaned.

"Whatever. Anyway," she breathed out, sniffing. "Enough about that. How are you? I've been really worried about you since you left Paris."

There was no way I could think of my petty problems. "Do you need me to come home? I'm coming home. You shouldn't be alone. I'll see about getting a flight—"

"No you will not," she said, cutting me off. "You and Ryan need this time together."

"But—"

"No, I'm good. You stick to the original plan and I'll see you when you get home in a few weeks," Marie insisted.

After we had said our goodbyes, Ryan nudged me, frowning. "How is she holding up?" One look was all I needed to give him. I could barely contain the tears and rage within myself. "He repossessed her car?"

I nodded. "Came into the bar and demanded the keys."

"I can't believe Gary's being such a prick." Ryan gave me a consoling rub. "Seems out of character."

"I can. They've been fighting and I'm sure she's said some things she might regret. But now he's trying to prove a point by stripping away everything he's ever given her. God, I need to do something. She has the keys to my car so she's got a way to get around, but still."

"She needs to hire a good attorney is what she needs to do. He can't do shit like that. And I tell ya, if he's fucking around on her, then I want nothing to do with him. You *know* how I feel about that."

Ryan snuggled next to me and I rested my head on his shoulder. "I need to go home soon. I can't strap her with running the pub while her life is crumbling. I want to be with her when she goes to the lawyer. It's important to me to be there for her. She's my best friend."

He sighed. "I know." He laced our fingers together. "She's got my support, too. Whatever she needs. You know we can afford it. After all, I do owe her a *huge* debt of gratitude. She helped me see things clearly when I wasn't."

I knew just by his expression that he was referring to all that she had done to keep him and me together, even when it seemed that we'd never get over our trust issues. Should I be doing the same for her? Trying to patch things up between her and Gary before they became irreparable? One thing was for sure—I'd pay for an attorney before I'd let Gary do more damage.

"Tar, tell me the truth. The way he's acting . . . did she cheat on him?"

My head popped off his shoulder. "No. No, never. I suspect it's the other way around."

He rubbed my shoulder. "Honey, I know you're torn up. And I know I'm being a totally selfish bastard when I say this, but I'm not going to lie and say it's okay for you to run back home right now. I know you want to be there for her but *we* need this time together."

"I know. And I'm not running anywhere."

He gently tugged my chin up. "I don't want shit like this to ever happen to us. I won't let our love go there, Tar. I won't. I swear to God. I told you that you will always come first and I mean that. I want to give you the world and never take it back and I won't let anything stand in the way of that. But I'm also under contract here. No matter what, I still want to provide for my wife and family."

I snuggled into his chest. "I know, babe. This is your job and I fully support it. I know where your heart is."

Ryan's fingers drifted over my faint scars. "I really want you to know what it's like to be on set with me. You asked me to help you understand it all and I don't know of any other way to do that except to have you experience it all."

I nodded. "I want that, too. But I also know that she's back there dealing with my bar and going out of her mind at the same time. Of course my only reaction is to want to fix it." *And kill Gary.*

"So let Cory run the bar for a couple of days and tell her to come to Vancouver. She probably needs to get the hell out of there anyway. Change of scenery would do her good."

I pondered that for a moment, wanting to be sure his offer was genuine. "Are you serious?" I had no qualms about closing the bar for a few days, knowing Cory couldn't handle running the bar by himself. He'd only been working as a bartender for me for six months.

He nodded and gave me that small, crooked smile of reassurance. "She's your best friend. She needs you. And I start conditioning training in the morning. You girls can hang out, do girl stuff."

Gripping his cheek, I kissed him. "Thank you. Your understanding means the world to me."

His hand locked around my wrist. "Hey! Where are you going?"

"I want to check flights and buy tickets."

Ryan rolled out from underneath me and playfully pressed my head back into my pillow. "Stay put, love. We have a travel agent at our disposal, remember? I'll take care of it."

After everything was arranged he was back in my arms, answering my question of how I could repay his kindness in whispered replies, all of which revolved around orgasms numbered seven and eight. I was so willing to pay up.

THE MINUTE I saw Marie in the terminal, her wry smile instantly turned to tears. It had taken some convincing, but I finally got her to agree to come. My heart sank and constricted hard from her misery. We'd been through so much together, so much loss and heartache and devastation, but our emotional support for one another was unwavering.

Time after time our friendship had been tested, like a battle-worn ship that refused to sink. She'd been my rock when my mom died and my salvation when the guilt and pain had been too much. She held me while I trembled as the paramedics took my father's body off the floor of the pub and away in an ambulance.

I nearly went out of my mind when she wrapped her car around a tree just nine days after we had graduated from high school; I spent every waking moment thereafter nursing her back to health. I was her maid of honor.

And now, today, we were adding another heartbreaking page to our eternal-friendship history book.

I stroked her long brown hair and hugged her fiercely. "We'll get through this. I promise."

When Ryan returned later that day after spending his morning being trained to rock climb, he gave Marie a long hug. "You need me to kick his ass for ya? Anything you need, just say the word," he said softly.

Mike stood off to the side, a case of beer in his hands. He looked like he was sorry for interrupting.

Ryan shrugged. "I thought maybe you ladies would like some time to yourselves, so Mike and I are going to watch the hockey game later, okay?" Like two little boys, they appeared hopeful that they'd get permission.

We sat in the living room with the men when the pizzas arrived. Marie was slowly getting into better spirits; she seemed to be a little more relaxed.

"Here, let me get that for you," Mike said, almost jumping out of his seat to open a bottle of beer for Marie. If he only knew how many bottles of beer she'd opened by herself in the last umpteen years working behind the bar. His gesture was endearing but almost laughable.

It was around eight thirty when Ryan decided he couldn't live without salty junk food, so the four of us piled into Mike's rental. Marie stopped abruptly, gasping in shock when Mike rushed to open the car door for her. Ryan, forever the gentleman, always held my door for me. He always treated me like a lady.

"I don't need a map. I have the GPS," Ryan joked from the passenger seat as he fumbled with the in-dash navigation.

"Good thing Mike's sober or we'd be driving in circles," Marie teased.

Ryan turned and leered at her. "Hey, don't talk about my man, Mike. He's an important part of this mission."

"Thank God. Lord knows someone's got to defend you when all those horny housewives try to assault you in the aisles," Marie joked. "How much you want to bet that someone asks you to autograph their rump roast?"

Mike laughed. "Wait. Does his signature actually have to go on meat or are all groceries included in this bet?"

Marie raised a brow at me. "All groceries," she clarified. "Why? You seriously want to bet against me?"

"Why yes, darlin', I believe I do. Women always dig in their purses for paper first," Mike replied. "I'll give you a few minutes to think about what you're willing to lose in this bet. Choose wisely."

His flirtatious comment surely didn't go unnoticed in the backseat.

I grabbed a cart before we went into the store, sensing Ryan's apprehension. He tugged his baseball cap lower, glancing around nervously.

As usual, Mike entered the store first. He did that wherever we went, getting the lay of the land before allowing Ryan entrance. After he did his quick visual sweep of the produce section to make sure the vegetables weren't staging an attack, he sidled up next to me and bumped my arm. "Jeez, woman. I thought we were here for Doritos. How much do you intend to buy?"

"For how much food you two pack away, I should get two carts. And unless you like wearing the same crusty underwear every day, I suggest you zip it and pick out your favorite fabric softener." I gave him a playful elbow bump back.

Mike looked aghast. "Did you just threaten me with laundry?"

"Considering that we don't qualify for on-set laundry services like some people . . . uh, yeah."

Ryan was already piling the cart with fruit and some cookies that were on display when we first walked in. He frowned at Mike. "There's no food in our place and if she stops cooking for me because you're being an ass I'm going to kill you."

Mike held up his hands in surrender. "You don't have to tell me twice. If it weren't for Taryn I'd never get a home-cooked meal and if she's willing to wash socks for me . . . Consider it shut."

I grabbed some lettuce. "Marie is a better cook than I am. She can make soup from a stalk of celery and a rock."

Marie smiled broadly at me. It was one of our private jokes from back in the starving college days.

Ryan waved the pack of cookies in Marie's direction. "There you go. Get your own cook."

I took the pack of cookies out of the cart. "Not on the approved diet from your trainer, babe."

Ryan's pout was heartbreaking. "No cookies?"

I felt like the mother of an overgrown baby. "No cookies. No doughnuts, either."

While Ryan glared at me, Mike stealthily gazed at Marie. Our dear bodyguard's face might have been impassive, but his eyes definitely gave it away that he was considering her, weighing out his options. Marie had a hell of a figure on her, including the kind of boobs that got women into trouble.

There were several times I wanted to dig into Mike's business, beyond knowing he spent ten years in the Marine Corps and was capable of killing someone a hundred different ways with his bare hands, but I never wanted to embarrass him. His love life was something that never came up in conversation. I suppose living on the road like he was was not the most conducive situation to try to maintain a relationship.

The possibility that he could be gay flitted through my brain once, but that quickly dissipated when Mike took a bit of an interest in Trish. That interest, however, was nothing compared to how he was now hanging on to Marie's every word as if she were the most intriguing woman on the planet.

A woman in aisle three did a less than inconspicuous gaze when she spotted Ryan. Her skin flushed as if she was both excited and unsure, but still she never approached. Too nervous, apparently.

I pushed my cart, enjoying the view of Mike trying to talk to Marie, attempting to be casually cool as he spoke.

"You never did specify the terms of the bet. Ten, twenty? Decide quickly. Stretch Pants Lady is fumbling with her purse."

Marie looked confident but slightly bashful. I noticed she rubbed the finger that used to have a wedding ring on it. There was nothing there now but bare skin and the hopes of a fresh start.

"How about dinner?" she tossed back. "If you win, pick out anything in the store and I'll cook for you. But if I win, *you're* wearing the apron."

Mike laughed, surreptitiously placing his body between Ryan and some older man coming down the aisle. "You may want to rethink that, unless you really love mac-n-cheese and ramen noodles and want to see me in an apron. Then who am I to disappoint?"

Nothing but an apron, I amended silently for her. *Yeah, she's smirking. Dirty minds think alike.*

She quickly recovered. "Not much of a cook?"

"Well, I have tried to make celery-rock soup once before. It probably wasn't as good as yours, though."

Ryan grabbed a jar of spaghetti sauce. His arms were piled with things. He walked up to Mike. "Wait, I thought we planned on taking them *out* to dinner tomorrow? That's what you said you wanted to do."

Mike looked like he wanted to throttle Ryan on the spot, that is, until several customers started leering down the aisle. One girl pulled out her cell, aiming it to take a quick snapshot.

Son of a . . . why, people? Do you think that famous people don't eat or shop? Come on! I darted to Ryan's side, bumping shoulders with Mike and blocking Ryan as much as possible. He couldn't be left alone for two minutes without someone taking a piece of him.

Marie whipped out her phone and aimed right back. The girl quickly started to back up. "Wait! Where are you going? I need to update my Facebook page."

Ryan frowned, showing his disapproval. "Don't do that. Just let them take their pictures. You start saying shit and that gets recorded . . . Just do me a favor and don't."

"Sorry," Marie said quickly, not looking sorry at all.

Mike gave her an elbow nudge. "Troublemaker! Seems as though you need a keeper, too."

I was starting to wonder if he was volunteering.

I smiled at Marie. No matter what Gary thought he could do to hurt her, I had no doubt she'd bounce right back on her feet.

THE FOLLOWING evening, Marie and I shared the bathroom mirror to get ready. She was in a much better mood after we spent a full day shopping with a nice, leisurely lunch in between.

I was still a bit peeved that Ryan hadn't returned my personal credit card, leaving me no choice but to use our joint card. I knew it was his way of making sure he was taking care of me, but I didn't like being at someone's mercy. I figured some new risqué bras and panties were a nice way of saying thank you.

Marie tugged at her new top and then abruptly stopped to hug me. "Thank you for buying this outfit for me. Once I get financially stable again, I'll pay you back. I swear."

I rubbed my hand over her back. "Not necessary. You're the one who told me I'd have to get used to spending my future husband's millions, remember? Consider it a gift from the 'Ryan says he owes you big-time for what you did for us' fund."

She dismissed my words with a wave of her hand. "I still feel bad, though. I hate not being able to afford the things I want without relying on Gary's money. This totally sucks."

I looked at her knowingly.

"Okay, okay, I get it now," she said. "I won't tease you about spending Ryan's money anymore. You and I weren't raised that way. We're used to earning our keep."

I put my makeup away, straightening up the counter. "Exactly. Oh, I'm sure there are millions of women out there who wouldn't even blink at becoming a pampered little house pet, doing nothing but gossiping and shopping all damn day. But that's not how I want to live. You remember Melanie's favorite saying?"

Marie smirked.

"'I don't owe you shit,'" we said in unison.

A second later Marie huffed, tucking her extra cleavage away. "Cripes. Mike is going to take one look at me in this getup and think that I'm some sort of desperate psycho ready to pin him to the wall. I just wanted a break from the stress to get my head together, not force the first warm, completely gorgeous body I come in contact with into an uncomfortable situation."

"I'm sure he doesn't view it that way." *At least I hope not.* "No one is forcing either of you into a situation here. And by the looks of it, Mike seems *more* than willing to spend time with you."

Marie rolled her eyes, but it was the truth and she knew it. His eyes had traveled up and down her body quite a few times, often fighting to decide between her face and her endowed chest.

"Is it too soon? Shouldn't I be in mourning or something for a year?"

"I don't know. I guess if you don't feel sad then what does that tell you?"

She didn't hesitate. "I've been unhappy for a long time. He's treated me like crap for so long; I guess I'm numb to it. But when I just *look* at Mike, I feel it all the way down into my toes."

"I can tell you he's a great guy. I've really gotten to know him better these last few weeks. But I feel bad for him. His life consists of waiting on whatever Ryan has to do. Most of the time he thinks he's intruding on us, and when he escorts us safely someplace and then quietly steps out of the picture, my heart breaks for him. He's probably looking forward to hanging out and *not* feeling like the third wheel for once."

"Well, I'm not looking at this like it's a date. I'm sure he is just being nice so I'm not going to read into anything."

The doorbell rang and Marie gasped. It was go time.

"Sorry I'm late." Mike had on a pair of black dress slacks and a thin gray button-down shirt that left no curve of his upper body a mystery. As soon as I closed the door, I noticed something shimmer on his back.

"Turn around," I said discreetly, pulling the XL size sticker from the fabric. I quickly balled it up in my hand. I'd never seen Mike blush before.

"Oh shit. How embarrassing is that?" he mumbled.

I was delighted that he felt the need to buy a new outfit for tonight. "Don't worry about it. It will be our little secret. You look really nice, by the way."

Mike seemed genuinely nervous, brushing his hands over his slacks. "Thanks, Taryn."

The minute Marie stepped into the room I saw it cross over both of their faces—that flush of excitement caused by extreme attraction to another human being.

Mike had eyed Marie quite a few times in the past, but he left it at that. I also noticed him scowl at Gary once or twice as well, when Gary was being less than polite to her. But Marie was unobtainable at the time. Now the playing field was wide open. Her wedding rings were off, leaving only a faint indentation on her finger of a period in her life that would eventually fade and fill in time.

"Oh wow. You look, um, amazing," Mike stammered, a hint of red staining his cheeks.

Oh how adorable! Look at him blush again.

Ryan also noticed the electricity zooming through the room. "Tar, can you help me a sec?" I followed him upstairs into our bedroom.

"We need to talk. You see what's going on with them, don't you?"

I smiled. "Yes. And I'm okay with it. Are you?"

Ryan looked tense. "Are you sure? He said he'd forget about it if you weren't cool with it."

Mike actually said something to Ryan about Marie? Judging by the look Mike gave Marie when she came into view, I'd say he'd have a tough time forgetting about her in that outfit.

"I'm sure," I said. "But what concerns me is that I thought Mike was interested in Trish. I know he's lonely and it's not fair for him to sacrifice his personal life for us, but I won't let him play both."

• Ryan nodded quite assuredly. "No, me neither. He likes Trish. He thinks she's cute, but he didn't have that instant chemistry with her that he's feeling for Marie. Hell, I don't need to say it—you can see it as well as I can. But I'm pretty sure his dick is doing most of the thinking and chemistry-feeling at this point. He knows she's hurting and is in no way ready for anything serious."

Ryan rubbed my arm. "Hey, she's my friend too, you know," he went on. "And she's my future wife's best friend. I won't allow anything to jeopardize that. Mike knows her current situation and I briefed him on some of the crap she's going through. He's willing to feel it out, but seeing that in the kitchen was like walking into a wall of sexual tension. Heck, I'd be surprised if they make it through dinner."

He made me laugh. "That's what we get for leaving them alone to *talk* last night. They're both grown-ups. I'm sure they'll figure it out on their own."

Ryan didn't seem so sure. "Well, let's go find out."

Two hours into a wonderfully romantic dinner, Marie and I politely excused ourselves for a companion trip to the ladies' room. Call it what you will, but we all knew this was a chance for us girls to do our halftime checkup while the boys pondered what they had to do to score. Mike and Marie were so comfortable together; it was freakishly weird and exhilarating to watch all at the same time.

"Oh God, I think I'm in love already," Marie gushed, pacing the tiny, private ladies' room nervously, fanning herself to cool down. She brushed her long brown hair back, pulling it off her neck. "Or, at least, in very serious lust. Did you see him choke up when he talked about his last military tour? How close he came to that car bombing in Israel?" Marie wiped a finger under her eyes, fixing her makeup. "He tried to hide it but he's holding on to some seriously deep emotional pain, Tar. You can see it in his eyes. That was hard for him to talk about, but he's got to. He's got to get that out or else it will fester."

To say we were all moved to the verge of tears when Mike told us about one of their missions, and how he lost his two good friends to senseless Middle East violence, was an understatement. Mike was harboring some traumatic stuff behind his tough-guy image.

Marie took the single toilet first. "Shoot. I feel guilty for peeing. That first bottle of wine alone was almost two hundred dollars. Do you two splurge like this all the time? A family of four could eat for a month on what they're going to spend on this meal."

While neither of us grew up underprivileged, it was slightly unnerving to pretend not to care what things cost. "I know. And the answer is *sometimes*. Ryan wanted privacy tonight and I'm pretty sure Mike just wants to impress you."

"Well, mission accomplished." She pinned me with her eyes. "He knows what Gary did, doesn't he?"

I nodded. "Ryan told him. He also knows you're separated and staying in my apartment."

"Thought so. I saw him tense up a couple of times." She took a deep breath. "Yeah, well, what you don't know yet is that Jeff the UPS guy came into the pub the other day. Told me he delivered a package to my house and was wondering who the cute girl was that answered my door wearing nothing but a T-shirt. He asked if Gary had a sister. It was like nine in the morning, Tar."

I gasped. "Oh God."

I could see her anger holding back the tears as the painful recollection poured from her lips. "You know, I wondered how the hell he could do that. Move on so damn quick with some girl? And here I am, ready to do the same thing. I guess I understand now."

I leaned up against the sink counter. "Do you still love him?"

Marie snorted. "After all of this bullshit, hell no. Our marriage is over." Just saying those words must have been hard for her because she was holding back some tears in that weak smile. "Now I just want to get my stuff and move on. The scary part is not knowing where to move on to."

I gave her a reassuring smile. "You know as well as I do that life has a way of clearing that path for you. And maybe the good Lord above has dropped two hundred pounds of gorgeous path-clearing answer out there at our dinner table for you."

That made her laugh. "That's the problem. I'm too afraid to get my hopes up. Not right now, anyway. He probably just wants some casual sex, but I highly doubt one night with Mike would be enough. Well, unless he has a small penis and no skills. Damn, he's already got me tangled up inside."

"You know . . . I recall someone once telling me to go for a one-night stand with Ryan. How fast you change your tune when you're the one wearing the slut shoes."

Marie made a face at me. "That's different. Your *fiancé* oozes sex from every pore and happens to be one of *the* most desired men on the planet. You'd have been a complete fool not to jump that."

"Well, I could say the same. Mike's pores are oozing just as much hotness. And he's becoming quite famous, too, you know. He's in just about every picture and video taken of Ryan these days. They're like the dynamic duo poster boys of sexiness."

"I know." She grinned widely but it didn't last. Her face fell quickly as she leaned on the counter. "This moment feels so surreal, like I'm going to wake up and find that it's all been one big practical joke. I can't go out there." She started to hyperventilate and appeared ready to puke in the sink. "I . . . if he . . . I don't think I could survive rejection twice in one week. If I'm not good enough for a schmuck like Gary, why the hell would I ever be good enough for someone like Mike? I mean, look at him. He's tall and gorgeous and perfect."

I rubbed her back reassuringly. Oh how I knew exactly how she felt. "You're gorgeous, too, you know. And you *are* good enough. I think it's about time someone starts treating you like the goddess you are."

She grimaced at me.

"You know as well as I do that things happen for a reason. And by some freakish miracle, two of the most amazing men in the world are sitting out there at a table waiting patiently for us to come back to them. We are two of the luckiest women alive. But instead of spending these moments with them, we're holed up in a tiny bathroom worrying like two idiots. What do you say? Ready to see where the chips fall?"

Marie took a breath and righted herself. "Yeah, I'm ready. Time to trust in fate." She gave her boobs a bit of a lift and took a deep breath. "Let's go make our mamas proud."

"GOOD MORNING," I uttered over my coffee cup, even though it was close to ten. Marie's long brown hair was all bushy and tangled and she was wearing the Brown University T-shirt I got her eons ago.

The wench failed to look me in the eye. Instead she searched for another coffee cup, ignoring me.

"I can feel you staring holes in my back," she muttered matter-of-factly, pouring the piping-hot liquid into her cup. "No, I didn't sleep with him. Yes, he is fully aware of the location of *both* of my breasts, and yes, he is an uh-may-zing kisser." She turned and grinned like a girl who was definitely up to no good last night. Her lips were still puffy.

"And if the super-large, extremely hard bulge that I sent him home with is any indication of the potential he has to rock my world, I'm signing up for a full membership."

I couldn't help but laugh. I pushed out a kitchen chair for her with my foot.

"My nosey fiancé was quite worried about how you two were faring. Even got out of bed once to see if Mike's car was still here."

Marie shook her head from the news. "We talked a lot. He knows I'm in the middle of dealing with something ugly. And he doesn't want to push anything until I'm ready, which I thought was very . . . thoughtful."

Yeah, she had it bad for him.

MARIE HAD only stayed for four days and in that time we spent every night with Ryan and Mike. I was glad to see that Marie had a renewed sense of hope. Gary couldn't rip her heart out because she was well on her way to falling for another man.

Mike appeared to be genuinely sad to see her go. He had arranged for other security to cover Ryan so he could personally see Marie off at the airport. That scored major points for him in my book.

As we all hugged goodbye in the terminal, I smiled when Mike promised that he'd keep in touch with her.

Mike paid the toll to get us out of short-term parking. I watched his lips press down into a grumpy scowl. By the looks of it, he was majorly pissed.

"She'll be all right," I said softly.

He looked over at me and nodded once. "Yeah."

I stared at the bumper of the car in front of us, feeling relieved that Mike had been a gentleman throughout, not playing the game to get Marie into bed for a quick hit-and-run.

Still, I could see he was all knotted up. "How are you?"

His jaw flexed and his expression darkened even further. He didn't answer right away, but when he did he said, "Just tell me if shit goes down with her. I'm figuring she won't tell me so I'm telling you I want to know about it, okay?"

I stared at him for a minute, sort of in shock. "You sure you want to make it your business?"

Mike flicked his turn signal on and was watching oncoming traffic until his eyes locked onto mine. His anger quickly dissipated, replaced with softened but adamant sincerity. "Yeah, I do."

I recalled how it felt to find out your man was cheating on you. Was Marie ready for her "next" or did she need time to sort it out?

Some of his tightness came back. "You have a problem with that?"

Yeah, I do.

Instead, I said, "She's not just my best friend, Mike. She's just about the only family I have and I don't want her to get hurt. She's already got one guy breaking her heart. She doesn't need two."

He gave me another stiff nod. "Understood."

Marie had told me that Mike held her while she cried in front of him last night. She hated that she broke down like that but they were talking and he was asking why she ever settled for less and it just happened.

Mike turned the radio off. "Don't think me cold but I'm glad this happened to her. I mean, I'm not happy she's getting hurt, but I've seen how that asshole's been treating her and . . ." He slapped the gear shift. "You don't treat a woman like her like that. You just *don't*. You get a woman like that, you cherish her."

I couldn't help but smile at him.

He glanced back over at me. "What?"

Yeah, he liked her a lot. The sooner she scraped off Gary the better.

CHAPTER 9

Act

Monday morning, eight o'clock, Ryan and I were promptly whisked away in a tinted-window sedan for a breakfast meeting with Jonathan Follweiler and the principal cast of *Slipknot*. Mike was sitting up front in the passenger seat, looking all foreboding again, while another man drove us. He'd been in a funk since we dropped Marie off but the macho asshole wouldn't admit it. I knew better.

I cast my eyes over at the driver; he had a really thick neck and no patience when it came to fending off sidewalk onlookers after he parked in front of the hotel entrance. It was moments like these that reminded me how far from normal our lives were. Normal people drove themselves places and didn't have chauffeurs opening their car doors.

Jonathan's wife, Anna, who was an executive producer of this film as well, had arrived in town and requested that I come along.

She greeted me with a big, friendly hug and a smile and I couldn't help but feel like we were being "fixed up" on a date. I presumed furthering our friendship was the only reason I was included in this breakfast icebreaker. I was most definitely being sized up as a potential shopping partner. Anna was planning on staying in Vancouver throughout most of the scheduled filming, and she had already mentioned in the first twenty seconds that we would have loads of fun together.

Honestly, I was glad. Her excitement was infectious and her complete acceptance of me was a huge relief. Making friends in Ryan's social sphere was important.

I shook hands with producer Parker Shay, and then was introduced to Ryan's next co-star, actress Nicole Devin. I actually didn't know who she was when Ryan told me her name so I looked her up on Google prior to this meeting. That's how I found out that her father is a L.A. talent agent and her mother an accomplished scriptwriter. Nicole had a recurring role on a cable series before landing this lead role opposite Ryan.

Though we were just about the same height, she had shoulder-length caramel-brown hair, pouty lips, and a professionally sculpted nose. She looked tired; slight purple circles surrounded her eyes. Instead of shaking my hand she held her arms out, welcoming me in for a hug that lingered a little longer than what was socially acceptable in my book. It was right about then that I realized her surgically enhanced breasts were causing dents to form in mine, and I backed out of the hug.

I gasped slightly when actor Bill Pullman entered the room. I knew he was cast to play the FBI agent, but it was still a shock to see him in the flesh, clad in jeans and a camel-colored sport coat, walking toward our table. It was hard not to feel giddy when he flashed those trademark dimples. Damn, I loved his movies.

While we were served coffee, I caught Nicole periodically gazing at me. She'd smile strangely, sniff a few times, then bat her eyes in another direction, often landing her view back on Ryan. Great . . . another attractive actress drooling over my fiancé and sizing me up to see how easy it would be to take out the competition. I felt my grip on my butter knife tighten.

I was trying to hold a conversation with Anna, but Nicole's runny nose and her constant sniffing were quite a distraction. I dug in my purse to give the poor girl some tissues. I was hoping that she would feel better soon and be over her cold before Ryan had to do any kissing scenes with her, because knowing my luck, she'd end up passing it on to Ryan and I would end up with the flu or something.

I was wondering how someone so skittish-looking could become

so famous when Jeremy Irons made his way to the table. *Holy hell;*
this man is like a walking poster child for "successful actor." Seeing him in
person was quite intimidating.

I knew Ryan was nervous about working with such seasoned actors, especially since he had the lead role in this film. He was forever
fearing his own acting skills might be inadequate. I had a small taste
of how cynical and critical people in this business could be at the
Reparation after-party, when I accidentally overheard some deroga-
tory comments made about Ryan's lack of acting skills. Thankfully
Ryan didn't hear them; he would have gone into a downward spiral
if he had.

Still, he knew he was the new kid on the block and hadn't fully
earned his place. Ryan's good looks combined with one successful
movie role had garnered a lot of attention, but he'd have to prove his
worth to his peers if he wanted their respect.

And I was sure that fear of failure was his biggest worry, though
he'd never admit that out loud. Sure enough, his insecurities mani-
fested just after midnight last night. He'd been tossing and turning
and wrestling with his pillows, punching and kneading them into
submission, like they had angered him.

We had just had amazing, energy-zapping sex, so I knew it was
his mind that kept him from passing out.

"Can't sleep?" I asked, hoping to get him to talk it out so he'd curl
back around me.

He tugged at the covers again. "Just restless. Close your eyes, babe."

Yeah, his mind was working overtime. "Want to talk about it?"

"No. Go to sleep."

I rolled to face him. "Worried about tomorrow?"

He sighed, frowned, and then said, "No."

Yeah, that was an obvious little lie. "You're already there, you know.
Just takes time for the rest of them to realize it."

Ryan dipped his chin to look at me, brushing my hair back.
"Where's that?"

"To where you think the rest of them are in their careers and where you think you aren't."

He made a small, noncommittal noise.

"You're working with two men who have been in this business the same amount of years you've been alive. I know you worry about it."

Ryan wrapped his other arm over me, resting his chin on the top of my head. His tiny, pained sigh was confirmation enough.

"You're just as brilliant and talented as they are, Ryan. You just don't see it yet, but you will and they will, too."

I waited for a reply, but he remained silent.

"Besides," I added, nuzzling deeper into his chest, "you have something they'll *never, ever* have."

"What's that?"

I closed my eyes and felt myself slip for a moment. Blessed sleep was grasping at me hard. "Eighty million screaming fans," I mumbled.

Ryan snickered and kissed my head. "I love you. Go to sleep."

The last thing I remember saying was "I love you more."

RYAN STOOD immediately to shake Jeremy's hand, awkwardly dropping his cloth napkin to the floor. Even someone as famous as Ryan had his own celebrity gushing moments.

Fortunately Parker Shay joined them and eased some of the awkwardness.

After breakfast, Anna and I were placed inside a chauffeur-driven Lexus for our day of shopping. I could smell the credit cards burning a hole in her purse.

It was going to be a long day.

I used this opportunity to pick her brain, learning as much as I could about what it meant to be a film producer, as Ryan had also signed on to be an executive producer of *Slipknot*. She was like my own private tutor, filling me in on all the sordid details and nuances of the film industry and introducing me to the wonders of shopping as if things didn't have price tags.

Over the following days she gave me guided tours of the sets, introducing me to the different film crews, set designers, wardrobe assistants, and boom operators, explaining as best she could what everyone's job was.

During a break, I called my answering machine, weeding through numerous requests for interviews and questions about who was representing me. *Like what the hell does that mean? Do I need a freaking agent now that I'm engaged to Ryan?* Delete, delete, delete.

"Hello, Miss Mitchell, this is Sharon Palmer from United Fidelity Bank. I'm calling regarding the safe-deposit box rental fee for Daniel Mitchell, which is now sixty days past due. Please contact me at your earliest convenience." I fumbled with my phone, making sure I didn't delete that one since I didn't have a pen to write her number down.

Would this nonsense with my parents' estates ever be done? I had gone through all of Mom and Dad's files; how the hell did I miss this one? I wondered if I still had copies of his death certificate . . . My thumb clicked for the next message.

"Taryn."

I froze. Just hearing my name in that voice sent a shock through my body. Suddenly it became hard to swallow.

"Listen, it's Thomas. I stopped into the bar the other day but I hear you're out of town. Shit. Um . . . listen, I really need to talk to you. It's important. Call my cell. My number is . . ."

My mind raced. What the hell could he possibly need to talk to me about? A hundred different scenarios ripped through my mind, including him possibly having nude photos of me and having been hacked or something stupid like that.

Is he going to try to get me back into his life? It's way too late for that to happen. After witnessing his unbridled ass-pumping into that skank, and even if there were no Ryan in my life, I wouldn't take him back.

Jonathan Follweiler yelled for me, hailing me over with his hand. I shoved my cell in my pocket, wondering if I should tell Ryan that Thomas called me.

"Ah, Taryn dear, we're in a bit of a pinch," he said, somewhat flustered and breathless. "Would you mind standing over there on that mark? We need to check lighting."

"Mark?" I questioned, pointing to the X that was taped on the ground a few yards away, and beating down the echo of Thomas's voice in my head.

Jonathan and the three other men surrounding him appeared stressed, while another man, who said he was the grip, raised some sort of handheld device near my face. The uncertainty of whether I was doing this properly had me frozen in place while enormous cameras and large lights were adjusted around me.

The first assistant director, a man I had come to know by the name of Denny, trotted to my side. "Where? Here?" he asked, wrapping his rough, paw-like hand around my upper arm to relocate me.

Jonathan hurried over and pulled his headphones down around his neck. "Taryn, see that first mark? I want you to stand over there and then when I give your cue, I want you to walk from there to here."

"Sure. No problem." I walked to the first mark and waited.

I made the same walk from point A to point B several times while the commotion of filmmaking and lighting adjustments happened around me. I had no idea why I was chosen to walk back and forth, but it didn't matter; I was just relieved to finally feel like I was serving some purpose instead of being a useless body in everyone's way. Ryan was off giving some sort of quick interview so I really didn't know what to do with myself.

While I stood on the second mark, I noticed Mike escorting Ryan out to the set. I saw panic flash over Ryan's face a moment later. He ran over to me like a father removing his child from the middle of a busy highway. Thankfully his concern for me made thoughts of Thomas disappear.

"Sorry," Ryan said in apology to Denny. "Taryn—what are you doing?" he whispered furiously. He started to tug my arm, pulling me off my mark.

"No! Wait." I tried to hold my ground.

"No, no. Ryan, leave her there," Denny instructed. "We needed a stand-in for Nicole."

"Oh," Ryan uttered. Relief washed over his face.

"Jonathan has found a use for me," I explained, bouncing slightly on my tiptoes on the large silver-tape X, trying to keep warm. Even though it was sunny outside, the temperature in Vancouver was on the chilly side. I nodded when Jonathan told me to stick around, but he needed ten minutes.

"Jeez, I sort of panicked there for a minute."

I frowned at him. "I think I know better than to wander out in front of the cameras."

"I didn't know. Sorry." His lips curled in amusement. "Just think, your first official job in the movie industry is as an actor stand-in," he said with a laugh. I could see the hint of pride touch his face. "You know they have you on film now? We'll have to see if we can get a copy."

I nudged him softly with my elbow. "This isn't a job. It's a quick favor for Jonathan. So, are you ready? Know your lines?"

Ryan nodded. "Yes, I know my lines. I presume you know them, too."

As if he had to ask. "I've been given my own official copy."

"Of course," he teased. "Jonathan make you an assistant director yet?"

I nudged his stomach lightly for picking on me. "No. Denny has, though. They put me in charge of kicking your ass when you get out of line."

Ryan smirked, sparked by my challenge. He bumped me, knocking me off balance, but I quickly recovered and bumped him right back. His long fingers cinched around my upper arms as he glared down at me, his eyes half-lidded and challenging. "You think you're tough enough?"

I swallowed hard, turned on by his show of dominance. "Absolutely. I know all of your weaknesses."

His eyes darkened and he took my neck in a gentle but possessive clutch, instantly igniting a warmth inside me. "Yeah?" he growled,
biting his lower lip, daring me to defy him. "You think? Little do you
know, you're my greatest weakness. But don't get any ideas. Remember, I've had my hands and mouth on every inch of your body. I know
how to take you down—quickly."

Oh how I wished we were somewhere private where he could
make good on his threat.

"Promise?" I whispered, drawn to watching his lips twitch,
thrilled that we had this effect on each other.

"As soon as I'm done here, I'm going to prove it to you," he
breathed out.

Was that a simple statement or a vow?

"I look forward to it," I replied, feeling stunned and out of breath.

"I'm so hard right now," he told me, toggling his gaze between my
lips and my eyes.

One quick glance at his crotch and I could see he was being
truthful.

"I wish I could fix that for you." Thoughts of using my hand, my
mouth, rendering him helpless and moaning, danced in my mind.
"But I think you're going to have to hold that thought." I tossed my
chin in Denny's direction.

Ryan breathed out a curse and turned his frame slightly, readjust-
ing the erection in his pants as nonchalantly as possible. It was hard
not to laugh at his predicament.

"Stop it," he groaned.

"Apparently wake-up sex wasn't enough for you?" I teased.

He glared down at me in utter exasperation. "Four or five times a
day might be enough for me. Keep that in mind, future wife of mine."

A giggle erupted from my mouth. "As much as I'd like to take you
up on your challenge, right now I think we need to get you refocused.
So . . . Chase. What did the police say?"

Ryan groaned. "Taryn, I know my lines."

"Okay." No need to warn me twice. I turned my attention to watching crew members setting up a very large screen several yards away. *Where are they going to put that huge green screen now? That looks like a pain to move.*

Ryan sighed. "Nothing. They don't have any new leads."

I glanced back at him. "Hmm?"

"My lines? My next line is 'Nothing. They don't have any new leads.'"

"Oh. Sorry. I didn't hear you."

Watching Ryan's new set assistant try to figure out which pocket to shove her walkie-talkie in while tripping over power cords was quite entertaining. *She looks young and upset about something. The shimmery blue streak of color in her black hair is kinda cool.*

Ryan cleared his throat. "I hate when you pretend to ignore me. Well? Are we going to do this or not?"

The sudden bad feeling about this not being a good idea hit me. "I'm not ignoring you. Maybe you should rehearse with Nicole. I don't want to upset anything."

Ryan didn't agree. "We have ten minutes and she's still in makeup. Do you have a copy of the sides?"

I pulled my copy of the scene dialogue from my back pocket.

"You're standing on her mark. Ready?"

"Sure." I took two pretend steps to land on the X. "Chase, what did the police say?"

"Nothing. They don't have any new leads. Reed won't turn over my dad's client list without a court order. I sort—"

"Wait . . . is that how you are going to do it for real?" Even though he recited from memory, he rushed and stumbled through it.

Ryan's eyes narrowed on me. "Yeah, I guess. Why? What was wrong with it?"

"Are you just telling me your lines or are we doing this full-on like we normally do when we run lines at home?"

He crossed his arms, taking a defensive pose.

"Don't get mad," I said. "You just . . . I don't know. You just sort of barked your lines at me. I thought Chase is supposed to be frustrated and more depressed. Well, that's how I interpreted it anyway."

"Sorry, you got me a bit distracted. I'm horny and I'm pissed that I can't do anything about it right now."

"Margaret Thatcher in a thong." My attempt to redirect him with Austin Powers movie humor wasn't well received. He gave me "the glare." I knew that glare very well.

"Tell you what. If you promise to nail this scene, I promise I'll let you nail me in your trailer right afterward. How does that sound?"

That got him to smile. "Bribery, Ms. Mitchell? And what's this garbage that you'll let me . . ."

"Uh-uh. That's the deal. You have to make sacrifices for your craft." He groaned.

"Multimillion-dollar actor, big mega-million movie? Ringing any bells?"

His jaw clenched. "I'm going to nail you hard later, just so you know. It may hurt, too. Make your teeth rattle."

I planted a foot, loving his feistiness. "You nail this scene in the first two takes and I'll add in a bonus prize."

His eyebrows rose, intrigued.

"But first you have to act your butt off."

"You drive a hard bargain. All right, shit. Let's try it again." Ryan shook out his arms. "Ready?"

I took a deep breath, pulling myself into that mind-set I do when we practice in private, and recited my lines again.

Ryan pretended to glance back at the building, rubbing his stomach where the bullets from earlier in the story had supposedly entered his body, and hunching from imaginary pain. "They brought one of my dad's associates in for questioning, but it didn't turn up any new leads."

"Did you tell them about the van that followed you the other day?"

Ryan's lips pressed tightly together and he shook his head.

"What about the address you found on your dad's cell?"

"No," he answered abruptly, looking away. "I didn't bother."

"Why not?" I said, demanding an answer. If someone killed *my* pretend parents, I'd be hounding the police for every minuscule detail.

Ryan turned his gaze back to me, giving me that "I really have no valid excuse so I'm just going to stand here and huff at you for a few seconds" look. "Because . . . I went there and it's nothing, another dead end. Apparently I'm just wasting my time. Chasing ghosts," he mumbled.

Ryan appeared to be genuinely sad. I remembered this part of the script very well, for this was Chase and Emily's first fight, out on the sidewalk in front of the police station.

I disagreed, imploring him to give more information. "What about the bullet casing? Surely they have some results—"

"They have nothing, Em. Nothing!" Ryan said harshly. "Just forget about it, all right? No prints. No leads. Nothing. So just drop it! I'm done."

I pushed on, lightly grabbing his arm when he turned. "So that's it? Just like that, you're going to give up?"

Ryan glared at me. "What do you want me to do? Go back in there and force them to do their job? It's not that simple."

"But . . ."

"But nothing!" Ryan's hand sliced the air, halting my reply. "Detective Bennett told me to stay out of it. I'm not supposed to be alive, Emily! Remember? Whoever broke into my house and put eight bullets in my family intended for me to die that day, too. There weren't supposed to be witnesses."

"Yeah, but you didn't."

"Yeah, well, maybe I should have," Ryan snapped back, letting the role of Chase completely take over his emotions. It was a beautiful thing to witness, and I was so there with him. God. Losing both of your parents. I knew exactly how that felt.

"Is that what you want? To waste the precious gift you were given by wishing you were dead? Is that why you pulled that ridiculous stunt trying to free-climb that crack out on Viper's Pass, figuring if bullets didn't do the job that free-falling three hundred feet would?"

Ryan groaned incredulously, like my words stung.

"Look at me. Don't you dare do this to yourself. Do you think Megan would give up if she were here?"

Ryan's head snapped back. "Leave my sister out of this," he growled.

"I can't. Not when you wake up every night freaking out that you couldn't save her. Not when you see her ghost drifting through walls and ceilings everywhere you go. Chase . . ." I grasped his jacket in both of my hands. "She wants you to find peace just as much as I do."

Ryan knocked my hands free.

"Just go. Go home." He nodded his chin, telling me to take a hike.

"Chase . . . no," I said stubbornly, snagging his jacket again. "I'm just trying to help. I . . . I didn't mean to make you upset. Please . . ."

"Let. Go," he ordered, glaring at the hold I had on him.

I felt my teeth lock in place. "No. I will *never* let go. I will not stand off to the side and watch you destroy yourself."

"You can't keep saving me, Em. You can't."

"That's not for you to decide."

Ryan's face twisted with anguish, feeling pain that was only pretend.

"Don't push me away, too," I said softly. "I need you just as much as you need me."

Ryan scoffed, shaking his head back and forth. "My mind is becoming unhinged and yet you still want me to be this, this guy . . . this guy I just can't be for you."

I gazed at the fabric bunched in my hand and then up into his eyes, knowing that Ryan Christensen and some poor scripted guy named Chase Sheffield would always be more than enough for me.

"I've never asked you to be anything more than who you are. If the police won't help us, we'll find someone else who will."

Ryan nodded and then slowly wrapped his arms over my shoulders, pulling me in. My hands automatically slid underneath his jacket and up his muscular back; I nuzzled my cheek on his warm chest. For a moment, I forgot we were standing here rehearsing, just like we did all those times in the apartment when I ran lines with him.

Ryan blew out a relieving gust and whispered in my ear. "Satisfied?"

I couldn't stifle my smile. I laughed lightly and gave the flesh on his back a light rub.

"That was *really* good!" he continued privately. "I cannot believe you remembered all those lines. You really nailed it. Sure you don't want to be an actress?"

When I opened my eyes, I noticed Jonathan standing near the camera that was pointed directly at us, pressing the headphones to his ear. Next to him stood Nicole Devin, dressed for the scene, looking glassy-eyed and angry. I didn't need to be a mind reader to interpret her opinion about what she had apparently just witnessed. Her slightly raised arms slapped down on her thighs.

"Oh shit," I breathed out.

Nicole stormed over to us. I squeezed the back of Ryan's shirt into a ball in my fist.

"What's going on?" she asked, volleying her slightly angered glare from my face to his, sniffing from her head cold.

Ryan repositioned himself between us, pushing me behind him. "What do you mean? I'm just running through my lines one more time. Taryn's my coach. Why? What do you *think* is going on?"

"Oh," Nicole said, her face dropping. "I thought. Never mind. I'm here now."

I unclenched Ryan's shirt; now was as good a time as any to get the hell out of here before I caused permanent damage. "Ryan, I'm going to see if Jonathan still needs me."

Nicole crossed her arms. "Yeah. That sounds like a good idea."

My feet that were so ready to flee ground down to a halt. "I was helping him. There's no need to assume anything else. I would never . . ."

Nicole cracked a little smile, then broke into a sniffing fit. Some of Thomas's old friends used to have the same sniffing habit. It made me wonder.

"No, no. Believe me—I'm not. It's okay," she finally said, nicely. "I think they're almost ready."

Instead of meeting her gaze, my eyes locked on to the strange dark shadow on her upper lip. I was just about to walk away when I noticed the drop of crimson fluid drip out from her nostril. It pooled at the edge of her lip before dripping down to the ground, missing her foot by an inch.

"Nicole, your nose is bleeding." I was surprised she didn't feel that trickle on her skin.

Her hand flew up to her face. Shaky fingers confirmed the blood. We watched as she ran off in the direction of the trailers.

WHILE RYAN did some walk-through rehearsals, I found a quiet place to work in the wardrobe tent, where the Wi-Fi was the strongest. After all, I still had a business to run. Even though I thoroughly enjoyed seeing him in his element, joking with the crew, being lighthearted and having the time of his life, I also knew I was a distraction.

Marie was being really understanding about my long absence, but my guilty conscience wracked me every day, knowing I was strapping her with my obligations. Fortunately, paying bills and ordering stock were things I could do anywhere.

I thought about returning some phone calls but I really didn't want to hear Thomas's voice again. Not right now.

Dina, the woman in charge of wardrobe, took me under her wing like a warm mother hen. She cleared off a small wooden table in the corner for me to have some workspace while I secretly listened to her and her assistant, Darius, gossiping about the rest of the film crew.

Dina peered at me over the top of her narrow glasses, giving me a slightly disapproving look. "I'm surprised you don't want to be out there watching Mr. Christensen film. Surely that's a lot more interesting than hanging with us."

I shook my head. "Actually there's more action in here than out there. I find that you two are quite entertaining." I smiled.

"Mmhmm." Darius scowled. "If I were you, I wouldn't let that delicious slice of man out of my sight."

"Darius!" Dina shrieked.

Darius was young and sort of reminded me of Jet Li, but a drama queen version with two-toned black and white hair. He made me laugh.

"What? You know I speak the truth. That boy is fine. Damn, I should have been an actress." Darius sighed. "If I were you, peaches, I'd keep an eye on that Nicole girl. I'd cut her forty ways to Sunday if that was my man," he joked, waving a pair of long fabric shears. "Let her know. You keep back, beyotch," he mumbled to himself.

Dina laughed at him. "Someone sure sounds jealous."

Darius just rolled his eyes. "Girl, pa-leeze. If I had a boyfriend like that, there is no way I'd let some ho be all up on him. Then again, one taste of these lips and he'd never go back."

Visualizing Ryan's reaction to Darius's claim was equally entertaining.

"Ah, I don't think Taryn has to worry about Nicole. Ryan Christensen isn't her type," Dina said with a wink, pinning the hem on a pair of pants. After that comment, she now had my total attention.

Darius's face puckered. "Whaaat? Honey—gay, straight, that man is *everyone's* type."

I smirked at Darius.

"Not if you prefer women over men, he isn't," Dina muttered.

My head shot up.

Darius looked surprised. "Dee, I didn't know you were a homegirl!"

"What? No, not me . . . Nicole," Dina corrected. "Rumor has it that she prefers the company of women."

"Oh no you did not just out her," Darius squealed.

Something inside of me suddenly wanted to cheer, finding this new information to be most comforting. I needed more.

Dina removed the straight pin tucked between her lips and shrugged. "That's the rumor going around." Dina's walkie-talkie screeched. She pulled the radio from her hip holster.

"Is Ms. Mitchell with you?" the voice asked.

Dina held the radio to her mouth. "Yes she is."

A few moments later, a young man wearing khaki pants and a green hoodie whisked me away on a golf cart. I was paired up with Ryan's stand-in for another lighting check. I was told that Nicole's stand-in had completely succumbed to the stomach flu, but I still questioned Jonathan's true motives for selecting me as her replacement. Regardless, it didn't matter; I was having a ton of fun being with Ryan.

THE FOLLOWING morning we drove into an industrial part of the city that was not at all located where I thought he would be filming today. The building we pulled up to was long and squat, with security fencing surrounding the parking lot.

Ryan's fingers were woven with mine but I could tell his mind was elsewhere. I knew what was on the shooting schedule today and he was so distant and quiet, he was practically mute.

Mike escorted us quickly from the car, leading us to one of the camper trailers parked nearby.

I set my laptop bag and purse down and sat at the small dinette, dreading this day worse than open-heart surgery without sedatives. It was time to break our comfortable silence.

"I don't know how this usually works. Do you want me to wait in here today? I will if you're going to be uncomfortable."

Ryan stood there, staring at me.

I stared back, waiting for his decision. "Just be honest."

"I don't know," he mumbled, eyeing everything but me for the moment. "I want you there and then a part of me doesn't. It's a closed set but . . . Think you can handle it?"

My first instinct was to scream "no" very loudly. Images of him executing the dreaded scene were flashing through my thoughts. What was I supposed to say? *Oh yeah, no problem. I can't wait to see you making pretend love to Nicole. It's been on my to-do list, actually.* Fortunately I reined in my self-preservationist sarcastic thoughts.

He pulled a can of soda out of the small refrigerator and popped the tab open for me. "Gauging by your lack of immediate response, I think you need to be there. This—stuff—is all a part of acting, Taryn, and maybe if you see that it's nothing more than choreographed pretending, then maybe . . ." His eyes locked on mine. "I just . . . I just don't want what happened in Florida to ever repeat itself."

"Ryan . . ." My gut twisted. Memories of standing in a downpour watching what I thought was him cheating on me with Lauren Delaney when in fact he was filming were so vivid I swear I could feel a drop of rain trickle down my spine.

Ryan sat down and took my hand in his. "You had another one of your nightmares this morning and I think I know why. We've talked about this already. You're my soul mate, Tar. Maybe if you see all of the preparations that go into filming a scene like this and all of the people standing around watching us, you'll know it has nothing to do with sex. It's just an uncomfortable illusion."

I swallowed some of my doubt, trying not to have any of it fly out of my mouth, knowing that the black-haired boy with bloodied teeth was the cause of me waking up with a gasp. "I know it's fake. It's not like you're going to go over there and actually do it with her."

"That's right. I'm not. It's all pretend. You know that this is my job and scenes like this are going to be in my movies. I just don't want you to end up hating me because I have to fake it with other women."

If only faking it didn't include actual skin-to-skin contact. We locked eyes. "Truthfully, I don't know what to expect and I'm a little scared. I can't help it."

His eyes softened. His fingers caressed my wrist. "Okay, let's talk about it. What are you scared of?"

"This is all new to me. I'm not *accustomed* to the idea of having the person I'm involved with do that sort of stuff with someone else in front of me. And things are good with us now but what if we're having a rough patch and then you and someone else and the temptation and kissing . . ."

His hand covered mine, softly stroking his thumb over my knuckles. "I won't be tempted. Trust me."

On some level I believed him. I'd observed him long enough to know that Ryan never, ever looked at other women, even when they were standing on top of him.

"It's one of my biggest fears."

He straightened my engagement ring. "I know. But keep in mind that I've already kissed my fair share and now I've found the only woman I want to spend the rest of my life with."

His playful smile helped me relax.

"Okay." I grinned.

"So you're not going to get jealous when I have to kiss someone else?"

I chuckled with uncertainty. "I can't promise that. My jealousy comes from being madly in love with you. As long as it only happens when the cameras are rolling, I'll be okay. It's just . . . I need you to understand if I can't handle it right away. I mean, I've seen you kiss Suzanne and—"

"Stand up."

"What?"

"Stand up. I want to show you something."

I slid out of the booth.

Ryan gripped my hips, pulling me closer. "I want to show you the difference between a movie kiss and a real kiss."

"There's a difference?"

He nodded. "Oh yeah." His warm hands lifted my face, his eyes focused on my mouth. "This is a movie kiss. Ready?"

I felt his closed lips touch mine as if he were only kissing me to be kind. When his mouth opened, I followed him. Kissing him like this was kind of weird and actually rather frustrating, like we were doing an unfamiliar dance or an awkward first-date kiss when you were really trying to avoid kissing the guy. "Uh-uh. No tongue," he corrected.

"No tongue?" I repeated into his opened mouth.

"Never." Ryan pulled back and looked me in the eyes. "Now *this* is how I kiss my fiancée."

His hand slid into my hair, cradling the back of my head. His kiss consumed me. Desire to suck and chew on his hypnotic mouth had me making little whimpering noises. The moment his tongue brushed and swirled with mine, I felt tingles all the way down to my panties.

"I know you love me," I murmured, drifting my hands into the back of his pants, underneath the elastic band, and over his amazing sculpted ass, "but it's going to kill me to see you make love to someone else."

I felt him tense ever so briefly. "I will never make love to someone else, Tar. Only you," he purred, his tongue quite preoccupied swirling with mine.

I pushed his pants down low on his hips and scraped my teeth over his bottom lip. "Promise?"

He snickered in my mouth. "It was in the fine print when you agreed to marry me, sweetheart."

Ryan lifted my ID set badge, separating our kiss long enough to remove it over my head. With a devilish grin, his fingers curled under the front of my T-shirt, pulling it up so it was over my head but still wrapped around my upper arms, cinching them back. "And our contract *will* be binding."

He swirled a fingertip under the edge of my lace bra and tugged one side down, seeking out an already aroused nipple with his wet tongue. Fire shot through my body.

"Ryan . . ." I gulped hard from the sensation of his careful attention to both of my breasts. It was difficult to speak.

"Bed," he breathed his desire, towing me in a rush down the short, narrow hallway.

It took him slightly longer to undress, fumbling to toe off his shoes while stripping off his pants, so I crawled onto the bed and waited. Considering we only had twenty minutes, I had expected he'd want to skip all the foreplay and jump right into it, so it surprised me a little when he took his good old time.

It was so sensual, him kissing me like this, allowing me to pant in his mouth as if he needed my sighs to breathe. He drew my bottom lip into his mouth, grazing it through his teeth, cradling me in his arm while his thigh had my leg pinned. I was so aroused by his touch, fingers gliding with deliberate effort while the heel of his hand applied just the right amount of pressure. His thumb danced in a firm circle, then heel, then thumb again. I wanted to explode then and there.

God, if he actually had to go film a real scene like this with Nicole I'd have to fucking kill her with my bare hands first. For a split second I actually envisioned doing that. There would be no way in hell I'd ever allow another woman to feel his expert touch.

I could hear my own moans getting louder, more breathless, as I writhed with each slip. I was just about there, seconds away from spilling over the edge, when he withdrew his fingers and stopped. *What? Nooooo!* I mentally cursed him for not finishing me off first. *And I was so close, too.*

But instead, Ryan grabbed my thigh and shifted my hip so I was on my side, his chest warming my back, replacing the void with something much longer, thicker. I reached back, running my hand into his hair, feeling his groans, his breath on my neck as he pressed tenderly, allowing my body to adjust around him.

"Oh God you feel good." His forearm squeezed my rib cage and his hand palmed my breast, stroking into me with renewed force, returning me dangerously close to that edge again.

His left hand twined with mine, unifying us as one as he made love to me. Just when I thought he would slip out and roll me somewhere else on the bed, he pressed back in. Slowly, methodically, from tip to total; over and over again, driving me crazy.

His moistened fingers returned and splayed me open, rolling swirls over my sensitive skin with each thrust.

As he picked up the pace, I held the breath in my lungs, unable to breathe at any normal rate, feeling the intense sensations of my orgasm rolling to a peak.

"That's it. Let it go. Come on baby . . ."

I was giving myself a headache from squeezing my eyes so hard, feeling the crescendo of orgasm. His deep thrusts were unrelenting, pounding into me over and over again. I cried out from the sensations breaking over me in waves, practically choking myself as they hit. I coughed out onto the comforter as I buried my face into the bed.

Ryan's presses slowed; his fingers continued to rub, milking additional shudders out of me.

"Ah . . . good one," he crooned softly, proudly, still swirling gently inside of me. He kissed my shoulder softly.

I turned back to him, receiving a long kiss before he slipped out and relocated my body to the edge of the bed.

"You have no idea how incredibly beautiful you look right now," Ryan growled. His hands gripped my legs below the crease of my knees, pressing my thighs back, staring down at me with both admiration and lust. He rocked my legs, lifting my rear and raking my insides at different glorifying angles.

But the clock on the wall told another story, one of him being out of time. Sure enough, a few minutes later someone rapped loudly on the outside door. I watched the pleasure on his face harden as he slammed into me with more vigor.

"Hang on!" Ryan yelled out over his shoulder. "Son of a . . . I just need five more minutes," he breathed out, pumping harder. His hands hit the mattress, pressing my thighs back as far as they could go, practically bending me in half to climb up inside of me. A light sweat beaded on his forehead. "Can you go again?" he asked, breathing hard, clasping one hand around my ankle.

I couldn't believe his question! We were in the midst of filming a multimillion-dollar movie, someone was banging their fist on his trailer door to escort him to set, and his greatest concern was whether I could achieve another orgasm? God love the man for trying.

I pushed his hand away and flipped over onto my knees. "Don't worry about me. It's your turn."

Ryan's voice cracked and pitched when he yelled again, "Give me five minutes!" over his shoulder toward the door. His hands palmed my rear, digging fingertips into my flesh. I squeezed down on him with everything I had left, tightening my grip like a vise. Just as I started touching myself, Ryan moved my hand out of the way, replacing it with his own.

"That's mine," he growled, rubbing me with demanding ownership, bringing a second orgasm on like wildfire. My body bucked and shook while he continued to punish me with each thrust. His soft whimpers and grunts turned into one deep, guttural groan as his body released and stuttered everything he had into me.

EVEN BEHIND Mike's dark sunglasses and stoic face, I could still see the hint of guy smugness on his lips as he walked us to makeup. He didn't need to utter a word to Ryan to congratulate him on getting laid mid-afternoon; the hard pat on Ryan's shoulder spoke volumes.

Ryan chose this time to tease me, casually drifting his fingers under his nose as if he still wore my scent. I chuckled at our private joke when he licked his finger and raised his brows, savoring a phantom taste of me.

One of the male makeup artists, a slightly pudgy and excessively hairy man we had been introduced to before by the name of Buckley, was busy fashioning a "cup," for lack of a better word, over Ryan's exposed privates.

"It's called a merkin." Ryan answered my questioning gaze, pressing the sides of the cup into his skin to assure its adhesion.

I envisioned him popping that thing off like a tent way too small for its support pole. The adhesive would surely, painfully rip a few hairs from his skin. *Ouch.*

Nicole might get to touch his body intimately, but there was one flesh-toned package she'd never get to see—lesbian or not. Unfortunately, his nudity meant that those totally sexy muscular indentations in his incredible ass might get some screen time. That would definitely cause a few million "Charles Conroy" fans to blow a gasket for sure. Even more hype for *Seaside III*, which wouldn't start filming until the fall.

Ryan turned to face me with his fists on his hips, looking like a life-sized, naked Ken doll with obscured genitalia. "So, what do you think?"

He was so adorable, smirkin' in his merkin.

"And it's not even my birthday!" I laughed. "I'm wondering how painful it will be when you have to take that thing off."

"Just like a Band-Aid," Buckley mumbled. "Grit and pull."

Ryan blew out a tense breath and slipped a gray flannel robe on, tying the belt securely like a boxer headed for a fight.

It was time for him to go pretend with another woman below him and I was going to watch.

CHAPTER 10

React

CUT. RYAN, YOU need to drop your arm a bit. You're casting a shadow on Nicole," Jonathan instructed, sounding irritated. "No, that's still not working. We need to adjust the lighting. She's got a dark shadow running right across her face."

I watched the gaffer make a slight adjustment to one of the towering lights near the large bed, and was thankful for the momentary reprieve.

An hour ago, that naked body was between my thighs, loving me. Now Ryan was carefully seated between Nicole's bare legs, nothing but flesh-toned merkins keeping their bodies from actually touching.

Ryan and Nicole were holding light conversation while the lights were adjusted around them, but the sight of him lying on top of her was almost too much for me to take in. Like a sick, masochistic voyeur, I stood there, watching. Watching my fiancé slip his lips over another woman's body every time the director called "Action!"

I knew it was fake, completely staged, but still.

Ryan pressed Nicole's hair back from her face, gazing at her before crushing his lips down on hers. She gasped and the sheet that barely covered them rose and fell with the roll of his hips.

Slight tremors vibrated up through my shoulders. Instantly I was torn from the spot and pulled back in time, recalling every ounce of pain I felt when I walked in on my ex-fiancé, Thomas, grinding his naked ass into that emaciated slut, Cheryl Regan, with painful clarity. The overwhelming anguish blasted uncontrollably like lightning into my chest.

I had sworn to myself that day I had caught Thomas, made the most sacred of vows to the sanctity of my own soul, that I would never, ever allow myself to be hurt like that again. To step anywhere near a man who was capable of eviscerating my heart.

Loving someone should never end in all-consuming devastation.

But time and time again I set myself up to be ripped to shreds. And here I stood, torturing myself all over again watching this charade.

Certain moments were tolerable: those when filming had halted and Ryan and Nicole weren't all over each other. But the moment the cameras were rolling, my hands tightened into fists and I wanted to puke craziness.

I knew Ryan was uncomfortable with my presence, peering at me through worried eyes every spare moment when his pretend make-out session wasn't being carefully orchestrated. Still, it wasn't enough to end this insanity.

I don't care how other women would handle watching their man fake sex with another woman; I twitched when Jonathan yelled "Action!" yet again.

Ryan's mouth on her jaw, her lips, grinding her into the bed like he was actually fucking her, looked so real that the heartache seared its way up my throat.

It's pretend. It's fake.

The sheet covering them slipped and a good sliver of Ryan's ass was now in full view. No matter how many times I repeated my mantra it still didn't keep the bile from rising up.

I could see Ryan desperately trying to reach that detached mental space he needed to go to to pull this off. He needed to be "in the zone," so to speak, where he wasn't Ryan Christensen anymore. The place where his character persona, Chase Sheffield, took over and deviant actions became inconsequential.

God, could I do this again? Could I actually be secure enough in my heart and mind to deal with the knowledge that there would be more times like this in my future? More fake love scenes and more intimate touches shared between my lover, my husband-to-be, and random sculpted actresses? Would my eventual marriage become yet another Hollywood divorce?

It's one thing to be married and trust that your spouse never cheats on you. It's another when scripted fake make-out sessions are part of his career, and you know with absolute certainty that moments like this will reoccur.

For a brief time I carried this man's baby in my womb. *If we ever have children, I'm not going to be able to stand here and supervise his pretend sex each and every time. Knowing how easily a moment like this could get way out of hand, leading to a connection with another woman.*

One day I'll be pregnant—large and round, uncomfortable. One day sex won't be a priority; feeding and caring for an innocent infant will be. Staying home to raise a family with some sense of normalcy will be. Will Ryan be able to control himself and know in no uncertain terms where the lines of acting and cheating are firmly drawn? So many unanswered questions.

Ryan clasped hands with Nicole, raising their entwined fingers over her head—a move that I thought was reserved for our lovemaking sessions only. The sense of betrayal that came from it pierced into my heart like a hot knife and I had to consciously stop the whimper from breaking free.

Jonathan had called "Cut!" and Ryan and Nicole were listening to him intently. I couldn't look at Ryan anymore—not in the eyes, anyway. My focus landed on everything else—the towering lights, the black cords snaking across the floor, the black screen blocking shadows from forming, the khaki cargo shorts the boom operator was wearing.

Thousands of movies, thousands of onscreen kisses. Jake Gyllenhaal's kissed a lot of girls. I love his movies. When he filmed with Anne Hathaway—that sex looked real. They both were this naked, too. And that girl in Prince of Persia—*Princess what the hell was her name? Jake kissed Heath Ledger, too. Several times. Damn, that was hot. But they were acting. Making a movie for our enjoyment just like this. I wonder if these things are why he split from Reese Witherspoon all those years ago? And after all of this time, he's still single. Maybe he wanted to—*

A firm hand clasped my shoulder, startling me.

"You okay?" Mike asked quietly. His worried expression wasn't helping.

Damn, how I wished my defiant bottom lip would keep from quivering. I gave him a noncommittal shrug.

"He loves you, you know."

I bit that traitorous bottom lip of mine hard, trying to find that place in my brain where I could be nonchalant, cool and so *whatever—it's just another day in the office for him—no biggie* with all of this.

I turned to look up into Mike's eyes. "I know."

"Doesn't make it any easier to watch, though, does it?"

I crossed my arms over my chest. "No, it doesn't."

Mike sighed. "It's pretend, Taryn. In this business, actors treat kissing like it's nothing more than giving someone a handshake," he said in a hushed voice.

I glanced back at him to see if he was actually serious with that line of made-up bullshit. Somehow I couldn't equate it so benignly. I kept my voice hushed. "It's the temptation I worry about, Mike. It's one thing to admire the apple on the tree. It's another to take a small taste and tempt yourself with thoughts of what you might be missing."

"True, but you can't condemn him for having this be a part of his job. Temptation is all around every one of us, Taryn. Even you are not immune and yet he trusts you."

I knew I had to learn to deal. It was just a harder concept than I thought, bordering on insurmountable.

"I'm not condemning him, Mike. And I do trust him, but I can tell you that if the situation were reversed, he'd be livid right now."

Mike scraped a hand over his head.

"Sorry. I'm trying, Mike. Really I am. But I can't say I'm all right with watching the man I love be so intimate with someone else, fake or not." I tilted my head in Ryan's direction. "How would you feel if that were your girlfriend beneath him?"

Mike's eyes darkened. "I'm not going to lie. I'd probably hate it just as much as you do right now. But I'd also try to remind myself that it takes more than a few hours of filming a fake love scene to build the kind of relationship that you and he have."

Mike's penetrating gaze silently shouted, *Think about that one, sweetheart.*

Filming halted for a ten-minute break. Ryan was still tying the belt of his robe as he rushed over to me. Silent words passed between him and Mike as he grabbed my hand and hustled me away. We found a private corner and Ryan immediately pulled me into a tight embrace.

His hand held my head to his chest and I couldn't help but tremble. He kissed my hair and my forehead over and over again.

"AT LEAST you get to keep your clothes on in this scene." I couldn't stop myself. I was trying so hard to be cool about things, nonchalant and teasingly playful, even, but the bitter tone I thought I had under control kept rolling out with my words.

Witnessing a mostly naked Nicole writhe like a wanton whore under my very naked fiancé continued to twist poisonous thoughts around in my head. Ryan didn't know it, but at 3 A.M. I slipped out of our bed to have a private crying session in the condo's kitchen.

Agonizing pain from the paranoia of Hollywood and fame separating us one day squeezed my heart again. Besides John Travolta and Will Smith, I could not think of any other famous couples who stayed together for the long, long haul. Even the best poker players wouldn't bet on those odds.

Ryan leaned over and gave me a quick kiss after we departed out of wardrobe. He draped an arm over my shoulders. "I like this jealous side of you. Makes me feel wanted."

He had no idea how close I was to freaking out. "You having fun torturing me? I don't care what you say. Pretend or not, a kiss is still a kiss, especially those designed to sell *the illusion* for all it's worth."

Ryan frowned at me and took my hand. "I told you she tasted awful. There was absolutely nothing about that entire experience that even came close to pleasure."

Yeah? What happens when the next one doesn't taste so bad?

Several crew members hustled past us so I kept my voice low. "Well thank *God* for that." I laughed at the absurdity, trying to cover up how territorial I was feeling with humor.

He took a long drink from his bottle of water as we walked to the large catering tent. "I know it bothered you to see me doing that sort of stuff with someone else. I don't know what else to say besides 'I'm sorry.' In time, you'll get used to it. Or you won't."

I zipped my hoodie to block the chill. "'That sort of stuff' meaning grinding Nicole into the bed as if you were trying to fuck her clear through to the other side of the mattress 'sort of stuff'? Yeah, that was beyond painful, fake or not." A frustrated tear formed in the corner of my eye and I swiped it away quickly, hating that my lack of emotional control just flew out of my mouth.

Ryan stopped abruptly and spoke to Mike. "Can you give us a minute?"

"Sure." Mike folded his arms across his chest and turned away to give us privacy.

Ryan pulled me off to the side behind some equipment. "Sweetheart, come on. I know it was hard for you to watch. God, I'd never do anything intentional to hurt you like that. I wish you'd realize that there is absolutely no reason for you to feel sad or threatened."

"I know. I'm sorry, Ryan. I don't mean to be . . . I'm trying. I really am." I couldn't stop the flood of emotion once the dam had been breached. I knew I was being irrational, but I was also willing to bet that *most* women would go a little crazy after watching their lover fake-fuck someone for several hours. "You have no idea how hard that was for me. I wonder how you would feel if you had to watch me like that with another man." I shrugged. "Maybe you'd understand then."

The glare I received was deadly. "Since you're *not* an actress, that scenario better never happen, or you and me . . . we'll have serious problems."

I knew I was potentially instigating an argument, but I didn't care. "Why? Does the thought of seeing me being intimate with someone else make you jealous?"

Ryan's nostrils flared, a telltale sign he was getting pissed-off, too.

"I'm trying to be confident and secure, Ryan, but it was a new experience and I can't help but feel betrayed. I am not used to having to share my fiancé, fake or not. It was hard and I thought . . . ah, forget it."

"Wait, what? How the hell did I *betray* you?"

I planted a foot. "You did the hand thing with her," I growled.

"What?"

"When you were . . . you wove your fingers with hers and did the over-the-head thing. I thought . . . I know it sounds ridiculous, but I thought that was mine. Ours. I guess I was wrong."

"What are you talking about?"

"With Nicole . . . you did the hand thing with her." I raised my arm up over my head quickly to demonstrate. "I thought that was something you only did with me. When you make love to me, you always tie our hands together. I thought it was special. Mine. Sorry, but it hurts to find out it wasn't."

He looked at me like I had lost my mind. Maybe I had. "You're kidding, right?"

"Forget it. I don't expect you to understand."

He groaned. I knew I was frustrating him but yeah well too bad. I had old wounds that left deep scars, too—reminding me never to be foolish with my heart again.

Ryan seized my arm when I tried to wave off the last five minutes. "You're upset because of the way I held her hand?"

I tried to shrug it off. "Whatever. Apparently it doesn't mean anything to you, but it meant a lot to me. It's like you make us one when we have sex. I thought it was special." I bumped a small rock with my foot. "It's not special anymore."

Ryan cursed low. "Oh, babe. I'm sorry. I didn't think of that. I didn't realize."

"Well, now you do," I murmured.

He frowned at me. "Tar, despite what you think, it was *physically and mentally painful* for me to do that in front of you."

I could hear the sincerity in his voice. I knew he really didn't mean to hurt me.

"I saw the look on your face," he went on, "and I thought to myself, what if *this* is the moment that breaks her. What if *this* is the thing that causes her to bolt. I know you keep thinking that I'm going to fall prey to the Hollywood cliché. That kissing some fucking actress is going to be the final straw that brings the house down. But babe, do you ever consider what I'm feeling? How fucking paranoid I am that the only woman I've *ever* loved is going to run screaming for the hills because of what I do for a living?"

I shook my head. "Never. You're not the only one who pledged *forever* here, Ryan. I will keep on fighting for us no matter what."

I looked him right in the eye, feeling like shit for not seeing his side. "Seeing you like that with someone else made me a little crazy. I think I can handle the kissing. Yeah, I'm pretty sure I can, just please give me a chance to get used to it and I . . . No, I'm positive I can deal with it, but the total nakedness and boob touching and the fake sex? I'm sorry but that—that was just too much for me."

"I hated it, too." He took a deep breath, and then nodded, seeming to make some silent decision. "That's why I wanted you there, Taryn. You know it's fake because you watched it get set up."

Ryan pulled me into his chest and rubbed his lips over my hair.

"One good thing, though, is that I know you're truly here for *me*. It just confirms how right this is."

The tip of his nose brushed against mine as his hand threaded into my hair. Ryan kissed me softly—just a few feather-light touches, before nudging my lips apart with his tongue. I could feel both our desperation and our desire, fueled by the wetness of our mouths and the necessity to convey unspoken messages.

He bit my bottom lip gently, forcing us to stop, then rested his forehead on mine, calculating his next sentence while scanning my eyes for a reaction. "In there, in front of the camera, it means nothing. This, us, this is what's real."

"I know," I whispered, drifting my hand across his shoulder.

"Do you remember when I told you about the girl I used to date, Brooke—the one who came to Maine when I was filming the first *Seaside?*"

I remembered. The girl he told me about who wanted his agent more than him.

"I was filming a scene where I had to kiss Suzanne and instead of Brooke getting jealous or mad she actually critiqued my performance."

"So?"

"So . . . I'm wrapped so deep in you that something like how I held Nicole's hand hurt you. I'll never do that again now that I know. But I told you I would be envisioning making love to you to get into character."

I closed my eyes and felt the softness of his face on mine. "It was very convincing."

He nuzzled his face on my neck and I could feel his regret. It was almost tangible. "It was hard. She really did taste awful. Like, I don't know. It was just bad."

I noticed his hesitance, as if he were keeping something from me. "She's lucky I didn't kill her like I wanted to," I said. "You'll probably get her head cold now."

Ryan rolled his eyes at me but offered no more on the distaste she left behind. "I really do like this jealous side of you. I have no doubt that your love for me is real."

I clutched his arm harder. My love for him ran bone deep.

AT THE end of the week, we were back at the cavernous soundstage, my initiation into a higher level of trust with my fiancé behind us.

Ryan spun on one leg and kicked with deadly accuracy, planting a heavy black boot directly into the chest of the evil villain, Victor Mordorf, sending him hurling through the air. Stunt actor Timothy Hughes landed on his back; the specially designed dining table buckled underneath his crashing weight and folded in half. And then Jonathan yelled, "Cut!"

Next take, Ryan grabbed the front of Victor's shirt, swinging several right-handed punches. I felt my breath hitch, my pulse quickened, as a twisted attraction in seeing my fiancé kick ass like some barbaric he-man sent intense arousal through my veins. The early morning weight training combined with his rock-climbing instruction was turning Ryan's body into even more of a chiseled pack of muscle. And at this moment, that muscle looked very lethal—and sexy as hell.

I winced as Ryan performed his own stunt, taking a calculated fall from a return blow to his face. I was so worried about him taking these risks but at the same time I knew he was loving every minute of it.

Ryan tore the string of Christmas tree lights off the fake fireplace mantel on the set, lashing Victor Mordorf to the high-back chair in his parents' supposed dining room. Anger and hatred rolled and coiled off him as he tied the newly bloodied, dazed actor, wrapping the last two feet of cord around the actor's throat. Ryan recited his lines, spitting fine mists of fake blood from his lips as he delivered his threats.

Seeing Ryan like this, full of icy hatred and raw emotion, snarling as he bound his captive securely, both fascinated and terrified me. Ryan wore a horrifying mask of bloodlust, letting go of his reserve and completely saturating himself in the role of Chase Sheffield's tragic life of death and redemption. *This is what acting is all about.*

It was through our role-play run-through of this same scene in our condo last night that we determined Ryan's approach to binding someone to a chair with Christmas lights had to be executed in very specific steps. No one really considered how difficult it would be to tie a string of decorative lights into a knot. Ryan brought this up with Jonathan and the stunt coordinator, Paul Rothham, resolving the choreography before cameras started rolling.

Fortunately Ryan left out the part where he tortured the shit out of me with his tongue and gave me two incredible orgasms while I was tied securely to a chair with thirty-five feet of borrowed lights from the props master. Those were private details from our rehearsal that no one else needed to know. A grin formed on my lips as I recalled the pricks of painful pleasure the lights made biting into my skin and how being bound and restrained heightened every touch. *Yes, I'd like to do that again, please. Very soon.*

I listened to the dialogue carefully. Ryan didn't want to ad-lib in the middle of the scene, so he had approached the script supervisor earlier with the changes we had worked through last night. I was surprised that she and Jonathan approved them. The cadence of the original threat was off, but with the new changes, they flowed and were even more ominous. It just fit better with Chase's natural reaction in the scene than what was originally written. Ryan delivered it with a master's ease.

"And cut!" Jonathan pulled the headphones off, circling them around his neck. He patted Denny once on the back as he backed away from the enormous camera and then turned to me, wearing a broad smile and giving me a thumbs-up. Everyone looked extremely happy with the shot.

I abruptly sat up in my chair. *Yes! He nailed it!*

Jonathan called Ryan over to the monitors. We watched the scene
on the playback reel. "How did that feel, Ryan? You happy with that
one?"

Ryan rested his hands on his hips and blew out a relieving breath,
staring intently at the small screen. It's amazing to see what forty-nine
seconds could capture. He turned to face me and we gave each other
a high-five.

Jonathan beamed, shaking his finger in my direction. "She's good!
Real good! You marry this one and never let her out of your sight!"

His comment surprised me. "What did I do?"

Jonathan admonished my question with a conspiratorial look.
"What did you do? Ryan gave credit where credit was due, my dear.
You have a hell of a keen sense for script analysis and direction and
you just made that scene a hell of a lot better."

Oh shit. "But Ryan and I rehearsed . . . I only suggested . . ."

Ryan shut me up with a quick kiss followed by a playful crack on
the ass. "That's where I'm carving my initials later," he growled privately to me.

Jonathan was ecstatic. "Maybe one of these days we'll get to see
what kind of performance you inspire him to give when you're standing on the opposite side of the camera, hey, Taryn?"

I adamantly refuted his comment. Ryan, however, seemed to
rather enjoy that idea.

"Never say never," Jonathan advised. "And don't think your little
rehearsal with him the other day went unnoticed. I think you'd be a
natural."

I held my hands up to stop his line of thinking—immediately.
"Oh, no. I'm only here to watch."

"Well, I'd have to argue that," Jonathan continued, turning to
Ryan. "Would you be opposed to us using Taryn in the nightclub
shot? I think she'd be a better fit."

I shook my head so quickly, the blood sloshing in my brain made me lightheaded. Stand-in was one thing; to be on actual film was another.

Ryan leaned closer. "Which shot?"

A ripple of shock rolled through me next, watching Ryan actually ponder this idea with keen interest. I thought for sure he'd be against it.

When their discussion ended and the attention turned back to me, I had to take a stand. "No. That's okay. I'm very flattered by your offer but I'm fine right here, staying *way* out of the way."

Ryan's encouraging grins and nods weren't helping, gesturing with pinched fingers that I'd only be in the shot for a smidgen.

"Nonsense," Jonathan said firmly. "I have Ryan's permission, so you must do me the honor of one small cameo."

That one small request generated a flurry of activity. When the time came, I was swept off to wardrobe, where I was fitted with a pair of ass-hugging jeans and a really cool white flouncy halter top with tiny brown beads that nestled near my exposed cleavage. Instead of me wearing a bra, flesh-toned adhesive lifts were added under my breasts to give them more support. The likelihood of my breasts getting some quality onscreen time seemed to multiply exponentially.

After my makeup was applied and hair fussed with, it was off to the set. Tonight we were on location, having taken over a bar/nightclub outside of Vancouver to film in.

My job? To be part of the background. I hoped to hell I'd be able to blend with the other extras in the scene. The bar was supposed to be packed and Ryan had to squeeze through the crowd to make his next mark. I was one of the bodies he had to squeeze past—that was, until another assistant director told me the plan.

I was introduced to several other extras that I would be standing next to for the shot. We were just a bunch of girls supposedly standing around, swaying and grooving to the music. Problem was—there was no music. Actually the crowded bar filled with a ton of extras was rather quiet considering. The soundtrack would be overlaid in postproduction.

It felt weird to stand there pretending to dance and look sexy in silence. Some sort of liquid sheen was sprayed on our exposed skin to make it look like we were all hot and sweaty. It made my bare arms glisten.

We did a walk-through rehearsal; Ryan had a shot coming into the club, cameras followed him through the crowd, he had to squeeze past me, and then take his final place at the empty seat at the bar.

Actress Morgan Harper, who was playing the deceased sister of Ryan's character, Chase Sheffield, was dressed exactly like me; the costumes were identical. Ryan/Chase was to have another ghostly vision of his sister.

An enormous camera was pointed at me, and as I studied the ominous black lens that would capture me making a complete ass out of myself, the realization of me actually being in a movie pricked at my nerves. My slightly elevated pulse broke out into a full gallop. I might as well have been running in knee-deep sand on the beach for how hard my heart was pounding in my chest. Holy shit.

Calm down. Remember your instructions. Smile coyly. Eye contact with Ryan for a count of five, then look back to the brunette whose name totally escapes me right now. I can do this. I can do this. What the hell is her name?

"Cue background; action background."

Before I could entertain additional panic, it was over. I think I smiled coyly—however the hell "coyly" is supposed to look. I hoped I didn't look away too soon.

Ryan was cool and professionally distant. He showed me no special favor, no separate inappropriate acknowledgment while we were filming. I could have been just another off-the-street extra as far as anyone could tell. That was fine by me; I didn't want a fuss.

Without the extraordinary media hype and devoted fan adoration elevating his status, Ryan was just a regular guy; sweet, caring, humble, funny—trying to do his best being an actor. He was so in his element here. My heart rate stabilized under the surge of love and pride I felt for him and I breathed easier in his calm.

"But I would grab her with my right hand," Ryan stated as we did another walk-through. His hand was sealed around my upper arm.

"Do you want me to flinch or . . . ?" I asked, as we continued to work out all of the little details.

Within a few minutes, my big film debut was over and I was moved out of the shot so Morgan could take my place. I found an open space off to the side to watch Ryan continue on without me.

"You can relax now. You did really good, by the way."

I looked over my shoulder, not recognizing the male voice.

"I don't think we've ever met. Hi. I'm Aiden."

I blinked several times, toggling my eyes between the large-veined hand he extended toward me and the rest of the man standing before me. His hair was styled and colored exactly like Ryan's. He even wore the same clothes Ryan had on. The resemblance was freakishly uncanny, although Ryan had much nicer eyes and was a hell of a lot better-looking than this attempted copy. Regardless, sheer fascination had me staring.

"I'm one of Mr. Christensen's stunt doubles. I don't bite."

"Hi. Sorry. I'm Taryn." I reached to shake his hand, thankful that he didn't manhandle me. I noticed Nicole Devin walking toward me rubbing her nose, but she stopped to speak to someone else.

Aiden pointed his chin toward the camera. "I was watching. From over here you looked like you did a great job."

His compliment seemed genuine. "Thanks. I hope I didn't screw it up."

When Aiden smiled, two tiny dimples formed in his cheeks. "I think you did just fine. You looked like a pro." He offered me a cup of water, which I politely accepted. "Was that your first time?"

I took a sip and nodded.

"I guess you got pretty lucky then—getting chosen for that spot.

You'll definitely be in the final footage. Not many extras get to claim that much face time."

I shrugged. "Guess this is my big claim to fame then, huh?" I joked.

"I'm sure you'll get a lot of mileage out of this with your friends, too. You should be able to milk this one for months."

Visions of Marie and Tammy hugging me into a choke hold made me laugh. "I think you're right. My friends will definitely torment me for a long time over this."

I noticed Aiden's eyes dip down and linger on my chest while a sliver of his tongue swiped his lips, gazing with an apparent hunger to breastfeed. *Yeah, I know. No bra and it's cold in here.* I quickly crossed my arms over my chest.

Aiden shook his head infinitesimally, as if my gesture broke the spell to draw his attention back to my eyes. "Hey, he's coming this way. Do you want me to ask him for an autograph for you? Maybe we can get him to pose for a quick picture. That ought to hold your girlfriends off for a little while. I hear he's a nice guy."

A tiny laugh of absurdity slipped out. *This guy has no freaking clue who I am, does he? I guess it doesn't matter to him because he's mostly just staring at my boobs.*

I glanced over toward Ryan, noting his look of displeasure before he stopped to engage Paul, the stunt coordinator. Paul removed his baseball cap and was scratching with one hand and pointing out maneuvers with the other. "No, that's okay. I don't want his auto—"

"So . . . Karen. Are you from Vancouver?" Aiden interrupted, motioning toward the ground as if to accentuate that we were actually standing in Vancouver.

"No. Ryan's my—"

Paul waved his hat and Aiden heaved his body away from the wall. *I doubt he even heard a word I said.* "Shit. That's my cue. Time to go to work. I hope you don't run off anywhere."

Before I could say anything more, Aiden trotted away, glancing back at me briefly.

I found a discreet place off to the side where I could watch the rest of the filming. As per the script, a barroom brawl ensued. Even though Ryan filmed most of the live action, Aiden handled the more intricate stunts, like having chairs slammed down on his spine. I was glad it was his body taking the abuse and not Ryan's. I had other plans for Ryan's body, and they didn't include patching cuts or watching him writhe in pain all night.

Aiden winked and smiled when he filled his paper cup at the cooler next to me. "Why are you hiding all the way back here?"

I shrugged. "Just staying out of the way."

He pushed the edge of his T-shirt sleeve up, flexing beefy biceps as he crossed his arms. "Ah, where's the fun in that. I could have used your help in there."

I thought about the irony. "No thanks. I get enough of barroom beer muscles back home. It's purely a spectator sport for me." It had been awhile since I had to break up a brawl in my pub, though my trusty baseball bat was never out of reach.

Aiden glanced over his shoulder. "I could definitely use a cold one after that last stunt. We have to gather some people together and go out for a few drinks."

I knew better than to answer him, so I let his comment go and politely excused myself to relocate to a better vantage point.

After several more takes, my new friend found me again.

"Looks like we're just about wrapped. So, ah, you have any plans after this or are you going to let me take you to dinner?"

"Take me to dinner? No." I was shocked that he even asked. I walked away, staring off at the man I was planning on having for dessert, when Aiden followed me. Ryan's gaze met mine, and when he caught sight of me having another conversation with my new admirer, his eyes narrowed on me with a look of obvious displeasure.

"I see. You're hoping for a chance with him, aren't you?" Aiden uttered in a mix of mockery and what I perceived to be jealousy. "Well,

I don't mean to burst your bubble, but I hear he recently got engaged, so I'd say your chances are slim to none."

I wanted to say, "No shit. I'm his fiancée, dumbass," and then thank him for discouraging a random woman from hitting on Ryan, but Ryan was storming his way over to us with blatant concern plastered on his face. I wondered if all this casual flirtation on Aiden's part was pissing Ryan off, but in eight more seconds I was going to find out for sure.

"Hey, do you want me to ask—see if he'll give you an autograph or something? Now's your chance before he leaves." Aiden was too busy watching Ryan's approach to see my eyes roll.

Ryan offered a handshake to Aiden and gave him a firm, manly pat on the shoulder. "Hey man. That was some pretty awesome shit you just did. You going to be all right? That one hit looked pretty painful."

Aiden rocked on his feet from Ryan's "friendly" pat and then got all puffy-chested, shirking off with a roll of his neck the mere thought that *anything* could cause him pain. "Nah, I do this sort of stuff all the time. I'm good. Hey, um, Ryan? I take it you've sort of met this lovely lady already. Her name is Karen. Karen, Ryan Christensen," Aiden said smugly, as if he and Ryan were best buds.

Ryan's eyes narrowed. "Karen?"

I shrugged my *whatever*. What was the point in correcting him? I knew Ryan was wrapped for the night and that we could leave.

It didn't take long for Mike to come into the fold. *My faithful human Rottweiler. Attack!*

"I was just asking Karen if she wanted to go out for a few drinks. There's some pretty great clubs downtown, but I'm having trouble tearing her away from here." Aiden gave me a nudge.

"Oh really?" Ryan questioned me.

I hoped he could see I was annoyed. "I tried to tell him *no* but he—" *Keeps interrupting me.*

"Ahh," Aiden groaned. "You're just afraid of having a good time."

See what I mean?

He turned to Ryan. "Hey, before you take off . . . I don't want to embarrass her and she's probably too shy to ask, but do you think maybe she could get a picture with you?" Aiden fumbled and dropped his cell, mumbling how he would text it to me later.

I wrapped my arms around Ryan's waist, ready to go back to our condo. Ryan's shirt was damp with sweat. It had been another long day and I could tell he was exhausted. I also had a pile of clean laundry for Mike to take with him since the on-set laundry service was only offered to the talent, not the keepers of the talent.

"I can't turn my back for one minute," Ryan groaned in my ear, letting his restrained irritation be known. Even though he was acting jealous, I decided that this emotional flare of his was going to be rewarded handsomely in the shower later.

"Believe me, I did nothing to encourage it."

"I know, babe." Ryan squeezed me, brushing some of my hair back. He cupped my face in his hand and kissed me wickedly.

I heard Aiden scoff. "Dude! What the fuck?"

Slightly embarrassed, I took a step back when Ryan ended his territorial display. Aiden's mouth hung open, totally abashed. He also appeared to want to take a swing at Ryan.

Ryan stared him down for a few seconds, then tried to play off his level of anger as if he were teasing. "This one's *mine*. Apparently you haven't been properly introduced to *my fiancée*, Taryn. I'd appreciate it if you stopped hitting on her. We clear?"

THE FOLLOWING day, Aiden avoided me like the plague. I sort of expected that. He apparently had moved on from me, flooding Nicole with his attentions. His flirting was over-the-top.

Aiden tried like hell to be extra chummy with Ryan, which I could have called as well. Ryan was as friendly as he had to be, not taking too kindly to another wolf sniffing around his mate. It was things like that that made me question whether it was a good idea for me to be around him when he worked.

Nicole, however, appeared to be quite jittery.

I presumed it was because she and Ryan had to do a kissing scene again, which seemed to have him slightly agitated as well, but I wasn't sure. Ryan was usually so aloof, but this time he was eyeing Nicole warily.

I watched the scene get set up, cameras in place, actors on their marks, and direction given. I couldn't turn my eyes away no matter what my heart told my mind to do. Seeing the man I love kiss another, even though I knew it was pretend, twisted my heart in ways no words could ever describe.

Confusion tore through me when Ryan abruptly broke from the kiss. His face puckered like he had just swallowed a nasty bug coated in sour dirt instead of kissing a cute actress. His grip around her arm became less than friendly.

Jonathan pulled his headset off when Ryan started to curse at her.

Ryan spat onto the ground twice, right there where they stood. "Tell me that wasn't what I think it was."

"You don't understand. Things have been really hectic and I—"

"I warned you!" Ryan cast her off with great offense.

"Ryan, wait," Nicole pleaded. She looked crushed by his rejection.

"Where's Parker? I want a fucking meeting, in my rig, *now*," Ryan barked as he stormed away.

The second we climbed into Ryan's RV, he grabbed his toothbrush and started scrubbing his teeth, spitting and rinsing his mouth repeatedly into the small kitchen sink. I didn't say a word.

There was a loud rap on Ryan's door and I jumped up quickly to answer it. Parker Shay and Jonathan Follweiler were on the other side.

"Ryan, what's going on? You wanted to see me?" Parker asked.

Ryan was livid. "I want her gone. This is *bullshit*, Parker." He wiped his face with a small towel. "I can still taste the fucking crank in my mouth."

Parker appeared just as lost as I was. "The what?"

"Nicole," Ryan growled. "She's a fucking meth head."

Parker rested his hands on his hips, taking this new information in. "Meth? As in methamphetamines?"

Ryan nodded. "She's snorting the shit."

Jonathan looked like he'd just been struck. "Are you sure? Did you see her using or something?"

"No, but I just had her spit in my mouth a few minutes ago. Believe me, *I know* what the shit tastes like and I can tell you that I'm not going to put up with it. I tasted it on her before when we did the bedroom scene and I warned her about it, but that drip I just caught was fresh."

I felt my knees start to become unsteady, so I sat down in one of the chairs before I'd keel over from this revelation. I didn't know which news shocked me more—Nicole doing illegal drugs or my fiancé knowing what illegal drugs taste like.

Ryan spat in the sink. "What the hell, Parker? This is our second film together. I thought you had my back."

"I do, Ryan. Believe me. I had no idea she had drug issues."

"This shit may fly with the cable networks but it's so not happening with any project I've got my name on, I can tell you that."

"Ryan—man, I'm sorry. I didn't know. I'll take care of it."

"Damn right you will," Ryan barked. "Because I am not stepping one foot in front of any cameras until it's dealt with. We've only filmed for a couple of days. Fire her and get another actress. Someone professional that doesn't have a drug problem."

Jonathan looked just as angry and frustrated as Ryan was, glaring at Parker in his own way.

Parker sighed heavily. "You know it's not that simple, Ryan. We've already shot the promos, the stills."

Ryan continued to freak out and argue. His emotional rant was making this entire situation worse. I had to do something. The moment I locked eyes with Parker, I gave him a subtle nod in the direction of the door, hoping he'd give me time to calm Ryan down.

"We'll take care of this, Ryan. Just relax. Let me make some calls." Parker pressed his phone to his ear on his way out.

Ryan was behaving irrationally, even punching one of the cabinets with his fist.

"Ryan . . ."

"What?" he snapped. "And before you start, I tried it a few times back in college, way back when. You know I don't do drugs."

It was good to hear it, but him punching stuff was more my concern. "I know you don't. Honey, listen. I know you're furious, but lashing out and demanding that she gets fired is not the way to handle this."

"You're not the one with chemical poison in your fucking mouth, Taryn!"

"I know. But I also know what was written in the executive producer agreement that you signed."

That got his temper to come down a big notch. There were several pages of legal mumbo-jumbo tossed in his direction that day he signed the paperwork; of course he didn't read it all, trusting that his lawyer giving him the general okay was confirmation enough. But with several million dollars on the line, I read every damn word of his copy, not leaving anything to the chance Ryan's lawyer would filter it down.

"You have dual obligations to this film now. You accepted the responsibility to make sound decisions when you signed on for those rights. All of the producers are required to consult each other for any changes to main talent, so you need to support them and handle yourself professionally, not freak out on everyone."

Ryan flexed his fingers in the air. "I just want to wring her goddamned neck."

"I know, but you can't."

He wiped both hands down his face. "Grr. Fuck. What am I . . . how do I . . . ?"

"Sit for a minute and try to calm down."

Ryan's eyes were filled with dread, worry, fury—all vying to dominate as he gripped the cabinetry next to the built-in refrigerator. "I've never had to deal with this before, Taryn," he growled. "I'm at a complete loss here. I mean, what do I do with this?"

Part of me was worried that the drugs from her mouth had affected him, given the way he was acting. I had no direct knowledge of their effects or symptoms to call upon, though, so I presumed he was just beyond riled. "Babe, sit. We need to thoroughly evaluate the situation—rationally." I was surprised he did what I said even though he was still breathing hard like a rampant bull cornered in a china shop.

"Just take a deep breath. I want you to try to forget that you're an actor and her co-star for a moment so you can start thinking like a producer. This is a business.

"First, *calmly* talk to Parker. You know that nothing can be resolved with you yelling at him."

"I know," he agreed, "but I'm so fucking pissed and—"

"I know, honey. You put a stop to filming so now they have no choice but to deal with it."

"I'm not going back out there. There's no fucking way."

"Talk to Jonathan. Come up with a plan. Her drug usage has halted *production* and therefore is putting this film in jeopardy. They are going to act on this now. I'm sure there are a ton of legal and contractual ramifications here to deal with that we have to consider. Then discuss how to confront her and attempt to resolve this."

Ryan nodded. "I can't believe she'd be so stupid. I suspected something was up from the moment I saw her but I didn't say anything. And then during our scene yesterday . . . that's when I knew for sure."

Now I knew his odd behavior wasn't just because I was watching him have pretend sex.

"If she's stupid enough to risk what could potentially be a turning point in her career over drugs," I told him, "then she deserves to deal with whatever ramifications come from it. She isn't a child. This is all stuff you have to learn to deal with if you're going to be an executive producer of your own films. You have to consider everything objectively."

He seemed to acquiesce. "You're right. All of it. Especially if we start our own production company like we talked about."

I nodded. "But . . ." I waited until he made eye contact. "She's young and she's doing foolish things messing with drugs like this. You need to help her."

Ryan's face twisted. "*Help* her?"

"Yes, help her. Listen, I know you are furious, but there's obviously some serious issues plaguing her if she's using such a hard drug like that."

"And that's *my* problem?"

I knew he was lashing out at the situation and not at me. "Yes, babe, it is. Instead of filming, you're in here fuming. People just don't do drugs for the hell of it. Well, maybe some do, but meth? She's been looking strung-out for a week, so I'm pretty sure this isn't recreational usage going on. That girl is in serious need of an intervention."

"Because someone told her she was looking fat or something stupid, this is now my problem? Fucking great."

"Everyone deserves a second chance. You've just called her out on it in front of everyone. Who knows? Maybe she's scared straight."

Ryan laughed at the likelihood of that.

"Be a leader, a mentor to her. You know firsthand how it feels to be under pressure. She's doing drugs because she's trying to cope with something, and if you go on a tear to get her fired, you never know how bad she could get. Don't let her become another Hollywood statistic, Ryan. So many others have thrown their lives away on drugs and alcohol. All it takes is for one person to make a difference. Find it in your heart to be the difference."

His eyebrow rose. "Like she's going to listen to me."

"You never know which intervention breaks through."

At least he considered my suggestion. He stared at me for what felt like forever until he finally said, "You want the role?"

"What?" I recoiled as if he'd tossed a live grenade in my lap.

"Do you want the role?"

"Are you serious?"

"Absolutely. You know the dialogue better than she does and your delivery when we rehearsed was completely natural. You know you can do it. Question is, do you want it?"

Suddenly I was very aware of the wall behind me. "Ryan, you can't ask me that, nor do you have the authority to offer it."

Someone knocked on the RV door and then I heard a familiar female voice. "Ryan?" Nicole called out.

I could tell just by how wide his eyes got that Ryan was at a loss for a next move. I took him by the hand for a moment and then opened the trailer door.

CHAPTER 11

Departure

I MUST HAVE BEEN good today to come home to such a sight," Ryan said when he found me reading on our bed, the sound of his approval resonating around his lascivious grin. He was standing in the doorway, arms folded across his chest, smirking like the Cheshire cat.

It was late, almost ten o'clock at night, and I had anticipated him being wiped out, but I was so damn relieved to see his smile return.

Guess he liked my new cream-colored lace camisole top and matching panties more. It was as far as I had gotten dressed after my shower and exhausting day keeping up with Anna Garrett and her credit cards. I smiled at him, feeling that thrill he always manages to incite in me with nothing more than a look.

I hadn't seen him since he left with Mike that morning and I was glad to see he was in a fairly good mood, considering the heaviness of his day. Hopefully his good mood would stay, helping to cushion the talk yet to come. I'd been feeling sick about it all day, but after my phone call with Marie I couldn't put it off any longer.

My sadness from knowing I'd have to go home soon had me stuck to the bed while my internal giddiness from not seeing Ryan all day had me desiring to jump up and latch my legs around his hips. Ryan sauntered over; his finger traced over the fine spaghetti strap of my top and down the valley of my spine, sending quivers right into my groin. A soft, throaty growl rolled up his throat. I licked his fingertip when he seductively drifted it over my lip.

"I figure if I'm going to spend your money, I might as well get things you'll appreciate."

He flashed his million-dollar smile, the one that makes my knees weak.

Damn, I'll miss this every day.

Like a big cat mounting its mate, he crawled onto the bed and over the top of me, loving my bare shoulder with his mouth. "Oh, I appreciate. Very. Very. Much."

His thighs surrounded the outside of mine, dipping his hips to prove his appreciation by letting me feel his denim-clad erection in the cleft of my rear.

I twisted beneath him, flipping over to my back. His tongue swirled with mine, reminding me just how much I missed him today.

"You are so fucking beautiful," he breathed out on my lips, lowering his body to rest next to me. "I missed you today."

I smiled, thrilled to know he felt the same way. I brushed his hair from his eyes when he rested his head on my chest.

It had been three days since the methamphetamines meltdown and everyone's lawyer and manager was in town to hold hands and lord over the situation. "I heard you did an excellent job this morning," I said, kissing his forehead.

He sighed. "You're banned from hanging around Anna."

I pushed back a little to see his face. "Why? She's the one who gave me the nod of approval on this outfit."

Ryan held up one finger. "I retract the ban." He gave me a reassuring smirk. "I figured she'd fill you in."

He mumbled something about hens and gossip. If he only knew the half of it. After spending so much time with her, I had dirt on half of Hollywood.

"Anna was very impressed with the way you handled yourself. You still okay with the decision?"

His shoulder rose and fell. "Don't have much choice, do I? She cried again when I said she's lucky she didn't get fired today. Nicole better keep her nose clean this time. She gets caught using again and that's it."

His eyes locked on mine. "I'm almost hoping she messes up. I told Jonathan you'd be a good replacement."

Surprise and some annoyance jolted into my chest. "I'm not an actress, Ryan. You shouldn't have done that."

He propped his head up. "Why? What are you afraid of?"

Oh, not much. The media making a huge production out of my transition? False accusations of me using you to get ahead? Incorrect theories that this is some sort of publicity stunt? Having your career negatively impacted because of it?

"It's a *bad* idea."

He frowned at me. "You're a natural, you know."

The thought made me shiver, knowing his view was biased. "If I'm going to ever go that route I want to earn it, not have it handed to me."

Ryan's lips twisted. "You're the only person who would see it that way."

Somehow I highly doubted that. "The gossip magazines would have a field day, Ryan. You know it as well as I do. You don't need that looming around your public persona. It will be bad enough when things are said about my small cameo."

"Could be your debut."

I rolled my eyes.

"What?" he sniggered, dropping his arm onto my paper pile. He picked up a few of the pages I was reading and glanced at them. I saw his eyes turn skeptically quizzical. "What's all this?" He scrutinized the papers.

"Anna gave me some documents to look at; financials and stuff."

He flipped through several of the sheets, becoming more and more intrigued as he panned through. "This is for *Slipknot*. Why the hell do you have . . . ? Are you . . . are you supposed to have this stuff? This is the agreement with their production company, Light Reel Pictures."

He toggled from gaping at the pages in hand to gaping at me, as if I'd committed a horrendous crime. "Production agreements, Light Reel's contract . . . Holy shit, Taryn."

I took some of the pages from his hand, trying to lessen the breach, knowing that even he wasn't privy to some of the agreements made to get *Slipknot* filmed. "She gave them to me in confidence. We've been talking a lot and I had questions. I think she's made a pet project out of me."

"Don't let anyone know you have these," he advised, admonishing my risky behavior.

I snatched the last few pages from his hand, incensed that he'd think I was that careless. I made a nice, neat pile, forgoing the last page I studied for the betterment of recouping the evidence. "I know. Don't you tell anyone I have them, either."

His head tilted. "Why do you have all of that?"

I looked over at him. "Someone's got to run our production company."

Hoping to sidetrack his reproach, I pulled from the bottom of my pile the log home architectural design book he had asked me to get. "Here. I got this for you. Build me a house, oh Captain, my Captain."

Shiny object diversion. "Oh cool." He flopped over onto his belly, thumbing through it. "Did you see any designs you like?"

I shook my head. "I like them all."

A faint noise caught my attention. "Is Mike downstairs?"

"No."

His voice was tinged with a hint of sadness, as if he missed his friend.

"Ryan, I really don't mind if he hangs out here with us. He's not just your head of security anymore. Why don't you call him and tell him to come over. I'll make some of those quesadillas you guys love so much."

Ryan stalled, appearing apprehensive. "He's ah . . . got other plans tonight."

"What's he up to?"

Ryan ignored me to go take a shower. I had almost fallen asleep when I felt Ryan shift off the bed and then something pointy tickle my butt cheek. "What are you doing?"

"Never mind," he instructed, palming my thigh in his hand. "Just go back to doing what you were doing and don't worry about it."

I looked over my shoulder. "That's a freaking permanent marker, Ryan!"

"It will wash off . . . eventually. Hold still."

"Honey, please don't draw on my ass."

"Shush." He pushed the edge of my underwear out of his way. "This is *my* ass. Mine. Property of," he said matter-of-factly.

I groaned as he palmed my rear, his rogue finger brushing oh so cleverly between the juncture of my thighs, twitching, tickling. He knew exactly what he was doing to me.

"So," I breathed out, very aware of my bottom, "does that mean I own your ass, too?"

"Damn straight," he murmured. "Own. Rule. My body is yours. Feeling in the mood to play with it? I'll let you."

I felt the excitement that his words stirred in me. "Let me? I didn't know I needed permission to play with my toys. I thought that was the benefit of being an only child. Never having to share."

Ryan frowned, returning to his drawing. "Nick used to enjoy breaking my toys. Whenever he was pissed at me he'd snap my shit into pieces."

The thought of Nick being nasty to Ryan saddened me. I frowned, wishing I could take away those bad memories.

He was so engrossed, I peered over my shoulder. "Are you having fun? Did I get an official *Ryan Christensen* autograph?"

Ryan chuckled. "What are your feelings about getting matching tattoos?"

Several thoughts flashed at once, starting with "pain" and "needles" and then quickly followed by the question of whether he was seriously considering permanently inking my right ass cheek with his name.

The next thoughts flooded in like a film in fast-forward—all swirling around the several tattoos that adorned Thomas's luscious body; the tribal art that wrapped around Thomas's chiseled left hip like a beacon to Wonderland.

I had to clear my throat. "I considered a tattoo once. Never went through with it, though. Why? Are you thinking of other ways to mark your *property*?"

He shrugged, downplaying it, but I could tell that he was seriously considering it. "Just thought it might be cool. I've been thinking about getting one for a long time. Thought maybe we'd have the same symbol or something."

I tried to see what he was drawing, but it only looked like a box with scribbling next to it.

"What is that?"

"I'm making an airport. This is the terminal and this here is the landing strip. Stop moving! My jumbo jet needs to land."

I quickly rolled over onto my side.

"Hey! Oh, what—you don't care if hundreds of passengers plummet to their death in the ocean? You're so mean." His once-determined face now looked completely dejected. He was such a good actor.

I smiled at him, snatched the black marker from his hand, and climbed onto him. "Why? Is your jet packed with navy seamen? Let me draw on *your* ass. I want to carve my initials on *my* property."

Even though he had been up since five thirty this morning, he moved with lightning-quick speed to undo his towel and roll onto his belly, so willing to let me draw on his body.

"Property . . . of . . . Taryn . . . Mitchell." I wrote in script letters on his tight, bare bottom. I drew a little heart at the end to finish it off.

Ryan glanced over his shoulder. "You done?"

"Yep."

He grabbed the marker out of my hand and tossed it in the general direction of the nightstand.

"Come here," he said, slipping a hand behind my head to pull me

down to his mouth. He tasted deliciously minty. The fragrances of his
body wash and shampoo wove me into a familiar cocoon of favorite
scents. Gently, he rolled me over onto my back. His fingers wove and
tensed into my hair, holding my head in his hand, silently telling me
he'd never let me go.

For me, kissing Ryan Christensen was like drinking instant passion. Arousal tore through my body, awakening the hunger for his
touch that always lies just below my surface.

He kissed my cheek, that tender spot under my jaw, down to the
nape of my neck. His hand slipped over my stomach, brushing fingertips over my ribs, working my camisole top up higher to expose
my skin. His lips skated over the lace, finding my raised nipple with a
gentle bite of his teeth.

My top was unceremoniously tossed to the floor. I threaded my
fingers into his damp hair as he tongued and sucked my breast. His
hand slid under my panties; he groaned once when he realized I had
shaved myself bare and then a second time, louder, when he felt how
slick I was for him. "Fuck, baby," he breathed out softly, reverently,
slipping his tongue back into my mouth.

Slowly he climbed on top of me, using his knees to nudge my
thighs farther apart. Kneeling up, he reached for my panties, taking
them down painstakingly slow, as if he were savoring the view.

I raised my legs, feeling the silk pass over my ankles. Ryan took
my calf in hand, placing my leg back to where it rested on the other
side of his leg.

"Let me see." He whispered his request, and I parted my legs for
him. He sucked in a sharp breath. I could see the heat rising in his
cheeks, tinting him with a glorious flush.

His fingers drifted over my bare flesh. "God, you're beautiful," he
breathed out. I felt my own breath hitch as he gazed at me with such
raw and unfettered adoration.

I ran my hand down his muscular chest, over the ripples of his
defined abs, mesmerized by his amazing body as he worshipped mine.

"I love you," I said, holding his gaze. His head swayed and he lowered himself onto his forearms to kiss me.

"I love you more," he vowed into my mouth.

Ryan kissed his way down my body, licking the smooth skin of my stomach just below my belly button, pressing my thighs wide open. I gazed down at his blue eyes, so eager to watch my reaction. I watched his eyes close as he drifted into the fierce direction of pleasuring me. His free hand pressed up over my ribs, then pinched and pulled my nipple.

"Oh, oh God . . ." *I think I just said that out loud. Didn't take him long to send me flying over the edge.* He wiped his chin off on the back of his hand and crawled like a hungry animal up the bed.

Before I knew it I was on top of him, feeling my body adjust around each glorious inch as I slipped down to fully take him in.

"Oh, Tar," he moaned, pulling me tight to his chest, his forearm and hand holding my body to his while his other hand guided my rear. Our kisses turned to open-mouth pants, nose brushing nose, lips resting on lips for leverage. His long fingers threaded into my hair. "You feel so good," he breathed, gazing directly into my eyes, before locking his mouth back on mine.

Ryan's arm wrapped under my right thigh, spreading me wider across his body. His hips thrust into me so fast it took my breath away. My wetness spurred him on even more.

"Ah yeah, that's it. Mmm," he purred, and rocked me harder. His strong hands cupped around my ass and he began thrusting with renewed vigor. I was starting to see stars and not just of the celebrity kind.

With a quick roll and swoop, he landed me on my back, slinking down my body so his tongue could slip fervently back and forth once again. Gently, but with deliberate effort, he bit into my flesh, a little nibble here, a little there, into the interior of my thigh, adding pain that only heightened my pleasure. His fingers curled inside me, overloading me with powerful sensations while he flicked his wicked tongue.

I gasped when he entered me again. He wove his left hand into mine, pausing to kiss my knuckles. "Only yours," he uttered on my lips, then raised my arm above my head, sinking himself deeper with each twist. I felt the incredible happiness from his tender gesture fill my heart and I surrendered myself completely to his will.

He rolled me on the bed like a hungry croc wearing down its prey, flipping me over and pleasuring me in ways that should be illegal.

I could feel it coming, that warm rush of orgasmic bliss. He was so deep; his fingers strummed my flesh perfectly. I couldn't hold on any longer; my body ached for a release. I paused several times to breathe, scrunching my eyes from the sensations coursing through me. I crashed my face into the bedsheets and let the all-consuming orgasm have me.

After we cleaned up, we nestled together back in bed. Ryan's chest pressed to my back, his strong, warm embrace holding me. I ran my fingertips over the tendons in his hand, the fine hair on his forearm, dreading the moment when I'd be forced to sleep without him. I kissed his arm, appreciating this moment, thankful that we have this togetherness, right here, right now. I felt the steadiness of his warm breath on my shoulder, as I lay there listening to the sounds of him falling asleep.

Discussing when I'd go back home would have to wait another day.

IT FELT nice to sleep in since Ryan's day wouldn't start until almost 10 A.M. While we enjoyed a leisurely morning, I packed my copies of the production agreements and shooting schedules into my newly acquired messenger bag. All of my necessities to keep very occupied were carefully stowed inside.

Ryan's set assistant, Paula, was full of energy and very eager to please when we arrived, fetching coffee for both of us. Apparently Mike got special treatment; she had a chocolate-covered éclair stashed just for him. Even Ryan didn't get an éclair.

I reviewed the shooting schedule, noting Ryan's times and the scenes planned for the day, then decided to listen to the messages on the pub's line.

Hearing Thomas say my name, twice, was unnerving, as if some cruel joke were being played on my memory, twisting my hatred into longing. Both times he requested I call him, not wanting to tell me the true reason for his calls, only saying it was urgent. The second message had more information. Though still vague, it contained the one word that would get me to call him back—Melanie.

"The only thing he said was that Mel's real sick," I said to Marie. She was getting ready to open the pub and interview two people for bartender/waitress positions when I called. "He didn't say with what. Just that there might not be enough time."

"Shit. I'll try calling her mom. I'm surprised she didn't call me if she was back in town," Marie said, sounding distracted.

"When do you go to the lawyer?"

"Tuesday, one o'clock. You going to be back by then?"

"Yeah, I'll make sure of it."

I heard her sigh into the phone. "Good. Tammy's getting really grumpy. I think she's mad that we're not helping with their wedding but I'm not exactly sure what we're supposed to be doing. I talked to her mom about the bridal shower and we figured we could either use the bar or go to a place like Jake's On The Pier."

"I'm coming home soon. I'll call you when I have my flight info." I'd have to tell Ryan tonight.

WE WERE driven back to our condo by one of the set drivers, with Mike, as always, in the front seat. I presumed he'd be coming in with us to do his quick security sweep, so I was surprised when he hurried us along and left the minute the lights in our condo were on.

"That was weird. So where is he off to in such a hurry?"

Ryan shrugged. "I don't know."

I could tell he was keeping something from me. I smiled at his bad fib while watching him change into a pair of sweats. "Sure you do. He's been disappearing a lot. Why won't you tell me?"

Ryan sighed and then gave in. "Because you'll probably get pissed and I will never lie to you, so . . ."

Shit. After that comment, it's too late for him to hold back now. I traded jeans for my favorite yoga pants. "Who is she?"

"Who is who?"

Yeah, now's not the time to play ignorant, mister.

He huffed. "Paula, my set assistant."

I pictured her clearly. My height—five-sixish. Thin. Cute and spunky with short jet-black hair cut blunt at her chin. An inch-wide electric blue streak painted in her hair. Black framed glasses that gave her that naughty librarian look. "This isn't their first date, is it?"

Ryan gave me a look that said he wasn't denying it.

"Wonderful. Marie's going to be devastated."

Ryan groaned as I walked out of our bedroom. "He's just been taking her out to dinner, Tar."

"For all you know. And he's also been calling Marie every day, filling her with hope." I felt my disappointment come on like a burn. "I knew it. And I warned him, too."

I heard Ryan curse as he followed me down the stairs. "Look, he likes Marie a lot. Trust me. But that isn't happening for him right now, so what is he supposed to do? Quit living?"

I couldn't stop my swell of anger, knowing how torn-up Marie was just from all the crap Gary was putting her through. "I just wish he'd kept his tongue out of my best friend's mouth. This is going to tear her heart out for sure."

Ryan followed me into the kitchen. "So he kissed her. It's not like he pledged his undying love to her."

"I get that, Ryan. That's not the point. He said he wanted to be updated on what's going on in her life. He not only said that to her, he said it to me in private. You don't make that step and then date your boss's set assistant. You just don't. He could have kept his distance but he made a choice knowing she was extremely vulnerable at the time. And the daily phone calls? You can't do that kind of stuff to girls. She let him in even though she had brick walls up and now this is going to mess with her head even more."

Ryan put his long legs up on the couch, tangling them with mine. "I get it. Why do you think it took me *weeks* before I kissed you? I could have had my lips all over yours the very first day I met you, but I didn't."

Yeah right. "No you couldn't have."

His confident look said otherwise. "I could have and you know it. But I didn't want to rush into anything. Not with you. Kissing complicates things. I took it slow because I wanted you to know me, *really* know me, before we got physical. So I understand that them kissing has made Marie have feelings beyond friendship."

I climbed over his legs and curled up on his chest. "I know you."

Ryan shifted, getting us comfortable. He kissed my forehead. "I know."

My thoughts swirled. "Apparently those feelings beyond friendship aren't strong enough for Mike to abstain since he's on a date with another woman."

Ryan groaned. "You're blowing this out of proportion. You don't know that."

I nuzzled into his chest and closed my eyes. "Well, *what I do know* is that as long as he's picking dates from the production crew, I want him to stay far away from my best friend."

Ryan rested a hand on my rear. "Don't you think it's up to them to decide that?"

"No," I growled on his skin. "I'm deciding for her because I won't let her heart get broken by another idiot. Mike had his chance and he blew it. I hope he and Paula are happy together."

That got me a swat on the rear, followed by a squeeze. "Now you're just being grumpy."

I ran my fingertips over the defined dip in his chest. "Disappointed is more like it. After what Marie's been telling me that he's been whispering in her ear when they talk, I thought he considered her to be something special. But apparently she must have misunderstood."

He lifted my chin up and glared at me.

"Don't look at me like that," I said. "He's the one out on a date with someone else. I'm serious. I will not allow anyone to hurt her again. Gary never treated her right, which leads me to something else we need do discuss."

He tipped up an eyebrow.

"My best friend needs me to come home."

I BEGAN missing Ryan terribly the moment my airplane taxied down the runway. It had been almost a month since I'd been home, but everything seemed to right itself the moment I saw my makeshift family waiting for me in the airport. God, how I missed my friends. I didn't realize how much until I saw their faces light up.

Pete snatched me up first, lifting me off the ground. "'Bout time you got your ass back home. Missed ya, kid."

I hugged and kissed Tammy and then wrapped my arms around Marie's neck. It wasn't until we piled into Tammy's Camry that I sensed some tension between her and Marie. Marie had asked her a question but Tammy ignored her, which prompted Marie to appear disheartened.

Walking up the steps to my apartment felt familiar but somewhat strange, since I hadn't been there for a few weeks. Tammy pulled some aluminum baking pans out of the pub kitchen before following us up the steps.

"I thought you'd be hungry so I made my fried chicken that you love so much," Tammy announced. I turned and hugged her. God I loved them all so much.

I spotted a few boxes in my living room and presumed they were Marie's. "Were you able to get some of your stuff from the house?"

Marie shook her head. "No. Gary won't let me in the house." She pointed at two black garbage bags. "I went over there the other day and found those sitting on the side porch. It's mostly winter clothes and stuff I don't wear."

I growled, aggravated enough for the both of us. "What do you mean he won't let you in the house? Did he lock you out?"

Marie shrugged. It was obvious that all this stress was taking its toll on her. "It will get straightened out."

I was surprised she didn't just kick the door in. "I called the bank and verified that they changed the routing for your automatic deposit to your new account. Did you get your paycheck?"

She nodded.

"What about the check from the fifteenth?"

Marie massaged her temples. "Went into our joint account. I pulled two hundred out at the ATM and he called me bitching about owing him money for bills. I guess the money is his until the lawyers sort it out."

I quickly ran some numbers in my head. "So basically you have the shirt on your back, your winter clothing in a few garbage bags, and five hundred bucks."

Marie's face crinkled and big, fat tears pooled in her eyes.

I wrapped my arm around her shoulders. I'd never seen her this defeated—ever. "Don't worry. We will figure this out. I'll see if the bank can reverse the last deposit. And you're staying here. No ifs, ands, or buts about that. We'll get the spare room cleaned out and there's storage in the basement."

Marie leaned her head on my shoulder. Thankfully, she had an appointment to see her lawyer.

No matter what, I'd make sure she'd get her smile back.

+ + +

IT TOOK exactly one week for the first indiscretion to hit the front cover of the gossip magazines. To say Marie was livid was putting it mildly. Her initial reaction of "What the fuck?" near the cash register in our local Whole Foods Market had a few heads turning. When she continued with "that son of a" and a slew of other breathy expletives strung together into one long, creatively formed curse word, people started to gawk.

Marie glared at me. "You know about this?"

Fuck.

She slapped the paper down on the rubber conveyor belt. "Tar?"

I gave her my most innocent, compassionate look, knowing I had broken the best friend code.

"You want to explain this to me? Why I'm looking at this?"

No, not really. I continued to empty the cart, stalling for an answer. "I don't know. All I know is they went out to eat together after Ryan wrapped for the day."

She stared at me, incredulously. "And you didn't think it was important to tell me?"

I knew she was mad at me or at the very least, disappointed. Hell, if the situation were reversed, I'd be angry, too. And hurt. "And tell you what, sweetie? That he had dinner with another person?"

She glared at the cover. Big, bold letters announced that Ryan's newfound tryst had been stolen out from under him by none other than his bodyguard. Supposedly this is why I left Vancouver. "I can't believe I fell for this. Again! Unbelievable. Son of a . . . Who is she?"

"Ryan's set assistant."

"Whore."

I winced at her anger, hating that I knew he was dating someone else. But I hated lying to her even more. "It was dinner. A bunch of people went out." Acid burned in my stomach. All that time I trusted Mike. I trusted him to be one of the good guys. I couldn't break her heart all over again, telling her the truth. I wanted to punch the front cover and tear it to shreds. "Apparently Ryan's cheating, too." I handed it back to her.

Marie smashed the magazine back on the end cap, much to the obvious displeasure of the cashier. "Talked to him last night," she said ruefully.

"And?"

She shrugged. "He failed to mention he was a lying scumbag who's dating Ryan's assistant." Marie opened up her purse. "I *cannot* believe I fell for his sweet bullshit. God, I'm so damn gullible."

I set the bags of apples and grapes on the belt next. "Who are you calling?"

"Cheating bastard bodyguard. Going to tell him he can go fuck himself."

I snatched her phone right out of her hand. "You don't want to do that."

"Why? Give me that back."

"No. It was dinner. Mike's been with Ryan every night since. They are attached at the hip. And you just filed for a divorce an hour ago so you're not in a good place right now to make that call."

Marie grabbed another magazine. "Look at this. According to this one you're pumping Ryan full of drugs."

"What?" I snatched it from her hand, feeling the blood rush from my head from seeing another outlandish headline.

Another celebrity tragedy in the making? Seaside's Ryan Christensen fighting addiction to prescription drugs

Seems Ryan Christensen is set to follow in the footsteps of numerous celebrities who have fallen prey to the lures of prescription drugs. CV has learned that Ryan has been taking several different medications to combat depression. "The pressure is getting to him," says one insider. Sources also say that Ryan's new fiancée, barkeep Taryn Mitchell, isn't helping. "She openly enables him, often encouraging him to drug up before public appearances. Everyone can see it. If he doesn't get help soon, this could turn tragic."

"What the hell?" I felt my fury roll in like a tsunami.

Marie grabbed the pages, reading the small article.

I grabbed my cell and started a text to Ryan. "Oh my God. This is bad. Bad, bad, bad."

"Call me asap"

My cell chimed. I opened Ryan's text.

"working what up?"

I texted back.

"CV mag says I'm pushing drugs on you and Marie is not happy about cover of Starr"

"Drugs? cover? wtf"

"Mike and Paula"

"call me now"

This was not a conversation to have while paying for groceries.

"2 minutes?"

"ok-love you"

"Love you more"

I shoved my phone back in my pocket.

"Ryan freaking Christensen," Marie groaned. "He's a megastar. You'd think he'd have better friends."

The fact that she was lamenting over Mike and not about filing for a divorce from Gary was, I thought, a good thing.

"All I know is that they went to dinner. I'd talk to him before you get further bent out of shape. You of all people should know that those mags are nothing but poison."

She grabbed the magazine again and opened it up to the pictures inside. "His hand is on her back, Tar. He told me he was bored. That lying sack of shit. All the same; every one of them. Cheaters, liars, scum-fucking assholes."

When we got to the car, Marie flopped her little body into the passenger seat. "Are you ever going to give me my phone back?"

I snapped my seat belt on. "You going to refrain from jumping to conclusions and making a call you might regret?"

She held out her hand. "I promise I won't call him."

I dug it out of my purse just as Ryan called on mine.

"What's this message about drugs?" I could tell he was keeping his tone low.

"CV magazine has a write-up that you're taking antidepressants, hon. How would they find that out?"

"Whatever. Just about every person I know takes them."

"No, not 'whatever.' It said that an insider told them I force you to drug up before public appearances. What the hell, Ryan?"

"They printed that?"

"Yes. There are only a select few that know you take medicine for anxiety. Your parents don't even know. This is *not* public knowledge." I glanced over at Marie, knowing she knew about Ryan's medical condition.

Ryan cursed, loud and clear. "I can't deal with this now. Call Trish. Get her on it."

"Will do. I'll call you later."

Marie gave me an odd look when I turned left instead of right. "Where are we going?"

"I need to take care of this bank thing while we're over here. I got another call about late fees for my father's safe-deposit box."

Twenty minutes later I paid the fees to a box for which I didn't have a key.

"A hundred and eighty bucks to drill a lock out? Pete would do that for free," Marie said as we walked out of the bank.

I unlocked the car doors. "Guess I know what I'm doing today."

I set my purse and the copy of the bank bill down on the kitchen table when we returned to the apartment.

"The woman at the bank didn't even say what kind of key to look for," Marie said, going through the junk drawer in the kitchen.

I put the rest of our groceries away. "It wouldn't be in there."

I pulled out the top drawer of the desk in the third bedroom.

"Here, go through all these files and I'll look through these. Open envelopes, everything."

She started paging through the stacks of documents my dad had rubber-banded together.

"Tar, these are old gas and electric bills from six years ago. I'm pretty sure you don't need to keep these."

I took a quick scan and then placed the garbage can between us. "Toss anything that isn't financial. I don't need to keep old bills. What is in those new boxes over there? Is that your stuff?"

Marie tapped the bottom box with her foot. "Nope. That's all Ryan Christensen fan mail."

"Are you serious?" The stack was as tall as me and spanned the entire wall. I opened the top box, finding letters and packages addressed to both of us at Mitchell's Pub. "Oh holy hell."

"Yep. I didn't know where else to put them. Hey, here's a key. Looks like it belongs to an old Chevy."

"Make a pile." I grabbed the first letter on top, slicing it open with my finger. I scanned through the regular fangirl fawning—how he's so wonderful, sexy, marvelous. I tossed it into the garbage bag. I noticed another one addressed to me care of Mitchell's Pub. The address was handwritten in chicken scratch. I got as far as "you don't deserve him you whore" when I threw it in the bag. My hand slightly trembled.

"Do you remember the night of the *Reparation* premiere, how Ryan was sort of freaking out?" I turned to look at her sitting on the floor.

"Uh huh."

"He was worried that someone in the crowd might try to hurt us, shoot us, stick him with a needle while he was signing autographs."

Marie gaped at me. "Seriously?"

I nodded.

I opened a manila bubble envelope that had what looked like underwear in it. "Eeeewwwwee." Just looking at it made me want to disinfect my house.

Marie's face scrunched. "Oh my God. Is that some girl's underwear?"

I felt like throwing up. This was like eight boxes of Angelica the psycho-stalker all over again. "People on this planet are seriously screwed up."

I tossed the fan panty envelope right into the trash bag. Some fangirl's skanky panties were now going to pollute a landfill somewhere. "You know what's even scarier?" I kicked the stack of boxes stuffed with fan mail. "When you start to actually add them all up."

I rifled through the pile, grabbing a few that were addressed to me. The first letter was a weird mix of congratulations and warnings not to mess it up. *Unbelievable.* The next one wasn't so benign. My hands started to shake. *Not again. Not freaking again.*

Marie noticed me stagger back into the boxes. "What's that?"

It was hard to speak. "Um, it says someone is going to kill me if I don't end it with Ryan."

"Let me see that." She grabbed it out of my hand. "Where's the freaking envelope?"

I handed it over.

"No return address but it's postmarked from Ohio. You need to tell Ryan about this. This shit isn't funny. I know you don't want another Kyle incident but chicks out there are crazy."

She was right.

There was nothing stopping another person like Angelica from coming after me, and if the stacks of mail behind me were anything like the letter I held in my hand, there were a lot more psychos out there wishing for my demise.

CHAPTER 12

Skeletons

"Taryn, that guy sitting at the bar over there says he's from . . . Oh Jesus cripes . . ."

I instantly looked over at Marie, who was murderously glaring at the front door of the pub. From her reaction I fully expected to see Gary sauntering in. I couldn't have been more wrong.

Instant tightness gripped my chest and throat, causing my heart to thump and sending my natural fight-or-flight response into high gear. I couldn't form a rational thought while the adrenaline was coursing into my blood. *Why in hell would he ever think to show up here?*

I felt slightly lightheaded and dizzy as I watched him approach the bar, his head dipped low with humbled hesitance. Running into an ex is one of the most awkward things in life to endure, but this run-in was not accidental.

Unfortunately, sometimes the skeletal remains of past relationships don't stay buried forever. Sometimes the dead inexplicably rise and manage to crawl their mangy asses out of the dark hole that you put them in. I felt sick to my stomach, seeing my past coming back to haunt me. I thought I had buried Thomas deeper than that.

Part of me wanted to shout at him to stop and get the hell out of my bar, but as I took in his overall appearance and extremely forlorn look, a moment of compassion held my words back.

"Like we don't have enough crap to deal with around here," Marie said out loud. It had been a week since she stopped accepting Mike's calls and she was bitchy. "Either you tell him to leave or I will."

I quickly noticed that Thomas was wearing the black button-down shirt that I had gotten him for Christmas several years ago underneath his well-worn motorcycle jacket, and casually untucked from his blue jeans. Did he wear it on purpose?

My fingers had opened those buttons before. My hands had sought out the hard chest beneath it.

Damn him.

As if I needed to be tortured some more, my eyes quickly skimmed over the bulge near his zipper. How I once used to crave that ... him, voraciously. How he scorched his place in my soul, assuring that any man I dated would be measured against him.

I also noticed that the laces of his work boots were pulled apart and exposed; how silly that I used to find that so goddamned attractive, all those years I pined for him. I hated that something so simple as his looks was still able to pull an unwilling emotion of excitement out of me.

Thomas's shaggy blond hair was tussled into casual disarray, giving him that delicious "I just crawled out of bed where I was naked and sinning" look. But instead of appearing cocky and ready for my icy greeting, his eyes were sorrowful, red. Pained?

He dropped his keys, his old black motorcycle helmet with the "Anarchy" sticker stuck on the back of it, and a pack of Marlboro Lites down on the bar.

"You can't smoke in here so you might want to try another bar," I grumbled at him as he climbed up on the seat in front of me.

His tongue was busy poking at his back molars while he gauged my reaction.

"It's nice to see you too, Taryn," Thomas said in a low, gravelly voice, reaching into his pocket. He was almost apologetic and definitely not in the mood for a fight. His eyes quickly toggled between me and Marie. "Can I have a beer or should I expect to be tossed out to the curb?"

The low, red circles that rimmed his green eyes were definitely out of place on his face. Over the years, I had seen Thomas at his best and at his worst, and he was definitely in a new state of low. Something serious must have happened for him to gather up the nerve to come into my pub.

"I thought you quit smoking."

Thomas leaned his elbows on the bar and used his index finger to point to the first cluster of beer taps.

"Yeah, I know," I said. "You want a Sam Adams." I pointed to the sign behind me that blatantly spelled out that "Management reserves the right to refuse service."

"And here I thought coming here might actually make me feel better. So much for that idea," he muttered.

If he was looking for some sympathy he came to the wrong place. I crossed my arms over my chest defiantly. "Wow. You're capable of identifying your feelings now? That's new."

My comeback made him wince. I had definitely hit a nerve. He wiped a hand over his dirty blond goatee, the very same one I used to nibble on. "Well played. I guess I deserved that." He nodded.

I hated being such a hardened bitch to him. It warred against all those other feelings of first love that still lingered behind. I glanced over at Marie, wondering if she was going to step in and let him have it as well. Oddly she kept her distance, but I still heard her faint laugh after I dropped that last zinger on him.

I tried to lessen my severity. "Thomas, why are you here?"

I noticed that his right hand, the one still donning that stupid silver pinky ring with the tribal design on it, trembled when he finger-combed his hair back. The memory of that ring made me recall an intimate moment when I thought all my dreams had finally come true. Thomas had just made love to me. We were in his first shitty apartment, which was above a souvenir shop near the boardwalk; his roommate was out at some club so we had the apartment to ourselves. He was holding me in his arms when he slipped that silver ring off his hand and put it on my finger. A "symbol," he had said.

Those haunting green eyes that used to make me do stupid things just to get them to look in my direction gazed up at me. "So is that a *yes* or a *no* on the beer?"

I quickly pulled myself together. "Do you think it's a smart move, drinking while riding? I thought you got rid of the Harley."

Thomas shook his head. Those bad-boy lips curved up a little, but not much. "Why don't you throw in a free shot of Jack? Maybe I'll do you a favor and wrap it around a tree when I leave."

"Promise?"

As if he were looking for backup to fight my heartlessness, he glanced around the pub, only finding unfamiliar faces surrounding him. He let out a huff. "I see your hate for me still runs deep. You done throwing knives, because I'm just about all bled out today, sweetheart."

What the hell did he expect? He was my first love and the man who single-handedly shattered my heart into a trillion pieces. The scars that he made would stick with me until the day I died. I tried to be cold, indifferent. "You don't get to call me *sweetheart* anymore now. What do you want?"

Thomas appeared ready to say something but resigned under some invisible weight that was weighing heavy on those shoulders. "Since compassion seems to be off the menu . . . one beer. Please."

Something was terribly wrong.

All those years of being madly in love with him crumbled my will as if it were made of tissue paper. I grabbed a mug and poured his favorite.

He slipped his fingers around the handle and took a long gulp. In two swallows, he had most of the glass emptied. "Thank you."

I crossed my arms, waiting.

"Look, I know I'm the last person you want to see, but honestly . . . I didn't know where else to go." His hands wiped down his face to reveal very watery eyes and a grim expression set on his mouth.

Some of my iciness melted away and new concern clutched my heart.

"I came here to tell you that, ah, Mel . . ."

He couldn't finish. Tears I'd never seen him shed began to pool and it was hard for him to look at me. "Melanie um . . ." His lips quivered and he sputtered, "died this morning."

Utter shock clapped hard on my chest, pressing down in a painful blast, as the memories of my old high school friend and her cheerful smile and bouncy red hair flowed over me.

Melanie was the third member of Marie's and my closely knit gang and the only one of us who managed to fully escape the boundaries of Seaport. She had joined the air force after graduation and had traveled to more countries than any of us could have ever imagined. She had settled in Germany for a few years and with time and distance it was hard to keep in touch. But it was because of our friendship that began back in seventh grade that I started my secret crush on her gorgeous older brother.

"What happened?" It was hard to form the words around the burn in my throat.

Thomas was overcome with emotion. Seeing him so distraught like this was hard to take. He was always so overprotective of his little sister, threatening all the boys who came sniffing around after her with certain death if they hurt her. Mel had a magical aura surrounding her that was so infectious you couldn't help but want to be in her constant company. This magic certainly did a number on a few boys and their precious egos. Back in those days, Thomas had his work cut out for him.

"She um . . ." He struggled to speak. "She got cancer. It spread all over into her lungs and shit. She asked me to um, get word to ya when she was saying goodbye to people."

Thomas quickly sprang from his seat as the first tear escaped his faltering hold, dripping down over the curve of his cheek. He hurried for the men's room.

Marie grabbed my arm as I tried to rush past her. "What the hell is going on?"

"He just told me Melanie died this morning."

Marie's angered face fell and she gasped, releasing the grip she had on my forearm. "Oh God, no."

Wasting no time, I hurried after Thomas, snagging his leather jacket, redirecting him into the empty kitchen. I needed him to tell me what happened.

Before I knew it, Thomas pulled me into his arms, wrapping them around me tightly in a hold of desperate need. His fingers knotted into my shirt. I knew it was killing him to show this much weakness, breaking that impenetrable façade he wore for all the world to see. Sometimes I think that this was the true reason he broke up with me so many times. I was the only girl who could break past that façade and it scared him to death.

As much as it repulsed me to allow my first love this close to me after how deeply he had devastated me, the need to comfort him wiped my hatred away.

I breathed in his familiar scent of leather and spice and skin, causing thousands of memories to surge into my consciousness. There were times I would have killed to have his love, to have him show me the tenderness and raw emotion that I knew he was capable of. But he always held back—always kept me at a safe distance. But now, at this moment, all of his guards were down and he was sobbing uncontrollably in my arms.

"It'll be okay," I said, even though my silly words were nothing more than a reflexive attempt to console him. Things would never be okay for him, his family, or for any of us who loved Melanie. Death is final.

"I thought she was getting better," he whispered in a higher-pitched tone of pain. "Oh, Mel . . ." His fingers clawed into my shirt.

I let him release his pain for a few minutes before whispering, "Tell me what happened."

Thomas rested his forehead on my collarbone and sniffed. One of his arms released me so he could wipe his eyes, but the other remained firmly locked around my waist. I tried to put some space between us, but as quickly as I tried, he pulled me back to his chest.

"She gasped for fucking air for twelve hours. I'll never get that sound out of my head. Oh God. Why?" His entire body trembled. "I'm so sorry I hurt you, Taryn. God, I'm so sorry."

"It's okay."

His lips were awfully close to my neck. I could feel his breath on my skin. "No. It's not okay. And now it's too late. It's all too late. I should have never done what I did to you."

In that moment, I found forgiveness. Life is too short to hold such a monumental grudge.

"What the hell?" Tammy exclaimed when she came through the kitchen door, giving me the evil eye over the top of her sunglasses as she assessed our embrace. "Am I interrupting something?"

I quickly put some space between Thomas and me, not wanting her to get the wrong idea.

"Tammy, you remember Thomas," I started.

"Uh huh," she said with a reproachful tone.

"Woman, where did you put the Aspinall catering slip?" Pete stopped short, not believing what he was seeing. "Are you kidding me? Are you fucking kidding me?" he growled, stepping up to us.

I put my hand on Pete's chest to stop him and Thomas from squaring off. Pete had size but Thomas had years of practice; besides, Thomas was emotional. I knew Thomas would much rather pound the shit out of something than cry about it.

"Easy, Pete. Stop."

"What is he doing here, Taryn? You finally have a good thing with Ryan and you need to fuck it up? For this piece of shit?"

"Fuck you, Herman," Thomas bristled and growled, wiping the remains of his tears away. "Don't start shit you can't back up."

"No. Fuck you, Sager. You've got some fucking brass balls coming here. Don't you think you've caused enough damage?"

"Stop it! Both of you." I turned to Pete. "He came here to tell us that Mel . . ." Her name caught with a hitch in my throat. "Melanie passed away this morning, all right?"

Pete's angered death glare at Thomas instantly fell as he took in my words. "Mel?"

I nodded, trying to hold it together. It'd been a long time since I'd seen her but the tragic news of her passing cut fresh and deep. Marie slipped in and put an arm around me, noticeably pulling me away from Thomas. I'd thank her later for that.

Thomas covered his eyes with both hands and let out a sigh.

"Oh God." Pete hunched over as if he'd been punched in the gut. His unrequited feelings for Mel had messed him up for years. Tammy tried to touch him but he flinched. "What happened?"

"Cancer ate her, asshole."

I let that one slide. We were all sporting fresh pain.

Pete glared right at him. "Dude, for what it's worth. Sorry for your loss."

Thomas nodded. "Taryn, can I talk to you?"

Marie tugged me by the shoulders, walking me toward the kitchen doors. "I think we could all use a drink."

Thomas followed me out into the pub and grabbed his stuff off the bar, finding an empty booth.

I tapped two small glasses of beer and joined him. Last thing his mother needed was to lose her only other child to a drunken motorcycle accident.

"Thanks for the short," Thomas said as he spied the small glass with disdain, taking a sip anyway.

I wanted him to get this over with. Seeing him again was tearing me up inside. "You're planning on riding that death trap you call a bike. Just looking out for your well-being."

The edge of his lip turned up slightly. "I recall you used to beg me to be on the back of my bike."

"Yeah, well. I didn't know any better."

"Ouch."

"Look, your mom doesn't need another tragedy today."

I saw him wince. "Mom's not taking this well. They actually had to give her something to calm her down."

I felt bad for his mom. Mrs. Sager always treated me well, siding with me most of the time.

"If she can't pull it together, would you consider going with me to the funeral home? I'm going to lose it if I have to pick out her fucking casket by myself."

Why me? My caretaker gene immediately wanted to say *yes* but I stamped it out—quickly. "That's something her family should do, Thomas. I know your aunt Betty would help out."

He gave me that innocent, tilted-head look that used to melt my resolve. "So is that a *no?*"

"As much as I want to help, I can't. Sorry. That's a *no.*"

He nodded at the tabletop. "I really fucked up with you, didn't I?"

I crossed my arms. "Yes, you did."

He sort of shrugged and the gesture instantly angered me. "I hear you've been in the news. Dating some famous actor now?" He motioned toward my ring. "Rich, too, can afford that kind of ice. Good for you. You deserve to be happy."

I nodded at him.

"Not gonna lie," he said. "Right now, I'm wishing you were with me."

I felt that like a physical blow. It was at that moment when I realized I was glad it wasn't. Everything shifted one degree, significantly enough to make me realize that the broken man sitting before me was not worthy of my heart. Still, it angered me.

"You say that now? Don't say that stuff to me. Not now. I gave you my heart time after time. I said *yes* to you when you asked me. You were all I ever wanted. But you're the one who fucked some girl in our bed. It doesn't get any worse than that."

"I was mad at you that morning," he admitted.

I tilted the small glass in my hand, toying with the idea of tossing its contents in his face. "You cheated on me with Cheryl Regan because you were *mad* at me?"

He nodded. "Sounds stupid now, but at the time it felt justified."

I noticed Thomas's glare at Pete. "Justified?" The notion that I was ever head over heels in love with this idiot felt so preposterous now. "Because I had to do a favor for Pete you felt justified to bed that stripper whore on *my* pillow?"

"Every time he called, you ran. How do you think that made me feel?"

"He's my friend! That's what you do for the people you care about."

My cell rang, playing Ryan's song. Thomas tossed his hands up in angered disbelief when I pulled my attention away from him to answer it.

"Hey babe," I said somberly, sickened by Thomas's disclosure.

"Hey, hon, what are you up to?" he asked. His rather nonchalant tone reeked of suspicion. A tingle ran up my spine. I don't know how he knew but he knew.

I swallowed hard, knowing I had two ways to answer. I glanced at the man I once adored sitting across from me while the man who held my heart and soul as if they were precious jewels was pressed to my ear. I opted for full disclosure.

"I am sitting at a booth in the pub, having a beer with my ex, Thomas. Before you let that upset you, please know that he's just told me terrible news. His sister passed away this morning. He's almost finished with his beer and although I am greatly saddened by his loss and I'm *very* upset that one of my best friends lost her life to cancer, I imagine he'll be leaving shortly."

Ryan sighed as if he were holding his breath, sounding relieved. "Thank you for telling me. I love you." His breathy declaration seemed slightly off.

"I love you more."

Thomas rolled his eyes at me.

Ryan snickered once in my ear. "I know. I'm sorry about your friend, sweetheart. Are you okay?"

"Yeah, I'm okay."

"You sure?"

"Positive."

"Okay. Good. Now put the asshole on the phone."

I handed it over. "My fiancé would like to speak to you."

Thomas pursed his lips, reluctant to take the phone. He finally put my cell to his ear and said, "Yeah?"

Thomas smiled that sinister, toothy smile I'd seen a thousand times. "Those are awfully big threats from a guy who's not able to back up his mouth."

His eyes darted over toward the bar, where an older man with a high and tight military haircut had been sitting since we'd opened. The man tucked his phone in his pocket, got up from his seat, and walked straight over to us.

Thomas leaned onto the table, wearing his cocky smile as he eyed the guy's full height. "Yes, I'm meeting your goon right now as a matter of fact. It's Taryn's bar and she hasn't kicked me out yet, so I guess I'll leave when I'm done. Uh huh. Is that so? Yeah, I'd like that. We can swap notes. I see. Well, I'd love to chat some more but your goon is getting antsy. Yeah, fuck you, too."

Thomas tossed the phone over to me, chugged the rest of his beer, and stood. "You may want to tell him to wait on that restraining order until after the funeral. Just a suggestion as I'm presuming you'd want to be there when my sister gets buried."

He leaned onto the table, getting awfully close to my face. "I may have done some things that I regret but I never tried to control you like that asshole is. You might want to rethink the whole marrying-a-control-freak thing. Guys who can't control end up being wife-beaters."

Whoever the intimidating guy was with the military haircut, it was obvious that he was getting impatient. Thomas didn't move, only glaring over his shoulder at him. "Touch me and I'll bust your fucking hand."

When he returned his attention to me, I looked into his eyes, trying to find any semblance of the guy I once loved. His walls were up again and I was slammed out. This was the base truth about him. No one would ever truly have him for he was unwilling to let anything make him that vulnerable.

Ryan placed his heart in my care every chance he had.

Now that my rose-colored glasses were off, everything was crystal clear. I looked Thomas right in the eye and said, "I'm sorry for your loss."

His eyes scanned my face one more time, giving me that crooked, sad smile of his. I had no doubt he'd be so drunk later, he'd sleep where he fell.

"Despite what you think," he said, "I did love you."

"Fucking a whore in our bed was a funny way of showing it."

"You're right. And I live with that mistake. See ya 'round, Taryn."

I took a deep breath as I watched him leave, relishing the fact that he no longer held my heart.

As for the new military man in my life standing a few feet away, Ryan had some explaining to do. With slightly shaky hands, I quickly texted him.

"You have something you forgot to tell me?"

My phone rang twenty seconds later.

"Is he gone?"

I finished my drink. "Yeah, he just left. You pissed him off."

"Good. He better not make a habit of coming around."

"I love it when you get jealous. Makes me feel wanted."

"I'm serious, Taryn. He even stops in for a beer I want to know about it."

"I'm not going to run off with him. You don't need to worry. So when were you planning on telling me I am under surveillance?"

"You're not under surveillance, hon. We hired private security to keep an eye on things since we're not there. But we're coming home next Friday. I have four days off."

Hearing that made my day. "You're coming home?"

"Yep. We'll be in around two. I really hate that you're not with me. I can't sleep without you."

"I can't sleep, either. I'm so used to feeling you next to me . . . Thanks for hiring someone."

"Mike and I are splitting it."

My head spun. "Why is Mike paying for my security?"

"He's not. Security is for the both of you. Mike is worried about Gary. Apparently his security background check revealed that Gary owns a lot of guns."

"He does, but . . ." The thought of Gary attempting to harm Marie was infuriating. "Hang on. I want to go upstairs." I slipped out of the booth and grabbed Thomas's empty glass. Marie was behind the bar just a few feet away. I ducked into the kitchen, walking past quizzical looks from Pete and Tammy, and hit the apartment steps to continue my private conversation with Ryan. "I don't understand. Why does Mike care? Marie's not even speaking to him."

"Yeah, Mike said she's avoiding him but he's planning on fixing that. Listen, you have to talk to her. I know things looked bad but it's nothing like it appeared and now that those pictures were published he's pissed-off and miserable."

"What do you mean things aren't what they appeared to be?"

My mouth hung open as he told me the rest of what Mike was really up to.

As soon as we ended our call, I ran down the steps and grabbed Marie.

CHAPTER 13

Uncovered

I HATE FUNERALS," MARIE said softly as we drove away from the cemetery.

My heart was aching; the sight of a casket tethered above a gaping hole brought back too many bad memories.

Seeing Thomas looking so wiped out was painful.

Just seeing him a few days ago was enough to make me replay every word we'd exchanged, each fond memory I had of him—everything. I hated him for making me reminisce.

Marie stuffed a tissue in her purse. "I can't believe she's gone. I didn't even know she came home."

"I know. I'm glad they didn't put her on display. Melanie would not have wanted that."

"No," Marie agreed, wiping her nose again. "She would have bitched to high heaven if her family did that to her." I saw her look over at me. "How are you doing?"

I met her eyes. "I'm okay."

"Spending some time on Memory Lane?"

Marie knew me so well. "Kind of hard not to."

"Well, snap out of it. Ryan doesn't need to see that deep-in-thought pouty look."

I eyed her speculatively. "You may want to take your own advice there, missy. You still have to deal with Mike."

She grinned to herself. "I know."

"So, did you forgive him?"

"Yeah." Marie nodded. "He told me that she had some personal matters with an ex who was harassing her. He didn't go into details but I believe him."

"Good."

She twisted her hands nervously. "I just don't know if getting involved with someone is wise right now, you know? I spazzed over a stupid magazine cover."

I knew exactly how she felt. "Scary stuff when you see your man on those covers, isn't it?"

She groaned and I could tell just from her expression that she could finally relate.

"I understand," I said. "Believe me. Thomas's cheating made me question every man's motives. That kind of betrayal sticks with you forever. All I can say is follow your heart."

"Or my vagina," she said with a laugh.

I smiled at her.

"Speaking of confusion, where are you heading?" she asked.

"I brought all of those keys. Thought since we were over this way we could stop at the bank before the guys land."

After arriving at the bank, we sat in the lobby, waiting for the next customer service person to help us. Marie tapped me on the thigh, noticing that the woman approaching us was smiling like a fangirl at me. I let her gush for a minute about how wonderful Ryan Christensen is before getting down to business.

The customer service clerk helped sort through the random baggie of keys, narrowing them down to a handful that might get me into Lockbox 291. Marie and I had found forty random keys when we searched; unfortunately none blatantly screamed "safe deposit box." "Last key," I said, trying the small one made of brass. I almost felt giddy when it slipped in and turned.

We pulled the inner black metal case out and she set it on a table, leaving to give me privacy.

Marie raised her eyebrows, waiting in anticipation.

I pulled the top lid back, spying several stacks of letters rubber-banded together. The rubber was so old it crumbled around the envelopes.

I flipped through them, seeing that all of them were addressed to me from Private Joseph Malone. *Who the hell is Joseph Malone?*

"What is all of that?" Marie asked. "Who are they from?"

"I'm not sure." I opened up one of the letters, scanning writing I'd never seen before. There was also a twenty-dollar bill inside the envelope.

Dear Taryn,

I hope you had a fun birthday. Five years old now! I can't believe how much you've grown. I promise when I come home I'll take you to the toy store so you can pick out a new Barbie doll. I remember how much you liked playing with them. I'm at a place called Fort Gordon now. It's in Georgia. You'll be happy to know that they painted me green just like you said they would. I'm a real army soldier now. It's really hot here. I'm learning how to do all sorts of crazy things, like crawl through the mud and climb over tall obstacles. I'm a good climber. I hate crawling in the mud. I think you'd find the mud yucky, too.

I have another six weeks to go and then I might go over the big ocean in a huge airplane. I hope your daddy will use the money I put in the envelope to buy you a new dolly for me until I can see you again. Be a good girl like I know you are.

Love you forever,

Joe

"Who's Joseph Malone?"

My hands shook. I felt a trickle of sweat slide down my spine, or maybe that was just my nerves. "The only Malone I know is my aunt Joan. That's her married name." I dug through the piles, feeling nauseous. There had to be thirty or forty letters from him addressed to me from all around the globe. Was my father protecting me from a stalker?

At the very bottom of the pile was a thick white envelope with the word *Original* written in blue ink. I swallowed hard.

As soon as I opened up the folded papers, I felt a warm rush of panic roll throughout my entire body.

"Oh my God. No. No."

I couldn't get to the garbage can in the corner fast enough before I threw up the entire contents of my stomach.

"Oh no. Oh, Taryn," I heard Marie say as I retched into the steel can.

I faintly remember Marie driving us home.

I SAT at one of the booths in the pub, reading letters about Joe's army life, his travels to the Persian Gulf, trying to piece it all together while Marie hovered.

We had an hour before we'd open the pub and a band was scheduled to play, but I couldn't stop the tears. I wasn't even sure what I was crying about anymore. My entire world—everything I'd ever known—had been turned inside out, where truth and lies and real and alternate insane realities had reversed.

I didn't even know who I was anymore. Of all the things to find in a lockbox, this was something I wouldn't have ever guessed. It was all so overwhelming to process.

I was in a state of shock when Ryan and Mike arrived. I saw Marie run for the kitchen door.

The moment I saw Ryan standing a few feet away, calling to me, I lost it, hurling my body at him and clinging to him like a lost soul in need.

"Oh baby. Everything will be okay. I've got you. Shhh . . ." He let me cry for what felt like ages, rubbing my back and soothing me with comforting words.

"Come on. Let's get out of here. Let's go get some air." He put his arm around my shoulders and walked me slowly, patiently, to the beach.

The breeze coming off the ocean tossed our hair and tinged my nose with the familiar salty air. We walked for a while before he sat us down on the hardened sand. He put me between his legs, gently combing my hair back.

"Whatever names are on that paper doesn't change who you are."

New tears streamed down my face. I felt empty and twisted inside. "But it does. It changes everything. Everything I thought was real isn't."

Ryan shook his head, cocooning me with his body. "You can't look at it like that, hon. The people who raised you are your parents. They loved you. Just because someone else gave birth to you doesn't change who you are."

Nothing would ever be the same. "My entire life has been a lie."

"No, it hasn't."

I wiped my cheeks with my sleeve. "I don't know why I'm so surprised. I always knew I didn't look like either one of them. Eyes, nose . . . I used to stare at my face for hours trying to find a piece of them in me."

I snuggled into his shoulder, feeling the chill off the ocean mix with the chill ripping though my body. My face felt sticky from crying. The waves rolled in, misting the air, mimicking the push and pull of my own emotions.

As I watched the gulls fly and land, guilt crashed over me. "I can't believe this. I'm sure everyone knew except me. Well, I guess this explains why my mother and her sister stopped talking to each other. Now I know that I was the cause of that fallout."

Ryan rested his chin on my head. "Don't start blaming yourself. They were adults who made their own paths. You had no influence over that."

I took the paper out of my pocket, showing Ryan my original birth certificate. I left the official adoption papers back at my apartment with all of the letters. "According to the papers, my birth parents were both sixteen when I was born." I wiped my face and blew out a cleansing breath, trying to pull myself together. "I remember my mom telling me that the reason I was an only child was that because I was so special, she only needed one. It's always bothered me why I didn't look like either of them."

Ryan sighed and squeezed me with his arms. "Your mom and dad did a fantastic job caring for you. There are plenty of people out there who are unfit parents. You said it yourself; they were just kids, Tar. Probably scared shitless."

"Joe went into the army after he got his GED. I was three or four, I guess. Sent me money in every letter, trying to do right by me. I just feel like I have so many questions now."

He pulled me in tight. "You do what you have to to resolve this but remember, the people who raised you are your mom and dad."

"They should have told me."

His eyes narrowed, almost reprimanding me. "Why? What would you have gained from that knowledge?"

"I never had a chance to get to know the people who brought me into this world. I really think my cousin Joe wanted to know me. My parents kept that all from me."

Ryan swiped a thumb across my cheek, wiping away a tear. "Maybe they had their reasons. Look, I know you feel torn up. Anyone would. But your family *kept* you in the family. They are still all related to you by blood. I've seen pictures of you growing up and I can tell you that those two people who raised you adored you."

As we walked back to the pub, I made the decision to find out what those reasons were.

I KNEW making this phone call would be difficult. My heart clenched when she answered the phone.

"Hi, Aunt Joan. It's Taryn." I was greeted with silence and for a moment I thought I'd need to tell her who I was again.

I heard her breath hitch and then she stuttered. "Taryn?"

"Yeah, it's me."

"Oh. Sorry, I'm a bit shocked. I never thought you'd call."

There was no sense stalling. "I found a copy of my birth certificate, the original one."

She gasped. "The original? You . . . you know?"

"Not everything. I do know that you're my grandmother."

She didn't try to hide her tears, breaking down audibly in my ear. A few tears of my own dripped. Ryan walked by, pausing to kiss my forehead and drop off a box of tissues before giving me privacy again. I knew he was just around the corner listening. It gave me comfort to know that he was only a breath away.

My voice cracked. "Can I see you sometime?"

"Oh, sweetheart. I would love that."

"Me, too. Can you tell me where my birth parents are?"

I let her cry for a few minutes. I knew this was hard on everyone. "I wanted to keep you," she said ruefully. "Joey—he was just a kid—and my husband, Paul, had lost his job. Things were . . . this would not have been a good place for you. I . . . I need you to know that."

I chewed on my thumbnail, holding my emotions in. "Why did you stop talking to my mom? You were sisters. You, you didn't even come to her funeral. Was that because of me?"

"Oh, no, dear. Your mother and I . . . Things were strained between us before you were born. Please don't . . . please don't think that."

I wiped my cheek, sensing she was lying. "Where are my birth parents?"

She sighed. "Joe has a family of his own now. He's in California. Lake Tahoe."

I found my head bobbing with understanding from her subtle tone, to let it be. "It's been . . . It's been a long time. I suppose he doesn't need his skeletons to rise."

She hemmed. "He has a lovely wife and two young girls. I'm worried it might be a shock for him. I'm not sure his wife knows he fathered a child at sixteen. It might not be something he wants to divulge."

I swallowed back the tinge of rejection. "Okay. What about my birth mother? Kelcie Tremont?"

Aunt Joan sniffed. "Taryn, she, um . . . there was a car accident. She and Joey and you . . . It wasn't his fault. Her parents had kicked her out of the house when she got pregnant and then they blamed him after the accident. You were barely six months old when it happened."

It felt like a hot knife slid right into my heart. I had four parents who were all dead to me. *How cruel is that?*

"You look just like her. Just so you know. But you have Joey's blue eyes."

My lip trembled as I held back a sob. "Um, well, if . . . if you talk to Joe can you please tell him that I know and I'd really like to get to know him? He can decide if he . . . if he wants to contact me. All this time I didn't even get to know him as a cousin."

Ryan stood behind me, placing comforting hands on my shoulders.

"I'll tell him but I can't make any promises. Your father, Dan, was very cruel to him, Taryn, cutting Joe off from all contact with you, even claiming that Joe was mentally unstable when he returned from the Gulf."

"Was he?"

"Oh no. He had some post-traumatic stress but fortunately he wasn't injured."

"If you talk to him, can you please also tell him that I have all of his letters that he sent? I started reading them but it's . . . it's a lot right now. But I want him to know that I will read every one."

"Oh, okay. I will."

I gave her my cell number. "I'm going to be getting married soon. My fiancé and I haven't really discussed the details yet but I'm . . . I'm very happy. He treats me like gold."

Ryan kissed the top of my head.

"So it's true?" she asked with renewed enthusiasm. "You and that famous young actor are engaged?"

I nodded, looking up into Ryan's eyes. "Yes. And I'm madly in love with him."

He kissed my hand and smiled.

"He ran into Mitchell's Pub one afternoon avoiding an onslaught of fans and now—now he's mine."

Somehow just saying those words out loud to someone in my family made everything gel into place. Those eyes, that devastatingly handsome smile, even with his crazy hair sticking up—he was all mine.

"HEY MAN! Good to see you!" Cory said exuberantly, shaking Ryan's hand when we went down to the pub. I had to distract myself from the trauma of the day, and sitting in the apartment going slowly mad was not healthy.

I watched our new bartender/waitress, Kara, comfortably handle the crowd. She seemed like a really good fit. Cory's roommate, Trevor, was carding people at the door. It was weird having people I barely knew working for me.

Ryan yanked his Mitchell's Pub ball cap down on his brow and slipped onto a stool next to Mike, who was watching Marie as if someone might try to steal her.

"You still hear from Francesca?" Ryan asked Cory.

He opened a beer for Ryan. "Nah. She's filming in Australia right now. We tried to hook up a few times but I can't afford to fly around the globe while she's doing her thing. She knows where I am if she changes her mind."

I stepped behind the bar, hoping to feel as if I belonged there. I needed to belong somewhere. I tried to wait on a customer but Cory nudged me out of the way. Then I started to mix a drink but Marie told me she had it.

I stood next to Ryan, slightly dumbfounded. It was hard not to let the sadness of the day creep back in. Not only was I questioning everything I'd been brought up to believe was true about my life, but now the only place that had marked my identity didn't need me anymore.

"You okay?" he asked, concerned. He twisted around so I was between his thighs.

I shrugged, trying to spare him the depth of my sadness. I put a smile on my face instead. "I guess they don't really need me to help." I watched Marie and Cory taking care of customers, keeping the flow going. The new waitress, Kara, was mixing drinks and tapping beer as well as hustling around waiting on customers. I truly wasn't needed behind the bar at Mitchell's Pub. *Is it possible to be kicked out of your own life?*

"Taryn, want to sit?" Mike asked, offering up his chair.

"No thanks. You just stay there." I felt safe with Ryan wrapped around me. Mike was gazing at Marie, completely enraptured. "So I take it you and Marie made up?"

A sly grin appeared on his face and he nodded. "I took Ryan's advice."

I raised a brow, glad for the distraction. "And that was?"

Ryan laughed.

"Shut her up quick by kissing her before she has an opportunity to yell at me."

I laughed. "And did it work?"

Marie glanced over and smiled devilishly.

"I sure as hell hope so," Mike said with a chuckle.

Of course I had to find an excuse to get behind the bar and drill her for answers.

"So, did you do him?" I asked her privately, wondering if she took advantage of time and space when Ryan took me to the beach. I pretended to be occupied while watching the fangirls go berserk when they realized Ryan Christensen was sitting at the bar.

Marie twisted a cap off a bottle. She looked so damn guilty it was pathetic. "Not quite." She shouldered past me, only to mutter on her return, "but I know where he's sleeping tonight."

The fangirl thing was amusing, watching them practically faint in Ryan's presence. Ryan signed a few autographs and posed for a few quick cell phone pictures, but once he allowed it, it was like the floodgates opened up. Girls started lining up. Pete had just arrived and was sort of body-blocking Ryan while he sat at the bar, but a few of the brave ones still tried to get to him.

Ryan pushed his chair back enough to slip his arm around me when I came out from behind the bar to run defense. It felt strange hanging out like a patron while we listened to the band jamming on my small stage. Ryan and Pete were talking about ridiculously expensive sports cars when I noticed a familiar dirty-blond slide his way to the bar a few feet away. Had Pete been at the door, he would not have gotten in.

My shoulders tensed, angry that I had to deal with more crap.

With a swipe of her arm Marie halted Cory from serving him. Mike was already on alert, sitting up, ready to push off the bar in a split second if necessary.

Ryan took notice. "What's up?"

"Dunno," Mike murmured, never taking his eyes off the situation.

I moved out from Ryan's protective grasp when Thomas started to walk over toward us hesitantly, like a little boy about to get scolded.

"Hey," he said, looking so damn sullen. "Came to see how you're doing."

"I'm okay. How are you?"

I didn't need to hear Thomas's reply to know exactly how bad he was doing. His lips and eyes scrunched together in tormented pain. It killed me to see him this way. "I can't get the sounds and images out of my head. I don't know what to do." He straightened when Pete sidled up. Thomas held out a hand in warning. "Don't start with me, Herman. I'm not in the mood."

Ryan's chest pressed into my back. His left forearm slid across my chest, his hand reaching the cap of my shoulder. I envisioned being spun and relocated out of his way quickly. Mike was at Ryan's side in an instant.

Thomas twisted his frown into a look of loathing. Ryan had no idea that his grasp on me was a direct challenge to Thomas.

"Ah, the control freak movie star," Thomas said with a sinister smile, focusing his eyes on Ryan's protective hold on me.

"Ah, the cheating ex," Ryan retorted, grasping me tighter. "Whatcha need?"

Thomas rolled his head on his neck. "Lost my sister, dude. Came to see how her friends were holding up."

I gave them all a glare of warning. "Okay, enough. Before any of you get any bright ideas, this crap is not going down in my pub. You need to talk? We'll all talk in the kitchen. You want to have a beer? Find a place to sit down."

Ryan drew in an audible breath through his nose that meant *I don't fucking think so.*

"Sorry for your loss, but I can tell you that I'm taking care of what's mine, so you don't need to worry about Taryn. And I know my man Mike here has Marie covered. I can appreciate your concern but it's not your place anymore. So what else do you need here?"

Thomas grinned, welcoming the challenge like it was his birthday and he was getting just what he'd wished for. "He your spokesman now?" he asked me, pushing the situation. "I recall when you were with me you had your own opinions on everything."

I stepped into his path, fully aware of his habit of turning his sadness into a fight. *Fine.* If it was a fight he was looking for to ease his misery, I'd finally deliver. "That's because *you* left me to fend for myself all the time, not caring about my welfare." Something over his shoulder caught my eye. That's when I saw the first cell phone pointed our way. I turned back to Ryan, privately saying, "People are starting to take pictures of this."

He ducked down and whispered in my ear. "Get rid of him—

now—or I will." He glared at Thomas. "I think it's time you leave. There's nothing here for you, man."

Thomas's anger became evident. His hands balling into fists didn't go unnoticed, either. I knew he had come to talk to me and all he was getting was shit from guys he didn't know.

Ryan moved me to his side so I was out of the way. Mike instantly took a step forward. Ryan's eyes never left Thomas. "You feel the need to take a swing at me, do it. We can throw down if it makes you feel like a man."

"Cocky son of a bitch," Thomas spat out with disdain, smirking as if what Ryan had just said was funny. I'd seen him act like this before and I knew exactly how it would end.

Ryan stood his ground. "Whatever. I've taken and given plenty of punches. But I won't be the one going to jail for aggravated assault tonight, I can tell you that."

"Enough. Both of you," I warned.

Thomas smirked again, ignoring me. "She'll get tired of you controlling her eventually. And when she does, I'll be right here to pick it all back up. You see, you may have this now, but I still have a part of her that you'll never have. Even now, I know I still get to her." Thomas leaned in closer. "And when you're fucking her, know she'll always be comparing you to me."

Ryan's body stiffened and I snapped, stepping back in between them before Ryan reacted to his taunt. "Knock it off. You know, for a second, I pitied you. Now you're just being an asshole. Get out of my pub. Now!"

Mike moved in front of Ryan, squaring off to Thomas when it looked like he wasn't planning to leave. "Enough, dude."

"Who the fuck are you?" Thomas sneered.

"Insurance," Mike answered calmly.

"What are you going to do? Hit me?"

Mike was casual but oh-so-threatening. "If I have to. It's my job to shut you down before you do something extremely stupid."

Thomas looked at me. "Is he kidding?"

I knew Thomas knew how to fight but Mike had hand-to-hand combat training. There was no doubt who'd be the victor. "I've had people threaten to hurt me, Thomas. I suggest you don't irritate my bodyguard."

He gaped at me. "You have a bodyguard? Wow. You serious? Why?"

"Because I have what a lot of others wish they had."

Ryan shifted slightly, silently acknowledging my words.

Thomas scoffed at me. "You'd risk your life for him?"

"Absolutely. There are always risks when you love someone."

Ryan's chin tipped up a bit more, standing taller and more forbidding. He had my heart and I had his and there was no confusion there. I also had his back, knowing I would go after Thomas myself before I allowed him to get one step closer to Ryan.

"Huh. Well, when you get tired of all the people snapping your picture and shit, give me a call. Unless you've turned into a spoiled gold-digger, too . . ."

I was so livid, I shoved myself in front of Mike.

I felt Ryan's arm cinch around my waist, moving me to his side and out of the way in one easy sweep. "Get out!" I ordered around Ryan's lunging body as Pete and Mike blocked him from making contact.

Ryan was spewing threats dotted with profanity while Pete body-blocked Thomas. As soon as Thomas turned toward the door, Ryan hauled me toward the kitchen and right up the stairs.

I wanted to rant, scream, throw stuff, maybe even throw up, but instead I watched Ryan to see what he was going to do.

"Where are your car keys?" he asked in a furious rush.

I pointed a shaky hand toward the key hook. He shoved them in his jeans pocket and then grasped me by my upper arms.

"Babe, focus. Help me pack an overnight bag for you. We're getting out of here."

"Where?" I asked in a daze, feeling as if I'd been peeled apart and slammed back together. I could barely stand, my legs felt so numb. My real birth certificate . . . lies . . . Thomas . . . Ryan riled. It was all too much. Too much.

He tossed his bag near the door and took me by the hand. "I don't know, but we'll know when we get there. We just need to go. Change of scenery."

He tapped on his phone while fetching my small overnight bag from the shelf in the closet. "Andrea, hey, Ryan Christensen. I need a private, restful hotel off the radar within two hours of my home base in Rhode Island."

CHAPTER 14

Weekend

W HOEVER YOU CALLED to book this needs a raise."

Ryan opened the French doors to the private deck to let some fresh air in, stretching as he stepped toward the railing. We could see a few boats out on the water, their lights illuminating the darkness.

We ended up in Newport at a breathtaking inn on the coast. I could feel the stress lift as we were guided to an adorable private cottage decorated in soft hues with a wide, wooden plank floor. A wall of windows with billowy white curtains overlooked the ocean.

"Definite raise," I muttered, taking in the huge soaking tub made for two.

Ryan came back inside and slipped his hand across my shoulder as he leaned to turn the water faucet on. It was when he started to undress me that I felt uneasy. The day had been too mentally taxing for a rousing bout of sex.

"Ryan, I'm not . . ."

He kissed my shoulder and shushed me. "I know, baby. That's not the point of this."

He stripped off his clothes and climbed into the tub first, holding out a hand as I stepped in. The hot water felt magnificent and instantly leached some of the tension from my body. I rested my head on his chest, wishing that moments like these could be norm between us and for the most part, they were.

"You okay?" he murmured as I got comfortable on him.

I nodded. His soapy hands slid up and down my back, over my arms, up through the tenseness of my neck.

"Good. Just relax."

"You're so quiet," I murmured after a while, needing to break the silence.

"I was thinking about something you said to me on the first day we met." He sluiced more hot water over my arm, warming my exposed skin.

"Oh?"

He dipped us deeper into the water, seeming concerned that my shoulders were cold. They were. "I was sitting at your bar and you were doing your best to ignore me."

I remembered doing that, but didn't want to admit it. I chased a few soap bubbles around on his chest with my finger. "I was not."

Ryan squeezed me. "Yes, you were. Don't lie."

"Damn. Okay. Maybe just a little. I was freaked-out that you were even there."

With his lips on my temple, he said, "I wanted to get you to talk to me and I asked you if you were always this quiet and you said something like 'I'm sure the silence and peace is refreshing.'" Our gazes met. "I just want you to relax and not worry about things."

And just like that, he was making my world peaceful. "When I close my eyes, I can almost ignore it all," I said.

"Then close your eyes."

"If only it were that easy."

I felt his chest rise and fall, making the water ripple.

"I'm sorry about the Thomas thing. I—"

Ryan raised my chin with his fingertip, making eye contact. "Do I need to be concerned about it?"

I shook my head and quickly said, "No."

He let my chin go. "Then I'm not worried about it. I sort of expected it, actually."

I looked back up at him. "You did?"

His elbow came up out of the water and rested on the edge of the tub. "Tar, you and I are all over the news. Shit always gets dredged up.

It was only a matter of time before one of your ex-boyfriends tried to stake a claim. He doesn't have any dirt on you, does he?"

I winced from the thought. "I don't think so."

Ryan was silent for so long, I thought maybe he'd dozed off, but his tempered breathing told me otherwise.

"So what else is stirring in your thoughts?" His fingers skimmed along my jaw. "I can't read your mind but I know it's going a million miles an hour, so you have to tell me where your head's at."

"My head is still stunned, fighting with the feeling that everything has changed and yet nothing has changed."

His hand slid down to my rear, curling my leg over his thigh. "Dwelling on your ex?"

I heard the minute tinge of worry in his question. "No. Not dwelling. Not at all. But I am processing. He told me he slept with that girl because he was mad that I left him in bed to go help Pete."

Ryan made a derisive snort. "Are you serious?"

"Serious."

"What an asshole. His loss." Then he nudged me with his chin. "You upset about it?"

I rested my hand on his broad shoulder, feeling his heartbeat on my cheek. "No. I never knew why he cheated on me. I've spent way too much time thinking that I wasn't good enough."

His hand cupped my head and he kissed my hair tenderly. "Don't ever think that."

"It's hard not to. Whatever. At least now I know why he did it."

His cheek brushed my forehead. "Then I'm glad you got closure. There are too many past hurts standing in our way. Yours and mine."

I had to remind myself that we'd *both* been betrayed by lovers. "His infidelity broke me."

He tipped my chin up again and kissed me. "Nothing that I can't fix." He smiled gently, warming my battered spirit. I loved this man so deeply I could hardly contain it, knowing that he would weather any storm in our path. I needed to kiss him more than I needed anything else in the world.

Ryan's teeth grazed my bottom lip but then he pulled back, not letting himself get carried away, though I could see that he had to fight his body for control. Knowing that he was restraining his urges to care for me this way was more than any gift he could ever give me. I rested on his chest, content in knowing that he'd get me through whatever life had in store for me.

Regardless of my feelings for Thomas, seeing him cry at Melanie's funeral emotionally ravaged me and those thoughts of her passing were still swirling in my mind. "I can't believe Melanie is gone. It's hard to process that."

"It sucks. I had a good friend in high school die in a car wreck. For weeks after it happened, I could have sworn I heard his voice in the halls." He took a deep breath. "I was supposed to hang out with him the night he died. When I think about how close I came to . . . well, I think about it sometimes."

I glanced up at him, grateful to be able to share these things.

"Wasn't your time."

"Yeah, I guess."

"It's been a few years since I'd seen her last. I guess that put some distance in our friendship. And I know that Thomas is devastated by it. He came looking for comfort and we sort of jumped on him. I feel crappy about it, actually. They both were a huge part of my life for a lot of years. I shouldn't have treated him so callously."

Ryan sniffed and I could tell he didn't agree. "I know you two have history but he had to be told that that's where it stays . . . in the past. I have enough shit to worry about without having to worry about him trying to worm his way back into your life."

I groaned, wrapping my thigh over his. "He's not going to worm his way back in. You know you have nothing to worry about."

"Just making sure it stays that way. Still, he needed to hear that from me. You leave a guy an in and he'll take it."

"I'd say you got your point across. Doesn't matter. He's history."

Ryan cupped some water and poured it down his face. I could sense his frustration.

"Are you really that bothered by him?"

"No." He sighed and rubbed his forehead.

"Then what is it?"

He seemed hesitant. "We got other shit to worry about."

I held his eyes until he broke. "I know this isn't the best time to talk about this but I want to keep you informed before you hear it from someone else."

I closed my eyes, fearing what he had to say.

"Marla is threatening to sue me for breach of contract."

I actually relaxed and breathed a sigh of relief before fully processing his words. "*What?*"

"My lawyer, Len Bainbridge, called me yesterday. He and David are working it out but I have to settle up with her. Her bill was seventy-five thousand."

"Are you going to pay that?"

"I'm going to have to. But not until we get all the expensive lawyers involved first."

"God, she's infuriating. I still think she's the one who leaked your anxiety medicine to the press."

"I think so, too. Can't prove it, though, unless we find the source. I'll mention that to my lawyer."

"Well, I doubt it was Trish. She's got too much to lose being that careless. And it surely wasn't Mike. None of my friends know—well, besides Marie. Your family wouldn't talk to the press, so that leaves David, Marla, or the woman at the pharmacy."

"David wouldn't talk to the press."

"Well, then what does that tell you?"

"Tells me that the list of people I can trust just got smaller."

+   +   +

I WAS feeling mostly relaxed and right with the world when we came back to the apartment on Sunday—that was until we had to deal with the four fangirls camped out by my back door. I was shocked that these college-aged girls had nothing more important to do with their lives than hang out in an alleyway all day hoping for a glimpse of Ryan.

Ryan, of course, was gracious as always, signing crap and posing several times until they were all satisfied with the pictures they captured.

We have to move, I thought as we trudged up the steps, trying to be loud enough so we wouldn't walk into an awkward situation going on *inside* my apartment.

Mike was sprawled out on my couch, wearing nothing but baggy gray sweatpants, a black sleeveless undershirt, and a well-sated glow. He looked like a giant lion lying belly-up in the sun with his legs hanging open, licking his paws and airing out his balls. I figured Marie would be twined around him, enjoying their postcoital bliss, but she was in the kitchen making coffee.

"You both look well rested," she said, smiling at Ryan and me. Ryan winked at her and took our bags to our room.

I took a cup out of the cabinet. "We had a couples massage yesterday. I wish I could hire someone to do nothing but rub my shoulders every day. You look well ridden and glowing yourself."

"You know it." Marie gave me a high-five. She carried a cup of coffee out to Mike. Ryan had his feet up on my coffee table, looking just as relaxed and contented as his buddy. The lascivious grins flying around my living room were humorous. I felt my body heat up just from thinking about what Ryan did to me that morning . . . and the night before . . . and after our couples massage yesterday.

The way Mike looked at Marie, I wondered if he was already falling in love with her.

Marie sat on the arm of the couch next to Mike. I liked seeing him reach for her with tender familiarity, as if he couldn't wait to touch her again. "Do you think you guys can help me today?" Her eyes traveled over each of us. "I'd like to get some of my stuff from my old house."

Within an hour, we were all standing in Gary's front yard. Seeing Marie have to knock on her own front door to gain access infuriated me. The bastard actually had the audacity to change all the door locks on her. Gary came out of the house, pulling the door shut behind him.

"Just let me get my clothes!" Marie screamed at him, shaking with frustration. The first few times she tried to ask nicely and beg him to let her in didn't work.

Gary jingled the car keys in his hands, blocking our entry into the house. "You should have called first. I've got someplace to be. Now's not a good time."

Marie groaned loudly. I knew how irritated she felt; I wanted to choke the asshole myself.

"Gary, easy." Ryan tried the friendly and nonthreatening approach first, placating him. "Let us just get some of her things. Just her clothing and stuff and then we'll be outa here. We won't take anything else. You have my word."

Gary snorted with derision, stepping into Ryan's path. "Screw you, Ryan. Stay the hell out of my house. This is all your fucking fault, you know. Shit was fine until you came around."

I bristled with horror when Gary said that. How the hell could Ryan be responsible for the demise of their marriage? In an instant, Mike shouldered up to Ryan, forever in protection mode. I could see the anger roiling through him as he squeezed his hands into fists. I had no doubt Mike desired to level Gary just for the sheer enjoyment of it.

Ryan appeared just as surprised as we all were. "My fault? You're kidding, right?"

Marie moved closer to the door. "What is wrong with you? How the hell is any of this his fault? You're delusional."

Gary sneered at her. "Oh, fuck you, Marie. I am so sick and tired of hearing how their life is so fucking perfect and ours isn't. Ryan does this and Ryan does that. It's like nothing I've *ever* done for you was good enough. So you know what? I just don't give a fuck anymore. Some other asshole can live up to your expectations now. I pity the next guy that puts up with your shit."

My eyes quickly bounced from Gary to Mike, catching a twitch in his jaw from Gary's verbal slap. Marie looked as if she were about to buckle at the knees.

"I hate you," Marie breathed out, holding back her tears.

"Whatever," Gary sneered at her as if he truly didn't care anymore. Watching her three-year marriage crumble was painful. How quickly people go from wedded bliss to murderous glares. My heart broke for her.

She started after him but Mike grabbed her by the wrist. Her eyes bounced from his hand to his face, watching as Mike silently told her to stop with a shake of his head.

Gary appeared affronted by Mike's intervention. "What, she's fucking you now? I knew it. I fucking knew it. How long, huh? How long you been screwing around behind my back, Marie? Couldn't get the fucking movie star you're so in love with so you settle for his baby-sitter. That's rich."

Marie gasped. "You bastard! You're the one who fucked some stupid skank, not me! You! Where is your little T-shirt-wearing whore, huh? She inside?"

"Only whore here is you," Gary retorted.

"Oh my God. I can't believe you just said that." I wanted to slap him so hard, he'd see stars for days. Ryan grabbed my wrist, keeping me from moving any farther across the lawn.

Mike stepped his hulking body into Gary's path, protectively guiding Marie behind his back. "Careful what you say to her, man."

Gary glared at him. "This doesn't concern you."

I was surprised Gary was brazen enough to pick a fight with Mike.

"Marie," Gary barked, expecting her to jump.

Mike never took his eyes off Gary. He pulled Marie back again, keeping his body in between the two of them. "You're done talking to her. You talk to me now."

Gary's hand curled into a fist, dropping some of his keys between the knuckles. "Oh, is that right?"

"She's not your concern anymore," Mike said low and deliberately, clearly meant to send a message. "You lost the right when you locked her out of her own house." Mike stood his ground, eyeing the gesture and questioning the absurdity of it. "Better make the first swing count because that's all you're gonna get," he added.

Gary took a moment to think about it, weighing his odds. Like he had a chance in hell to win that fight. He reluctantly backed down. "Marie, tell your friends to get the fuck off my property or I'm calling the cops." As if to heighten his threat, he pulled his cell out.

"It's my property, too, you know," she argued back.

Mike glared at him as if he wanted to kill him, then turned and took Marie by the hand and tugged her toward the car, guiding her body in front of his. "Come on. Let's go."

Gary stood in the driveway, enjoying his moment of victory.

I climbed in the backseat with Marie and put my arm around her shoulder while digging out more tissues.

"I hate him so much," Marie whispered through her tears to me.

"Babe," Mike said from the driver's seat as he drove down the block, "your house have a security system?"

Babe? When the heck did that start?

Marie wiped her cheek. "No."

"Gary own any weapons?"

My eyes flashed to Ryan, who was staring over at Mike.

"Yeah," she answered. "But everything is locked up in the gun safe."

"Everything?" Mike questioned again.

Marie sat up. "He used to keep a revolver in the nightstand drawer in our bedroom. The rest are hunting rifles."

"And where are those?"

"Gun safe is also in the bedroom."

Mike nodded once. "You know where he's going today? How long he'll be gone?"

I heard Ryan mumble something. Mike held up a finger for him to wait.

Marie sniffed. "No idea."

I caught Mike's eyes in the rearview mirror. "Taryn, directions. I need a hardware store."

Forty minutes later, with the aid of a small tool kit, Mike gained us entry into Marie's house. And I thought my public takedown in Paris was a big deal; I could only imagine what "breaking and entering" would look like on the front page. I felt like I was going to rattle out of my skin and then maybe hurl lunch.

"Stop worrying, Taryn," Mike said, using one of Gary's shirts to keep his fingerprints off the revolver he'd found in the nightstand drawer. I watched him unload it with familiar precision. "This is Marie's house, too. There's no legal order for her to vacate."

Just seeing a gun in proximity to my body was nerve-racking enough; thinking about us getting caught and Ryan's picture plastered over every gossip magazine had me reevaluating this as a very bad idea.

Mike pointed a finger at Ryan. "You, out. Marie, grab what you need. Try to be quick about it." He guided Ryan by the shoulder, steering him toward the door. "We're waiting outside—off the property line to avoid trespassing charges."

I grabbed a garbage bag and started frantically packing whatever Marie told me to take, starting with her clothes.

Whatever shit we were in, we were in it together.

"WELL, THAT was fun," Ryan sarcastically joked, hauling the last garbage bag in through the back door. "Damn, something smells good."

Mike took a big whiff. "Heck yeah. Taryn, go get us some of that." He made me laugh. "I'll go beg Tammy to cook us supper."

Ryan threw the black bag of clothes over his shoulder. "Invite them up tonight. We can all hang out."

I opened the door from the hallway into the pub kitchen to see what Tammy was up to. It was a welcome distraction to the breaking and entering we'd just committed. "Hey, Tammy. Smells fantastic in here."

She was busy adding ingredients into her industrial-sized mixer. "Oh, hey, Taryn."

"I had to keep the guys from breaking down the door. What are you making that smells so yummy?"

She pointed to a rack. "Cherry tarts right now. Sorry, but I don't have any extras."

I eyed the cooling rack with longing and invited her and Pete to join us upstairs for dinner later.

She dusted her hands off on her apron. "Hey, before you go, can I talk to you a minute?" Tammy appeared troubled as she wiped her hands over and over again on a wet rag. "Is everything okay between you and Ryan?"

I wasn't sure why she was asking. "Yeah. Things are great. Why?"

She tossed the rag into the sink. "I don't know. Just wondering about the whole Thomas thing. I figured you might be fighting."

"No. We're not fighting. There is nothing to fight about."

"Oh. I just thought he'd be mad about you hugging your ex like that. I figured you told him anyway."

I felt myself getting slightly defensive. "There was nothing going on between Thomas and me. Melanie has been a friend of mine for years. I hope you don't think that I was doing something inappropriate."

"Oh no. No. That's not what I meant. It's just that I know how jealous Ryan is. I thought maybe he was mad and that's why he came back here."

"No. He had a break in filming so he came home."

"Oh, okay. So what's up with Marie? Is she dating Mike now?" she asked.

I shrugged, wondering why she wasn't asking Marie these questions. "I'm not sure. They like each other. You do know that Gary has a new girlfriend, right?" Something was up. She wouldn't make eye contact with me.

"This whole thing is putting us in a very awkward situation," she said. "I mean, Pete and Gary have been friends for a long time and it's like we're being forced to pick sides."

She definitely caught me off guard. "No one is forcing you to pick sides, Tammy."

"Well, yeah, they kind of are. We're getting married in four months and they are both in the wedding party. Pete and Gary have been friends for years. It's not fair that he'd have to ask him not to come. No one seems to care how it affects us."

"Tammy, I don't know what to say. It's your wedding. Gary made a choice—Marie is just dealing with that. He just locked her out of her own damn house. What kind of man does that?"

"Well, she's with Mike. Can you blame him?" she snipped.

I was beginning to think she'd lost her damn mind. "How would you feel if Pete locked you out and wouldn't let you get any of your stuff?"

"I didn't know he did that. She's been so busy around here and it's not like we hang out together a lot when you aren't around."

"Everyone's been dealing with a lot. Trust me. I don't want you to think that we don't care."

"Oh." She turned to take something out of the oven. "Well, since Ryan is here now, do you think that you can ask him if he's going to be a groomsman or not? I mean, he hasn't said anything to Pete and he avoided the topic on Friday when Pete mentioned it. It would be nice to know if I even have a freaking bridal party or not."

I bristled at her anger. "Yeah, sure. He's been busy filming a movie so I'm sure he's not been avoiding anything on purpose. I'll make sure to ask him to confirm."

Tammy snorted as if that answer wasn't good enough. "I'm sure he's been in a great mood since your ex-fiancé has been coming around. Like he needs that crap."

Like *I* needed that crap—or her crap right now for that matter. I was starting to wonder if all this wedding stuff was turning Tammy into a bridezilla. I certainly wasn't going to become confrontational even though I wanted to.

"Well, I'll let you get back to running your business. I'll make sure to get an answer to Pete."

I didn't wait to give her an opportunity to respond, hurrying through the door and up my stairs as if the floor were on fire.

Ryan's unbelievably nice ass was poking out of my open refrigerator door when I found him in my kitchen. "Everything okay?"

I wrapped my arms around his waist, burying my nose in the neckline of his T-shirt. "Can we elope instead?"

Ryan snickered and rubbed my back. "Sure. What brought this on?"

"Planning weddings apparently makes women go insane. I'm pretty sure Tammy's growing fangs and claws."

"Oh. That sucks. Is it contagious?"

"God, I hope not."

He whispered in my ear, "You can always hire a wedding planner to do that shit for you."

My head popped off his chest when I heard a loud crash and Marie's high-pitched yell for help coming from the spare room. I found her surrounded by a few boxes and a whole lot of crap spilled out around her feet—clothing, books, and a slew of old videocassette tapes.

"Sorry," she pleaded, still holding a box from tipping off the top shelf in the closet. I had to laugh at her panicked expression. "I tried to move one and they all came crashing down."

Mike took the box out of her hands.

"Are these boxes full or what?" Ryan asked, opening one of them.

I folded up one of my mom's old sweaters and set it aside, trying to clear a path. "That's all of your fan mail from the last few weeks, hon. You need to either go through it or we need to pitch it."

He looked astounded and confused. "All of this?"

"All of those boxes." Marie pointed. "Including skanky underwear, sappy praise, and more death threats."

He turned on her, and then turned his questioning glare on me. "Death threats?"

What could I say? As sick as it was, it wasn't anything new. Several thousand of his fans hated that he was with me.

Some unspoken message passed between Ryan and Mike before Ryan cursed and then hauled one of the boxes out to my living room.

I boxed up all of the videos, noting that my name was written on the majority of them. Memories. Childhood memories. Memories that Dan and Jennifer Mitchell made for me.

Without even thinking, I grabbed the box of tapes and sat on my living room floor in front of the television, pressing the tape marked "Fourth of July 1986—Taryn 4 yrs old" into the aging VCR.

Ryan sat on the ottoman behind me. "Look at you! All curly blond ringlets."

I smiled at my innocent babbling about swimming with my Barbie doll, pushing my oversized sunglasses up my sun-kissed nose. I had on a little pink one-piece swimsuit with a blue fish on the hip.

Ryan pointed over my shoulder. "Is that? Yeah, that's your pappy's cabin." I saw the familiar gray cinder-block garage behind me.

And then I saw him. Like a ghost out of my innermost thoughts he appeared, coming out of the garage behind me. Tall, thin, and lanky, walking with the stinted lope of a teenager.

There he was, captured forever on film.

The boy with the black hair.

I felt as though someone poured ice through my veins.

CHAPTER 15

Discoveries

I STARED AT THE television for so long my eyes hurt. It was like he walked right out of one of my nightmares and presented himself to me. *Here I am—the one who haunts you.*

Ryan had moved behind me after telling Mike and Marie we needed a few minutes of privacy. He sat on the floor, holding me while I quietly broke down again.

I didn't even realize I was touching my own mouth until I felt Ryan's hand smooth around my wrist. "In my dreams, he always has bloody teeth. Just blood—everywhere. I never . . ." It was hard to speak.

"Is that Joe?" Ryan asked softly.

I nodded. "I think so." I rewound the tape and paused to see him in still frame but the tape made squiggly lines on the screen, obscuring his face.

I felt Ryan's lips, his breath on my neck. "Is this one of the things that has you jumping out of bed sometimes?"

"Yeah. All this time, I didn't know who he was. He's not in any family pictures. I thought . . . I thought he was someone I made up."

Ryan slipped the remote out of my hand and pressed play again. The tape rolled on, mostly capturing me playing with beach toys in a round plastic wading pool on the grass. Every so often, Joe would make an appearance, a ghost in the background, lurking, but always keeping an eye on the camera's direction. I suppose, keeping an eye on me.

"I want to know him."

254

Ryan's hand skated across my face, taking in my plea. "Mike can find him if you want," he said.

I thought about it for a second. "I want him to want to know me, too. It can't be one-sided. He's got to want to know me but it's been so long—people change."

Ryan held my face, pressing a soft kiss on my lips, but he was distracted by the heavy thudding of footsteps coming up my stairwell.

I heard Pete's hearty greeting when Marie let them in.

Ryan crawled around me, pressing the eject button. "You change your mind, just say the word. We can hire someone to track him down. I'll let you decide if you want to share all of this with them."

My gaze was locked on the tight skin of his body, graciously exposed when his T-shirt rode up his stomach. It was just the jolt I needed.

Pete instantly scrutinized me and jerked his head for me to follow him to the dining room, where he cornered me. "Red-rimmed eyes. All puffy. You okay?"

Nothing got past Pete.

And I couldn't lie to him. I gave him a noncommittal head bob while his mouth silently said "bullshit." I decided talk therapy was what I needed.

I pulled out a chair and asked Tammy to join us. No sense having to repeat myself. After a string of introductory words, I then uttered the two words that churned like acid in my stomach.

"... I'm adopted."

RYAN CLOSED our bedroom door and peeled his shirt off, exposing a body I'd never get tired of looking at. "You know I don't care, right?" His words were as gentle as the eyes that watched me with apprehension. I'd spent an evening discussing my origins with my friends; it was emotionally exhausting.

"I know."

"Doesn't change anything about how I feel about you. The only thing I want to know is if you're going to take my last name when we get married, which I'm hoping to hell you will."

I blinked at him, processing what he said, and then sort of melted inside. "I had intended to."

He breathed out a contended sigh and hugged me. "Thank you."

I heard the toilet flush and Marie's and Mike's low murmurs outside our closed door.

"It's weird having other people here," I muttered conspiratorially.

"Yeah, I know. I totally love your apartment but I hope you know I don't want to live above your pub for the rest of our lives."

"Or listen to Marie giggle before sex."

"That too," he chuckled, palming my rear. "You do realize that Mike and I can't leave here until both of you are bowlegged and glowing, right?"

I grinned. "You should make it a competition. See which one of you folds first."

Before I could react, Ryan let me go and grabbed the doorknob. "Hallway meeting," he called out loudly.

I felt instant mortification. "Ryan!"

"Shush." Ryan crossed his beefy arms, waiting. God, I loved his biceps. Mike came out of the room, sans shirt as well. Damn, he was built like a linebacker who spends his life in a gym, not to mention his chest was as smooth as a baby's bottom.

"Two things," Ryan started, holding up his fingers. "You come out of your room for any reason, you put something on. I don't want to see anyone else's bare ass other than my woman's. Number two, Taryn suggests we make a wager on this evening's festivities."

"Ryan!"

He pushed me back with his fingertips. "Shush."

Mike leaned a hand on the door frame. "Wager?"

"First man to fold."

Mike's eyes cut to me once, quickly. "Interesting. I'm in. Time or quantity?" he asked as casually as if they were discussing the weather.

"What time is our flight again?"

"Eleven forty-five. We're gone by nine," Mike's deep voice rumbled.

"Time. We can sleep on the plane."

"Agreed. Bet?"

"Two bills?"

"Sounds fair. Women keeping time?"

"Yep," Ryan quipped. "Time gets written down so there's no cheating."

"Anything else?" Mike asked.

"Nope."

"What time is it now?"

Ryan leaned around to see my alarm clock. "Ten after eleven."

I watched as they shook hands.

"Have a good night," Mike said with a nod.

"You too, man." Ryan tapped his shoulder and then locked our bedroom door.

Me and my big mouth.

The lascivious glare Ryan gave me instantly made my heart beat faster, warming me in all the right places, effectively distracting me from all of my woes. I was the rabbit and he was the hungry wolf and it was obvious that I was about to be eaten alive. Perhaps this wasn't a stupid suggestion after all.

He walked with purpose, stalking over to my side of the bed.

Game on.

MY ALARM went off at eight o'clock. I wanted to hurl it against the wall and smash it to bits. Ryan's arm was pinning me to the bed and he was out. Even the shrill of the alarm didn't stir him.

I heard the shower turn on so I hit the snooze button one more time before dragging my butt into the kitchen to make the guys some breakfast.

Marie came shuffling in, rubbing one eye, and mumbled something that sounded like "morning." "You write your time down?"

"No."

She stretched. "Damn, my body hurts."

My body ached, too. I could feel the pain in my hips. "Yep."

She grabbed a piece of mail off the counter, tore it in half, and grabbed a pen. "Was this shit really your idea?"

I took four coffee mugs out of the cabinet. "I said it as a joke."

"It was brilliant." She pushed the torn envelope and the pen toward me. "But I think he broke my vagina."

I spit out some coffee after that one, staining my envelope piece. I wrote down the last time I looked at the clock: 4:50.

Marie had written 5:10.

"Looks like Ryan's out two hundred," I muttered.

Mike came in all fresh and looking mighty fine in a pair of worn jeans and a gray tee that hugged every muscular curve. "Morning, ladies. Who won?" He ran a hand tenderly over Marie's shoulder.

"You did." She beamed up at him.

He smiled and kissed her as if they'd been together for years. I didn't miss his hand possessively palming her butt cheek, either. It made me smile.

"Pay up, shorty," he teased Ryan when he came into the kitchen.

Ryan motioned for the results. "I lost by twenty minutes?" He groaned and tossed the papers onto the counter. "That's bullshit."

I poured a cup of coffee for him. "Sorry, babe."

"Twenty freakin' minutes." He towered over me, giving me the stink eye. "You made me quit, too."

"Sorry. I was done. You want me to pay half?"

"No," he grumbled, scowling at me, making me question whether he was truly upset. "I got it. But you owe me and I will collect."

I followed him into the bedroom, worried. "Are you really mad at me?"

He smirked. "No, babe. I'm just teasing. I was tired and wiped out, too. It's okay . . . until I collect what you owe me." He cracked me hard on the rear.

I sucked in a breath, imagining him collecting. I hated watching Ryan pack. He was always in motion.

Like two sad sacks, Marie and I hugged and kissed them both goodbye in my living room. Marie looked just as forlorn and reluctant to let them go as I was. We stood there for a moment after the door closed behind them, staring at each other in silence, feeling empty.

"That was the best night of my life," she uttered. "Thank you for that."

"I heard you scream a few times."

Marie rolled her eyes, abashed. "I heard you, too."

We gave each other a high-five, just because.

She yawned. "Well, I don't know about you but I'm taking my broken vagina back to bed." I watched her walk funny, doing the "I've been fucked hard" swagger down the hallway.

I shuffled behind her, feeling her pain echo in my own sore hips and thighs. "Yep. Me too."

I crawled my achy body into my cold, empty bed, thinking about how much sleeping without Ryan sucked.

A FEW days later I was Skyping with Ryan when the separation hit me hard. "I hate being away from you."

He tilted his head, studying me. "You don't have to be, you know."

I pulled my fingers back, as if his words had bite. "I know."

He regarded me for a moment before turning his attention back to the documents in his hand. "Sell it. Cut yourself free."

As much as I'd thought about it there were several reasons why I couldn't. "I can't. Marie and Tammy rely on me, on this place. I can't screw my friends like that. Besides, I need to work, Ryan. I'm not good with doing nothing or shopping every day."

"I need you to manage my life," he said simply.

"You just don't want to deal with your mother," I teased.

He scratched his head, distracted, seemingly frustrated. "That too."

I frowned at his lack of attention, which then had me tapping my finger on the image of his face, as if that would do the trick.

He finally looked up. "Listen, parties, family gatherings, holidays, vacations, all of that personal stuff is in your realm, Taryn. She wants to throw an engagement party for us—fine. Work it out, block out the dates, and put it on the calendar, and then when you're done with all of that explain to me what these numbers are on my investment statements because I can't figure out how I could lose so much in one quarter."

That was an easy one. "Your accountant sucks. Money needs to be managed, not resting in a coffee can until you have bills to pay. He should be making more strategic investments for you."

"Well then, you need to fix this. I'm adding this shit to your wifely duties. You feel comfortable and you want to manage it, I'll fire him. It's that simple."

As good as that made me feel, part of me was freaked that I might screw up. The fact that he trusted me with his millions was humbling. "If you want me to."

He was all business, still reviewing documents. "I want you to, starting now. I'm emailing the files to you. Let's get this shit straightened out because I am so not liking losing five fucking figures on market fluctuations."

I could do that. "Okay. By the way, are you ever going to give me my debit card back?"

He didn't bother to look up, simply saying, "No. And don't ask again."

I was startled by his abrupt, authoritative tone. "I seemed to remember you threatening punishment if I tried to steal it back."

That got his attention. "You want to defy me?"

It was worth considering. "Maybe."

His eyes heated with the challenge. "Just make sure your lovely ass is on a plane on Tuesday. I'll deal with you then."

"Trish is taking me dress shopping and then I've arranged for us to have dinner with Cal and Kelly Wednesday night."

I watched the hint of a smile spread across his lips. I knew it pleased him that I was making ties within his circle of celebrity friends. "Good. Very good. They'll be at the MTV Movie Awards, too. You nervous?"

This would be my first awards show—ever. I hadn't really checked my nerves with everything else going on. Ryan looked over his shoulder. That's when I saw Mike's head flash in the background. "Problem's been contained," Mike muttered. "Ten minutes."

"Okay, thanks." Ryan turned back to me. "You still flying back with me to Vancouver on Thursday?"

"What's going on there? What problem?"

I could see him trying to decide whether or not to share. "Some overly enthusiastic fans got onto the set. They were mingled in with some of the extras. We had to take a break from filming to sort it all out."

My skin prickled. "Are you in danger?"

"No."

For some reason I didn't believe him. "Would you tell me if you were?"

My eyes met his on the screen. "I'm not in danger, babe. I don't need you worrying for nothing."

I was just about to argue when Marie came in, carrying an enormous bouquet of red roses in a clear crystal vase. "Someone got flowers." She beamed at me.

I smiled widely at him, deeply touched that he'd do something so sweet. "Ryan! God, they're beautiful." I shoved my nose into one of the open blooms, savoring the fresh smell. "Thank you."

He appeared confused, then pissed. "I'd like to take credit, but I didn't send you flowers. Who the hell is sending you flowers?"

I opened the card and read it out loud.

Dear Taryn,

I know you don't know me but I am a huge fan and I hope these flowers brighten your day. I thought this might encourage you as well . . . "For I know the plans I have for you," declares the Lord, "plans to prosper you and not to harm you, plans to give you hope and a future." Have a wonderful day lovely lady!

Jeremy

I suddenly felt sick. Ryan's murderous glare was enough to make me go pale. "You don't leave the house without an escort. Ever. Got me?" He yelled over his shoulder for Mike.

"I can't live in fear, Ryan," I muttered, annoyed that my once-peaceful oblivion was now convoluted by psychopaths and unknown birth certificates. I pushed the vase off to the side as if it were a ticking bomb.

I knew he was angry; that much was evident. "The shit is coming to your house, Taryn. To your damn door." He dialed someone on his phone and seconds later, Mike rushed into Ryan's trailer. After briefing him, Ryan asked for Marie. He made her read the card, out loud. "She doesn't go outside without someone by her side—*ever*."

I was mad, disgusted. Stupid flowers, sequestering me to my own home, making me feel as if I were a prisoner.

I WAS on the telephone with Andrea, who works for Ryan's agent, ironing out my travel arrangements to L.A. for the MTV Movie

Awards next week, when someone pounded on the apartment door, startling the crap out of me.

I was relieved to hear Tammy's voice answer back. I opened the door to see her standing there, visibly shaken. I had heard her down in the kitchen, but it was barely noon so I had no idea what had her so frantic.

"'They just took Pete to the hospital," she sobbed. "He dropped me off this morning so I don't have a car."

I yelled for Marie and grabbed my purse and keys.

"He fell off a roof. That's all I know," Tammy said as we rushed down the alley to my car.

Marie gave me a concerned look, knowing I was violating Ryan's direct order.

"He said I don't go out alone. He didn't specify with whom." I really didn't care about my safety; I was more worried about Pete.

Tammy hopped in the front seat. "What's going on?"

Marie climbed into the back. "Oh nothing. Just the usual whack-jobs stalking Taryn. Someone sent her roses yesterday."

I didn't want to think about it for too long or else I'd be inclined to run and hide in my closet with the baseball bat. "It's nothing. Just flowers."

"It's creepy as shit," Marie muttered.

I drove as fast as I could to the emergency room, knowing Tammy was beside herself. We were all fraught with worry. The three of us stormed through the automatic doors at St. Luke's and into the large waiting room.

I saw the color drain out of Tammy's cheeks when the girl behind the desk asked if Tammy was immediate family. Her fear for the unknown, thinking the worst, mirrored mine.

"Go." I gave Tammy's elbow a nudge for her to follow the nurse. Marie and I found an empty corner of the waiting room.

"God, I hope he's all right," Marie uttered, scrolling through her cell.

I shoved my keys in my purse, beating back my worry for Pete. Hopefully we'd hear something soon. "Did you talk to Tammy this morning?"

She shook her head and concentrated on her phone. "What am I supposed to say to her? I guess I'll just bow out of being in the wedding, since Gary seems to be hell-bent on staying a groomsman. You know what pisses me off? He hates weddings. We almost didn't get married because he didn't want a big wedding. You remember that? He's doing this crap out of spite. I know it. I don't know what I ever saw in him."

"Doesn't matter much now, does it?" I nodded at her thumbs, busy texting to Mike again.

Marie gave a wry smile and snapped her phone shut. "He's pretty incredible. I'm trying not to mess this up."

I gazed at the Weather Channel on the waiting room television. "I wish you could go with me to L.A."

"Yeah, me too. I hate that you're doing all of this world traveling without me." Her eyes cut over to me. "I miss him."

I could hear the longing in her voice. "Can I ask you something?" She met my glance.

"What are your thoughts about managing the bar full-time?"

She looked away, shaking her head as if she didn't like the idea. "You know, if you would have asked me that five months ago, I would have jumped at the chance. Now?" Marie shrugged. "I never thought I'd be twenty-eight and going through a divorce. Sometimes I want to run from this town and never look back."

"I know the feeling."

"Besides you and my dad there's not much else holding me here."

I nodded. "You and that bar are the only things keeping me here," I said. "I can't . . . I can't be in two places at once and I definitely know I wouldn't be able to trust the pub to just anyone. And you and Tammy . . . I can't sell it. I won't do that to you."

"You can't worry about us. You have to do what's right for you."

She sat quietly for a moment. "We'd need to hire more staff to replace you. You know I can run the pub, but, honestly Tar, I'm not sure I want to anymore. I've been doing a lot of thinking myself wondering what I'm going to do next."

I knew exactly how she felt. She and I had fallen into a rut where keeping the bar running after my father died was almost like a moral obligation.

"What do you want to do?" I asked.

She seemed reluctant to share. "Well, Mike mentioned that there's a huge demand for female bodyguards. A lot of celebrities are using females in their security detail now. I don't know. I'd have to learn self-defense and do some weapons training first but ... He's been trying to convince me to give it a try."

"That something you'd be interested in doing?"

"Well, it sounds really intriguing and he's even willing to train me, so ... Gary said I was a bitch; might as well get paid to be a professional one."

Surprisingly, I wasn't overly stunned. Marie was lithe but fierce at the core. What did surprise me was her newfound fire for doing something completely different.

"You can be my bodyguard," I teased jokingly, but as I said it, I thought about how cool it would be if she were.

"Well, yeah. I was actually thinking that. You seem to attract a whole lotta crazy."

We both snickered at that until the realization that I had no defense skills of my own trickled in.

"I don't know if Mike and I have a future," she continued, shirking it off, "but with or without him there's so much more world to see than just the inside of the pub. You're traveling and seeing places, Mike has been all around the freakin' globe ... I just want—more. This thing with Gary? It's been brewing for a long time. And now ... well, I just want to cut my losses and move on."

I saw the desire in her eyes, and wished she had been with me in

Paris; none of that embarrassing nonsense would have gone down if she'd been with me. "Are you seriously considering it?"

She nodded and then her shoulders slumped. "I think I'd be real good at it. But it doesn't matter what I want. There are courses I'd have to take and Mike told me about this four-week certification program that a friend of his runs. Problem is, I don't have the money or the time. And the last thing I want is for Mike to view me as a career clinger."

I'd sell the bar before I'd let her give up hope. We'd been to hell and back and I'd give anything to see her happy again. I dug out my phone and called Mike. He answered on the third ring.

Marie was still glaring at me when I hung up. "I can't believe you just did that."

I tried to defuse her with the same admonishing glare. "You want to get out of Seaport or not?"

"Yes, but you just tossed that on him. Of course he wouldn't say no. He's going to think I'm a whack job."

Her mouth snapped shut when I smiled at her. "He was *very* enthusiastic so quit worrying." I texted Ryan, telling him Pete was in the hospital. "Besides, the man nailed you for six hours straight. I'm pretty sure that allows you to ask a favor or two."

"That was just sex," she muttered. "I'm not reading anything into it."

"I don't think so. He's smitten."

She twisted her lips at my word. "I've had guys *smitten* before. It never lasts. Once they get into your pants it's just a matter of time until the novelty wears off. I'm actually surprised it hasn't happened already. He'll sleep with some other girls soon and then I'll be a distant memory, so I'm not getting my hopes up."

I frowned at her doubt but I totally knew how she felt.

"And what happens when Ryan doesn't need him anymore? He'll have to find other clients. He can't drag his girlfriend around in a suitcase . . . well, unless he buys one of those inflatable ones, although I highly doubt he'd ever go plastic."

I chuckled. "He *is* a damn good-looking man."

"That he is. Looks even better naked." She grinned.

"Is he being weird or anything since? You seem happy, so I guess he hasn't turned into a flaming asshole yet."

"No." She laughed modestly. "He's been super-sweet. Almost too good to be true sometimes."

"He calls you all the time."

She was glowing with that look of dreamy love. "I know."

I read Ryan's reply, asking me to fill him in once I knew Pete's condition. "Then quit your worrying."

She huffed. "But then you'll be strapped."

"I won't be strapped. It will all work out."

I practically jumped out of my seat when Tammy came through the double doors. Her face was ashen and worried. "Is he?" I started, not sure of what to ask. I handed a tissue to her.

Her hand shook when she pushed her hair behind her ear. "He's awake but he's banged up pretty bad. He just had an MRI and now they're taking him for X-rays. He's got a big lump on his forehead. His left arm is definitely broken and his knee and ankle are all swollen. The doctor wants to make sure that he doesn't have any internal bleeding or swelling since he hit his head. They said he was unconscious for a bit on the job site."

I wrapped my arm around her back, guiding her to sit down for a moment. "What happened?"

Tammy wiped the corners of her eyes. "Apparently he was carrying a pack of shingles and slipped. He fell like eight feet."

Marie grabbed the box of tissues that was on the table in the waiting room and took the seat next to her. "He'll be all right. He's tough."

It took about an hour, but I was relieved when we were finally able to visit with him. I almost wanted to cry seeing him bandaged up with a big white cast on his arm. Pete gave me a weak smile, as if he were embarrassed. I slipped my hand into his and he squeezed my fingers while I tried not to think about how bad this day could have been.

The large purple lump on his forehead and a few cuts near his eye were frightening reminders of how things could have turned from broken bones to tragedy.

CHAPTER 16

Limelight

I CLIMBED INTO THE large, black Suburban that had been dispatched to take us to the MTV Movie Awards; I was holding the edge of my thigh-revealing dress so I wouldn't accidently flash my undies. Thoughts of my friends, of Pete's slow recovery and that I wasn't there to help, were with me even though my friends were thousands of miles away on the other side of the States.

I sat quickly in the single seat, ridding myself of my stilettos to make the climb into the bench back seat easier, tamping down the budding nervousness growing from the anticipation. Ryan climbed in behind me, looking devastatingly gorgeous. He was wearing fitted black jeans, a black V-neck tee, a gray blazer, and his game face. The scent of his cologne was enough to make me want to strip him bare and nuzzle his neck for a few hours.

He leered over at me, smirking with those wet lips that knew my secrets, reminding me that all of this celebrity ass-kissing, management team ordering, fan-pleasing hoopla came with the game.

"What?" His question came out as a low, hungry purr.

All I could do was smile and keep the overwhelming craziness in perspective. Nuzzling his nakedness would come later. I bit my bottom lip, thinking about rolling my tongue over all of his secret spots. My mouth was actually watering from thinking about it. His eyes darkened. "I like the way your mind works. Can you hold that thought for a few hours?"

Mike cleared his throat and by his private little chuckle I could tell we weren't discreet enough.

David sat in front of me, playing with his Rolex again, going over the details of our evening. Trish sat in the single seat in front of Ryan, reviewing some papers and then giving Ryan the rundown of what was expected at our arrival.

I could tell by his concerned look that he was more worried about me than another public appearance. Leaning his head toward me, he softly asked, "You okay?"

My mind initially screamed "hell no" after seeing the huge crowds gathered. Instead I nodded sharply, giving him my most assured smile. "Oh sure. This is old hat," I joked. I felt the warmth of his hand when his fingers laced with mine.

Ryan gave me a tug and a trademark smart-ass smirk, finding the humor in my response. "Old hat. Cocky. Love it."

That still didn't ease the stranglehold of nervous excitement twisting my stomach as we slowed in the line of cars depositing other celebrity attendees. Mike, David, and Trish exited the car first and closed the doors. Ryan and I slid to the middle seats by the doors, where I put my shoes back on, waiting for our cue to exit. Mike would not let us get out until our other security escort was present and he'd had an opportunity to do a scan of the scene. I knew the drill: stay in formation, keep moving. Mike was always positioned behind Ryan on his right side.

Ryan was agitated by the sheer number of people milling about. "I'm not talking to any press." He growled a low reminder at Trish when Mike opened his door.

No sooner did his toe hit the ground than people started screaming and yelling for his attention. It was so comforting when he turned back to take me by the hand; I knew we were going in as a team.

"We're to the left for press photos," Trish advised, steering us toward a huge wall with the MTV logo and year printed in a repeat pattern.

I wanted to let go of his hand so I wouldn't have to pose for pictures. This wasn't about me being here; I had come to terms with that.

This was all about the celebrity making an appearance that drove the frenzied crowd to near madness. Ryan faltered a bit, unsure at first of what was expected of him. There was always someone instructing, guiding, telling him to go there, stand here, head in that direction. No matter how many times he'd done this before, I could see through the façade that he was nervous.

I watched him take a deep breath and steel his shoulders. In an instant, my humble lover transformed back into the revered A-list movie star. He posed his body with empowered confidence, gave his signature smirk smile, and oozed that natural sexiness that was so graciously captured in thousands of pictures.

It was difficult not to be awed by it.

I panned the entire crowded entrance, the beginning of the red carpet, scanning for familiar faces, for danger, for clarity in the chaos. I stood back while Ryan posed in front of the wall for the throng of photographers. He was moved down the wall in what seemed like five-foot increments while photographers shouted for him to turn in their direction. When he got to the end of the wall, I could see the glaze forming over his eyes from enduring flash after flash.

He held out his hand to me, reclaiming his hold.

"We have—" David started, but Ryan cut him off, tugging me back to the space he'd just occupied on the wall. His hand slid to my ribs, pulling me into his side where I fit perfectly, posing us for the cameras.

My nerves were humming with excitement as I put on my best smile for them, for him.

"We look smashing, darling," he uttered near my ear, joking with a funny accent to lighten the situation. I felt myself relax a bit more, knowing I was exactly where I was supposed to be, supporting my future husband.

After the prerequisite photo op, our entourage hurried us down the standard red carpet—avoiding all of the microphones, from every media outlet imaginable, that tilted out from behind the barriers—

while other lesser-known actors and actresses were basking in the attention. Ryan was scheduled to be interviewed backstage, where he would talk the talk.

We were ushered to an open section of outdoor concrete where I spotted Suzanne Strass, Ryan's co-star in the *Seaside* films. She was chatting it up with a man and another woman when she spotted me; her smile quickly faded as she eyed me up and down, as if I'd offended her by making an appearance here. Call it cattiness, but something in me made me twist the huge diamond on my finger, my silent way of telling her to *suck it*.

I knew that they were going to be presenting a sneak peek of the second *Seaside* film tonight to ramp up the pending premiere, not to mention that he and Suzanne were up for several awards. She wasn't a threat as much as she was a thorn in my side. I'd never forgive her for the trouble she caused when Ryan and I first got together, her silver tongue crafting stories, leading me to believe I was just a foolish conquest of his. I'd have to deal with her a few hundred more times, since Ryan had one more film and two press junkets to go through before he was rid of the franchise. I didn't even want to think about all the interviews and magazine shoots to come.

Before I knew it, Suzanne was standing next to Ryan, pretending to tease him in her own playful way with mock punches. "Hey stranger," she said on a giggle. Ryan gave her the obligatory distant hug but that was the extent of it. She leaned and gave me a quick shoulder hug as if we were long-lost friends who quite possibly were moments away from stabbing each other in the back. "So good to see you."

I was shocked by her overt gesture but played it casual. "Good to see you, too. How have you been?" I figured it was benign enough. I could see she was straining to be polite just as much as I was.

Suzanne became animated, displaying exhaustion from an obvious busy career. "I had literally no time to even get ready for this. I just flew in from New York this morning."

Even though Ryan was involved in another conversation with some man and woman who were blatantly sucking up to him, he entwined his fingers with mine and brought them up to his lips, kissing my left hand while sliding his eyes to Suzanne. I was confused at first until Suzanne scowled, which then had me smiling.

I let her babble on and pretended to be enthralled with her stories even though her presence alone evoked unpleasant memories of my first encounter with this wretched girl. She was the epitome of every diva story you've ever heard about spoiled rich girls, even going so far as to tell us how deplorable the filming conditions were. If her fans ever knew what she was like in real life they'd probably all stop going to see her movies.

I felt Ryan squeeze my hand twice, a silent reminder that he was paying attention to my situation even though he was busy having his career manhandled by David. His thumb skated over my skin, comforting me with his unspoken acknowledgment. I felt cherished by his private gesture.

"Ryan," Suzanne interrupted, "we need to discuss what we're going to do if we win." A twinge of jealousy struck me as she enthusiastically discussed how to accept their award, thinking of clever ways to act out their "best kiss" onstage. Thinking of him kissing anyone made me slightly crazy. I wanted to grab her by the hair and twirl her around but then what would that accomplish? No. I had to get a grip on my jealousy. *He's an actor*, I reminded myself. *Shit.*

Small hands wrapped around my waist, startling me. It was such a relief to see Kelly Gael and her husband, Cal Reynolds, smiling back at me. I hugged her fiercely.

"I can't wait for September," Kelly uttered, bringing up the multi-country press junket for *Seaside II*. The first stop was Berlin. "I need a partner in crime. Please tell me you're going with Ryan."

Ryan leaned back and answered for me. "She's going." And just like that, he resumed his other conversation.

I smiled, slightly astonished that he was even listening, considering all the commotion that was going on around us. Kelly squealed excitedly and clapped her hands, almost springing up and down in her designer pumps. She had just grabbed me to hug me again when I saw another familiar face, though the expression on it appeared sad.

I moved my head to peer around Kelly's hair to get a better look at Ryan's co-star from *Slipknot*—Nicole Devin. I wondered why she was so distraught. Too many people blocked my view, so I stepped back out of Kelly's grasp and took a few sidesteps to my left, forcing Ryan to release my hand.

Nicole was apparently pleading with someone as if she'd done something that she'd regretted and was beseeching forgiveness, but I couldn't see who it was. There was so much drama painted on her face that the desire to find out why became a burning need.

If the guy in the dark suit would just move, I thought, trying to will him to obey my mental plea. It shocked me when he turned his head, as if he'd actually heard me. I squinted, not sure that my eyes were accurate at this distance. He showed more of his profile, and that's when I fully recognized him. I sucked in a deep breath, hoping my vision was betraying me; after all, I did have several glasses of champagne in me.

He glanced completely around, fortunately failing to connect with my gaze, which gave me a false sense of relief considering that I had no idea why he was here, nor did I want him to see me.

Ryan recaptured my hand, breaking my surveillance. "What are you looking at?"

I wanted him to wait so I wouldn't lose track of my targets, but he moved in closer.

I looked up into his eyes, which were showing his concern. "Kyle is over there."

I felt him go rigid. "Where?"

"He's wearing a dark suit. Over there next to the woman in the light gray dress. See him?"

Ryan spotted him and then scowled, none too pleased that he was here. "The guy just won't go away," he growled, seething now.

"Nicole is over there." Some of the crowd moved along and that's when I noticed who she'd been talking to, which confused me even more. "Is that . . . ?"

Ryan drew in a quick breath, exhaling out her name as if to purge his body of toxins. "Lauren."

Wonderful. The bitch from Florida, in the flesh. "Are they arguing?"

"Appears so."

Now I was even more curious, like watching one of those pathetic reality shows where the drama is over-the-top, but for some reason you just can't shut it off. "I didn't know they knew each other."

Ryan's hand tightened on mine, almost to the point of pain. "I didn't know, either."

It obviously bothered Ryan to see them all interacting, although judging by the way Kyle glanced around, he seemed bored with the whole thing. I watched as Kyle's gaze lingered on the very short dress and long, bare legs just a few feet away.

Lauren seemed to be making a point, trying to placate Nicole now. Apparently the heated conversation had taken a new turn. Lauren pulled Nicole in for a hug. I was shocked by their overt friendliness; Nicole had her face pretty much buried in Lauren's neck, and then for a moment I swore they were about to kiss.

Ryan tugged my hand, irritated by it all. "Come."

I wanted to resist, reluctant to tear my eyes away from the girl drama, but his tone left no room for arguments.

BY THE time we reached the after-party at the Soho House in West Hollywood, I had met and mingled with more famous people than I ever thought imaginable. My mind and body were buzzing with the glitz and glamour that came along with Ryan's chosen profession, not to mention being blinded by hundreds of paparazzi flashes on our way in the door.

As we hurried away from the throng of photographers screaming, shouting, and chasing us, I wondered how Ryan managed to stay humble and grounded with all of this attention. Even I felt a tinge of supremacy from being with him, knowing that several of the people around us at this lavish party would kill to be in either of our positions.

Ryan had won three awards tonight for his role as Charles Conroy, and I was so damn proud of him it was hard to not be smug about it. Even when he and Suzanne won the award for Best Kiss, I felt extremely proud. I was glad he didn't kiss her onstage. He promised me he wouldn't, stating that *I* would be the only woman he kissed in public.

As I glanced around the packed affair, my eyes landed on the very lovely ass of Ian Somerhalder. Zac Efron was standing a few feet away, deep in conversation. To hell with the MTV swag gift bags; this was definitely more of a gift than anything. I was morphing into a freaking fangirl being so close to them. My fingers itched to take out my cell, capture a few photos, and send them on to Marie so we could squeal about them.

Screw it.

I tried to stifle my starstruck enthusiasm. Marie would die if she knew I could hit Ian with a spitball, he was that close. I snuck my cell phone out and took a discreet picture, needing to torment her.

"What are you doing?" Ryan asked. He seemed partially amused and slightly disappointed.

I created a new text message. "Tormenting Marie."

He gave me that "are you kidding?" glare, but I ignored him. It was Ian *Smolder*halder for cripes sake and honestly, this close, he was even better-looking. Marie would be jumping over chairs if she were this close to him, asking the poor guy to sign his name on her body somewhere close to her boobs with indelible ink.

I heard Ryan scoff when he spied over my shoulder to see who I captured on my cell. "His ass? You took a close-up of his ass?"

I knew I should feel guilty but altruism warred with those feelings. "It's a gift for Marie. She's going to flip."

"I thought she only had eyes for my ass." The tiny pout on his face was pathetically endearing.

I was glad he was being playful about my paparazzi moment. "She's used the bathroom after you've been in it, Ryan. The mystery and allure are gone now. You've effectively killed it for her."

He rolled his eyes and then frowned at both me and Ian. "That guy takes a shit, too, you know."

I shook my head to disagree. "No, he doesn't. He's still in god status and we all know that gods don't poop."

"Oh, come on! For real?"

"Yes. You didn't poop, either—ever—until she discovered you were a mere mortal."

His eyebrows almost hit his hairline. "So I was a pseudo-god?"

It was hard to text and debate at the same time. "Or a constipated, time-traveling demigod."

Ryan almost spit out his beer. "I can't believe you just said that about me. We're not even married yet and I've lost my god status."

I shrugged while my thumbs kept typing. "I was on to you the moment I saw blood on your face. I knew you could be wounded. Gods can't bleed. Everyone knows they are protected by mystical forces."

His hand landed on my hip, pulling me into his groin. "But you've called me 'God' hundreds of times now. Have you been lying all this time?"

I met his darkened eyes, and was excited by his aggressiveness. "If I tell you the truth, there will be no living with you and your *huge* ego. You know I worship you, so that should count for something."

I watched as his devilish tongue slid out to wet his lips. I wanted those wet lips on me, wanted to taste the flavor of bliss on his tongue.

Ryan held out his cell, angling it. "You want a picture? I want a picture, too," he uttered close to my lips. "Look at the camera and smile, baby." After he captured our smiles, he captured my mouth.

And then someone bumped into me, on purpose.

"Hey! No making out." I looked over into the goofy, disapproving face of one of Ryan's *Seaside* co-stars, Kathleen Jarrett, and took in her awesome black sequin dress and gorgeous eyes. Behind her, her handsome actor boyfriend, Ben Harrison, beamed, flashing those adorable dimples.

"She's taking pictures of Somerhalder's ass," Ryan said dryly, tipping back his glass of beer while he discreetly indented his partial erection into my hip.

Kat gapped at me. "Really?"

I sucked in a quick breath from feeling the unspoken need in Ryan's pants and the silent point he was trying to make. Kat was waiting for an answer, so no sense denying it. "It's for Marie. She'll get a kick out of it. I've got to get one of Zac Efron, too. She'll freak."

"Ooh, I know him. You want to meet him?" Kat asked, bouncing excitedly.

"No, she doesn't," Ryan answered for me.

Kat rolled her eyes and finished her drink. "Jealous much?"

Ryan scoffed, taking another sip. I patted his gloriously tight abs. "He knows I love him and only him."

Soon we were surrounded by most of the *Seaside* cast, all of us laughing, joking, and downing plenty of expensive alcohol. Even Suzanne was tolerable.

Kat set her glass down on the table. "I need to use a bathroom. Taryn, go with me?"

Ryan leaned over and gave me a quick kiss. "Don't get lost."

I took my hand off his thigh and followed Kat through the tightly packed crowd. Why is it that when you're slightly buzzed and wearing uncomfortable shoes, the ladies' room becomes a half-mile walk? Kat squeezed past some people, turning to grab my hand to pull me through. I couldn't help but giggle with her when we got to an open space.

She wrapped her arm around mine. "That was fun."

I was still laughing, having a blast when I sort of fumbled in my tracks, unsure if my eyes were deceiving me. Sure enough, two girls were making out hot and heavy in a darkened corner.

Holy hell. Welcome to Hollywood.

Should I be shocked or turned on by their blatant public display? The whole thing had me quite bemused until one of them broke away and made eye contact.

I staggered. *Holy hell, that's ...*

Lauren Delaney.

Sucking face with Nicole Devin.

Never in a million years ...

The second Lauren saw me she pulled back from Nicole, shoving her away, apparently flustered from being caught.

"What are you looking at?" Kat asked, yanking on my arm.

I nodded my chin and Kat guffawed loudly, apparently just as shocked as I was.

"Oh my God. I ... Wait until I tell Ryan." I thought Kat was going to double over with laughter. "He's turning all his leading ladies into lesbians."

I gave her a stern look. "That's not funny."

"Oh yes it is! What are the odds?" She looked over her shoulder. "That means Suzanne is next."

We were outside the women's bathroom when my cell rang. It was Marie, probably calling to squeal in my ear over Ian Somerhalder's exquisite derriere.

"I almost touched it!" I blurted excitedly, not even bothering to say hello.

I could tell by the first sound she made that she was upset. "Taryn, listen. Tammy just called. Pete was just rushed back to the hospital. I don't know what's going on but she said that he tried to walk and couldn't feel his leg so she called the ambulance. I guess he fell in their bedroom."

My slightly inebriated condition mixed with a power shot of worried adrenaline made me feel lightheaded. I covered my other ear with my hand, trying to hear her over the chatter and noise. By the time I hung up with her, I felt as if I'd been socked in the stomach. I left Kat behind in the bathroom and hurried back to the table to tell Ryan.

Ryan halted in mid-sentence when he saw me. "Tar?" One word that said, *You only went to the bathroom. What the hell happened?*

I glanced at the cell still in my hand while horrible visions of Pete not being able to walk down the aisle of his own wedding plagued my thoughts. "They just took Pete back to the hospital." I filled him in with what little I knew.

He took a deep breath then Kat suddenly bounced up behind him, all too excited to tell him what we witnessed on our way to the bathroom.

Ryan's mouth fell open. "You're shitting me."

Kat was having too much fun teasing him like this. "Full-on tongue action."

I actually saw him shudder. "You're positive it was Lauren and Nicole Devin? Positive?"

Kat looked at me and we both nodded.

Ryan ran a hand through his hair, digesting this new information. "Wow. Good for them, I guess."

I tried to change the subject, talking about anything that didn't involve things that Ryan would stew over, but I could see that the news had affected him, slightly changing his mood. He was with Lauren for a while when they dated a few years ago; they'd been intimate for months. Ryan was not the type of man who could switch off his emotions.

Instead of letting it affect us, we mixed and mingled with so many celebrities that I was awestruck. It seemed that everyone asked the same sort of questions: What are you working on now? Did you hear about this person or that person? Most of the conversations ended with enthusiastic promises of keeping in touch and "hope to work with you sometime" comments. It was hard to discern between true intentions and crafted bullshit, but I'd like to think I guessed accurately.

Ryan had just made a private comment to me when I saw Kyle storm through the crowd on a direct course for Lauren. Someone else had engaged Ryan in conversation and after being introduced, I kept part of my attention on watching Kyle and Lauren. Kyle was pissed. I could tell because I'd seen that face before. Lauren looked stubborn, planting a foot and crossing her arms over her chest in defiance.

Kyle reached for her but she rolled her shoulder away from his grasp. He apparently wasn't going to take no for an answer, snatching her wrist and pulling her off balance so she had no choice but to follow him. He towed her along like an insolent puppy fighting the leash, and never looked back at her as she struggled.

As much as I was curious about their interactions, I was glad that he seemed to have found a new outlet for his misguided attentions.

PHOTOGRAPHERS SURROUNDED us like hungry jackals as we hustled through LAX. My heart pounded in my chest from the chaos that ensued when we stepped into the terminal. Men were yelling, running sideways, aiming those nasty black cameras at us. So the famous Ryan Christensen was getting on another plane. Why is that even remotely newsworthy? Such nonsense. Ryan tugged his duffle bag up on his shoulder and grabbed my hand as Mike and three extra hired bodyguards moved us through the entrance. Two airport police officers flanked us, telling the paparazzi to mind the other passengers and to keep their distance.

We were ushered down a separate row to go through security and I nearly tripped over my own feet trying to walk as fast as possible. Ryan glanced back at me when I stumbled, then he stopped long enough to put my body in front of his.

"You okay?" he uttered quietly, walking his fingers over the small of my back as he nudged me along.

I nodded, slightly mortified by the prospect of having my little stumble be on the next episode of *TMZ*.

"This is fucking annoying," Ryan growled to me privately under his breath.

I tried not to spy over his shoulder but the paparazzi were still taking photos and filming us as we came to a halt in the security line.

Ryan tapped Mike's arm. "Why are we stopped?" We were standing in a special line but there were still like twenty people in front of us with a pack of rabid idiots forty feet behind us filming and photographing.

I heard a faint chime just as Ryan asked, "Is your cell ringing?" I thought I had turned it off, knowing it would have to be off for the flight. I didn't recognize the number and considered ignoring it until thoughts of Pete being in the hospital crossed my mind.

"Is this Taryn? Taryn Mitchell?" the unfamiliar male voice asked hesitantly.

As quickly as the notion came, I pictured some obscure religious-message, flower-sending weirdo named Jerry or Jeremy calling me. I had the sudden urge to just hang up. "Who is this?"

"It's ahh . . . Joe."

I gasped from the slight shock.

"Joe Malone," he continued, clearing his throat nervously. "Your um, father."

CHAPTER 17

Reconnected

RYAN NODDED HIS chin at me. "Who's that?"

"Joe," I whispered, both to answer Ryan and to assure my brain that I was actually talking to the man who fathered me. I had almost convinced myself that he'd never call.

Ryan pulled his sunglasses off, hooking them over the front of his T-shirt, and focused all of his attention on me. The man on the other end of my phone sounded close to tears as his breath stuttered in my ear. I knew how he felt; I wanted to cry with him.

"Yeah," he choked. "Oh God. I, um . . . never thought I'd . . . that we'd . . . Oh God, I don't even know where to begin. It's been so long. Please, let me hear your voice. Say something. Anything."

"I don't know what to say. How are you?"

Joe laughed uncomfortably. "I'm good, sweetheart. I'm good. A little speechless right now, though."

"Me too."

It was hard to concentrate. Airport security officers were surrounding us, moving a section of the nylon barricades out of the way to usher us through into another pathway toward a TSA security agent.

Ryan nodded at me. "Tar, you're going to have to call him back."

I knew I needed to move, to get through security and away from the spying paparazzi, but my feet didn't want to move. My hand gripped my phone tighter, fumbling through an awkward apology for our bad timing. Joe nervously chuckled in my ear, being quite understanding that I was not able to give him any more of my time at the moment while going through baggage scan.

As I stowed my cell away in my bag, sadness mixed with my elation. The most important part was that he reached out to make the
first connection. That was a huge step.

Ryan pulled his shoes off, dropping them into a plastic bin. I
slipped my purse from my shoulder and followed suit, hating with a
passion this part of flying.

It wasn't until we were in the air and getting served our first bev-
erage that Ryan asked me about the call. "Talk to me. What did he
have to say?"

It was hard to talk with several passengers blatantly gawking at
us. "He mentioned getting together."

Ryan's expression said *that's good and is that something you want
to do?*

I answered his nonverbal question with "Yes. I need to."

He squeezed my hand and gave me a resolute nod, assuring me
that he'd make that happen.

"OH MY God, Taryn. I'm gonna choke her," Marie announced loudly
and in no uncertain terms into my ear. After spending a few hours on
a plane, a forty-minute drive to the hotel, and a restless night's sleep
on a very stiff hotel mattress, I was not awake enough to understand
her reasons. I set my coffee cup down and held my cell away and
could still hear her clearly.

Ryan was rubbing the sleep out of his eyes as he took the silver lid
off the omelet that room service had just delivered. We had slept in,
since Ryan didn't have to be anywhere until one o'clock.

"You know that girl Gary has been seeing? Well, I just found out
that she's a friend of Tammy's."

I winced as my stomach felt drop-kicked. "You're kidding?"

"Nope. I wish I was. I am so mad I can kill them both."

"How did you find this out?"

Marie scoffed. "Because the whore is in *your* pub kitchen right now helping Tammy out, that's how. I just came down to prep and stock and there she was, baking and shit like it's no big deal. I cannot believe Tammy would do this to me! I thought we were friends, but friends don't hook up their other friends with *my* scumbag soon-to-be-ex husband."

I pulled the sheer curtain back, looking out at the gray skies over Vancouver, thinking about how quickly wonderful things can turn to shit.

"Did you say anything to her?"

Marie hemmed. "No. I thought she looked familiar, until it dawned on me how I knew her. She'd better stay the hell out of the pub, that's all I have to say. She sets one foot in here and I swear to God I'm going to hammer-fist her. As a matter of fact, screw it. I'm going back there and giving *both* of those hags a piece of my mind."

I could hear her on the move. "Wait a minute! Stop! I don't think you want to do that."

She groaned in anger. "Oh yeah, I do. She crossed the line by bringing her here. I'm gonna—"

"Wait." I scrambled, watching Ryan saunter in his boxers over to the dining table. "I have a question first."

She huffed. "What?"

"Boxers or briefs?"

"*What?*"

"Mike. Is he a boxers or a briefs guy?"

Ryan's eyes glared up over the top of his laptop screen while he chewed his breakfast. I held out a finger for him to hold on to that disapproving thought for a second—I had a point to make.

Marie sucked in some air. "Boxer briefs. Best invention ever. With that elastic band riding real low." She sighed a bit. "He's got those Ken doll leg-hinge muscle-gap things going on. You know what I mean? The V pockets?"

I'd just so happened to have been staring at my own set of amazing leg hinges, which disappeared like an arrow into his shorts, moments before. "Yes, I do." Ryan smirked at me, apparently taking my dirty purr and hungry eyes for what they were worth.

"Thanks," Marie whispered out, sounding a bit calmer. "I know you're trying to calm me down but I still want to go back there and confront her. Bringing that girl here is *not cool*, Tar. I don't care how you color it. Is she doing this to rub my nose in it? I mean, why?"

"I honestly don't know, but I promise I'll find out. Just swear to me you'll stay out of the kitchen until I get to the bottom of it, okay?"

As soon as I hung up with Marie, I took a deep breath and scrolled down to Tammy's number, knowing loyalties were about to be tested. Right off the bat she greeted me with a snarky snip to her voice, which didn't bode well.

After getting a quick update on how Pete was doing, I got to the second purpose of my call.

"I don't know how to ask this so I'm just going to come right out with it. I know you have someone there with you today, and I want to know if it's the girl that Gary is seeing."

Tammy sighed—loudly. "What difference does it make?"

Cocky was not the way to deal with me right now. "Are you kidding?"

"I have a business to run and I needed the help. What do you want me to say?"

If I could have climbed through my phone and shaken her, I would have. "And you didn't think that this would be a problem? My God, Tammy. Are you that insensitive?"

"I'm not trying to be insensitive, Taryn. Pete is laid up, I've got orders to fill and a wedding to cater tomorrow, and I don't see anyone else offering to help. You know with Pete out of work I'm the only one earning any money. And now we have hospital bills piling up and ambulance bills to pay. I'm sorry if that upsets people, but I had no other choice."

Now I was rubbing my forehead. "And your only choice was to enlist the help of the girl who broke Marie's marriage apart?"

Tammy growled. "Amy didn't do that. Look, I don't have time to talk about this now."

I wanted to scream. "Fine. But I would prefer if you didn't rub it in Marie's face."

"I'm not rubbing anything—"

"You brought her there, Tammy! Are you forgetting that Marie lives upstairs now because her cheating husband locked her out of her own damn house?"

I could hear her frustrated huff. "I didn't think she'd care. She's moved on with Ryan's bodyguard, hasn't she?"

"That's not the point. No woman wants to see her replacement, Tammy. Ever."

"Well, she's going to have to get used to it sooner or later. I might as well tell you now that Pete and his brother, Jim, are not speaking to each other and Pete's had it this time. He wants Gary to be his best man now, which means that I don't have a maid of honor since my sister-in-law, Deb, was it. So I've asked Amy to be my maid of honor so Marie doesn't have to feel obligated."

"Unbelievable . . ."

"What? She said she didn't want to come if Gary was going to be there anyway, so I don't know what the big deal is."

My anger bumped up to an entirely new notch.

"I thought Marie would be relieved since she's busy running the bar now that you're not around much," Tammy said. "She doesn't have time to help me anyway. Neither do you. You're never home anymore."

I didn't need to be a rocket scientist to figure out why she was being so pissy, but her tantrum was uncalled for.

"That's a little unfair, Tammy."

I heard what sounded like a metal tray hitting the floor at the same time Tammy said, "Oh, shit . . . Marie, just wait a minute . . ."

I could hear Marie's voice loud and clear. "It's a simple question. I just want to know how long you've been fucking my husband, that's all."

Oh, shit was right. "Tammy, get your friend out of there." I heard the girl, Amy, stuttering in the background, saying something about not knowing he was married when they met.

"Marie, he never told her he was married—"

"Don't even fucking talk to me right now, Tammy. You mean to tell me *your friend* didn't know he was married? You think I'm that naïve to believe that you didn't have a hand in this?"

"I didn't," Tammy pleaded. "I didn't know about it until after they'd met."

"We went to L.A. together and you didn't think to tell me that he was screwing around?"

I felt like I was in the middle of a war that was being broadcasted over cell phones. I felt completely incapable of fighting for the cause.

"It wasn't my place to tell you that."

What? Oh, bullshit.

Marie's voice got even louder. *Good.* "Wasn't your place? I thought we were friends, Tammy. Friends that have each other's backs through the good, bad, and ugly. But I guess I was sadly mistaken."

"I am your friend! You are blow—"

"Not anymore!" Marie shrieked. "And you . . . You even think about setting foot inside my pub and I will beat you to within an inch of your life. Understood?"

I heard the girl mumble something.

"Good. I hope you two are very happy together. He's a cheap bastard and a lousy lay and he's all yours."

And that's when Tammy hung up on me, leaving me rattled and riled and hanging in the wind three thousand miles away.

"I was afraid of this," Ryan said, staring at his laptop while waiting on a call of his own.

I was clutching my cell, chewing on the edge of it, wondering when and how everything started falling apart. "Afraid of what?"

He glanced over the opened screen, then went back to doing what he was doing. "Friends. Fights. Anger. Jealousy. All of that shit."

I was scratching my head, trying to figure out what he meant.

"I didn't think that it would happen, though. I mean, one of the reasons I even considered pursuing you and pulling you into my crazy life was because I saw how tight you were with your core friends. I didn't think that they'd break their bonds once we started getting serious. Guess I was wrong."

Either he was speaking man mumbo-jumbo or I was still dazed from my call and missing the point. I squinted at him. "Um. Huh?"

"The fighting. It's started. I used to have a huge group of friends, but once the first movie came out, one by one they started dropping like flies. Things get fucked-up. Same shit is happening to you."

Ryan squatted down in front of me and leveled his eyes on mine. "I'm sorry."

"Why are you sorry? My friends are fighting, Ryan, not us. I don't know what you caught of that conversation, but I just found out that the new girl that Gary is seeing is one of Tammy's friends, who just so happens to be in my pub kitchen helping Tammy out right now. Marie went down to open up and ran right into the girl."

Ryan frowned. "I thought maybe . . . Friends get weird and shit when all of a sudden you have money and they don't, you're traveling and they aren't. I just know that the petty shit comes to the surface and the next thing you know you're fighting and at each other's throats. So many people want fortune and fame but what they don't realize is that it comes with a ton of heartache."

I rested my taxed brain in my hand. "I still don't get where you're going with this. My friends are fighting—"

"And you feel compelled to pick a side."

"Well, yeah, to a certain extent. Especially when one is purposely causing hurt to the other. I'd take a stand regardless, and whether or not my future husband was über-famous shouldn't be a factor."

"Yeah, but—"

"Yeah, but what? *You* are who I've chosen to be with. If my friends have a problem with that—which I don't think they do, but regardless—if they can't be on board with my happiness and they feel threatened by my choice, then they really aren't good friends to begin with. And if they *are* jealous, then I'd hope they'd keep it to themselves, as I am certainly not flaunting anything under their noses. Tammy is under a lot of stress and she's lashing out. I get that. We girls go crazy every now and then. I can even forgive her for keeping her nose out of other people's marriage problems. But what I will not excuse is her knowing that her friend is banging another good friend's husband and bringing that nonsense to my house."

Ryan put his hands on his hips. "I love you."

I smiled. "I know you do. I love you more."

That earned me a trademarked lip smirk nose wrinkle. "You think Tammy hooked them up?"

I hated to think the worst of people, especially friends in my closest circle, but over the years I'd seen so many show me their dark side that I now knew even the sweetest, the kindest could turn horrid.

SPEAKING OF people turning horrid, I was just about to shut the lid on Ryan's laptop if I had to listen to another minute of his manager's condescending bullshit during their online video conference.

I was having my own conversation with our publicist, Trish, over some changes to Ryan's schedule when Ryan hammered his fist into the table.

"I lost forty-five grand in the last six months, so you can shove all of the 'let Mercer handle that' bullshit. Fucking people need a wake-up call that I *am* paying attention to my financial statements. If they are incapable of keeping me from losing money then I will find another firm to manage it."

I was updating my master calendar when Ryan's elbows hit the table. I heard him end his call and when I looked over, he was holding his head in his hands. He had so many people poking their noses into his business, telling him how to run his life, I wondered how long he'd be able to endure the constant pressure of it all.

I set my pen down and crossed the room. As soon as he looked up at me, I straddled his thighs, wrapping my arms around his warm, bare shoulders, and pulled him in tightly.

I closed my eyes and rested my cheek on his head, rubbing my fingers over his hair, his neck, while his arms cinched around me. We sat in silence for a long time, just breathing and being, chasing the insanity away as best we could.

Ryan's eyes met mine and we softly kissed, reassuring each other with weary smiles.

"Change your mind yet?" he asked warily, locking his thumb through the belt loop of my jeans.

I shook my head, knowing what he was asking. "Never. You're mine."

That definitely pleased him. He gave me a crooked, unsure look. "Till death do us part?"

I gave him a soft kiss. "Maybe just a bit beyond that."

"So, tell me. Tammy's stressing out. Makes me wonder what we'll be up against when we're planning our wedding."

I took a little breath. "Honestly? I really don't want a big to-do, Ryan. I'm thinking sweet and simple."

"Sweet and simple, huh?"

I nodded. "You know—family and friends. Romantic. Elegant. Maybe some twinkle lights in the trees."

He wiggled his thighs, bouncing me a bit. "Twinkle lights. Okay, what else?"

I paused to think about it. "Outdoors maybe."

"Like tents and stuff?"

That thought made me wrinkle my nose. "I don't think I want the big, white tent thing."

Ryan scratched his cheek. "You want to do the church thing or . . . ?"

I really had no preference. "I'm not set on anything and honestly, I haven't been in a church since my dad died, so ... What do *you* want?"

His noncommittal shrug was the easy way out. "Naked on a beach?"

I frowned and gave him a nudge.

"Really!" he went on. "I don't know. Outdoors sounds good. Or inside somewhere. I'm completely open to suggestions."

"I think we have time to figure it out. Maybe we should work on living together in sin first."

Ryan slid his hands over my rear, tensing his fingers. "I like that idea. I started drafting some designs." Suddenly he was completely rejuvenated, as if he had a new fire burning in his gut. He flipped open the sketchpad he always doodled in.

"All right, time to start designing our house."

RYAN WAS back on set filming when I got to talk to my birth father again. We spoke on the phone for almost an hour, neither of us really minding the time. Joe was easy to talk to and although we kept the conversation light and informative, I could tell that his words were filled with regret.

While Ryan filmed, I stayed in his trailer, going over everything from our latest financial statements to picking out front doors for our future house.

Ryan's set trailer rocked a little when he bounded in. "Hey babe," he said, eying me over. "What's going on?"

I watched as he set some papers on the counter. "Oh, where to begin? You sure you want to hear this?"

Ryan took a bottle of cold water out of the small refrigerator. "Not when you start off that way, Taryn. But yeah. Start sharing."

"You have time?"

He took a sip and tilted his head. "I have fifteen minutes. Can I have the abridged version?"

"Okay . . . Marie and Tammy are still fighting, Pete is miserable being laid up on his couch and out of work, your mom said that she's throwing our engagement party at their house on July twenty-second, which is on both of our calendars now, and somewhere in the last week Cory started sleeping with the new waitress Marie hired." I wiggled my cell. "Oh, and I talked to Joe."

He looked a bit surprised. "Wow. I thought all the drama was out there." He pointed. "Cory nailing that short blonde I met, or did Marie hire someone else?"

"No. It's the one you met—Kara."

Ryan nodded. "Well, good for him, I guess."

"Not so good for me. Especially if there's a dramatic breakup."

He slid into the dinette and sat across from me. "That's the shit you have to deal with being a business owner. Although it's really Marie's problem, I suppose."

"It's my bar. It's my problem. One that I've been avoiding for weeks now. She's got her own drama to deal with."

Ryan scratched his eyebrow with his thumb and frowned at me. "I can't tell you what to do, but you know you can't be in two places at once. And Mike is so miserable, I'm about to send him off to Seaport if he doesn't get to see Marie soon."

He was rather grumpy lately.

"She wants to become a bodyguard."

I was surprised when he didn't seem fazed by that. He took another swig of water and I watched him swallow. Something about that was quite sexy, actually. "Mike told me."

The news that Mike talked to him about it was also surprising, since Mike wasn't one to share much. "Mike told you?"

He nodded. "Yeah. We talked about it quite a bit."

"According to Marie, he's being extremely supportive about it."

Ryan twisted his lips as if he were hiding a secret. "Love will do that to ya."

That surprised me. "He's in love?"

"Isn't it obvious? She's very attractive, but she also is a bit of a scrapper. Feisty little thing, ya know? That's exactly what he needs."

I smiled. "Yeah, I know. She doesn't take a lot of crap. She's worse if she's been drinking."

He crawled out of the bank seat and sat down on the couch, putting his feet up. "And what are your thoughts on all of that? You'd lose your bar manager."

"I think she should do whatever makes her happy."

He rested his head back into his hands. "I agree. Especially if she and Mike stick. Would be best if their jobs complemented each other. That's just a win-win for us."

"Win-win?"

He gave me his *isn't it obvious?* eyes. I wasn't about to ask. I was sort of stuck on his other innuendo. "You want me to sell the bar." It wasn't a question, but it definitely came out of my mouth as a whispered realization.

His frown said it for him. He took another drink of his water, eyeing me before he spoke. "I want you to do what's right for us. Having the business is great but you being constantly worried about it isn't, so something needs to give."

He was right, in a way, but then again we'd been engaged only a few weeks. Was I wrong for wanting a fallback plan? One ace stashed up my sleeve in case of emergencies? After all, I had my own sense of self-preservation.

"Can we discuss this some other time?"

Without hesitation, he said, "Yep."

"How are things on set? How's Nicole doing?"

Ryan seemed undecided. "She's been toeing the line."

"You think she's staying clean?"

He scratched his eyebrow. "She doesn't have much of a choice since I insisted on her getting weekly drug screenings. She can be pissy toward me all she wants; while she's here working on *my* film, she will keep that shit out of her body and her head in the game."

I nodded. "Did you talk to her about getting some drug counseling?"

I knew he was not keen on intervening. "No, but I did have a private chat with her. One slipup and I'd see to it that she gets hauled off set in cuffs."

"You didn't?"

"I most certainly did. I don't have time to babysit. She has to deal with her own shit or else. Anyway, that's not our problem. I have to go back soon. I came to get you. I need you there."

"You need me there?" I gave him my best *are you for real?* look.

He picked at his costume, which was a blue pair of very cool rock climbing pants, a look that I'd be sure to buy for him the next time I went shopping. "Yeah. I like knowing you're there."

"I don't want to be in the way. I figured I was a distraction."

"Taryn, you just breathing is a distraction. Knowing you're on the lot, holed up in my trailer doing God knows what that I can't see, is a distraction."

Ditto.

And here I thought I made him nervous. Hearing that he wanted me there made my insides warm. I was learning so much by being a silent observer and I'd much rather be out there than in here. "Well, since you need me . . ."

Ryan knifed his body up and then he was inches from my face, letting me know his thoughts. "I need you. You're my muse."

I knew he was messing with me but his sexy lips made me think about how damn lucky I was, especially imagining him being all athletic and sweaty on set. "Your muse, huh?"

He grinned and nodded. "Uh huh."

"I thought I was your sex slave."

That got me a wider grin and a sexy-as-hell kiss. "That, too," he breathed, tasting of the mint gum I had slipped into his pocket.

I wanted his tongue again. "You taste good."

"I'll let you taste me all over if you want—later. Reminds me, there's this one position we haven't tried yet and I was wondering if you'd be game?"

His face was so close; I had to lean back. "Just one?"

Ryan's eyes narrowed. "You have a dirty mind and a mouth that makes me have all sorts of ideas. That's why you're perfect for me."

I met his lips and gave him a wicked kiss, growling from the strain of having to separate us. "Before you get carried away . . ."

"Then you better come up with another distraction besides putting your tongue in my mouth."

I fought his pull and murmured, "I talked to Joe for almost an hour."

He looked surprised, edging back a bit. "Yeah? And?"

I fought back my disappointment and sudden sadness, trying to stay positive on the subject, but it was hard. The man who fathered me was keeping me at arm's length, and well, it hurt. I felt more rejection than acceptance in that hour.

"It was good, but . . . well . . . He told me about his wife and his family. He has two young daughters who apparently are huge fans of yours."

Ryan's eyes narrowed, reading me like a book again. "Is that so? Apparently he also said something that upset you. I can see it in your eyes."

I sat back. "He said that he'd always regretted giving me up but he was young and didn't know the first thing about raising a baby and . . . I can tell he's full of remorse."

Ryan sat down next to me. "I can imagine. So we going there to meet him?"

"No."

"And why not?"

"Ryan, I have not been a part of his life for a very long time."

"So?"

"It's not that simple. We talked and, well, he's glad I know the truth about him but said he's not ready to tell his wife about me yet.

He's not sure how she'll take it since he's never told her about fathering a child when he was a teenager. He's afraid the news will upset her too much."

Ryan rubbed his forehead, appearing annoyed. "Well, that's too fucking bad."

"Ryan, it's his choice. I can't expect him to put his family's happiness in jeopardy, no matter how much I want to meet him."

Ryan shrugged a bit. "A man should own up to his situation."

"He was a kid when I came along. I can't put that on him. He's got to decide what's best for them."

He seemed to disagree. "What's he do for a living?"

For a moment, it sounded like he was being protective, like he needed to know if Joe was good enough to be my absentee real father. "He's a master electrician. He owns his own company. He said he does a lot of new construction and they're so busy they can hardly keep up." There, that ought to be good enough.

Ryan's lips twitched and he nodded his silent approval. "Good, honest job. Sounds like a hard worker."

Who are you and what happened to my twenty-seven-year-old fiancé?

"Does his wife work?"

I nodded. "She's a dental hygienist."

That got an eyebrow raise and a few more head bobs of approval. It was almost like saying she was related to his dentist father, in the way he seemed good with that information.

"And the girls? How old are they?"

"Abby is fourteen and Eli is eleven. They sound like great kids."

With that Ryan seemed to relax a bit, but still he said, "Listen. I know that you've been dealing with this . . . this shock. And I'm going to continue to be patient and supportive, but I will not allow someone you barely know to upset you. Before you opened that box, things were fine. Well, as fine as they could be considering, but now this has tossed you for a loop and I don't give a shit if he's the king of Siam. If he doesn't bring goodness and happiness to you, then he's going to be cut off very quickly. Mark my words, Taryn. I won't let this eat at you. If he doesn't want to own up to his shit and be a man about it, then he can go back to being unknown to us. You've had enough hurt for one lifetime and I won't stand for someone bringing more sadness on you. I won't."

"I know," I grumbled quietly.

"No, I don't think you do. Your entire life you've been obliviously happy. Now you question everything more than you did before. But what you need to focus on are the things that are right and true in your life. Me. My family. We are constants. I'm not going anywhere and you know that. But some guy you don't know who donated some sperm is not worth the head space he's taking up. Dan and Jennifer were your parents and I know they were taken way too early from you, but you need a mom or a dad; my parents are all too willing to step up and give you what you need.

"This guy . . . this Joe person, he makes no difference to our lives. You and me—that's all we've got. And if your friends want to make choices that don't include a future with us, I've got no problem with that, either. None. Cut that shit clean off and we'll make new friends. We surround ourselves with people who care and love us. That's how we roll."

He was right. So freaking right, as usual. I'd recognized my fears of abandonment when I thought Ryan's parents were moving him out of the apartment right before we got engaged. Everyone I loved eventually left me. Everyone. And now some guy I didn't even know was tugging on my emotions and twisting my thoughts just because I needed to get something back; needed to validate why this information about me being adopted was even dropped on me.

Still through all of that, I almost wanted to laugh at him. "That's how we roll?"

"That's how we roll," he said, serious at first until the edge of his mouth tipped up. "You have no relationship with him. He doesn't want to make one with you, no problem. One less person fucking with our happiness, as far as I'm concerned."

I smiled at that thought; how he was able to make me love him more and more every day.

His eyes dropped down to my lips, his head tilted in the opposite direction, and he murmured, "C'mere" as he leaned down to kiss me. I wrapped my arm over his shoulder so I could pull my body even closer while my other hand found those soft curls of hair by his neck. He groaned in my mouth as I tugged on his hair.

"I need to spend an entire day kissing you," I breathed out on his lips.

He pulled on the tips of my hair hanging right next to my breast. "Tomorrow. All morning. No phones, no computers. Your mouth and your body are mine."

Someone banged on our trailer door. "Ten minutes, Ryan."

His shoulders slumped, as did mine. His eyes skittered over to my laptop screen. "What you got there?"

I'd forgotten about my Internet searching. "The totally awesome front door for our new house. You like?"

"Yeah, let me see it." His lips curled just a bit and he sat up, moving the computer closer to get a better look. "*Nice*. Add it to the list."

Well, that was easy.

"You want to see more?"

"Why? You design the whole house?"

"No, but Marie sent some pictures. She said this is where we should get married." I opened the email and made the attachments full size on the screen.

Ryan's eyes scrunched together before going wide. "Wow. No, scroll back. Back. Stop. Holy shit, that's cool. Where is that?"

"Italy. A place called the Grotta Palazzese. What do you think?"

Ryan's smile widened, taking in the restaurant. It was located inside the opening of a cave and had breathtaking views of the vast

Mediterranean Sea. "That's wild. Italy? Is that what you want? Something like that?"

I shrugged, not firmly decided on anything. "I don't know. But that definitely looks like a cool place to have dinner."

He gave me his look, the one that said he'd fly me anywhere I wanted and give me the wedding of my dreams as long as I said *yes* along the way.

"I think we need to go there and check it out, even if it's just for dinner. Brings us back to freeing up your responsibilities, though, Tar."

"I know. And I think I have a solution."

Ryan raised a brow. "You do?"

After I told him my idea, he was more than happy. He was downright relieved.

GOING TO Italy was easier said than done. After spending another few days with Ryan in Vancouver, I flew back to Rhode Island by myself. The month of June was almost over, Marie was slightly miserable, Tammy wasn't really speaking to either of us, and Pete was drowning in debt, his days of climbing ladders and doing manual labor for a living on hold indefinitely.

To say I was looking forward to returning to all of this would be a lie. At least the paparazzi and gossip rags were being somewhat nice, printing photos of our happiness when they caught Ryan and me out shopping a few days ago.

Ryan and I had a nice time wandering around, taking in some sights and spending some money on stuff we didn't need but could afford. I was sporting a gorgeous antique diamond bracelet that Ryan spent a small fortune on and he bought himself a nice platinum chain with a stainless steel dog tag that had a tribal design on one side and my name engraved on the other.

But now I was sitting in the passenger seat of my car, Marie behind the wheel, since she picked me up at the airport, and the amazing time I had with Ryan sadly becoming another memory.

I watched the landscape zoom by once again, feeling a sense of déjà vu, and wondering if things would settle.

Going back to Mitchell's Pub was starting to feel like a burden, and that was not good.

"Did you book your flight?" I asked, wondering when the other shoe was going to drop.

Marie glanced over quickly. "Yeah. Class starts July ninth."

My mind flipped through the calendar, knowing I already had a problem, but I wasn't about to let it halt her plans.

"You're going to miss Ryan's wrap party because of me."

I felt my shoulders tense as I glanced over at her. "Mike needs to keep his big mouth shut."

Marie barked out a laugh, "I know you're supposed to be in Pittsburgh at his parents' on the twenty-second as well, which you failed to tell me about."

"I wasn't keeping it a secret." Well, I was, but I wasn't going to tell her until after she'd left.

She passed a slow-moving camper in the center lane. "Liar. You said you didn't have anything firm until the Teen Choice Awards on August seventh."

And therein was my problem, right in a nutshell. Since cloning wasn't possible, something had to give, just like Ryan had said. "You need to worry about your schedule and leave me to worry about mine," I growled, teasingly of course.

"I thought you were trying to go to Italy the week before that?"

"No. Ryan's not sure if he'll have to go to L.A. earlier. He's waiting to hear." I dug around in my purse for my calendar. "When are you coming back then?"

"July twenty-eighth." Her voice did an excited upswing, making it sound like a question. I could tell she was treading lightly. She also knew that I had no one to fall back on.

"You'll come back a lean, mean fighting machine," I joked, trying to let her know I was totally supporting her decisions.

Marie gave me a weak smile. "I don't have to go for this session, Taryn. I could put it off. Give it a year, maybe. I dunno. I know I'm putting you in a tight spot."

I adjusted my ring. "No. Definitely not."

"Taryn, I'm rushing this. I don't even know if Mike wants a relationship with me. I'm fighting with Gary over who gets to keep the damn toaster and shit. I shouldn't be making any big moves."

"If this is what you want then you go for it now. Time to do what you want to do for once."

"But—"

"But what? Are you going to doubt your desires because you're unsure of Mike's intentions? You want to be a bodyguard, knowing what it entails, then do it. And no buts. I haven't seen you this excited about something in years. You want to forge a new career path, then now is the time. You're wasting your education and talents being stuck behind the bar."

"I'm not stuck . . ."

"Yes, you are. We both are. It's time for the next chapter."

"I need an income, Taryn," she countered. "I can't go without a job."

I sighed. "We've had this discussion already."

"Taryn, you can't pay me a salary that I didn't work for. You've already loaned me money for the lawyer. And it's going to be awhile until I see a settlement from my divorce so I can pay you back."

"Marie, what did I say?"

She huffed. "It's not right. You can't keep bailing your friends out."

I turned in my seat to look at her, keeping the fact that I was going to cash out some of my inheritance to cover things if I needed to. The bar was making more money but not enough to cover several full-time salaries. "You would do the same for me and you know it."

"You're going to have to hire another bartender or two and someone will have to be there to manage the place. And I can't expect you to hire someone for only two weeks and then fire them when I get back. Cory is great, but you know as well as I do that he's young and isn't ready to take on that amount of responsibility. And what happens if I get down there and find out I can't handle it? Mike said this is pretty intense stuff—like combat training, firing a gun while rolling on the ground and stuff. I mean, what the hell do I know about disarming someone or kicking someone's ass? Last time I was in a fight was when we were in high school and I punched Sophie Lithgow in the face for calling me a slut."

I laughed. "It's a start. And *that* was classic, by the way. She deserved that—calling *both* of us sluts."

"Yeah, but I at least earned the title," Marie boasted.

"No you did not."

Then she gave me a crooked stare, insinuating that she did.

We were silent for another half mile when I finally said what was swirling in my thoughts. "Ryan sort of hinted again that I should sell the bar."

Marie's mouth popped open. "Why?"

"Because I can't be in two places at once."

She groaned softly. "You sure you want to do that?"

My knee-jerk answer was no, but I said, "I don't know. I'm thinking about it."

She shook her head adamantly. "I don't think you should sell it."

I was thankful she said that. "Is it wrong of me to want to have a fallback plan?"

"Hell no! Look at me. Bastard locked me out of my own damn house! I barely escaped with the clothes on my back and now he's threatening to smash our china that his aunt got us just so I don't try to take it in the divorce. I don't know where I would have ended up if you hadn't taken me in. That's not to say Ryan would do any of that nonsense to you. Honestly, I think you'd be just fine doing something else if you did sell the bar but the part of me going through a shitty divorce says you should keep your safety net."

The smart woman inside me had been burned too many times by men, and so maintaining self-preservation was a moral imperative. "I hate feeling like that."

"I know," she muttered. "What did your mother always tell us?"

"The one where you can find trash on any street corner, but you should always hold out for a man with a heart of gold?"

"No, no. That was a good one, too, but the one where she always said that you should make sure the man loves you more than you love the man," she said. "According to Ryan, the sun rises and sets on your ass so I think you're good."

Thinking back to those times when my mom gave me her little quips of wisdom spread warmth up from my heart. "My mother was a wise woman."

Marie grinned. "Yes she was. Too bad I didn't listen."

I scratched my head. "Yeah, that makes two of us. This time I am, though."

"Yes indeed. Trading in the bad boy for the *badass* boy."

For some reason, a picture of a shirtless, beefy Mike Murphy flashed through my thoughts. "Mike's pretty badass."

"Yes he is." She smiled. "He's the reason why I'm sure things need to end between me and Gary. I didn't realize just how bad I had it until Mike came along. Gary has never made me a priority. Not once did he ever put my needs ahead of his own. When I look back at our relationship, even before we got married he never made me feel as if I was important. You've seen it. After a while, that shit starts to wear on you. But Mike . . . I know he's pulling in a few favors to get me into this school. He hasn't hesitated once about taking care of me. Not once."

"Mike's been really grumpy," I told her. "Ryan's ready to ship him here—*soon*. Fortunately, they're just about wrapped on *Slipknot*."

Her face lit up. It was such a beautiful thing. "Really?"

I smiled just as broadly. "He thinks Mike's in love with you."

"Really?"

"Really, really."

After a few seconds of grinning from ear to ear, she said, "Ryan's madly in love with you, you know. Still . . . please don't sell the bar."

I bristled a bit.

"I'm sad that I'm going to miss your engagement party at Ryan's parents'. I'm sure Ellen will stuff you full of food." She didn't have to tell me that those words hurt her to say.

That reminded me of one more thing I had to do: time to see if my next bright idea would pan out.

"I WENT to visit Pete today," I told Ryan when we Skyped later that night. Poor Pete. I could completely relate to the torturous itching that came from sporting a cast. His new limp also didn't go unnoticed.

"How's he doing?" Ryan asked while lying on the bed with his laptop on his legs. He wasn't wearing a shirt and obviously had just gotten out of the shower, as his skin was flush and deliciously dewy. Damn, it was a beautiful sight on my computer screen.

"Do you have any idea how hard it is to talk to you while you're looking like that?"

Ryan's face scrunched. "Like what?"

"Naked and all . . ." My hand waved since I was at a loss for words.

Ryan grinned, running a hand over his bare chest. "You like what you see?"

"You know I do."

He flipped his laptop to the side, making sure the camera was showing what he was now stroking in his hand. Like a teenager watching a porno, I had my very own Ryan Christensen nudie show. "See anything else that you like?"

I blushed, feeling extremely nervous. "Oh my God, Ryan! What if some hacker can see you like that? That's how private sex stuff . . . stop! You want videos of you whacking off to go viral?"

He nudged his screen, aiming the camera back on his face, which now showed demanding authority. "No one is going to see. Take your laptop back to our bed and take your clothes off."

I jumped a bit at his stern tone, feeling oddly compelled to comply. Still, I was very apprehensive to do anything so risqué over the Internet. "Ryan . . ."

His expression was meant to show that he wasn't going to be denied. "Now, Taryn."

It worked.

Begrudgingly, I carried my laptop to my room and flopped down, still fully clothed.

We were both on our sides, one arm propping our heads up. I watched as his fingers moved toward the screen. "I miss you," he said softly, cracking my resistance as if it were made of tissue paper. "I miss the feeling of completeness I have when you're in my arms. Do you ever feel that way? Like a part of you is missing when we're apart?"

I wanted to reach through the screen and touch him back. "All the time. I sort of feel incomplete."

He wiped his finger over his lips. It was the sexiest damn thing, as if his hunger for me was palpable. "Do you know what my favorite part of your body is?"

I swallowed—hard—figuring he'd go for the obvious. I wasn't going to give him the satisfaction of guessing.

"No guess? It's your lips. And not for the act that you might think I love them for. The curve of them makes me always wonder what's going on in your head. Between your lips and your eyes I can more or less guess and I'm usually pretty accurate. You may not realize it, but they are the windows into your soul."

I studied his face—the softness of his cheeks to where they met up with the shadow of beard growing on his jaw, the incredibly long eyelashes that framed those million-dollar bedroom eyes, the square cut of his chin. "Your eyes give you away, too, you know."

"If you were here, I'd kiss you right now. I wouldn't stop until you were naked underneath me, sighing in my mouth. I can almost feel the silky smoothness of your skin as I run my fingers beneath your undies."

I was beginning to believe there may be some wonderful advantages to video chatting. He was seducing me with the soft cadence of his words and the visuals he created in my thoughts.

"Take your finger, run it slowly down your neck, down to the base of your throat. I want you to feel me kissing you as I make love to you."

Obediently, I did as he instructed. Each time he told me to wet my fingers or pinch my own flesh turned me on more and more until I was drenched with excitement, panting and moaning. I'd touched myself plenty of times during those dry spells between dating, but this was a million times better.

A million.

RYAN HAD conveniently turned the screen so I could watch him clean up. My pounding heart was finally slowing when he nudged his laptop back to display his face on my screen.

His satiated smile lit up my heart. "You should video-seduce me more often," I said.

He laughed lightly, finger-combing his hair back off his forehead. "I'd much rather do that to you in person, but we do what we have to do in the meantime."

"I didn't realize watching you would be such a turn-on."

His lips twitched. "Oh, I did. Just hearing your voice is a turn-on for me; everything else was just a bonus."

I rolled over onto my stomach. "Yeah, right. My voice excites you that much."

His expression said he was dead serious. "Future wife, we've had phone sex before and now not only can I see your face, I can also see your naked boobs. Trust me. Now tell me about Pete, unless you want to go for round two, which I must say I'm getting ready for." I watched him stuff a few pillows under his head and then he flashed his semi onto the screen again just to show me his exclamation point to that statement.

After I regained my ability to speak, I muttered, "Pete's miserable."

"You iron out that crap with Tammy?"

"No. But I will. I'm presuming we're still in the wedding. You still want to be a groomsman? He asked if you were still in. I'd understand it if you don't want to. You haven't known Pete that long and—"

Ryan interrupted me. "I already told him I would. I gave him my word. They should know that my presence is going to cause a stir, so if they're good with that, I'm in. They've been warned. Besides, there's no way I'd let some other guy walk you down the aisle, Taryn. No way in hell."

I loved his possessiveness. It made me feel safe and cherished. "Is that your final answer?"

He glared at me over my screen before saying, "That's my final answer *forever*. You good with that, babe?"

Considering that Thomas had left me at a party once, not giving a shit who drove me home or even if I got home alive, I was more than fine with it. "Yes."

"That's my girl."

Say what you will, but I was damn glad to be *his* in no uncertain terms.

"And what did he say to your other proposition?"

The memory of Pete's reaction when I asked him made me smile wider. "You'd have thought I'd offered him a miracle."

"So he's on board with it?"

"Yes. He starts training with me tomorrow."

CHAPTER 18

When It Rains

IT WAS COMING down in buckets outside. It was the kind of heavy rain that you swear just might come through the roof because it's falling that hard. I wandered to the front door of Ryan's parents' home, cracking the door to watch the rain pour down.

Ryan had wrapped filming on *Slipknot*, and the cast wrap party was something else. Pete was doing an excellent job managing the pub, so I was able to meet Ryan back in Vancouver. Nicole had gotten quite intoxicated, slurring at us and insinuating it was Ryan's fault that her lover, Lauren Delaney, wasn't there. I knew for certain that her love life wasn't even on Ryan's radar when we arrived at the party, but she was under the impression that he'd banned Lauren from the guest list.

Maybe he overdid it just a bit when he said she'd be lucky to get a job waiting tables once the media catches wind of her drug habit, but it definitely shut her up quickly.

So many people only see the smiling public photos of celebrities at premieres and junkets; if the general public only knew some of the shit that went down on major movie sets, they'd be shocked. Personality clashes, overinflated egos, differences in acting methods and scene interpretations—it all happened.

But that was two days ago, Ryan finally had some downtime, and we had a family engagement party to brace for.

Ryan slid a hand over my khaki shorts and gripped my hip, peering over my shoulder. "Go," he nudged, pushing me on through the threshold. "Let's go stand out on the porch."

The sky at 7:30 P.M. was dark and ominous; the heat of the day was being quenched, causing the steam to rise up off the hot macadam driveway. I held my hand out into the thick stream of rainwater that was flowing over the lip of the storm gutters that edged along the porch roof.

"Nick and I washed my dad's car in a downpour like this once. We had a blast. Dad gave us a bucket and sponges and put us to work, though we didn't know we were working at the time. We were all soapy and soaked but damn did we have fun."

The water pelting my hand was cool and refreshingly chilly as I imagined two mischievous boys running around with soap sponges. "Wow, it's really pouring!"

"I'll say. Last time I saw it rain this hard, we were—"

I instantly stiffened. Ryan stiffened up, too, stopping himself.

Streaks of car lights flickered through drops of rain in my thoughts; the sounds of tires screeching on wet road and a horn blaring at me to get out of the middle of the street in downtown Miami swirled into one painful flashback. That horrid memory, that feeling as if I'd just been eviscerated seeing him kiss Lauren, that wishing to have all the pain just go away washed over me. It was distant but instant. Thankfully, I was able to keep that memory separate from this current moment, not allowing those bad moments to pull me under.

"I shouldn't . . . I didn't mean," Ryan fumbled, followed by the whisper of a curse to himself.

I gave him my attention, trying not to let it blow out of proportion. "It's all right."

Suddenly he snagged my wrist, pulling me to the opening on the porch. "I. *Fuck.* Come," he ordered.

"Where are we going?"

Ryan stepped off the porch, then stood directly under the water overflowing from the gutter above.

"What are you doing?" I asked as the water poured onto his head.

He smiled wickedly and shook the water off his head before bending and catching me behind my knees. I felt the whoosh as I was hefted over his bare shoulder and then cold rainwater pelted my hair, my shoulders, and my back, causing me to squeal.

"Ryan!"

"Come on, baby." He walked us down the flooded driveway in his bare feet. He only had a pair of track shorts on since we were lounging around the house.

The rain was cold but refreshing and instantly blocked my thoughts out, giving me the space to only worry about getting soaked.

"What are you doing?" I giggled as he hustled down the long drive.

"Makin' new memories," he said in a rush, stopping when he reached the torrent of water flowing down the street.

Just when I thought I couldn't love him any more than I already did, I fell another few miles deeper in love with him. He twirled us around, holding my legs out so I was balanced over his shoulder on my stomach. Heavy rain pelted my legs as I laughed from his playfulness.

"You're crazy!" I felt so giddy and free.

Ryan motioned like he was going to dump me on the ground. "Do you love me?"

I grabbed the back of his wet shorts. "Yes!"

He raised my legs higher. "What?"

"Yes!" I giggled louder, exposing the top crack of his ass as he hung me down his back.

He splashed into a huge puddle. "Say it!"

"I love you!"

Ryan spun us in a circle. My wet hair whipped around, sticking to my face. "What? I can't hear you. It's raining. You'll have to speak up."

"I love you!" I shouted, wiping the wet hair out of my eyes with one hand while holding his shorts with the other.

"You what?"

I smacked his perfect, soaking-wet ass. "I love you!"

"You love me?"

He was making me dizzy, jumping and twirling us around like that. "I love you!"

His hands gripped my thighs. "You gonna marry me, Mitchell?"

"Yes! Don't drop me!"

He dipped me back farther; my wet shirt gathered uncomfortably under my breasts. "Yes? Yes, what?"

I was laughing so hard, I was getting one of those side-stickers in my ribs. "Yes, I'll marry you!"

He set me down in the cold, streaming rainwater; one hand grasped my hip while the other got stuck into my hair at the base of my head. And then he was kissing me. In the downpour. In the stream of water running against the curb in front of his parents' house outside of Pittsburgh. Kissing me with everything he had and then some. Smoothing back my wet hair. Biting my lips. Swirling his tongue with mine. Mingling our hungry breath into one.

Marking my memories with new thoughts of the rain.

Shining his brightness on me in the midst of a dark storm.

My hands were on his smooth, muscular back, his ribs, his neck and face.

Mine.

Mine, mine, mine.

"I love you," he murmured.

"I love you more."

He broke away to grace me with his killer smile. His happiness, knowing I was a huge part of it, was like a gift. One that I'd cherish forever.

But I still had to get him back for spinning me upside down. I bent down, gathered up a handful of water, and tossed it at him.

"Oh yeah?" He skimmed his big foot through the stream, sending water splashing all over my shins.

I hadn't felt so free in such a long time. I kicked water back at him. When he bent for his own handful, I kept kicking and splashing, until he was sufficiently drenched.

Ryan straightened, glared down, and said, "You'd better run."

I took off through the rain, running only the length of the neighbor's yard barefoot in the street before I got tagged and scooped up off the ground.

Ryan was smiling as he carried me down to the corner where the street storm drain was overflowing. The rain was coming down so hard, the water was flooding the street.

"We used to play down here," Ryan said, walking with me pressed to his chest. "Me and Nick. Ricky Beidler used to live in that house over there. We'd get into all sorts of trouble."

He set me down in ankle-deep water. That's when the serious splashing started. Water soaked into my bra, trickling down my back.

"That all you got, Christensen?" I kicked, sending a blast of water at him. He laughed, tossed his wet hair back, and grabbed me around the waist, sitting me down on my ass in the water. I squealed again when cold water flooded down my butt crack.

Ryan plopped down, sitting next to me in the stream. "Come here," he ordered low, snagging me by the armpits to haul me across his lap.

The rain was slowing down but it could have been hailing for all I cared, being in his arms next to the curb in the street, sitting in rushing storm water. Ryan wiped the matted hair off my forehead, tilting his neck down to kiss me.

There was no denying that look of love in his eyes; that gaze that said a million words. I wrapped my arm over his shoulder, sliding my hand up his wet neck and into the tangles of his hair, feeling his kiss and all its meaning down into my bones.

We were the only two people in the world.

Sitting in the street.

In a small stream.

In the rain.

And just like that, my gorgeous man replaced bad with another slice of great.

IT WAS almost one o'clock the next afternoon when I heard Ryan's mom, Ellen, huff for the thirty-second time—or was it the thirty-third? I was on my laptop at the kitchen table and Ryan was outside working on his car and ignoring his mother's desire for him to keep a scheduled feeding time.

I made a silent deal with myself that the next huff would get me moving and sure enough it did.

"Ask him if he's ready for a sandwich," Ellen said in a rush, making sure I carried her message out to the garage.

I silently added "Yes, mother" to my "Sure. No problem."

I found Ryan, or should I say Ryan's legs and khaki cargo shorts, which were riding very, very low on his hips and exposing all sorts of tight flesh and happy trails of hair. He was on his back underneath the front end of his Shelby, and by the streaks of grease on his very sexy, low-riding shorts, I guessed he was changing the oil. The guy had $29 million but was too much of a *guy* to pay someone to change his oil. God love him and all of his humbleness.

I tapped his foot. "Hey, hot, sexy mechanic. How's it going under there?"

Ryan curled up enough to grin at me. "Going good."

The sight of him with dirty, grease-stained hands, a smear of it on his plain white cotton V-neck tee and one on his forearm, and some tools in his hands added to his sex appeal.

"You're looking so delish under there; I might be tempted to have you change *my* oil, too. What do you think?"

That earned me another smug smile. "I think you need more than your oil changed, ma'am. I'm thinking you'll need a tune-up *and* a lube job as well."

"At a minimum!" I joked. "And a buffin' and a waxin' too."

"Keep up with the dirty innuendos; you're making me hard."

"Keep up with the hot, dirty mechanic act and I may just do you out here in the driveway." That earned me a few eyebrow waggles. "Your mom is having a slow meltdown because you haven't eaten yet today. How long until you're finished?" There was no way he'd be able to hold a sandwich with all of that motor oil on his hands so no sense making him something to eat until he was cleaned up.

He groaned. "Doesn't she have anything better to do? I'll eat when I'm hungry. I'm still full from last night."

I was just about to give him a comeback when his cell rang. It was sitting on a towel next to an opened bottle of Gatorade.

"Grab that, would ya? Who is it?"

I crouched down and picked it up, tilting the screen so I could see it in the bright sun. "Your lawyer, Len Bainbridge."

"Answer it. My hands are too greasy."

I tapped the screen and said, "Hi, Mr. Bainbridge, it's Taryn Mitchell."

"Oh hello, Taryn," he said jovially. "How are you?"

After a few pleasantries, he asked for Ryan.

Ryan's legs were still sticking out from underneath his car and he'd already given his instruction. "I'm sorry. He's indisposed at the moment. He's asked if I can take a message for him."

Ryan cocked an eyebrow at my formalness.

"Yes, please tell him that my office is emailing the settlement documents with Brown and Sullivan PR. He needs to review them and if all is acceptable, we will proceed with the disbursement."

"Okay, great. I'll let him know."

"Thanks. Oh, yes, one moment. Thanks, Miriam. Yes, I almost forgot, Miriam is sending the requested prenuptial agreement template for his review. He'll need to mark it accordingly as to what your wishes are in the event of dissolution of marriage. It's all quite self-explanatory. He, of course, should call me if he has any questions."

My brain seized up at the word *prenup*.

"Taryn, are you still there?"

I think I formed a spit bubble first, which caused an involuntary reaction to choke.

At the second calling of my name, I managed a nod. "I'll tell him," I rasped.

Ryan rolled out from underneath his car, wiping his hands off on an old rag. He looked up at me, squinting one eye at the bright sun. "What did he have to say?"

Did you ever have that warm rush feeling—the kind that hits you right before you either freak out, pass out, or throw up? Yeah, I was there.

"I don't want your money, Ryan," I managed to say, even though I felt numb and disconnected from the conversation. He had millions in the bank. I thought we'd gotten beyond that, but apparently my assumption was incorrect. Of course he would want an escape clause.

"Not one cent," I sort of choked out through the lump in my throat. "I'm capable of earning my own way and if we bring babies into this world I'd expect you to help me raise them right and healthy, but I'll keep the apartment should you ever decide you need dissolution and I need a place to live. I guess that stuff will just be a given in the divorce proceedings anyway but I would never touch your money or demand a piece of it because *you* earned that money. I would *never* do that to you. You're building the house on your property—it's not mine nor will it ever be. I need you to know that. I would never take it from you." I didn't realize I was tearing up until he went blurry.

Ryan stood quickly. "Babe, you're freaking me the fuck out. What the hell are you talking about?"

My arm moved, holding out his phone. I should have been angry, but I wasn't for some reason. I was more desperate and wounded than anything. "Your lawyer is emailing you the prenup agreement you requested. I want you to know I'll sign it. It's only right. You should have peace of mind."

Ryan looked like I'd just punched him. "Whoa, whoa. Hold up. What prenup? I didn't ask for a prenup."

I shook the phone in my hand, making a point. "He says different."

Ryan ducked down, making sure he had my eyes. "Taryn, honey, I swear to *God* I did not ask him to write up a prenup. I swear. I am just as blindsided by this as you are. But I will get to the bottom of it, you can be damn sure of that. Give me my phone. I'm calling him right now."

Just as I was ready to hand it over, thankful that he didn't think I was going to empty his pockets or even imagine me being that greedy that I'd do such a thing, I pulled my hand back.

"Wait." I wiped the hurt from my cheek. "Before you do that we should talk about it. I know that there are no guarantees that people stay together for life, but I want it written down that I don't want your money. You help me pay for your children's care, should we have any, and that's it. I don't need alimony or any of that because I've gotten spoiled or feel entitled that you owe me or something."

Ryan took my arm firmly in his hand. "Hey, hey, stop. Stop this— right now."

Once the floodgates had opened, I couldn't. "No, we need to discuss this! You have *a lot* of money, Ryan. I didn't work hard to earn that; you did. That's yours—all of it. I don't expect you to fork over gobs of cash I didn't earn because we didn't last like we'd hoped. And then there's the property you bought and stuff. That's all yours, too. Just because it's next to my family's cabin doesn't mean I'm entitled—"

"*Stop!*" he ordered, loud and firm. "I am *not* talking about this."

I don't know why that frustrated me, but it did. "We need to," I insisted.

"No, we don't." Ryan frowned at me, tugging my arm slightly. "You want to give me peace of mind, then stop talking about this shit right now."

"We're going to need to talk about it eventually. You know that as well as I do. There's too much at stake . . ."

He glared down at me. "Let me ask you something. Did Dan and Jennifer Mitchell have a prenup?"

"Ryan, that's—"

He raised his voice over mine. "Your parents have a prenup, Tar? Yes or no?"

"I'm pretty sure my parents didn't, but still, that's not the point."

He held up a halting hand. "You think *my* mom and dad in there have a fucking prenup?"

I just stared at him, avoiding having to answer.

"I can tell you they don't," he said. "And I sure as hell didn't ask my lawyer to draft one up, either." He started jabbing his finger on his touchscreen phone.

Ryan was breathing heavy while being placed on hold. "When he gets out of his meeting, you tell him I want to know who the hell told him to write a prenup on my behalf." He hung up abruptly, without even saying goodbye.

Ryan stormed off toward the kitchen door and I had no choice but to follow.

"Ryan? What's wrong? You look mad," Ellen questioned, while he used the kitchen sink.

"I'm not mad, Mom. I'm *pissed*."

Ellen quickly looked at me, trying to ascertain if I had caused his anger.

"What's going on?" she continued to pry.

"You have a prenup with Dad?" he asked with a definite growl.

I saw the confusion blanket her face. "No."

Ryan glanced over his shoulder, casting me his *see, I told ya* look.

Ellen was smarter than I gave her credit for. She held up her hands, backing up and out of the conversation as if there were a ticking time bomb sitting on her kitchen floor.

"Ryan, things were different for them. Our parents didn't have the amount of money that you do and—"

Even though his back was turned to me, the hand that shot out, slicing the air in my direction, was a definite cease-and-desist order. I stood there in silence, watching him hunch, his arms pressing into the stainless steel rim of the sink as if he were pressing his emotions back together.

"Time and time again, we keep coming back to the same spot," he muttered at the sink. "I know there are no guarantees"—he turned to face me—"but the reason why neither of our parents had a prenuptial agreement was because they didn't start out in their marriage by preparing for it to end."

I pulled a chair out at the large oval dining table, feeling the need to anchor myself. He said the words that were in the back of my mind. "I know."

"You want us to start out that way? You want some paper that says if I fuck around or if I don't sit down and talk shit out and work through our problems that you'd get a few million tossed at you?"

I shook my head. "No, I don't. But apparently your people think differently."

Ryan's lips squashed together in frustrated anger. He pushed his hair back, scratching his head, venting his anger in an audible huff. I knew that one wasn't because of me.

"I'd never take from you regardless."

His shoulders dropped. "That's why I want to give you everything."

My breath hitched. "I already have the part that I want. Love is priceless."

He came over to the table, pulled out the chair next to me, and sat down, our knees touching.

"You have a lot of other stakeholders concerned about your bottom line, Ryan. Even agreements for our wedding photos and stuff, like you said. All of those things; it all has to be legal."

Ryan took my hand in his. "You need to realize that I'd cut them all loose before I'd risk losing you."

I leaned into the other hand cupping my cheek. "I want you to feel safe with me forever, even if that means signing something to give you that."

"Tar, I know you're not a taker. You're the most giving person I've ever known." His frown softened. "I do not want that kind of paper looming between us."

"Escape clause," I muttered.

"What?"

"Escape clause. It outlines how everything gets divvied up in the event of a divorce. Did you know that Marie and Gary are fighting over who gets to keep the TVs and dishes?"

Ryan sighed, disgusted. His eyes met mine. "And you think that might happen between us."

I felt my head shake, but facts were facts. "I'm watching my best friend get her heart torn out and working on a new relationship at the same time while arguing about who gets the toaster. She and Gary made it three years. I just don't want you to ever worry about me taking your TV."

He leaned forward, placing a soft kiss on my lips. "We are going to blend our lives together. We're going to have a family. But I'm not starting our marriage with a paper that outlines how we end it. Family is important to me. Baby, we will go to counseling to straighten our shit out before we start picking fights over a damn toaster."

"You really mean that?"

"I do. Taryn, I know being in a relationship with me comes with an entire set of stressors that normal people never have to deal with. But you cut that away and I'm still me. I'm just a man."

"I know." I drew in a deep breath. "The prenup thing really surprised me."

"It threw me, too. And you're right. We need to talk about all of this. And if you need me to put it in writing that I'll never stray, then that's what I'll do."

Mom's quips of wisdom flooded my thoughts. "No. I don't need that, because I know that inside, my man has a heart of gold."

Knowing he was fully invested in our relationship made all the difference in the world.

CHAPTER 19

Roots

"AND THIS LOVELY lady is my crazy cousin Shannan," Ryan said jovially, hugging the next person lining up to greet us with playful familiarity. Ryan's mom had apparently invited every relative and their entire neighborhood to our engagement party. My brain was reeling from meeting so many new people.

He hoisted Shannan up by her waist, her long brown hair curtaining her face.

"Ah! Ryan! Put me down!" Shannan squealed, thrashing a bit. She had to fix her shirt when he set her back down, all flustered. She gave him a nudging slap. "You're a nut."

It was so magnificent to see Ryan so relaxed and happy, seeing his extended family again. I couldn't stop smiling.

"And who is this handsome young man?" Ryan asked, patting the head of an adorable little boy. He must have been around seven or eight, holding a black skater's helmet in his hand.

"That's Caden," Shannan said. "You haven't seen him in a while."

Ryan looked stunned. "Caden? Dude, you've grown. You were like this big when I saw you last."

Caden regarded Ryan with a scrutinizing gaze. "You look like that guy who's in that movie my mom likes so much."

Shannan appeared mortified by his disclosure, silently nudging her son to go and play.

Ryan crossed his arms. "You telling me that your mommy likes my movie? This lady, right here? The one who told me that I was wrong for the part?"

Shannan gave Ryan a shoulder shove.

Ryan rolled with the punch, obviously loving this information way too much.

"Oh, yeah. Aunt Nancy and Aunt Stacy, they come over and watch it a lot. Aunt Nancy boos every time that girl, Gwen, comes on the TV, though."

"Caden!" Shannan squealed.

"Mom, I'm hungry. When are the hot dogs going to be ready?" Caden asked.

"Mom, I want a hot dog, too. And can I go in the pool?" an adorable little blond girl asked, tugging on Shannan's shorts.

The pool sounded like a good idea. July in Pittsburgh was hot.

"Soon, baby. Say hi to Ryan and Taryn. They're going to get married. This is my daughter, Lauren," Shannan said proudly.

Just hearing that name made me flinch. But this adorable child and the evil Lauren that I knew were polar opposites.

As I glanced around the yard and patio loaded with smiling people I was overwhelmed by how large Ryan's immediate family was. His mother, Ellen, was one of five, all sisters, each of whom had several children and grandchildren. And on his father's side, Bill Christensen was one of three. Even Ryan's eighty-two-year-old grandfather, Nels Christensen, was there, congratulating Ryan on his "beautiful choice."

I ended up at the long table on the patio after being introduced to more aunts, uncles, cousins, and kids. We'd already been asked several times when we were getting married and received numerous suggestions on everything from churches to caterers to what type of flowers are best. Just the thought of having to plan and decide on all of these details were enough to send me into a small panic.

I envisioned Ryan's side of the church tilting over, filled to the rafters with his boisterous family, while my side had maybe two dozen poor souls clinging to the pews, and several rows of crickets. My mother only had one brother, Bobby, and a sister. I hadn't heard from Aunt Joan since I had called her to tell her I knew about my birth parents. Uncle Bobby was living in Texas—we never saw him. My dad had his brother, Al, and they had two kids. That was it.

Suddenly, I felt alone.

Ryan sat next to me in his wet swim trunks, his plate overflowing with food, a stacked hamburger I was sure was painted with ketchup and mayo balancing precariously on top of the pile. I drifted my fingers over the droplets of water that clung to his sun-kissed shoulder, loving the simplicity of our engagement party. His parents could have easily made this into an uncomfortable affair, hiring caterers and servers, but to my relief this was a good old-fashioned family barbecue. His dad and other random men worked the grill while all of the women clustered to make their famous macaroni salad or swap recipes for the forty different types of pies and cookies on display. Life was simply wonderful.

"Have you given any thought to when you're going to get married?" his aunt Rita asked. She had a short silver hairdo and that healthy glow that comes from living a carefree flip-flops life in the Florida Keys. She and her husband flew up here just for our party. Her cute little Yorkie pup named Katie was perched attentively on her lap.

Ryan was double-fisting his burger. I saw him glance in my direction.

"We've looked at some dates but we've been so busy that we haven't really discussed it. Maybe next year. His schedule is quite hectic." *There. That ought to be good enough.*

Aunt Rita pursed her lips, showing a hint of antipathy. "See, that's the problem with being a celebrity. You all put your careers in front of your relationships. That's why most of the marriages are a farce. She films, he films, and no one has time to tend to the marriage."

I saw Ryan stiffen. I knew every fine nuance of his body language and could sense his shift into defense mode. He set his burger down and wiped his hands.

"Taryn's not an actress," Ryan corrected her, wiping his mouth.

Aunt Rita pegged him with that maternal familiarity that silently spoke volumes. "Yes, but you are."

His forearms hit the edge of the table like a lawyer ready to argue. "So? What does that have to do with it?"

I glanced over at Shannan, who was doing her best to pretend that she wasn't paying attention to the conversation, but the way she clutched the arms of her chair with clawed hands said that she wasn't going anywhere. I watched the nonverbal communications going back and forth between her and her sister, Nancy, which said, *Uh oh, Mom's going to let him have it* and *rather him than me.*

Aunt Rita pet little Katie with loving strokes. "My point, dear boy, is that you need to take the time to tend to what's important here"—she patted over her heart—"or else all that glitz and glamour is going to turn you into a celebrity cliché."

"A cliché?" Ryan said, offended.

"Yes. Honestly, the philandering behavior of actors is appalling. Don't forget how you were raised."

His fork hit his plate, rising to her challenge. "Have I ever?"

"No, but I want to remind you not to be like the rest of the celebrity riffraff out there and shame our family."

"Well, you can all rest easy. I have no intentions now or ever to shame our family."

Aunt Rita seemed pleased by that. Still, she said, "You want to know why all of these high-profile relationships don't last?"

"Oh, here we go," Nancy groaned.

Shannan sat up. "Mom, maybe now is not the best time to be opinionated."

"No really. Listen," Rita continued, ignoring them. "You all think I don't know what I'm talking about, but I read and watch the news all the time. What all you young kids fail to remember is that the excitement and freshness of that new relationship doesn't last. Everyone—every relationship—hits those rough patches when you argue and don't get along so well and it's so easy to be tempted to go for that freshness again to feel appreciated and desired. If not—bam, you're miserable and getting your kicks elsewhere. But if you keep that freshness alive in your relationship you'll get through it. Mark my words."

"Spoken like a true champion that divorced her first husband," Ryan's aunt Betty teased in passing.

Rita squirmed in her chair. "Jerry was an idiot. There are exceptions to the rules."

"Oh, now there are exceptions. You better fill me in so I don't disgrace the family," Ryan said dryly.

"Yes, exceptions, smart aleck. Having a drinking and gambling problem are two of them. Being too drunk to hold a job is another. Exceptions I hope I don't ever see with any of our children, including you, hot shot."

Ryan took a sip of his beer, making that sucking-through-his-teeth sound that happens whenever he gets aggravated. "What I want to know is did you give this same lecture to your two sons-in-law over there as well or is this wisdom you're imparting just for me?"

"Oh believe me, they know I'd skin their hides if either of them was unfaithful," Aunt Rita said assuredly.

Ryan sat back in his chair, putting her under the same scrutiny. "That's a good deflection but you're avoiding the question. Did you or did you not give them the same lecture?"

"My sons-in-law are not surrounded by promiscuity and temptation."

Nancy looked mortified. "Mom, that's not fair—"

"What does that have to do with anything?" Ryan interrupted her. "There is nothing keeping Brent or Jake from hooking up with the cashier at the grocery store or the flirty secretary at the office or even trying to nail the babysitter. You're posing a question of morality. My occupation has nothing to do with my morals."

"It is widely known that celebrities tend to have more of a propensity for infidelity than do most—"

"No, you're questioning my integrity and judging me for no reason other than that I'm an actor," Ryan said, stabbing his macaroni salad with his fork. "I don't deserve that and I don't appreciate it."

Janelle just so happened to be walking by with a full plate of food in one hand and holding her daughter, Sarah, on her hip with the other. I held my hands out since I was done eating and needed to buffer myself from the hostility around me. "Let me have her. Come here, baby girl. Hi, sweetheart. You keep me company while Mommy eats her dinner, okay?"

Sarah was a welcome distraction, banging her juice bottle on the table. I put some ambrosia on the tip of my spoon, finding a hungry little mouth opening wide for it.

Ryan gazed at me and then bumped his head in my direction. "You see this, Aunt Rita?" he said, waving his hand at me. "I've got everything I need right here, and then some, so don't you worry about my ability to remain committed."

Once the fun of making Ryan feel like shit was over, people started moving away from the table.

"Bora Bora," I mouthed when Ryan glanced up from his plate. "First flight out."

He snickered softly and leaned over, wrapping an arm over my shoulder. "I don't know what I'd do without you. You keep me sane."

I smiled up at him and that was all I needed to do to garner one hell of a kiss, as it if was a reward or a thank-you. "I'm guessing Aunt Rita won't be invited to the wedding."

"Screw them all. We're eloping."

THE FOLLOWING day we had a smaller party of our own; just a few of Ryan's friends that I had met at the birthday party I threw for him back in November and plenty of burgers and liquor. Ryan dove into the pool, surfacing right next to my raft. He jostled the edge of the raft with his forearms, rocking me off balance.

I gripped the edges, laughing and holding on for dear life. "No! Please don't dump me."

Ryan smiled playfully, tugged my raft into his chest, and kissed me senseless. I brushed his wet bangs back off his forehead, tasting the chlorine from the water on his lips as he twined his tongue with mine. "Mmm, potato chips and beer."

He snickered in my mouth. "Then I guess you should have me for lunch." That devilish glint in his eye told me he was up to no good. He dipped the edge of my raft down into the water.

"Please?" I whined. I was enjoying the hot sun, hoping to get a quick tan out of it.

"Okay, I'll be nice."

I rubbed my hand over his arm, feeling the heat radiating off his skin. "Your shoulders are starting to get really red. You want me to put some lotion on them?"

"Nah, I'm good."

Yeah, he'll be good until he is complaining that he can't sleep. "You're going to be uncomfortable if you burn."

Ryan glanced down at where my fingers were trailing. "I feel it on my back more than anything. I'm not going to stay in long, hon. Scott and Laura are actually taking off soon. I want to talk to him about getting some parts for the Shelby." His finger brushed over the edge of my bikini top. "This one of the suits you bought in Spain?"

I nodded, fondly remembering our small shopping spree in Barcelona. "You bought this for me."

"Nice. I have good taste. Well hello there my little nipple friend. I'm glad to see you, too." Ryan spun my raft around, placing his back to the rest of the party. That's when he pulled me in closer, dipped his head, and grazed his teeth over the fabric.

So much for being discreet. The sensation made my belly clench. "Ryan." It came out as a breathy moan.

"Shhh." He stopped my weak disapproval with a passionate kiss while his finger and thumb slipped under my top, causing me to arch up into his touch. He moved the edge of my suit over far enough to swirl his tongue over the sliver of flesh he'd exposed, sucking so hard I felt it in several different places all at once.

I was losing the fight as to why he should stop. "Someone might see us."

"He returned his mouth to mine. I don't care. I want you so bad right now. Climb down on me. No one will see."

I glanced over at everyone lounging around on the patio furniture, drinking and shooting the breeze. "They're less than thirty feet away. I'm sure they'd figure it out."

"I'll tell them to leave."

My eyes swept back to the patio. Janelle was rubbing sunblock on little Sarah. "Ryan . . ."

"Fine. We'll come back out here tonight after I tell them all to leave."

"Why, Mr. Christensen? You want to play water polo?"

His face was right in mine, speaking on my lips again, discreetly pinching my nipple hard enough to make me gasp. "No, I want to play hide the submarine. And motorboats."

The sun was so bright that even though I was wearing sunglasses, the reflections off the water were almost blinding. I used my hand as a visor just so I could see Ryan's face. That's when I noticed something sparkle in the neighbor's tree. I moved my swimming suit top up to cover what he'd exposed.

I looked back and saw the flash of brightness again. "What is that?"

Ryan looked over his shoulder to see where I pointed. "Where?"

"Up there, in the tree." I saw movement, first thinking it was a raccoon or someone's cat and then I saw a knee.

"What the hell?" He swam to the edge of the pool and pressed his body out of the water.

I saw the man crawl down from the tree as I hurried to get out of the pool. I made it to the driveway when I spotted the rogue photographer come out through the neighbor's hedgerow, distracted and clutching his camera. He noticed Ryan just as Ryan made his way between the rows of cars in his parents' long driveway.

The photographer started to run.

Ryan took off like a bullet out of a gun.

Mike pushed past me. "Oh, shit."

Scott and Matt were tight on Mike's heels. Scott tossed his plastic cup of beer to the ground just as Ryan's body became airborne, tackling the paparazzo in the neighbor's front lawn.

By the time I reached them, Ryan was straddling the guy, trying to wrestle the camera free. The guy tried to hit Ryan, but Ryan dodged his swing. He clipped Ryan's shoulder instead.

"You son of a bitch." Ryan hauled back and punched the photographer in the face, making that sick popping sound that could only come from fist hitting flesh and bone.

"Ryan, stop!" I screamed as he continued to swing.

Mike grabbed Ryan around his chest and pulled him off the photographer, tossing him like a 180-pound sack of potatoes onto the grass.

"What the hell is wrong with you?" the scrambling paparazzo asked, wiping his fingers over his bloodied lip.

"Ryan. Ryan. Easy, man." Mike had to use his weight to hold Ryan down.

"Scott, get the fucking camera," Ryan ordered, pointing. "Rip the card out."

"No! Don't touch it," Mike yelled.

Ryan scrambled to his feet. "He's got pictures of Tar and me, Mike. Those prints will never see the light of day."

"Don't touch my camera," the photographer said vehemently.

"Give me the fucking memory card or I'm going to finish what he started," Scott threatened.

"Go to hell. I don't have to give you shit."

Ignoring Mike's commands to stop, Scott kicked the guy's hand, knocking the camera free.

Just as the paparazzo tried to grab for the camera and Scott's leg, Ryan lunged and tackled him again. The guy rolled and elbowed Ryan in the face. Blood instantly gushed from Ryan's nose. Matt wrestled the guy until he had him pinned face-first in the grass.

I heard the police sirens in the distance. Mike was trying to break it up, but the second that Ryan got injured, Matt joined the rumble. The boys from Pittsburgh were giving this guy an ol' fashioned ass-kicking.

Ryan staggered to his feet and spit a wad of blood out of his mouth. Then he picked up the camera from the grass, removing the memory card. He set the camera near the guy's head.

The sirens were getting closer. Ryan's hands were bloody from his nose bleeding all over the place. Now the entire neighborhood was alerted to the melee. The elderly couple that owned the yard we were in came out of their house.

Scott took off his shirt and handed it to Ryan, who proceeded to wipe his bloody face with it.

"Sit down," Matt yelled at the paparazzo and gave him a shove when he tried to stand. Ryan balled up the bloody shirt, rolling his gaze from me to the shirt and back again, then handed it to me.

The cruiser's engine gunned and then screeched to a halt at the curb. As soon as the police officer got out of the car, Ryan and the guys were ordered to lie facedown on the ground. Tears ran down my face watching Ryan get handcuffed and patted down like a criminal. Another police SUV came blaring down the street from the opposite direction.

Ryan's father and Mike were trying to explain things to the cops while the photographer blabbered on about how he was assaulted and his camera destroyed.

Ryan looked worn and battered; his bare chest was bloodied and stretched from being handcuffed. Blood splatters were all over his swim trunks with a smear of it on the upper part of his knee. He motioned for me to come to him.

"Baby, are you okay?" I wiped the edge of his chin with the shirt.

"I need a towel. Wait . . ."

I knelt back down on one knee. His eyes instructed me to come closer.

"Careful with that. Make it disappear."

I clutched the shirt to make sure nothing fell out, knowing what was wrapped up in it. "Are you under arrest?"

He squeezed his eyes shut for a moment. "I don't know. I'm gonna need you to call David," he muttered quickly. "And my lawyer. Oh, and call Trish." He spit out more blood, cursing to himself.

Now that the adrenaline was subsiding, I could see the magnitude of the last ten minutes crashing down on him.

While Ryan was being interviewed by the police, an ambulance came zipping down the street. I felt like my bones were going to rattle right out of my skin from shaking so hard.

"Are they taking him to the hospital?" Ellen asked in a panic as she ran back with a bath towel.

The ambulance crew attended to Ryan first, swabbing the blood off his face and nose. I knew exactly why he refused to be taken to the hospital. That would have set off a media feeding frenzy for sure. We had to keep this contained.

The elderly neighbor, whom I had met yesterday when he and his wife came to our party, ambled over to talk to Ryan. "How are you doing, son?"

"I've been better, Mr. Doughten. Sorry about all of this."

The old man scowled at the paparazzo. "So that bastard was in my tree, was he? Spying on your family?"

Ryan nodded, staring mostly at the ground. "He was taking pictures of us, sir." It was apparent that he was embarrassed to be standing there talking to a man he obviously respected while wearing handcuffs.

"Pictures, huh? Oh Jesus, Mary, Joseph." He scrubbed his bristly gray whiskers. "You can't catch a break, can ya kid?"

Mr. Doughten's lower lip quivered as he eyed me up and down.

The police officer sidled up to Mr. Doughten. "Huh? Hell yes, I want to press charges." He raised a crooked, arthritic finger. "That son of a bitch was in my tree, trespassing on my property. Damn right I'm going to press charges. This is ridiculous."

"And Mr. Christensen?" the officer asked. Another police cruiser sped down the street, red and blue lights whirling.

"Hell no. That boy knows my front lawn better than I do. Been cutting my grass since he was old enough to run the tractor. He's a good boy. And his two friends there. Been helping Lil and me for years. Planted every one of them arborvitaes over there for me. And Scotty put in my brick walkway. They're all good boys from good families. Now do your job and get those damn handcuffs off of them. Let them go back to their party."

The officer turned to Ryan. "Mr. Dooley claims that you stole the memory card from his camera."

Ryan confessed to removing it. "But I don't have it. I dropped it in the grass somewhere over there."

After a few moments of scanning the yard with a flashlight, the officer gave up. Finding it was obviously not one of his top priorities. Just when I thought they were going to release him, the officer informed Ryan that he was under arrest for disorderly conduct.

Everything became brighter as I heard the whoosh of my blood pulsing in my ears. It felt as if the ground were about to give out under my feet. Ryan's father grabbed his mother as she lunged toward the police car. She was crying and in just as much shock as I was.

Both Matt and Scott were under arrest as well. All three of them were getting crammed into the backseats of the cruisers. The officer guided Ryan into the car and closed the door. As I stood there, watching him from the grass, he wouldn't look at me.

"I'll get the car and follow them," Ryan's dad, Bill, said. Mike followed him.

I WAS surprised when they came back in a little over an hour. David was not pleased to hear my voice when I called him, but too freaking bad. I was still on the phone getting talked down from the rafters by Trish when I heard the car doors slam in the driveway.

Ryan barely looked at me, passing me in the kitchen with a sideways glance. I heard him jog up the steps and then the shower came on.

Bill tossed his keys on the counter, answering his wife. "They got processed and released. They'll all have to go to court, then find out what the fine is."

I wanted to go to Ryan but I could tell he wanted space. Mike sat in a chair outside with his head in his hands doing his own private browbeating.

I sat down opposite him, leaning my elbows on my knees. "You okay?"

Mike stared at me for a moment before silently shaking his head. "This should have never happened today. I screwed up."

"No you didn't."

"Yes, I did. I'm too close."

"Too close to what?" *Snapping? Join the club.*

"You and Ryan. Been too lax. I'm not paying attention like I should be. I didn't even do a basic perimeter check today."

"Mike, you can't see everything. The guy was way up in the tree."

He sat up abruptly. "It's my *job*, Taryn. You and Ryan are paying me to protect you from shit like that. I failed you both today. I've got to resign. He needs someone new, someone who can put distance between the threats and the clients."

"Oh no. You are not resigning from our detail. That idiot was so far up the neighbor's tree there is no way you would have seen him unless you were standing in the middle of the pool. I only saw him because the sun glared off his lens. There's no way you would have spotted him from the ground, so quit beating yourself up about it."

"My charge got arrested today," he growled through his teeth.

"Your *charge* could have easily sent you after the photographer but he didn't. You are not responsible for Ryan's actions."

"He shouldn't have had to if I'd been doing my job."

His dedication and conviction were admirable. He wouldn't be so torn up if he didn't love us. I wondered if Marie got to see this side of him. "Are you always this sensitive?"

His eyes popped wide open. "What?"

"One slip in an entire year and you're ready to quit."

"Not quitting. Just placing you in better hands. I've compromised my position by blurring the lines and that puts you both in danger."

He was being overly emotional. "Well, you can't quit."

"Why not?"

"Because I won't allow it," I said firmly.

"Look, if this is about Marie, I won't let—"

"It's not about Marie. It's about having someone *I trust* watching him. Mike, you are the only one within his immediate circle of management that I trust. I breathe easier knowing you are with him wherever he goes. Your presence alone gives him a level of comfort and peace that he's not going to get from just anyone."

"Comfort and peace do not keep him safe, Taryn."

"Mike, you could surround him with armed guards and it would not have kept that idiot from climbing a tree and using a telephoto lens. Ryan has enough stress on him. He wants to feel normal. Who would have ever thought he couldn't do that in his family's backyard? And you need to have some downtime, too."

"Yeah, but—"

"But nothing. You're not quitting, so get that out of your head."

Ryan came outside wearing a pair of shorts and a deep scowl. "Where's that camera card at?"

I followed him in the house and handed it to him, wondering how much space was required. I mulled it over at the kitchen table before I decided to suck it up and be brave. I knew firsthand the humiliation that came with wearing handcuffs.

He was sitting at his desk in his old bedroom, glaring at his laptop. I noticed he plugged the card reader from our camera bag into the USB port.

"You okay?"

His eyes flashed up to me. "I was arrested for the first time in my fucking life. What do you think?"

"I know the feeling."

He gave me an angered scowl. I could see a deep purple bruise starting to form under his left eye.

"Want to throw shoes?"

He let out a deep sigh, as if he was pushing all the bad out. His eyes closed for a moment. "No. Don't want to throw shoes."

My next words came out on a whisper. "Do you want me to leave you alone?"

He huffed again and rubbed his forehead. I took that as an unspoken yes so I turned for the door.

"Tar, wait . . ." He held out his hand. "Come here." I reached for his offering.

I let out the breath I didn't realize I was holding when he pulled me onto his lap. His arms cinched around my body and he buried his face in my neck. I drifted my fingers through his damp hair, pressing him tighter.

"I'm so tired of this, Tar. So freaking tired. Can't even have a day off without them following us." He looked up into my eyes. "He came to my parents' house. *My parents.* That's crossing the line."

I touched the skin below the bruise on his cheek. "I agree."

"People don't realize . . . they don't know how it is to feel stripped of your privacy. All they want are pictures of whoever I'm with or what personal shit I'm doing—as if they have a right to know that.

And for what? To see that I'm just like anyone else? Christ, Tar. You got hit by a fucking car because of me."

I held his face. "That was *not* your fault. Don't say that."

He jerked away. "Yes, it was. That crazy girl was stalking you because of me. Huge boxes of fan mail showing up at your place? Threat letters? What happened in Paris? Nah, I'm not having that anymore. Uh-uh." I could see him steel his resolve.

One of his arms released me so he could click the mouse. Rows upon rows of pictures dotted the screen. He let out a curse, rubbing his forehead. "He's been tracking us since we landed here. Son of a bitch."

"Oh my God. Are those from yesterday?"

"Yep. Bastard got shots of my entire family. There's one with us when I was holding Sarah. Damn it!"

My eyes widened as he continued to page through hundreds more. I felt as if I'd swallowed a rock seeing close-ups of Ryan's tongue on my breast in the pool. The idiot took so many pictures, it was almost like live action seeing shot after shot of Ryan and me in private, intimate moments. I wanted to puke.

"That's it. No more. After the third *Seaside* is filmed, I'm done."

CHAPTER 20

Rebound

He was arrested, Taryn. There's nothing I can do. His mug shot is public record now," Trish explained. I didn't care. It had been four days since the incident; every tabloid and news outlet was circulating and publishing the picture of him bruised and tinged with blood and I wanted them to end.

I hid in the far corner of the bar office to make sure Ryan couldn't accidentally overhear my conversation, even though the last time I saw him he was still in bed. That was at one o'clock. I was feeling like I was at the end of my rope. "I know. Ryan's lawyer called. Even if they get the charge dropped the picture is still out there. He's not taking this very well, Trish."

She sighed. "I wanted to talk to him, see if he wants me to spin this, but he won't take my calls. He's not the first celebrity who's had their mug shot posted. Either we counter with positive press or just let it naturally blow over, which it will."

"Yeah well, right now the press is having a field day." I was starting to pick up Ryan's forehead-rubbing habit. "Ryan's lawyer alerted us that the photographer has hired counsel. He's attempting to sue us for a million. Can you believe the bastard wants us to pay for the lost income he would have made selling pictures of us to the media?"

"I believe it."

"Ryan's not himself anymore. This has pushed him into such a depression; I don't know what to do. He's even lost weight. He's barely eating. All he wants to do is sleep or lie on the sofa. He's becoming a recluse."

"Let him have a few days to get it together. His ego has taken a blow."

I chewed on my fingernail. "This isn't just about his ego. He says he's retiring."

"What?" Trish shrieked. "No. Bad idea. Bad. That will kill his career. Comebacks in this business are hard to make. He's at the top of his game right now. He pulls out and you can kiss his box-office draw goodbye."

"Trish, the guy had over a thousand photos of us. The cops found soda bottles filled with pee in the neighbor's yard. He'd been wearing this camo netting stuff to blend in with the damn tree! Who knows how long he'd been up there."

"Oh, boy. I've heard of him. They call him 'Fast Freddy.' He freelances for one of the largest celebrity photo agencies in L.A. He's the idiot that almost got Bieber into an accident two weeks ago, chasing him down the Santa Monica Freeway for a shot. These guys know no boundaries."

"They're like jackals." I looked at the calendar in my hand, wondering what I could do to get Ryan back into the swing of things.

"Why don't you two go on vacation? Get out of there for a few days?"

"I've suggested it but he doesn't want to deal with airports or any place that's public. I told him that hiding is not the answer and that he should show the world he's fine and doing his thing but it's like talking to a brick wall. I've had reporters and press staked out in my pub since we got back. I have two guys working the door because we've been inundated with curious fans. It's crazy. I need to get him away from here but he refuses to go."

Trish sighed. "I hate to even bring it up, but I heard about Marla's latest stunt."

I took a deep breath, cringing from just hearing that woman's name. "I don't know how she thinks she could get away with overcharging us. I'd like to stick her lawsuit up her ass."

Pete peered around the office door, waving his cell at me. "Tar, Ryan's calling for you."

I quickly ended my call with Trish and tucked my cell in my pocket. Ryan refused to set foot in the bar, saying that it caused too many problems for my business for him to be seen. His fans just didn't know when to quit. It was getting to be assumed that if I was here then he was, too. There were spotters watching out for me now.

Ryan frowned at me when I came through the apartment door. "Why aren't you answering your cell?"

"I was talking on it."

"Oh. Who were you talking to?"

"I was dealing with something. Why?"

Shoulders that used to stand tall and firm were hunched as if he'd been defeated. He hadn't shaved in several days, nor had he done anything more than shower and run a hand through his hair. He had on a torn T-shirt and a pair of threadbare cotton shorts, looking more like a homeless person than a multimillionaire celebrity.

He rubbed his eye with his knuckle. "Nothing. I woke up and didn't know where you were, that's all."

I hated seeing him reduced to this state of despondency. "Are you hungry? You want some lunch?"

He shrugged, shuffling barefoot down the hall to his second-favorite place: the left side of the couch.

I sat next to him and tried to snuggle up. He seemed less agitated when I was under his protective wing. "You still have those pictures of places you wanted to see that you gave me at Christmas?"

He scratched his bare feet together while he flipped through the television channels. "They should still be in the drawer in the bedroom under my T-shirts. Why?"

"I think we should pick one and go someplace. Get the hell out of here for a few days. Fun? Sun? What do you think?"

He took a big sip of one of the many cups of water he had stashed around the apartment. At least in his depression he hadn't started drinking. "Tar, we talked about this. How many times do I have to tell you that I don't want to go anywhere right now? Can't we just stay put for once? Please babe? I feel as though I've been around the world eighty times. I just want to relax."

He slid into the couch, wedging deeper into his depression.

I understood his desire for taking a break, but this was beyond his normal behavior. He hadn't been out of the apartment since we got here.

"What ever happened to those sketches you did of our massive home?"

"They're in my messenger bag. Why?"

I got up, tired of watching him flip through one hundred channels over and over again. I set his drawings next to my laptop and turned on the printer. First thing I searched for was a copper farm sink I saw in a magazine once. I found one that I liked, printed it out, and taped it to another blank page in his tablet. I knew he was watching me so I pretended to ignore him.

Curiosity eventually won out. "What are you doing?"

Trying to get you thinking of other things, like our future. "I found something I wanted to add."

He leaned on the back of the couch, studying his impressive sketches. "Maybe I'll go back to college, finish my degree."

And just like that he frowned.

"Who am I kidding? I can't go back on an open campus." He tossed the sketch pad onto the table and moped back to his spot on the couch. I hated this. I hated seeing him so withdrawn. Even our sex life had taken a hit. His passion was gone.

It was time for something drastic. I hurried down the hall, hanging our little Do Not Disturb sign on the apartment door so Marie or Mike wouldn't come in unexpectedly, and took off my clothes in the bedroom.

He at least gave me some attention with a questioning glance when I came back into the living room wearing nothing but my white bikini underwear. I grabbed the remote out of his hand, turned off the television, and straddled him.

"What are you doing?" He breathed out his question with a hint of admonishment, as if me being mostly naked and on his lap needed a reason or clarification.

"I want my Ryan back."

His lips twisted into a frown, and then his expression rolled into what scarily resembled rejection.

"Talk to me."

His hands slipped around my hips, tensed, and seemed to push back and up, raising me a smidgen off his crotch. "You had to get naked to talk to me?"

"I figured it was a good way to get your undivided attention. We should be on a beach somewhere having a grand time, making love, having fun, being young, enjoying life. You've been so closed down. You don't want to talk to me. You barely touch me anymore. It's scaring me."

His hands pushed my hips back, a definite sign of his unwillingness to further this conversation. I grasped his forearms, unwilling to let him push me aside.

Desperation clawed at my throat. "Please don't push me away. Please. I can't take it anymore." His despondence was taking its toll on my heart.

He tried to squirm out from underneath me and just like that a new fissure cracked into my patchwork heart. "Ryan, don't. Oh God, please don't. You promised me!"

He resigned back into the couch. "What do you want?"

His momentary rejection unnerved me. I'd been down this road once before and I'd be damned if I was going to let history repeat itself. Fucking men giving me false hope and promises that they so easily yanked back when it was convenient. Well fuck *that*!

"You're breaking my heart! Don't you see that? Is that what you want? You want me off of you, pushing me away like that? Is *that* what you want?" I knew my voice had risen in volume but damn he was pissing me off.

"I just want to chill. That's it. Is that so hard to understand?"

I glared at him for a moment, shocked at his harsh tone. "Fine. You want to *chill*, have at it." I started to climb off his lap but his hands clamped my thighs.

"Where you going?"

"I'm getting off of you and going to live my life. You're not *chilling*, you're rotting away here, letting that shit in your head fester and eat you alive. You don't want to talk to me, get it out and move forward, then you can sit here and continue to *chill* on your own. Let me know when you're done."

"Stop," he groaned.

"Why? A second ago you were pushing me off of you."

He studied me for bit, his eyes scrunched and pained with so much mental poison. "I'm sorry."

I picked up one of his hands, curling it in my own and pressing it between my exposed breasts, pulling it as close to my heart as it could go. "Don't be sorry, babe. *Talk* to me."

He shook his head, fighting it, not able to find the courage or the words.

"Tell me," I pleaded softly. He was tight-lipped and scowling. "You said once that a man should own up to his situation. You also said we'd always talk it out. You promised. Talk to me!"

Ryan was so forlorn. "I can't shut it off. Can't shake it."

I placed soft kisses on his fingers, patiently waiting, trying to encourage him to go on.

"God, you're so fucking beautiful," he said softly but with so much conviction. His eyes drifted downward, landing on my stomach while he pondered. I let him take his time, glad he was at least touching me again.

"You would have been seven months pregnant by now." His fingers drifted over my flat belly button.

"Oh, honey . . ." I breathed out my warning plea for him not to go there.

"I think about it all the time. I wonder if our daughter would have had our blue eyes or if our son would have taken on some of my traits. What their face might have looked like."

I wished I could hush his sadness by kissing his skin. "We'll have beautiful babies . . . when we're meant to bring them into the world. I promise."

He tapped the tip of his finger lightly on my tummy, seeming to disagree. "That was our first and I took that from you. My *career*"—he sneered as if the word was dirty—"took that from us."

I tipped his chin up, aching from seeing him look so lost. "No. Stop, Ryan. Things happen for a reason. Things that you have no control over. We would have managed, but we weren't ready for a baby. We need to be strong together before we bring a child into this world. What happened to me—you can't take that on your shoulders. You can't. I won't let you."

Ryan disagreed again, stuck in something powerful. "There was so much blood when you lost the pregnancy. I thought you were dying on me." He bit into his bottom lip while his eyes got watery.

"I'm here." I nuzzled his hand. "I'm right here, baby."

He stared at my thigh, tracing an invisible line with his fingertip. "Sometimes I forget how strong you are. *Resilient* may be a better word. Life keeps throwing you punches and no matter what, you keep getting back up."

I laced our fingers together. "That's because I have something worth fighting for. You. A promise of forever. You make me want to be stronger."

He snorted and squirmed underneath me. "That's because I'm doing such a bang-up job keeping you safe. What a great job I've done."

I clutched his neck and pressed his shoulders back into the couch. "Stop it. Don't say that. I have never felt as protected and cared for as I have by you."

His head swayed, defeated.

"You're letting them win."

I combed my hands through his hair, tugging until I had his eyes back on me. I took his mouth with desperate longing, kissing him as if I could break the wicked spell that was pulling him under. "Fight with me," I breathed on his lips, which seemed to refuse me passion. "Please, baby. I can't do this without you. I need you. I need you."

His jaw tensed as the pain he'd been holding in so tightly finally cracked. A soft sob slid up his throat. "I'm so tired, Taryn," he croaked, his voice stuttering from trying to keep it in check. But the hurt had nowhere else to go except out. "So tired. All I do is bring us pain."

A tear slid down his cheek. And then another. I knew it was killing him to show me this much weakness but it all needed to be purged, excised from his system like a soul-sucking demon. Seeing him cry was my undoing. He'd finally succumbed to the pressure and that made me mad.

"No you do not! You are the love of my life and my best friend! No matter what life throws at us, we take the good with the bad, Ryan—the good with the bad. We roll with it because that's how we roll."

He pulled me down to his chest, clutching me as if he needed me to get his air back.

I held his head while he buried his face in my neck. "Oh, babe. We'll get through this. Honey, you know how to fix this. You stopped taking your medicine."

He frowned, sniffing. "I'm not taking shit, Tar. No pills."

"Ryan, you've tossed your body into confusion. You can't just suddenly stop taking them."

"Pills to cope . . . What's next? Pills to sleep? Pills to keep awake? That's a sure way to die. You know how much I hate that shit, Tar!"

I held his face in my hands. "Ryan, look at me. I did a lot of research when the doctor put me on antidepressants after the accident. My situation was temporary. You've suffered from anxiety attacks for a long time, even before all of this. It's when you stop taking them that your system gets out of whack."

Resistance to that slipped over his face. "I don't want to rely on drugs, Tar. I don't."

I wiped his cheeks with my thumbs, erasing the physical evidence of his stress. "Doesn't matter. You need them. You need to regulate the serotonin. It's not a sign of weakness, Ryan. And it doesn't make you any less of a man. It's a body imbalance, that's all. There's no shame in that."

He closed his eyes. "I tried to work through it on my own but I feel like I can't shake it. It's like a never-ending loop. Seeing the disappointment on my father's face when they put me in that squad car; I know it broke his heart. I did that to him. Me." Ryan rubbed his palm over the center of his breast plate. "It presses in on me, right here. Like I have an elephant sitting on my chest. Sometimes it's hard to breathe."

"I know, but we can change that. You don't have an addictive bone in your body, Ryan. You need to take one little pill to regulate your body chemistry. That's all."

"Okay," he whispered, conceding. "I'll start taking them again. I can't live like this."

"I'll make an appointment for you to see my doctor. We'll get your smile back. I promise."

IT WAS Monday. We'd been back in Seaport for two weeks when my birth father called again. Ryan, Mike, Marie, and I were at Seaport's Sandy Cove Beach enjoying the hot weather and gorgeous day. Ryan and Mike were tossing a football back and forth while from the comforts of our beach chairs Marie and I enjoyed the incredible sights of them shirtless and tan.

It was pure elation seeing Ryan smiling and having a great time.

It was like he'd been totally rejuvenated. He was on new medication for hypothyroidism, and the differences were almost night and day.

I waved at Ryan to come over.

He opened the cooler lid, grabbed two bottles of ice-cold water, tossed one at Mike, and used the cooler as a seat. "What's up?"

"I just talked to Joe."

Ryan pushed his sunglasses up on his head, looking at me quizzically. "And?"

"He'd like us to come out to Lake Tahoe."

He made that audible exhale noise, seeming none too pleased with that idea. "I don't know."

Okay, so he wasn't even in the same ballpark with my enthusiasm. We had a silent standoff until Ryan said, "I've got to be honest. I'm not seeing the benefit here. The man hasn't been in your life at all and I'm inclined to keep it that way."

I was momentarily distracted watching Mike, who was holding his hand out for Marie. I felt my heart flutter just from the look he wore on his face. He tugged her up from her chair and, without saying a word, walked off with her as if she were a prize, holding her hand as he did. I couldn't help but fall in love watching them enjoying each other, walking in the surf, bumping into each other, Marie gripping on to his muscular arm with both hands. Her beaming up at him and him beaming right back. It was like watching the best part of a love story.

"They make a great couple."

Ryan glanced over his shoulder and then back to me. "They have what we have." He smirked.

I smiled. "I know."

He tossed his chin. "It's a much better fit for both of them."

I was so damn happy seeing their love blossoming, it was hard to contain it. "I agree."

Ryan's smile fell. "Back to this Joe business. Taryn, I want to trim all the variables off. Things are finally getting back on track for us and

I'm not looking to add any crazy onto the pile. You want to meet him, we'll set it up, but not without me being there. First sign of potential bullshit, I'm pulling you out and we're on a plane."

"I want to meet him."

Ryan chewed on his bottom lip. "Did he come clean with his wife?"

"Yes. He said she was understanding about it and she and the girls want to meet me."

Ryan nodded before putting me back under his scrutinizing gaze. "This really a road you want to go down?"

I knew he was just trying to shield me from further hurt. "Yes. If I don't, I'll always wonder. I need to put that part of me to rest, Ryan."

He reluctantly agreed. "Okay, if that's what you need, I'll get our flights booked."

I grinned at him. He didn't need to utter the "I love you" words for me to know how much he did. "Thank you, babe."

He dropped his shades back down. "Pete going to be all right managing the bar while we're gone?"

I reviewed my mental calendar. We had the Teen Choice Awards coming up, and then Ryan had to do some fittings in L.A. for the third *Seaside* film.

I nodded, quite confident that I'd made the right decision. He'd lost all of the bookings he had for the summer, having to sub out the work to another guy, so he was more than thankful for the job. "He'll be just fine. He's been helping me for a long time, so he knows what needs to be done."

"Tammy seems happier, too."

I recalled the talk she and I had the other day, ironing out some of our issues. She and Marie were still walking wide circles around each other to avoid confrontations, but for the most part, Marie was over it. Having Mike tell her to get her ass in his bed every night, even though *his* bed was my guest bed, was helping to soften Tammy's betrayal. "We're going to try serving a limited menu in the pub. See how that works out before we go further. Maybe she'll name a sandwich after you."

Ryan rolled his eyes.

I glanced at my cell to see the time. "We've got to get going. We meet the builder in two hours."

Ryan stood, straightened his dog tag necklace—the one with my name written on it so he could "keep me close to his heart at all times"—and tried to see where Mike and Marie had gotten to. "You okay with the addition we talked about?"

I watched Mike whirl Marie around in the surf, and wished Gary could see how much happier she was. His callousness deserved a bit of retribution. "Is Mike?"

"My head of security needs a command center and I'm thinking I'd sleep better at night knowing your new guardian was conveniently located."

As much as I loved that idea, he was presuming a lot. "She just took a course, Ryan. Who knows where that will take her."

His wry grin told me he had info he wasn't sharing.

"What do you know that I don't?" I asked, grinning right back at him.

Ryan casually shrugged. "Let's just say whatever it is we've got planned, you two ladies can't do shit about it." He held out his hand. "Come on. If you want to meet Joe, we've got to book a side trip to Lake Tahoe."

CHAPTER 21

Unguarded

STOP FIDGETING. YOU look official," I teased Marie while she tugged at her coat sleeves. Mike made her wear a plain black suit jacket and pants with a cream-colored blouse and sensible, low-heeled shoes for her first red carpet assignment in L.A. Even though she was nervous as hell she at least looked the part.

Mike had been working with her since she'd returned from the intensive training program, going over everything from limousine procedures to how to handle a physical altercation. He also schooled her on the different code words she'd need to use to communicate with him. It was actually quite interesting to learn all of the things Mike did behind the scenes to protect people.

He'd become such an integral part of our daily lives that sometimes it was hard to remember that he was "working" when he was with us. Half the time it felt as though he was hanging around because he and Ryan were best friends.

"I still think I could have been all kick-ass in a hot little dress," Marie groaned. "You're all gorgeous and I look like an uptight schoolteacher."

"Remember the formation we practiced," Mike muttered from the front seat of our chauffeured car, his subtle way of reminding her she was "working" and not here to be rocking hot with me. I knew he'd dressed her to blend in, not to stand out. Ryan and I had done quite a few "run-through" scenarios with them in my living room to the point where Mike had even shown us some self-defense techniques—should we ever need to protect ourselves. I could understand his reasoning that wearing a skirt would not be the smartest idea.

"You going to kneel on someone's head?" I muttered to her, teasingly. Mike had shown her how to subdue someone to keep them immobile while we were being removed from a "threat." Executed properly, an assailant might get a good crotch view or a "Vagina Crunch" as Marie and I called it.

Marie just rolled her eyes at me. "I've fired seven different guns over the last few weeks and I've got a pretty good aim. Watch it."

I sneered back. "Don't be overwhelmed by the camera flashes. Try to keep from looking at them or else you'll be seeing spots the rest of the night. It's almost like you're temporarily blinded."

We waited in a long line of cars snaking along the road that led to where all the celebrities were arriving at the massive Gibson Amphitheatre for the Nick Teen Choice Awards. It was Marie's first assignment as my guard, working the detail under her new boss, Mike Murphy.

I had been wondering how the boss/boyfriend relationship would work, but so far things were going fairly smoothly. She was more than willing to take his orders, which I think just really turned him on. He'd bark a command and she'd immediately submit to his orders. Then he'd stand taller with that hint of secret smile lifting one corner of his mouth. He tried to be all badass but his little giveaway was just enough to be his downfall because Marie would play it for all it was worth.

Regardless of what Mike thought, Marie really had the upper hand in this relationship.

I saw her touch the hidden microphone in her ear. "Yes, okay. We're green."

Ryan leaned into me. "It's like *Spy vs. Spy*, you know?"

"They're practicing their BDSM code talk. Whip me, Master. I've been naughty." I giggled and elbowed him when Marie chucked me the finger.

Ryan tilted his head, smirking. "It's been a while since we did the bondage thing. I'm feeling inspired by all of this ass-kicking show of dominance."

Mike leaned over the seat. "If you two are done, we're up next to exit."

Marie had her game face on, looking all serious and on edge when I climbed out of the car.

Ryan tugged me a few feet before he was pulled right in to give autographs and greet his fans. I stepped back out of the way, as I'd been instructed at all his other appearances. Marie was on my right side, keeping watch. Mike had her practice "shielding and removing" me from potential threats, and since she was right-handed, her left arm would be the one she used to grab me. Who knew there was a science to all of this? Mike knew the routine. He handled Ryan's autographing and posing better than any publicist or manager could ever do, having been with Ryan at every public appearance he'd made in the last year.

"See how Mike keeps things away from Ryan's face?" I said to her. Mike was holding a hand up, keeping all of the things fans were shoving at him to sign from getting too close.

"Holy shit, Taryn," Marie muttered, taking in the hundreds of screaming fans lined up behind barricades, hungrily vying for a second of Ryan's attention. "I thought the premiere was crazy; this is insane. They're like rabid teenagers."

"This is almost how it was in Paris."

Her head snapped in my direction. "Like this?"

I nodded, keeping a handle on that memory. I was getting used to it, but this was only Marie's second time experiencing the "fande-monium" that followed Ryan Christensen the movie star wherever he went, and I could see she was visibly shaken by it all. Ryan seemed so much more collected, cheerful even, giving his fans what they so desperately craved.

"Mike was on the phone with event security all morning coordinating this."

I acknowledged her with a nod, and then glanced around. I noticed the extra security milling behind us. I knew both Ryan and Mike wouldn't leave her to her own devices should anything go down.

"So is this basically what I do then? Just stand here with you?" Marie asked, glancing around, looking all official as she scanned for possible threats.

"What? Babysit me? Yep. You're doing it."

She twisted her lips at my poor attempt at humor.

I nudged my chin toward Ryan and Mike. "Those two chumps think we have no clue what's going on."

Marie nodded. "After the Kyle thing, it's pretty obvious why Ryan would want you to have a female bodyguard. I gathered that awhile ago when Mike first started talking to me about the wonders of being in personal security. He sort of slipped once when he told me that Ryan wanted a female to guard you."

"Yeah, I'd say their little scheme is pretty transparent."

"Do we let them know that we're on to them?"

"And miss an opportunity to mess with them? Nah. This is all part of his master plan to ensure that I don't get bored and into trouble while he's busy being famous."

Marie peered around me, keeping up with her vigil. "I sure as hell won't be complaining. I get a gorgeous man who fucks like a machine and to travel the globe with my best friend. I have no problem babysitting you while we shop."

I couldn't help but laugh at that.

"I will start taking yoga classes if Mike gives me my own charge card—I'm telling you that now."

"Just think of the trouble you could get into if you were a contortionist."

She broke into a fit of giggles. "So does this job come with health insurance? I may need it."

"Not sure, but I'll let you stare at Ryan Christensen's ass for an extra ten minutes a day."

She looked aghast. "Only ten minutes? Hah! You know, if you would have told me a year ago I'd be part of Ryan Christensen's entourage, I would have questioned your sanity. This is surreal. And no offense, but his ass is stellar."

I watched all the faces of his fans light up the moment Ryan stopped in front of them, grinning, too. "What did my mom always say? Dreams come true when you point yourself in their direction."

"Your mother was a brilliant woman," Marie stated emphatically, both of us casting our gazes back to Ryan's and Mike's stellar asses.

I pulled a vision of my mom's smiling face into my thoughts, hating that as the years passed since her death, I had to sometimes struggle to remember what she looked like.

Ryan smiled and waved a final goodbye to his screaming fans, then walked with purposeful strides to where I stood waiting. He took me by the hand, raised it to his mouth to softly kiss my fingers, twined his fingers around mine, and continued walking. His random public display of affection left me breathless. I don't even think he knew how his unconscious actions made the entire outside world disappear around us or how he set my heart fluttering like a hummingbird's wings from his natural chivalry. I knew we were going to pose for the press photo op next, but I would have stood in any firing line just to be next to him.

NOW THAT I was paying more attention to all the behind-the-scenes details, I realized just how much Mike truly did for us. The rest of the award show went off without a hitch and Ryan received a large surfboard for winning Choice Movie Actor, Drama. I loved watching him onstage, thanking his fans. His acceptance speech was short and sweet and hanging out with the old *Seaside* cast backstage was a blast.

When the award show was over, Mike and Marie were waiting to take us to our next destination—a late dinner with them and Cal and Kelly at the decadent restaurant Koi.

Thank God Marie was with us as we were bombarded by paparazzi when we came out of the restaurant. Mike had made sure our driver was waiting at the curb before allowing us to leave the safe confines of the building. Ryan had my hand, Marie was flanking me, repeating Mike's orders for the throng of photographers to back up and let us through. After two and a half glasses of wine and being blinded in the dark by all of the camera flashes, I was glad I didn't have to drive.

"No wonder celebs get into accidents," Marie muttered. "I can't see for shit. Look at them! Why the hell are they blocking the front of the car?"

The paparazzi were elbowing each other out of the way, trying to get more shots of us inside the vehicle. Ryan had his hand cupped over his eyes. I noticed Marie was doing the same thing. "You know, I always thought famous people did this because they were hiding from being photographed. Now I know it's also to protect your damn eyes!"

HER VOICE flashed back through my mind as we endured the same gamut of photogs trying to catch our flight out of LAX. Fortunately, only a few passengers with cell phone cameras were on hand when we landed in Reno, Nevada.

I was nervous, excited, and petrified as we hurried out of the airport, climbing right into a chauffeured SUV waiting at the curb. I had always wondered how celebrities were able to get carted away so quickly; it was all a matter of precise coordination.

Mike held the door, guarding our entry. Even getting into cars was choreographed. I always got in first, followed by Ryan. Once the "principals" were stowed, Marie was in next. Mike always sat in the front passenger seat—always. He also handled receiving our luggage. Ryan Christensen didn't wait at luggage carousels—ever.

I was beginning to think that Mike needed a big, fat raise. Giving him my best friend in the world with a big, red bow wrapped around her didn't seem enough.

Ryan took my hand in his, giving me a reassuring squeeze and a smile. He didn't need to ask me if I was nervous to meet my birth father; he knew. I'd barely slept a wink last night.

While we waited for our luggage to be loaded, Ryan toggled through his missed messages. "We've got a problem."

My first thought was that the paparazzi had followed us, assuming we came to Reno to get married. Well, that's what Trish's first thought was when I mentioned our destination. I did not need any more problems and from his distinct tone I could tell it was personal.

He turned to meet my waiting stare. "Got an email from Trish. Apparently one of Tammy's friends posted on Twitter that she's going to get to meet me at their wedding in September."

My nervous energy burst into a blur of outrageous fury. "You're kidding?"

"I wish I was." Ryan shoved his cell back into his pocket. "Well, there goes that. I told them to keep this to themselves. No one ever listens. Their wedding is going to be a media circus. Son of a . . ."

He glared over at me. "You know it's going to be crazy now. I told Pete how this could turn out. News travels that I might be stepping into a church and you'll have fucking helicopters flying overhead."

Marie snorted from the backseat. "I wonder which idiot friend of hers did it."

"Be nice," I muttered, digging out my phone.

"Not likely," she retorted with defiant sarcasm.

I rolled my eyes and started to call Tammy while the driver stowed our luggage in the back. "She's not answering."

"Of course she's not answering. She knows I'm with you," Marie added.

Ryan knew how much this dissension bothered me, having these moody, snippy attitudes floating around between what used to be the greatest of friends. I could only hope that it was the stress Tammy was going through making her crazy.

"I have to fix this," I groaned.

"Why?" Marie snapped. "She wanted to have the bragging rights that Ryan was going to be in her wedding. This is her mess, not yours. She should have kept her damn mouth shut."

"I agree," Ryan muttered. "This isn't your problem, Tar."

I mostly agreed with them. Still . . . "When we get to the hotel, I'm going to try to call Pete. He has a right to know what's going on, especially if there's any chance his wedding might get ruined."

The look in Ryan's eyes said that it was already too late to prevent that.

THE VIEW coming up to the Ritz-Carlton hotel in Lake Tahoe was spectacular. The tall pines, majestic mountains, and impressive hotel complex beckoned us to come and enjoy luxury at its finest. Inside, a massive stacked-stone fireplace took central stage, towering "fifty-five feet tall," as I had been informed by the concierge.

We were directed to a private floor, entering the most lavish suite I'd ever seen.

"Wow," Marie breathed out. "I'm so glad you're my friend," she said to Ryan.

He smiled and took my bag off my shoulder.

Our suite had huge windows with gorgeous views of the mountains. Only one person we knew would know how to find this sort of decadence. "Andrea?"

Ryan winked. "Yep."

"That girl needs a huge raise."

"Who's Andrea?" Marie asked, wandering around in a tight circle so she wouldn't miss anything.

"She's the goddess of all travel agents," Ryan answered. "There are supposed to be two master bedrooms. Pick one. Mike and I will be here drinking this complimentary bottle of cognac while you ladies decide."

Marie and I wandered from room to room. "This place is bigger than the apartment," she breathed.

I felt the elation hit my toes when I saw the extensive tiled shower stall. "I know."

"I love having rich celebrities as friends," she muttered, petting one of the white, fluffy towels folded on the counter as if it were alive.

"When is Joe coming here?" she asked.

"Tomorrow. He's bringing the wife and kids."

She wandered into another room that looked like a small living room or a den with a gorgeous view of the barren ski slopes. "Why aren't you going to his house?"

My fingers skated over all the rich fabrics as I followed her path. Even the draperies were luxurious. "Ryan wanted neutral ground, but by the looks of this place, he's got the upper hand. He also didn't want a public meeting in case things didn't turn out so well. It's Ryan's version of controlling the situation."

We wandered through the central living room, checking out the other side of the suite, getting lascivious smiles from the boys on our way through.

Marie breathed out a curse. "With accommodations like this, Ryan can get his control freak on any day he likes, as far as I'm concerned."

"I'm calling dibs on this room."

"Fine. They're pretty much identical anyway. I'm glad there's a huge room separating us." She gave me a nudge. "Just try to keep it down tonight, all right?"

I followed her out, noting that just looking at Ryan, standing there in a plain gray tee untucked from his jeans, was enough to make my heart skip a beat. "Marie, what say we make a bet?"

She turned, confused at first, before she caught on. "What *kind* of bet, Taryn?"

"First woman to fold."

Mike barked out a hearty laugh.

I put on my most confident smirk, even though I was actually quite tired. "I've got two hundred in cash. Men can keep the time."

Ryan drummed his hands on the raised bar. "Yes! Now we're talking. I like where your head's at, hon."

Marie whipped her head around, looking for some support from Mike. I knew she didn't have two hundred dollars on her but Mike's reassuring nod said that he did.

Her long chestnut hair flew back around. "You're on."

I SLAPPED two hundred on the polished six-person dark mahogany dining table right next to Marie's plate and kept walking. I knew I had lost so there was no point contesting it.

Mike started laughing to himself.

Ryan came out of our room, finger-combing his hair back. "Keep your comments to yourself, Murphy. She didn't sleep at all the night before."

I poured two cups of coffee, wishing I could mainline one right into my vein. Right after my second wonderful orgasm last night, I must have passed out. Let's just say after *coming*, the last thing I remember was *going*.

Mike slipped the bills off the table, folded them nicely, and tucked them right into Marie's cleavage. She smirked, wearing my money like a booby badge of honor.

The momentary laugh was not enough to keep me calm. My nerves were on edge from the moment I woke up. *What will he look like? Will I see any of me when I look at him? Will he turn out to be a ginormous ass, making me regret my decision to meet him?* So many unanswered questions drew me away from the fun of losing our little contest.

I NEARLY sprang out of my skin when our room telephone rang later in the early afternoon. I knew the message even before Mike hung up.

"They're here. They're being seated at the Chef's Table down in the restaurant."

Ryan cupped my face in his hands; his thumbs skated over my cheeks while his concern-filled eyes bore into mine. "No matter what, I will not allow this day to end on a sad note. Things go good—we invite them back to the suite here. Things go south—after lunch they go and we put it behind us. Okay?"

I nodded. "Okay."

"Okay, baby." He leaned down and took my mouth, dotting his vow with a kiss.

It was hard to breathe; I was filled with so much trepidation, it was stifling. Ryan led the way, holding my hand the entire time, almost pulling me along. He walked with confidence, as always. Those broad shoulders taking on my worry.

I noticed the two young girls first; their wide-eyed shock and amazement at seeing Ryan Christensen walking their way was almost comical. There was no doubt they recognized him since they were absolutely giddy with delight.

I don't know why I was surprised when I saw Joe for the first time. Maybe it was because I had only seen him as a lean and lanky teen with hair as black as midnight, but this solid man with the Tim McGraw vibe was not what I had expected.

My eyes traveled from his broad shoulders and tall frame up to his closely shaved goatee and matching short brown hair. His cheeks were glowing with a bit of a summer tan showing everywhere. As I approached, his eyes crinkled when he widened his smile.

All of the air vacated my lungs when I took in his deep blue eyes, which were a spitting image of my own. That moment of *finally* having some familiar facial recognition hit me hard, as if some force of nature had just slammed into my chest. I felt a sob bubble up and lodge in my throat.

Oddly, I had expected to meet someone older, considering he'd fathered me, but I had to remind myself that there were only sixteen years separating us. Joe was forty-four now but didn't look old enough to have a daughter my age.

As Joe's blue eyes scrunched, his hand tightened on his wife's shoulder, and I noticed his lower lip start to quiver. He stepped around his wife to make his approach. I could see the tremors tweaking his muscles, causing his steps to be somewhat shaky.

Ryan tugged my hand and pulled me in front of his body; his fingertips nudged the small of my back, releasing me make this journey on my own.

"Oh my baby girl," Joe stuttered out, sucking back his own sobs.

That's when I lost my tenuous hold.

Hot tears of my own started to fall. I didn't know this man from Adam, but something about him just felt so right. Next thing I knew, strong arms were surrounding me, his hand gripping the back of my head, burying my face into his chest.

"Twenty-eight years. I have *never* stopped thinking about you for twenty-eight years. Thank you for giving me this," Joe sputtered, keeping his voice low.

I nodded, unable to speak, feeling his pain, feeling his joy. I could only imagine what he must have gone through, having to give up his flesh and blood.

Joe took me by the shoulders, pressing me away from him a few inches. "Let me look at you some more. I can't believe it. I thought . . ." He choked up. "I never thought this day would come."

Knowing he was just as affected by this reunion as I was was a relief.

He drew in a short breath. "You look just like your mother, Taryn."

I found myself nodding and agreeing with him, even though I'd never seen a picture of the woman who gave birth to me.

"I wish she was here to see you all grown but I'm sure she's smiling down on us from heaven today."

Joe tried to wipe the tear from my cheek, which made me automatically wipe my own face. "It's nice to finally know where I got my eyes from."

He smiled wider, making me wonder what else we had in common.

While I gave his wife, Jill, a hug, Ryan and Joe shook hands and exchanged greetings.

After a nice lunch, Ryan extended an invitation for them to come back to our suite.

Marie was doing a wonderful job keeping the two young girls entertained while Ryan and I sat with Joe and his wife to have a private conversation.

Joe appeared sincere but cautious. "I can only imagine how hard this must be on you, finding out like that. I was under the impression that your dad destroyed all the records. I never thought he'd keep them."

I took a sip of my coffee, trying to disconnect myself a bit from the emotional overload. "He had it all together in a safe-deposit box."

Joe nodded. "My letters and everything?"

I set my cup down. "There was about two thousand dollars as well."

He scratched his head, mashing his lips together for a moment. "I'd always wondered if you got the money I'd sent. Figures your dad wouldn't spend a dime of it. Probably thought it was drug money or something."

Drug money?

His hand rubbed over his mouth. "I had some problems before I went into the army. Let's just say Uncle Sam kicked that shit out of my system quickly."

I had no doubt about that. "I have savings bonds for both your girls. I want them to have the two thousand dollars."

Joe held out a hand, ready to rebuke me, but I spoke over him. "Joe, it's for their future. I appreciate your generosity, but it's not necessary."

Joe's wife, Jill, overrode his disapproval. "Thank you, Taryn. That is very thoughtful of you. The girls will be going off to college before we know it so we'll make sure it goes to good use." Jill looked over at Ryan. "Although meeting you is going to be priceless to them. They haven't shut up about it since we told them. Our oldest thought we were playing a practical joke on her up until the moment you walked into that dining room. I can't thank you enough for *all* that you've given my family today."

Ryan smiled but waved it off as no big deal. "I'll make sure they get some pictures of us together to take back with them."

Both Joe and his wife seemed exceptionally pleased by that. Then Joe turned his attention back to me, studying me as if I were made of glass. "You probably have so many questions now."

That was an understatement. "I have so many questions, I don't know where to even begin."

Joe rested his elbows on his knees. "Ask me anything. Jill has a right to know, as well. I know I shocked the hell out of her, too"—he reached over and took his wife's hand—"but like I told her, I never thought I'd see you again, so what would be the point of upsetting her."

Jill gave him a reassuring smile, rubbing the back of his hand. "I'm not upset. You were a teenager, Joe."

Joe shrugged, seeming to want to atone for his sins. "A kid that got his teen girlfriend pregnant."

Ryan crossed his foot up on his knee and reached for my hand. "And for that, I thank you," he said, pulling my hand up to his mouth to grace me with a kiss. "You created the woman I love. There is no better gift than that."

Something silent seemed to pass between the two men, a mutual understanding of sorts.

Joe seemed relieved. "At least I did something right. I'm glad to know she's in such good hands."

I felt a blush warm my cheeks. I was in the best of hands. How vastly different my life could have turned out had my parents not given me up. Bits and pieces of the army letters Joe had written to me came swirling back. All of them hinted at the fact that Joe was a bit of a hellion when he was a teenager.

I squeezed Ryan's hand. "You dated Kelcie in high school?"

Joe glanced at his wife, silently seeking her approval to talk about this. She gave him a thoughtful smile in return. "Yeah. She sat by me in math class. I used to cheat off her paper. We were fifteen when we started going steady."

I could see he was recalling fond memories.

"We were like kindred spirits; both of us were hell-raisers who hated our parents. When I got Kelcie pregnant, I honestly thought my life was starting over. I'd hoped that her mom would at least be understanding, but instead she kicked her own daughter out onto the street. And Kelcie's dad . . . that bastard ruled with an iron fist. To this day, I still think he used to beat her mom, but I could never prove it. Both of them were not good people."

Thoughts of having "not good people" as a set of grandparents I'd never meet crossed my mind.

"Anyway, I tried to get her out of there. We even thought that if she'd get pregnant my parents would take sympathy on her and let her move in." He laughed. "Yeah, that wasn't one of our brightest ideas."

Ryan sat forward. Something had unsettled him.

"Don't get me wrong, we both wanted you," Joe said, backpedaling. "It's just, well, my dad got laid off and my mom wasn't making all that much at her job. Kelcie tried to get on welfare to help feed you. We were just kids, barely able to wipe our own noses."

"I always dream about you having black hair," I said, unconsciously touching my hair.

Joe appeared taken aback. "You do? Huh. I actually used to dye it. I wanted to be a punk rocker. My mom almost cried when I traded in piano lessons for a guitar with an anarchy sticker on it."

Ryan glanced over at me. "Well, now we know where your musical talents come from."

I smiled. My mom couldn't even tune the car stereo.

Joe's eyes widened. "You play?"

I nodded. "Started on piano and taught myself acoustic guitar."

Ryan brushed my arm, smiling. "And she's got a beautiful voice, too."

Joe seemed impressed. "Wow! That's excellent!"

After a few moments of silence, I went for the question that burned the most in my mind. "I dream about you quite often, Joe. Whenever I do, my dad, Dan, is always there, too. And you two are fighting. I mean, physically *fighting*. And then there's blood. *Lots* of blood. Your teeth, your mouth."

Joe winced, shaking his head. "Taryn . . ."

"No, I need to know. It's always the same dream and after all of these years, I need answers. I have nightmares—scary, horrible nightmares."

Ryan's mouth opened, realization dawning on him. I nodded at his silent conclusion, knowing I'd never fully explained why I sometimes woke up terrified. Now he understood. I squeezed his hand harder.

Joe stared across the short distance between his seat and mine, his lips mashed into a hard line.

"And they always end the same way. You say 'I'd never hurt you, baby girl' and then your teeth turn red with blood." I knew I was goading him, but I didn't care. It was time to find out just how fucked-up this situation really was.

Ryan's face fell, coated with pitiful sorrow. This was news I'd never shared before. I thought he might be miffed about finding out this way, but I'd just have to deal with him later.

"Taryn," Joe started, using a tone that was obviously a warning.

"No, I need to know. Why? Why do I have the same dream over and over again?"

He hesitated, holding his breath, but I was tired of waiting. My dream was always the same, and now I knew it wasn't just a figment of my imagination. I'd been recalling a memory over and over again.

"Just tell me. Please."

Joe huffed, then rolled his gaze back to me. "It was the Fourth of July, right before I shipped off to boot camp. You know your birth mom got killed in a car crash, right?"

I nodded. "Your mom told me."

Joe frowned, pained by this walk down memory lane. "It was right after Christmas when it had happened. You weren't even two yet. Your mom—Jennifer—and Uncle Dan, well, they were both doing well financially. He'd just gotten that big promotion at Corning and my parents were just about to lose the house."

I swallowed hard as answers started to fill the empty spaces.

"Aunt Jennifer wanted you real bad. And I did something really stupid. I . . . I was up to no good, and I got tangled up with the wrong sort of people."

I held up a hand, not wanting to know I was used as barter. "Is this the reason why our mothers stopped talking to each other?"

Joe's face blanked, and then he gave me one nod of confirmation.

"Taryn," Ryan groaned. I knew he was telling me not to feel guilty about that.

I gave Ryan my own pleading warning. I still had unanswered questions. "So then what happened on the Fourth?"

Joe hesitated, gazing at the ornate rug beneath his feet instead of answering.

"Joe, both of my parents are gone. I have a right to know the truth. What happened?"

"Nothing, really. It was a family picnic, no big deal."

Somehow I highly doubted that.

I could see him caving a bit more, his broad shoulders slumping. "I may have been a bit surly, considering the circumstances. Part of the agreement was that you were never to know that they weren't your natural parents. I had to swear I'd never reveal the truth. It"—he gasped, choking up—"it killed me to do that, Taryn. You were my baby girl. *Mine.* I held you from the moment you came out of your momma's belly and I *promised you* . . . I promised that I'd never stop taking care of you. I rocked you and fed you and read stories when you had colic and wouldn't sleep. And then when that asshole drove too fast on the icy road and smashed into us, I was all you had left. I knew we shouldn't have taken you out, but all we had to do was put you in that car seat and drive around a bit and you'd be out like a light. I couldn't just let them take that from me!"

Jill rested her hand on Joe's thigh to comfort him, her hand trembling slightly.

My own hand started to tremble as well. In the dream, I know I'm alone with him and I can feel him touching my hair, talking to me as if he's sorry. And then my father pounces, ready to kill him. Maybe my intimacy and fear-of-abandonment issues have atrocious origins?

I felt my chest tighten even more, fearing the answer to my next question. "Did you hurt me?"

Joe winced. "What? Oh, Lord, no. No."

"Then why did my dad hit you? He beat the crap out of you until you bled. He was a levelheaded guy. Why would he attack you so brutally?"

Joe was glowering at me, his breathing labored with his frustration. "Because I told you the truth! I told you about your real mom and I told you that I was your real dad and no matter what they did, they would never take you from my heart. You are *my* daughter. That's why!"

CHAPTER 22

Fiasco

I COULD FEEL OUR plane descending on its approach to Providence. I'd been watching the arrival time on the screen, counting from one to sixty to help take my mind off the change in pressure squeezing my ears. I was all out of chewing gum, slightly in pain, and flat-out exhausted.

A huge part of me, though, felt relieved. Meeting Joe and his family, being able to reconcile that part of my life, was emotionally taxing but very necessary.

I departed Lake Tahoe hoping that my disrupted soul could finally find peace.

Joe had shown me a picture of Kelcie, and after the shock wore off at how much I really did look like my birth mother, he told me I could keep it. I squeezed my carry-on bag, hugging the picture that I'd placed inside my wallet. Kelcie Tremont was two months away from her eighteenth birthday when she died on that icy winter night.

The last thing she did before leaving this earth was tend to my needs, even though it was obvious from this meeting that Joe had been harboring the guilt since he was the one that suggested taking me out in the car. I held his hand for a long time while he and I had a private moment to talk about forgiveness.

Ryan reached over the armrest and patted my leg, rubbing his palm over my denim-clad thigh. I met his gaze, understanding his thoughtful look. Right after that, I had a revelation. Somewhere along the line, Ryan and I had developed the ability to say a hundred words to each other with just one look. I could read him just as easily as he could read me, and what he wanted to know right now was what I was dwelling on.

"I have to talk to Pete," I answered. With all of the other revelations we'd been dealing with over the last three days, speaking with Pete had been put on hold.

Ryan nodded but I could tell he was concerned. I knew he had a lot to do; the third *Seaside* movie was scheduled to start filming in three weeks and he'd be on location in New Orleans for three and a half months. "We'll talk to him together. I've got to tell you, Taryn, I'm not happy about Tammy having an attitude. You've allowed her to run her business out of that kitchen for pennies. Pete's got an income now because of you, and I know you've been friends with him for a long time, but if she wants to keep playing bitchy bride, she can do it on someone else's dime."

My mouth popped open to speak, only to be shut by him continuing with his small rant.

"I've got no tolerance for nonsense anymore. And if planning a wedding makes a girl that crazy, we're keeping ours small and simple."

Is that so? "No opinionated aunts then, huh?"

He laughed. "Definitely not."

I wanted to say "Pete's my friend and I own the bar," but that reminded me of how Thomas used to draw lines between what was mine and what was his, and that was not the way I wanted my relationship with Ryan to be. Ryan was entitled to give me his opinion and I knew he was protecting me the only way he knew how. After so many years of having his own experiences dealing with users and takers, he was leery of everyone.

By the time we landed and drove back to my apartment, I was wiped out and ready for bed. The last thing I needed to see were more boxes blocking my hallway.

"What the hell's all this?" Ryan groaned.

Mike opened up one box while Ryan opened another. "Looks like more fan mail," Mike muttered.

Ryan shoved the box flaps back together and grabbed his bags.

I didn't need sharp hearing to pick up on Ryan telling Mike that he wanted to toss it all before I saw any more threat letters or hate mail. Surely with the volume sitting in boxes, there had to be a few unkind letters in the mix.

Ryan's phone chimed. He'd been avoiding someone and I was pretty sure I knew who that was. "You can't keep ignoring him."

He tossed his suitcase on the bed. "Yes, I can."

"He's your manager."

Ryan groaned. "He had no right doing what he did."

"Then tell him that."

"I'm still too mad not to fire him."

I shrugged. "Then fire him."

He toed his sneakers off. "I can't."

"You're ready to kick Tammy and her business out of the kitchen downstairs but your manager took it upon himself to order a prenuptial agreement and you don't think that requires a bitch-slap?"

His hands rested on his hips while he stared at me. "You want me to fire him."

I made a pile of dirty laundry, noticing the similarities between the task at hand and this conversation. "Is that a question or a statement?" I was hoping we weren't headed for an impasse.

Ryan shrugged. "Both."

Drat.

"He's not my manager. I don't have to deal with him as much as you do so it's not my call to make."

Ryan set his bag on the bed. "You don't like him."

I met his gaze. "Another question or a statement?"

"Statement."

I resumed sorting laundry. "No, I don't like him, but you already know this. He's been underhanded too many times, which makes him untrustworthy in my book. He has a difference of opinion with you of how you should lead your life, what roles you should consider pursuing, and he's made it blatantly clear that he views me as an intrusion. Then again, I know nothing about hiring a talent manager. I do know that you have to have a certain level of trust in the people you employ. So the question goes back to you. Do you trust him?"

He took a deep breath, his shoulders falling in disappointment. I knew this had to be weighing heavily on his mind for a while and I was glad he was finally addressing it. "I used to."

Being diplomatic and not wanting his decision to be swayed by my opinion, I asked, "And why don't you anymore?"

"Len Bainbridge is *my* lawyer. David had no right speaking to him on my behalf about a prenuptial agreement, regardless of inquiries for photo exclusives."

I couldn't agree more. I was glad he drew that conclusion on his own.

THE NEXT day I faced another possible impasse.

"Your friend Amy posted about him being at your wedding on Twitter, Tammy." I tried to be sympathetic and compassionate but direct and to the point as well. I knew she wasn't the one who leaked the information, but she'd have to deal with the aftermath.

Big, brown eyes that just weren't getting it gazed blankly back across the table at me. "So?"

Either I wasn't explaining myself properly or she was missing the point. I folded my fingers together, trying to keep calm. "So, what that means is on the day you two get married, there is a high probability that your church will be surrounded by a swarm of photographers, press, and fans. Most of the gossip sites have already posted that *our* wedding date has been leaked, Tammy. They don't care if it's your wedding or not. They see a tweet about Ryan and a confirmed wedding and the news channels explode with it. *CV* magazine's website even has a fake wedding invitation posted with the date."

Pete groaned and sat back in his chair, turning an angry glare on his fiancée. I hated seeing them like this, torn up about things they had no control over.

I could see the light dawning on her. It also became quite obvious to me that when Ryan and I did get married, keeping the date and the location secret would be the top priority.

"So now what?" Pete asked.

Ryan drew in an audible breath. "You know I want to be there for you, man, but the shit that surrounds me can get out of control. Your wedding date was posted in one of the replies to the original Twitter post. It spread from there."

Pete turned and glowered at Tammy. "You fucked up."

Her face fell. So did my heart. "Pete, it's not her fault."

Tammy was on the verge of tears. "I didn't do this!"

I clutched his arm, hoping to get his attention before this blew up, but it made no difference. His other fist hit the table. "No? Then who did?"

Tammy appeared indignant, holding it in. "I don't know why you're so mad at me."

Ryan cautioned them both. "Listen. What's done is done. I'm just worried about your day being ruined because of this, that's all. Taryn and I are huge media targets right now."

Tammy swiped a tear away. "Ruined? Like how? Do I have to cancel everything now?"

I could see the panic welling up in her. "No, sweetie, you don't. It's your wedding day—it's *your* day to shine. We just don't want to do anything to detract from that."

Pete was obviously fuming. "Amy couldn't keep her damn mouth shut, could she? I warned you about her, time and time again, and now look what she's done. I do not want that bitch in our wedding."

Tammy fell back and cowered in her chair. "She's my maid of honor, Pete. You wanted Gary as your best man."

"Yeah, well I also didn't know that he was nailing your friend behind Marie's back. Not only is she a loud-mouthed whore, she's also a home-wrecker. I don't want you hanging around her anymore. She's no longer welcome in my house."

Tammy stood up abruptly; her chair scraped the floor. If looks could kill, he was a dead man. "I can't believe you just said that."

"What? That your girlfriend is a whore or that's she's a home-wrecker?"

"Go to hell," she growled.

Pete relaxed back into his chair. "Babe, sometimes I feel as though I'm already there."

Tammy let out a frustrated groan, chucked her middle finger at Pete, then stormed out of the pub and back into the kitchen.

Ryan was scratching the back of his head, appearing just as dumbfounded about the last ten minutes as I was. "Dude, I'm sorry. We never meant to cause problems for you."

Pete waved his hand, casting that off, and then rubbed his face. "It's not your problem, Ryan. This wedding is creating so much stress, she's driving me crazy." He glanced back and forth and then held his gaze on me. "I didn't know Gary was messing with that girl. I swear. Amy was over at our place one time when Gary came over. They sort of hit it off right away, but I didn't think anything of it. I just thought they were being friendly. I told Tammy to tell Amy to back off because Gary was married but apparently that message never made it through."

I believed him. Through all these years, Pete had never lied to me. He told me everything straight up, whether good news or bad.

"What are we going to do?" I asked him.

Pete shrugged. "I just banned my best man's date, Marie and Tammy aren't speaking, the paparazzi are going to hound you if you show up, and I just pissed off my bride. I don't know. I honestly don't know."

FOUR DAYS later, Ryan caught a flight out to L.A. to start rehearsals for the third *Seaside* film while I stayed in Rhode Island. Pete had an appointment at the physical therapist, so Marie and I were back behind the bar together, mixing drinks and tapping beer, just like old times.

I saw Tammy walk out of the kitchen, her eyes totally focused on the paper in her hand. "Taryn, I have the first draft of the lunch menu." She stopped abruptly when she almost plowed into Marie.

Like two magnets repelling each other, I watched as they quickly sidestepped, avoiding even the smallest of acknowledgments. Marie turned her back, swiftly moving to the opposite end of the bar. Tammy's lips curled down into a frown.

She still held the paper in her hand, but her attention was focused on Marie's cold rejection. I couldn't say I blamed Marie; after all, betraying a friend is enough to get you permanently kicked out of the sisterhood. But for the sake of my own sanity, I had to remain neutral, even though I knew my relationship with Tammy was forever altered as well.

"Is she ever going to talk to me?" I could see the hurt, the longing for reconciliation, in Tammy's expression.

I wiped my hands off on my bar rag and tucked it back into my pocket before reaching for Tammy's printout. "I don't know. I suppose you'll have to work on earning her forgiveness if you want to be on speaking terms again."

I felt my cell vibrate in my front pocket. I hated answering numbers that I didn't recognize but I decided to answer anyway. "Hello?"

A deep, husky male voice responded. "Yes, good afternoon. May I speak to a Miss Taryn Mitchell, please?"

Reporter? Stalker? Crazed fan? Hacker? My mind ran through the possibilities. "Who's calling?"

"My name is Todd Brandwell. I'm calling from the chief medical examiner's office in New York City and I'm trying to reach a next of kin by the name of Taryn Mitchell. Your number was listed as a contact."

Dread sank heavy into my gut. "Next of kin? I'm sorry, you say I'm listed?"

"Yes, if you're Taryn Mitchell."

My throat constricted and panic swept through me. I started mentally listing the current locations of everyone that mattered in order of importance, beginning with Ryan. He was in L.A. He called me when he'd landed and I had just received a naughty text from him not more than twenty minutes ago. Other possible names started to scroll. "I am. What's this about?"

"Miss Mitchell, I'm sorry to inform you that James Pantelanio passed away last night. If you could write down our office number—"

Suddenly I was able to breathe again, not recognizing the name. "I'm sorry. Who?"

"James Pantelanio," he repeated, enunciating slowly. The Los Angeles address he recited wasn't familiar, either.

"I'm afraid I don't know him. I wish I could help."

"He had another emergency number, which is registered to a Mitchell's Pub. I've tried to contact that number as well but I am only receiving an answering service."

My heart lodged back up in my throat. This person had both of my numbers listed. The lengths some stalkers go to—

"Mr. Pantelanio is a seventy-two-year-old male, approximately five foot, seven inches, one hundred and forty pounds, dark peppered hair."

None of these descriptions—

"He was a heavy smoker. We believe he was also employed as a photographer, but we cannot seem to locate any employment—"

"Wait. You said 'James,' correct?"

"Yes, ma'am."

My heart sank. Could it be? "I think I do know him. Can you please send me a photo?"

Ten minutes later I was looking at the driver's license of the man who had once saved my life, who'd dropped to his knees in the slush and snow, and had given me CPR after I'd been hit by a car. I couldn't stop the tears from pouring, knowing that the sweet Italian celebrity photographer known to all as Jimmy Pop was dead.

CHAPTER 23

Wedding and Ashes

H<small>E'S IN A</small> small, mahogany box. It's actually quite lovely."

Ryan sighed. He wasn't overly thrilled about me going to New York to claim the remains of a deceased celebrity photographer, especially one who'd been chasing him for the last three years, but I was the only one who had come forth to even say they knew the guy so I'd felt obligated. But Marie had gone with me on the two-day trip, which made Ryan relax. "And what are you going to do with it?"

"I'm thinking about putting Jimmy Pop on the top shelf between Jim Beam and Johnnie Walker."

That got him to laugh. "Perfect place for him."

I leaned against the back bar. "I thought so. I figured he can keep an eye on the place. I have three of his Nikon cameras, too. The coroner gave me everything that was on his person. I even have three copies of his death certificate. Why would he list me as his 'in case of emergency person,' Ryan? It makes no sense. We barely knew each other."

"I don't know. Maybe he just didn't have anyone he could trust?"

I drifted my finger over the pewter cross that adorned the lid, feeling the anguish looming in my chest that you feel when people you care about die. It resembled the cross that was given to me before they closed my father's casket. I drew in a deep breath. "Maybe. But why me?"

"He knew you were smart and savvy; I wouldn't be surprised if there is a small fortune with your name on it."

I groaned. *Not another estate to deal with.*

"He probably figured you'd do good things with his money, Tar. He didn't have any children or family; who else could he leave it to?" I heard someone speaking to Ryan in the background. "Listen, hon, I've got to go. I'll call you later."

Marie carried our little stepstool behind the bar. "I heard you say you wanted to put Jimmy Pop up there. We can move the Patrón and Cabo Wabo over and then you'll have room."

She handed down a bottle just as another flower delivery was being made. Mike had sent flowers to Marie only two days ago; I wondered if he was kissing up for a specific reason.

This batch of flowers, however, was less than impressive. It looked like the kind you buy at the grocery store.

The deliveryman was tall and young, maybe mid-thirties, but with severely thinning brown hair that did that eight-strand greased comb-over on the bald head thing. He wore tinted glasses that were too large for his face. He might have had those same glasses since they were popular in the eighties. What was even creepier was that he was completely focused on me.

I was glad there was a thick bar separating us. "Can I help you?"

He was nervous; I could see his jitters physically shaking him. "I have flowers a . . . a delivery, Tah . . ." He seemed slightly confused as his eyes locked on mine. "For you."

Marie came down off the ladder, immediately putting him under her scrutiny. We had just opened the bar for business and there were no customers.

I nodded at the bouquet. "Thank you. You can leave them at the end of the bar there, okay?"

The deliveryman didn't move, just continued to oddly stare at me with a deer-caught-in-headlights look.

Marie's gaze was guarded as she scanned him with trepidation. "What flower shop do you work for? There is never a store name on the ones you deliver."

He took a step backward, appearing ready to flee, as she took a step forward, reaching her hand in the two-and-a-half-inch gap between the top of the new front-load cooler and the underside of the bar.

"I, um . . . they're for Ms. Mitchell. I'm . . . I just wanted to give her . . . flowers."

I watched Marie out of the corner of my eye, hesitant to take my eyes off the stranger.

Marie's hand obviously found what she was looking for; her hand started to withdraw.

He was wearing a short-sleeved, blue button-down shirt and what looked like uniform pants, but nothing about what he wore indicated he was a deliveryman. "They're just flowers," he continued to explain. "Women like men who bring them flowers. It's customary. It's part of the whole wooing process."

Marie's questioning glare was agitating him. I wanted him to drop off his stupid flowers and leave. He was creeping me out. "Thank you for the flowers. They're lovely." I tried to smile, hoping that would be enough to let him know I was appreciative. "But, sorry, I can't accept them. I'm engaged and not—"

"Taryn," Marie snapped in a hushed whisper.

"I've been trying different ones," he continued to mutter, talking to the flowers this time.

What?

"I know you hate daisies and carnations. Believe me, I've learned my lesson with those. They always end up in the Dumpster in the alley. You tend to keep the roses longer—like a week until they wilt. I check to see which ones you don't like all the time. Do you press them in books?"

Press them? He'd lost me. I'd never seen any roses or any other flowers for that matter. "Pardon?"

"The ones you keep?" His mouth turned up into a quirky smile.

"The red ones? There were a dozen but only ten were thrown away. I counted them. It upset me at first that you'd just toss them away, but then I realized that it was the flowers you didn't like. I know you can't keep them all, even though I hoped you would. If you put them in wax paper they keep longer. I'll only get you roses from now on."

"I'm sorry, I don't know what—"

"They remind me of your lips—soft and red. You kept the red ones the longest."

Marie waved her hand low and urgently at me. "I'll handle this, Taryn," she growled out, never taking her eyes off the guy.

He frowned at Marie, glaring at her. "Don't speak to her like that," the weirdo reprimanded.

"Listen carefully, sir. Do not deliver any more flowers to Ms. Mitchell. You are no longer welcome in this establishment. Do not attempt to contact her in any way. Please take your flowers and leave—immediately. I will contact the police if you refuse to leave or if you attempt to return. Do you understand?"

He looked wounded; his lips were moving but no words came out, which alarmed me even more. Adrenaline was pumping through my blood. I started mentally assessing escape routes and defense maneuvers—the pub telephone was behind me to dial 911, but that would be too obvious and not stealthy enough. My cell was in my pocket, but I'd have to unlock the screen first. The security panel for the upstairs hallway was too far away. Our trusty baseball bat was in the corner but I'd have to step around Marie and the small stepladder to reach it.

"Do you see the cameras up there in the corner?" Marie pointed.

Cameras? When the hell did we get cameras? We'd talked about them but that was just talk as the system was expensive. Someone is going to get their ass chewed out for failing to inform me that I now have a surveillance system installed inside my pub.

My unwelcomed suitor gazed up at them, appearing just as puzzled as I was.

Marie was assured and composed. "Now the security company has your picture."

This definitely pissed him off. He paid no attention to Marie. He was mad at me. "All I wanted was to finally take you on a date and you make me feel like some, some common criminal? Who do you think you are? You think you're better than me? I'll have you know that I have my master's degree in chemical engineering! Perhaps you would have found that out prior to wanting to call the cops on me, hmm?"

Marie cautioned him with a new, soothing voice. "Sir, calm down."

"No! I will not calm down! After all of the money I've spent to get you to like me? You women are all the same. You flaunt your bodies, enticing men to be attracted to you, and then what do you do? You cut them off at the knees as if they were helpless soldiers wandering the desert, just begging for a sip of water."

Soldiers in the desert? My God, this guy is beyond cuckoo and now he's becoming enraged.

I suddenly noticed what Marie slid out from the top of the cooler—a very intimidating black handgun that she seemed to have no problem holding.

Dear God . . . cameras? Guns? What's this place turning into? A Twilight War Zone? Surely Mike will be beamed into the middle of the room in Doctor Who's TARDIS ship at any moment.

"Sir, I'm asking you for the last time to leave the premises or else I will call the local authorities." Marie's voice left no room for debate.

Completely dejected, the guy huffed, scowled at both of us, called me a heartless bitch, and then scared the hell out of me when he whipped the flower bouquet at us.

It all happened so quickly, I didn't react fast enough. The flowers caught my arm and then ricocheted off the back bar countertop.

My heart rate went into overdrive. This guy was completely mental. While distracted by tangles of baby's breath and palm fronds, I noticed that Marie had taken a shooter's stance, her badass black gun pointing right at him.

"Freeze!" she shouted. "Taryn, call nine-one-one, now!" Her command didn't seem to matter to him; one view of her gun and he was taking wide backward steps toward the door.

Pete walked into the pub from the kitchen, whistling and completely oblivious to the standoff. He stuttered to a halt. "What the ... ?"

While we were distracted by Pete, the crazed guy seized the opportunity to run.

Pete stood gaping in shock at both of us while Marie lowered her weapon. "Jesus! What the hell did I just walk into?" He rushed over and locked the front door.

Marie fiddled with the gun before placing it back inside a black holster. She snapped the holder thing on it and pushed it back into its hiding spot in the gap above the cooler. I knew she was aware of me watching her, but she was doing a fine job of ignoring me.

I felt almost out of breath. "You have a gun behind my bar?"

She gave me a casual glance and then shrugged. My blood heated up another notch. Like *hell* it was no big deal! "I had it hidden."

I leaned onto the bar for stability. "Whose gun is it?"

Her face was stoic but she was breathing just as heavily from the incident as I was. "Mine."

"Since when the hell do you own a gun?"

Marie grabbed a beer glass and filled it halfway with water. "I got it after I graduated from the course. It's a Glock nine-millimeter. Want to see it?"

People holding guns kill people. My answer was quick. "No."

"I should take you to the range and teach you to fire it. It's so much fun!"

"Marie, why the hell do you have a gun?"

She shrugged. "Mike bought it for me. It was my graduation gift. He's worried that Gary might try to shoot me so he wants me to be prepared to shoot first. I can't believe that crazy guy coming in here like that. He scared the crap out of me."

Yeah, that was a load of lies. Gary was no longer contesting the divorce and was too busy fooling around with that Amy woman to even bother. As long as Marie didn't try to take more of Gary's money, she wasn't even a blip on his radar anymore.

"Just so you know, I've applied for a permit to carry a concealed weapon, so whenever we travel locally, I'll most likely be armed. Stop looking at me as if I've grown another head."

Pete was standing in the middle of the pub, glaring at both of us. "You care to tell me what the fuck that was that I just walked into?"

I waved him off. My best friend drawing weapons on people to protect me was more important. "Why am I just hearing about this now?"

"Pete, call the police. It's protocol. All threats need to be reported." Marie took a sip of water, averting her eyes from me. "Tar, the way this works is that you are supposed to go about your day without worrying about security. It's *my* job now to worry about it, and it's also my job to be as transparent as possible and not allow you to be worried about your safety. Bodyguards should be visible but invisible. Understand?"

"I thought that you were just going with me to public appearances and stuff? I didn't realize you were taking this so seriously." The thought of my best friend actually putting her life on the line to protect me suddenly became very real and very frightening. It was almost too much to bear.

Her eyes opened wider. "Of course I'm taking this seriously. *Very* seriously!"

Guilt swept over me, pressing hard on my chest. Somewhere in my mind I'd thought that we were just saying she was my bodyguard as an excuse to allow her to travel with Ryan and me—like it was a cover story or something. After seeing her pull a gun on someone, the reality of the situation became clear. I rushed right over and threw my arms around her. "I wasn't thinking. I'm sorry. Thank you. I love you."

Marie patted my back. "I love you, too, Tar. We have a lot to learn about stalkers and how to handle them, but I promise to keep you informed from now on, okay?"

I nodded, hugging her neck.

Pete cleared his throat and showed us his cell phone. "Cops are on their way."

My eyes sought out the cameras up in the corner. There was also a small, dark dome directly above the cash register. "Someone care to tell me when they got installed?" I asked. "Since no one thought it important to tell me."

"Oh, shit," Pete groaned. "I forgot to tell you. They were installed yesterday while you were in New York fetching the paparazzo guy's ashes. It's a good thing, though. We got that guy on camera."

Marie pulled her hair off her shoulders. "I made him look directly at it, so we should have a pretty clear shot of his face. God, I hope I'm not in trouble for drawing my weapon. Mike will have my ass for that."

That might not be such a bad thing?

"You know what I mean," she groaned at me. "Taryn, I hate to say it, but I don't think it's a good idea for you to be down in the bar anymore."

"What?" *Am I being kicked out of my own bar now?*

"I agree," Pete said solemnly.

"You're too accessible to them," Marie continued. "That wasn't the first time that particular weirdo came in here. He's been trying to deliver flowers to you for several weeks. Besides, this is a public place. There is nothing to prevent anyone from just waltzing through the front doors and posing a threat. I'm afraid that the only option we have is to remove you. Like it or not, you're a celebrity—a public figure. Your status has put you in a precarious position."

My body went rigid. This was *my* pub and now I was being told not to enter it? "I'm not famous."

"Oh yes you are!" Marie countered. "Even *People* has published several articles on you. I know you don't believe it, but this is the way it is."

I disagreed. "But plenty of celebrities own businesses—restaurants and stuff. I'm no different."

Marie laughed lightly. "Yeah, they do. But you can't walk into one of Robert De Niro's restaurants and chat him up while he makes you a cheeseburger."

I felt indescribably hopeless about being told I was no longer welcome in my own pub. And then a split second later, I felt pissed, too. All of this because of some misguided idiot and his stupid flowers.

Pete wrapped his arm over my shoulders. "I know it's hard to stomach, kiddo, but Marie's right. You're a public figure now."

"That guy just admitted going through your trash, Taryn! For what? To see that we threw his flowers away? That's messed up. You saw how angry he got. I'd hate to imagine how things could have turned out if one of us *wasn't* in here with you. You think Ryan's paranoid? He has every damn right to be. There are a lot of sick fucks walking this earth."

As much as I hated to admit it, both of them were right. "So now what do I do?"

"Let Marie run the pub," Pete suggested. "She'd be perfect for managing the entire operation."

"No," Marie said adamantly. "Sorry, but Taryn knows my heart isn't into it anymore. I have a new career on the horizon."

I knew Pete was just being diplomatic. There was longing in that guy's soft puppy dog eyes. "Pete, you're running things now; how would you feel about making that permanent?"

Marie glanced at Pete, feeling him out. "This something you want to do for the next few years? Taryn wouldn't have to deal with it then."

Pete nodded confidently. "Yes. I'd love to. Tammy's business just keeps growing. She's making more money than I did working construction. And if we go ahead with serving food here with a lunch and dinner menu, this place will just become busier."

I was still pissed about the security system. "All capital expenditures get approved by me first. Clear?"

"Even the ones you don't pay for?" Pete questioned.

My eyes narrowed. "Who paid for the system, Pete?"

"I think I hear sirens." He walked off toward the window.

I had this overwhelming desire to tackle him and force him to speak. "Peter?"

"Who do you think?" he asked with a knowing glance. "They made me shake on it—*both* of them. And don't even bother being pissed. You'll have no argument once they find out what happened in here today. None."

Damn it—Pete was right.

I ZIPPED the back of Marie's knee-length black dress, smoothing out the gorgeous satin, careful not to snag any of the soft tendrils that hung lose from her upswept hair. It had been almost three weeks since the pub incident, during which I used my newfound downtime to force a reconciliation between Tammy and Marie. Well, forced may be a bit of a stretch, but I most certainly had my say in the matter.

Their final argument started over mozzarella sticks. Really. I still don't know the full extent of their ridiculous fight because neither of them was making much sense, but both of their voices were so damn loud, I could hear them all the way upstairs.

I ended my conference call with our architect and builder just to see what all of the ruckus was about. I knew Marie was still pissed about Tammy's friend hooking up with Gary and the fact that Tammy did nothing to stop it, but after Tammy and Pete had their big showdown two weeks ago, Gary and Amy were out of the wedding, leaving them with absolutely no bridal party and Tammy in full bride-to-be meltdown.

I'd had enough of the insanity.

I was also wise enough to know that they were at each other's throats because deep down they wanted the hostility to be out and over with. And the longer it lingered, the longer it festered.

But after thirty minutes and a whole lot of crazy accusations, I managed to get the two of them to hug.

The day before Pete and Tammy's wedding, Ryan and Mike flew back to Seaport. Come hell or high water, I was going to make sure my dear friend Pete married the woman who had captured his heart and that his woman would have a beautiful wedding to remember.

Marie and I stopped dead in our tracks in my living room when we took in the sights of Ryan and Mike dressed to the nines. Both were devastatingly handsome in their black tuxes and crimson neckties. They were standing near the front windows; the afternoon sun making them appear dreamlike.

"Oh my God," Marie breathed out.

I knew exactly what she'd meant. All of that gorgeousness should be illegal because it was lethal.

"Mine," I whispered, basking in the reality that Ryan was in fact, mine.

"I get the one on the left," she muttered softly.

Marie and I had been given simple instructions: wear a black satin cocktail dress. But with Ryan in his Ralph Lauren tuxedo I felt grossly underdressed. Ryan sauntered around the couch, his eyes boring into mine. Something about seeing him dressed up always took my breath away.

Ryan, forever the gentleman, took my hand and raised it to his mouth for a kiss. "You look absolutely stunning." He held me at arm's length and then his brow furrowed. "Something's missing."

He looked over at Mike. "Is it me or is there something missing from this gorgeous picture?"

Mike inspected Marie from head to toe, even doing a walk-around. "Hmm. Yeah. Something's off. Like it's *almost* perfect but just not quite altogether—*there*."

I had to laugh; both of them were examining us like pieces of art. "Is it the hair?" Mike asked.

Ryan carefully touched one of the curls that touched my cheek. "No. I don't think so," he said reverently. "Your hair is perfect."

I smiled. Marie and I had spent almost two hours at the hair-dresser this morning getting dolled up.

Ryan was staring at my lips when he said, "What about the shoes, Mike?"

"Shoes?" Mike echoed. "Let me check." He crouched down in front of Marie, lifting the hem of her dress to start his examination mid-thigh. I heard his lascivious groan from across the room. His fingers skated slowly down her thigh, pausing while he kissed her knee. I was watching him watching her. By the time he got down to her ankle, it had grown very warm in my living room. "Shoe's good, Ryan."

Yeah, their little game was working both of them into a lather.

I watched Ryan's tongue slowly sweep across his bottom lip: wetting, inviting, taunting. Damn, I wanted to suck it into my mouth and end this teasing. He pulled me into his chest, drifting his nose near my neck. "God, you smell good." He breathed into my ear. "Delicious."

I felt his fingertips drift down my neck, following the square-cut neckline, causing my belly to flutter and tighten. He placed a small kiss at the bottom of my throat. "I'm thinking it's the neck," he whispered, grazing his teeth over my skin.

He rose up, slowly and deliberately. "Mike, check her neck."

I grinned when he resumed his nuzzling. "You keep this up and you'll have to make love to me instead of taking me to this wedding."

I felt him smile. "Promise me you won't turn crazy when we get married."

I clutched his waist, feeling the liquid heat building low in my panties. "I promise." He was so close; I could feel his erection. I caressed my hand over it. "Are you happy now? You have all of this and no time to play with it."

He moaned. "That's a present for later. I'm going to do you slowly tonight."

Just as I started drifting off into that blissful image, I heard Marie squeal. She held a flat box.

"I have one for you, too." Ryan slipped a hand into the back of his trousers and pulled out a thin, flat box with the iconic HW logo embossed on the lid.

My breath caught when I removed the felt covering. "Oh my God, Ryan! This is absolutely beautiful." I touched the diamond wreath necklace, noticing the small *R* in white gold, dangling next to the clasp.

Marie's wreath necklace was just as stunning, though it was a different design. And sure enough, dangling from the clasp of hers was an *M*.

"Did we just get collared?" Marie teased, touching the diamond necklace.

Ryan smirked. "Something like that."

"You've got a problem being owned?" Mike asked her.

"By you?"

Mike took Marie's hips into his strong hands, drawing her in. "Yeah. By me. You good with that?"

Her smile was priceless. "Oh, yeah. I'm real good with that."

I heard a horn honking.

"I believe our ride is here," Ryan said.

Just as I had expected, my alley was inundated with a swarm of paparazzi, caging in our black stretch limo. Despite what people might think about the luxury of riding in a stretch limo, they were actually a pain to crawl around in—especially with heels and a dress.

"Damn," Ryan breathed out. "I thought we'd thrown them off with that posted appearance at Chateau Marmont. So much for that."

Mike was the last one in. "Yep, didn't work. I figured as much. Plan B is still in place."

I entwined my hand with Ryan's. "Plan B?"

He nodded. "We hired event security. That will keep them out of the church and out of the reception."

"Does Pete know this?"

Ryan kissed my hand. "I called him a couple of days ago. It's all arranged. Just remember how this goes. We need to keep ours completely exclusive and private."

"Maldives," Mike murmured.

Ryan gave him a nod in agreement.

The outside of St. Andrew's Episcopal Church was surrounded by a small mob. My heart sank. Our worst fears were coming true. Ryan squeezed my hand.

Mike held the door open for us. Marie was the second person out, blocking the photographers' prying cameras.

Ryan and I had made it a few feet toward the church steps when he paused and turned us around. As if we were at any other public appearance, Ryan and I posed for the press. We turned, smiled, and gave them what they all so desperately wanted. Except that Ryan did not give out any autographs.

He tried to speak over the frenzy. "We are here to celebrate the wedding of dear friends. I hope you give them the courtesy of your respect and privacy today. Thank you."

Inside the church, I had a private moment with Pete, which caused a few tears of happiness to fall from my eyes. We'd been through hell and back, enduring the ugly side of life together.

Marie walked down the aisle first. I could see she only had eyes for Mike, who didn't know Pete from Adam, but who had willingly stepped up to be a groomsman to make this day special for them.

I took a step through the threshold, imagining making this walk on my day.

I saw Ryan draw in a quick breath; his smile was breathtaking, standing tall and proud near the altar, watching every step I took with nothing but love in his eyes.

I wanted to marry him now more than anything.

CHAPTER 24

Face-off

I N THE FIVE months following Pete and Tammy's wedding, we'd been to California, Portugal, England, Louisiana, Pennsylvania, New Jersey, and back to England while Ryan was filming the third *Seaside*.

Ryan's planning and scheming had paid off. While he spent twelve- or even fourteen-hour days filming, I was happy and content spending time with my best friend. I had long ago come to know that Mike's salary was paid mostly by the studios, since personal security was written into Ryan's contracts and it was part of his appearance rider and now that rider also included a security team. Marie had often joked with me that I was paying her to be my friend.

Marie and I kept ourselves very busy, planning everything from home décor for the enormous house that was waiting for the spring thaw to be built to naming the production company Ryan and I wanted to start. Spending time hanging out with the cast and crew of *Seaside* also made the days blur and blend into one hell of a good time. I had taken over managing Ryan's affairs, working like a personal assistant on most days. I didn't mind; our hectic schedule and active social calendar kept me out of trouble.

I even found a new friend in Ryan's lawyer, Len Bainbridge, when he helped me clear up the nearly $1 million estate that the sweet Jimmy Pop left behind. The Children's Hospital of Los Angeles was very grateful when Ryan and I presented them with a check in Jimmy Pop's memory.

That was a wonderful day.

Everything was going tremendously well at Mitchell's Pub, too. Pete had hired several new staff members to support the growing demand for Tammy's gourmet dishes that she was whipping up in the kitchen. Maggie, the elderly lady who owned the bakery opposite my pub—the one that Ryan had escaped through the first day that we met—was looking to retire and sell her store as well. Tammy had hired several people and was hoping to run the catering out of the bakery. So we were working on that plan.

Marie joked that I could run a multimillion-dollar corporation from my cell phone and laptop. I was starting to agree with her.

But now we were in Manhattan, getting ready to kick off the first day of press tours for the premiere of Ryan's film *Thousand Miles*. We'd landed in New York yesterday and everything was going rather smoothly until we arrived for his press interviews and I spotted "them." Suddenly my hands were sweaty, my senses were on high alert, it was hard to swallow, and I wished I was wielding a baseball bat—or better yet, Marie's fancy black gun.

Ryan noticed *them* about twenty seconds after I did. His eyes narrowed as he assessed them, he cursed, then he frowned down at me. I had no doubt that he'd drag me back to our hotel and force me to stay there if he had his choice.

I wrapped my hand into his, entwining our fingers into an unbreakable bond. "No way. We do this together."

He was furious. "Figures Kyle would be here with her. I really want to hit him."

I didn't take my eyes off the doorway where they were standing. "Yeah? You take him. I've got her."

Mike was busy dealing with the location's shoddy security, so he was the last one to notice his former coworker milling about.

A young man who was part of the crew approached us, holding a small box with wires. "Mr. Christensen, I have your mic." He clipped the small microphone onto Ryan's shirt, fishing the wire beneath his clothes. Ryan lifted his arm so the guy could connect it to a small box that clipped to the back of Ryan's pants.

David, Ryan's manager, strolled over, twisting his Rolex. "Okay, Ryan. You and Lauren Delaney are scheduled to do a joint interview with Moviefone in about ten minutes and then you'll do the rest of the press interviews individually. We have three interview rooms, so we'll be moving the press around in ten-minute intervals with a break every hour."

I couldn't help but keep an eye on the other side of the room—on *them.*

"Yeah, fine. Whatever." Ryan squeezed his water bottle, making the plastic crinkle from the pressure. "What's the deal, Mike? I'm not liking this one bit," he growled.

"Dunno. I know PSG relieved him of duty right after the incident. They wouldn't hire him back— not after that breach. He must still be working private detail." Mike leaned in closer. "Do you have a PFA on him?"

Ryan flashed another angry frown at me. "No."

"I didn't see a need to," I said, sticking by my original decision.

"I want him to stay away from Taryn. He comes near her or gets in my face, I'll kill him." Ryan was dead serious. "I need to talk to Lauren before we start. Can you find out if he's traveling the entire press junket with her?"

Mike nodded. "I'll see what I can find out."

David ditched the woman organizing the press interviews after looking over in the direction of our heated stares; he was finally clued in to the situation. He stormed right back over to Ryan. "Christ. Not this shit again. Time to put your personal shit aside and be professional, Ryan. Perhaps Taryn should wait at your hotel until you're finished so we don't have any additional problems?"

Ryan glared at him. "I think it's time we part ways, David."

I was surprised that Ryan was doing this now.

David jerked back, aghast. "What?"

"You want to keep your fucking job? That's the *last* time you dismiss my woman. We clear? I don't need you to remind me or to tell me what to do."

"I was merely suggesting that it might be wise to separate her from potential problems, that's all."

Ryan scoffed at him. "David, you're so full of shit. I think it's best if you just walked away before I fire you."

The woman with the clipboard walked over. "Mr. Christensen, we're ready to begin. You'll be in Parlor A. If you'll just follow me." She ushered, pointing the way.

"Yeah, in a minute." Ryan clutched my elbow. "Stay away from him. Find Trish and stick with Marie, okay?"

I gave him a kiss and went on a hunt for the ladies' room. Straight down the wide hallway, I found a buffet table with bottles of water stuck in ice. Just when I thought I was safe I felt the little hairs prickle on my neck, sensing him before he stepped beside me.

"Taryn."

No, no. Shit. The closer he came the stronger the scent of his cologne became.

I decided to avoid a conflict and be considerate. "Kyle."

He regarded me with a sideways glance. "You look well."

I gripped a bottle tightly in my hand, feeling the cold moisture seep into my palm, matching the chill rolling down my spine. "Thank you."

"I've seen you a few times but I haven't had the opportunity to congratulate you on your engagement."

I heard the faint strain in his voice from him trying to be sincere. I wanted to ignore him completely, but it was difficult, so I gave him a simple "thank you" instead.

"I heard Ryan was getting out of control there for a while, punching the paparazzi?"

I felt heat flame up my neck from him attempting to bait me.

Of course he couldn't pass up an opportunity to press my buttons. "When they climb up trees to intrude on our privacy, they deserve it. Besides, that's old news."

He took a swig of a bottle of water, contemplating my response. "I was just surprised that he'd mar his wholesome image like that."

I glared at him. "Are you done?"

Kyle reached for a napkin. "Things could have been different, you know."

"Yes, I could have sent you to jail."

He snickered. "Still have your starch. Good. Very good."

"Shouldn't you be guarding a door or something? Surely you must be breaking protocol by leaving your woman unprotected."

He leaned closer. "Should I be worried?"

I laughed. "Not in the least, though I highly doubt you being here is just a coincidence. I'm happy for you and Lauren. Really, I am."

I heard a purr roll up his chest. "Now who's being insincere? Or is there truly a hint of jealousy still lingering?"

I couldn't help but laugh. "Oh, no. Rest assured I feel no jealousy. None whatsoever. In fact, I'd say your partnership with that conniving bitch is a match made in heaven."

He actually had the audacity to cat-growl at me. "And still so feisty, too."

"What are you going to do, Kyle? Put me up against another wall to try to change my mind?"

He made a throaty sound of disgust and then turned toward me, his face painted with what truly looked like regret. "I hurt you. I know that. I get it. I know what I did was stupid and rash . . . I don't expect you to believe me but I truly wanted to protect you."

I wanted to slap him. "You're lucky I didn't have you arrested."

"And I appreciate that. Look, I've kept my end of the deal. Have I bothered you at all since?"

"No, you haven't. But the first chance you got you couldn't help but take another cheap shot at Ryan. And *that* bothers me."

"He has what I want."

I fought rolling my eyes. "You have Lauren."

His lips twitched as he shook his head. "Yeah, funny thing. Turns out I'm not her *type* these days. Doesn't matter because she's not mine."

"Well, that's too bad."

Kyle sighed. "Will you ever forgive me?"

I'd had enough. "Honestly? No. And while we're on this junket I suggest you do yourself a favor and stay the hell away from both of us."

I didn't know where I was walking to but I headed back to where I knew Ryan and Mike were last. My hands were shaking. Memories of Kyle pressing me into the door frame at the bottom of my apartment steps swept through me, spreading fear and trembles of terror through my bones.

I found Trish sitting in a chair taking a call on her cell. Marie was sitting next to her. My cell chimed with a new text so I dug it out of my purse and just as I was thumbing through the new message, I heard a familiar nasally, shrill voice that will forever be scorched in my memory.

Trish said what I was thinking. "What the hell is she doing here?"

Marla's head turned slightly, pausing her conversation for a beat when she noticed us. Acid churned in my stomach. I hadn't even previewed this film and already *Thousand Miles* was turning into a thousand miles in hell.

"I think I want to go home," I muttered quietly.

Trish shifted in her chair. "You and me both. Apparently Ms. Delaney has herself a new publicist. Figures she'd go for Ryan's old representation."

Ryan had texted me. I held up my phone to show Marie. "He's summoning me."

I found him in a room with what looked like a half tent made out of black fabric. The *Thousand Miles* movie poster was set up behind the chairs. Industrial lights were set up to illuminate the area being filmed and floor fans were whirling to keep the area cool.

Ryan looked like he'd been through the blender. "You hanging in there?" I asked, taking him into my arms.

Just then Kyle walked down the hall, glancing at us briefly on his way. I couldn't help but scoff.

"Did he say anything to you?"

I froze. I wasn't going to tell him we exchanged words. What good would that do? "You should know that Lauren hired Marla Sullivan."

Ryan took a step back. "What?"

"Marla is here. She just showed up."

"You're kidding me?"

"I wish. She's putting on quite the show of enthusiasm."

I thought Ryan was going to go through the roof. "Wonderful." He rubbed his forehead, then grabbed my hand to tow me along. He pinned a glare on Mike. "Where's David?"

A young woman came rushing over to Ryan. "Mr. Christensen, we're ready to start the next group."

He held up a hand. "I need a minute."

Ryan bounded right up to David, jerking his chin in Marla's direction. "You know about this shit?"

He was either caught off guard or an expert feigning ignorance. "What do you mean?"

"I'm talking about the woman who's suing me for breach of contract and the guy who assaulted my fiancée being on this junket. Now answer the question. Did you know about this?"

"I, well, I found out a couple of days ago that Lauren signed on with Marla's company, but I thought she'd give the account to an underling. How was I supposed to know she'd be here?"

Ryan groaned in frustration. "This puts me in a compromising situation, David, both physically and financially, and that's not good."

"Okay, I should have told you that Lauren hired Marla's PR company, but I didn't think it would matter."

"Well, it does," Ryan snapped. "You know she's contesting the revised settlement I paid her, saying I owe her more money. You could have given me a heads-up. It's getting to be that I can't trust you anymore."

David looked offended. "Ryan, don't say that. I've always had your best interests at heart."

"Is that why you took it upon yourself to have Len draft up a prenup?"

"Yes, I did. We have monies coming in that need to be protected."

"From who?" Ryan yelled. "She won't even use my money to put fucking gas in her car. The only one spending my money is *you*. I know what's written in my contract, David. You worried I'd screw you out of wedding photo royalties?"

David held his hands up in surrender. "I'd never do that and it's a damn shame that you think that way. Hey, you want to risk half your money on a girl that you'll divorce eventually, that's on you."

Ryan was livid. "That's the difference between you and me, David. After this press tour is over, I think we need to go our separate ways."

David clutched Ryan's forearm. "Hang on, buddy. Let's not take this there again."

Ryan glared at David's hand. "You best remove that hand and walk away. I'm not playing anymore."

I kept my eye on Lauren instead of celebrating David's dismissal. She seemed overly giddy and bubbly, as if she were enjoying watching us squirm.

Bring it, bitch. You're next.

I STRAIGHTENED Ryan's necktie before we arrived at the Manhattan premiere of *Thousand Miles*. I was glad he wore the black Hugo Boss suit with the purple and black paisley necktie that matched the color of my cocktail dress.

He ran his finger over the gathered material on the bodice of my dress and then over my beautiful diamond wreath necklace. "You look extraordinary."

Ryan's appreciation for me never faltered. I hoped I'd never take how lucky I am for granted. "You are quite the package yourself."

Attending my second movie premiere wasn't as frightening as it was the first time but the huge crowd and flurry of aggressive photographers was enough to make me quake in my stilettos. The flashes of hundreds of cameras, the roar of the crowd screaming for me to look their way . . . it was all beyond surreal.

I had to give Lauren and Ryan credit; both were exceptional actors, putting on a believable show of friendship and solidarity for the crowd and cameras. They had come to an agreement earlier that they'd be on their best behavior while out in public. Privately, however, Ryan had no use for her. He assured me that he'd never work with her again. Ryan wasn't big on forgiveness, especially where my best interests were concerned, and he told her so.

As soon as the screening was over, we were whisked away to the lavish after-party in the ballroom at the Gramercy Park Hotel. Fortunately, Ryan had stipulated that his security team go with him wherever he had to go, which meant that I had Marie close by for moral support.

She walked with me toward the open bar while Ryan was in deep conversation with the film's cinematographer. She glanced at me with weary eyes. "Taryn, I hate to say it, but that movie was awesome."

I found an open area of couches and chairs and sat down. "Yeah, it was. Ryan was fabulous again. But there were a few parts that were difficult for me to watch." The dinner scene where I thought Ryan was on an actual date with Lauren in Miami made my chest burn. I recalled that Ryan had squeezed my hand tightly during that part. He remembered, just as I did, what happened outside the restaurant that night—the night when I had left him.

And just as Ryan's character leaned over the linen-covered table to kiss Lauren on the screen, Ryan wrapped his arm over my shoulders, taking my face in his hand, and kissed me so passionately I wanted to cry tears of happiness. He didn't want me to watch them. It wasn't part of our reality. His mouth on mine, his hand clutching my cheek, his love for me—that was what was real.

Marie sat in the single blue armchair next to me. "I still can't believe I'm at another freaking movie premiere after-party. This is all just mind-boggling."

I took a sip of the white wine that I'd been nursing. "I know. I love how they decorate to promote the movie's theme. Ryan said they go all out for the *Seaside* prem—"

I was in mid-sentence when I lost Marie's attention to someone else. I turned and thought "oh shit" when I saw Lauren Delaney standing before us in her ugly expensive dress and matching scowl.

When she realized I wasn't going to be intimidated, she pasted on a forced smile. "I just wanted to congratulate you on your engagement."

Yeah, right.

What else could I say besides "Thank you"?

She flitted her eyes at me. "Yes, well, just make sure you treat him right or else you'll have to answer to me."

This was news. "Oh, really? And you care, why?"

She sniffed, not backing down. "Ryan's been an important part of my life for many years."

Marie crossed her legs and raised a skeptical eyebrow. "Was that before or after you fucked around behind his back with Lucas Banks? I know the gossip magazines don't always get it right. I'm just trying to keep the timeline straight."

I wanted to give Marie a high-five for that one.

Lauren was taken aback for a moment, and then she righted herself and smirked. "You think you know everything. Why don't you go back to the little hick town that you crawled out of."

I looked up at her. "Seriously? Out of all the comebacks out there, that's the best you could come up with?"

She smiled and crossed her bony arms. "You think you have him. Enjoy your fifteen minutes."

I flicked my diamond engagement ring with my thumb, sending her a message. "I think I'll have him a lot longer than that. See, I'm not *ever* going to be a dumb bitch like you were and screw around on him. But what I don't understand is why you even care? If something should ever happen that we're no longer together, I'm positive you wouldn't even be on his list."

Lauren looked as if she'd been sucking on a lemon. "Getting him back would be easy."

"Why, do you think he'd be interested in a four-way with you, Nicole, and Kyle?" I snorted. "Highly doubt it."

I could tell she was grinding her teeth. I was getting to her. *Good.*

"You just saw our film. You think all of that was just acting? I'd watch my back if I were you."

Marie sprang out of her seat. "You threatening her?"

"Why?" a familiar deep voice rumbled.

My head snapped, seeing Ryan come up behind Lauren after I heard his angered question. Her face went white.

Ryan nudged her out of the way so he could sit on the arm of my chair. "I'll ask again, Lauren. Why should my fiancée watch her back?"

She hemmed. "It was just a figure of speech."

Ryan stood up, moving into her personal space. "I'm only going to say this once. For the duration of this junket, you will stay the hell away from me and my future wife. That also goes for your little meth-head girlfriend and your asshole bodyguard. We clear?"

Lauren smiled coyly. "Since when did you become such a prude? I recall you used to be quite adventurous when we lived together. You should embrace the lifestyle our careers afford us before you're too old to enjoy it. Playing house is boring. You're missing out on all the fun, all the parties. You had your tongue in Nicole's mouth, too. Imagine the possibilities."

Ryan blanched. "Yeah, that will never happen."

"You seemed to like it when we fucked that little set director together." Lauren leaned toward me, making sure I heard her. "Did he ever tell you about that, Taryn? The three-ways we used to have?"

Ryan grabbed her arm. "Do not fucking talk to her. And do not make the *one-time* seem like more."

She giggled. "Homophobic now, are we?"

"I have zero issues with what people do. But what I do have a problem with are conniving bitches who go out of their way to destroy my relationship, and their drug-addicted girlfriends fucking with my livelihood. Your little fuck-friend is damn lucky I didn't have her fired when I had the chance. As for you, I cut you a break when everything in my gut told me not to. I won't make the same mistake twice. You even breathe in Taryn's direction, you *and* Nicole will be lucky to find a gig at some shithole theater when I'm done."

I was glad he stood up to her, but the last thing I ever expected to deal with on this night was finding out that Ryan had had sex with two girls at once. I had to realize that the wild version of Ryan was a thing of the past.

I GLANCED out our hotel window, basking in the beautiful sunrise over Rome. It was our last stop on the *Thousand Miles* press junket and in a few hours we'd be on another plane heading back to the States.

I felt Ryan's warm chest press into my back. I wrapped my hands over his. "I don't want to go home."

He kissed my neck. "We're not."

I looked up to see if he was kidding. "We're not?"

"Nope. We are taking a three-day detour."

That sounded wonderful. "Can I even ask, or is it a surprise?"

Ryan smiled. Well, it is sort of a surprise, but there's this awesome restaurant built inside a cave on this cliff that my woman said she wanted to see."

It was better than winning the lottery. "For real? You're not just teasing me, are you?"

He patted my rear end. "I'd never tease. Mike's taking Marie, too. The four of us are going, but I don't expect to see much of them."

I was so happy, I started bouncing on my toes and clapping.

He bounced with me, mocking me. "You want more good news?"

I smiled wider. "Yes!"

"We're going by helicopter to Polignano a Mare."

I wanted to bounce out of my skin.

"So pack up, because we catch our ride in two hours."

After kissing him wickedly for this huge surprise, I dashed around the room, packing up our stuff.

Ryan folded up the dress shirt he wore last night. "Pack only what you'll need in your backpack. There's not a lot of room for luggage inside the cabin."

I had to do a carry-on overhaul. I had so much crap in my bag that things were starting to fall out.

"I want to call Mike, see if we have a car coming," Ryan said.

I took the big manila envelope that the woman at the press panel gave me the day before out of my backpack. I was starting to believe I was turning into Ryan Christensen's briefcase. I had receipts and notes and signed documents galore.

I made a pile of important paper stuff, thinking that the manila folder would be a perfect place to shove it all; unfortunately, it didn't work out so well. I dumped the contents out on the bed, trying to reassess what was really important to keep.

Papers, brochures, you name it. *Junk, junk . . .*

Something fell and hit the bed when I opened up one of the brochures from the manila envelope. It was a small piece of folded magazine paper, made into what looked like a tiny envelope.

What the hell? I opened it up and gasped.

My hands started to shake. "Ryan?"

Hearing the alarm in my voice, he came right to my side.

"What's this?" It looked like chunks of compressed baby powder, and there was a lot of it.

He studied the item in my hands before attempting to take it away from me. "What the fuck? Don't spill it."

"What is it?" I asked.

I watched him take a careful sniff, and then his face twisted. "I'm not exactly sure, babe, but I think this is cocaine."

CHAPTER 25

Done

I PACED NERVOUSLY WHILE Mike and Ryan analyzed the contents of the little envelope.

"I think Ryan's right," Mike announced. "I'm pretty sure this is cocaine."

I felt my throat tighten. That was in my backpack.

Mike pegged me with inquisitive eyes. "Where did you say you found this?"

I pointed at the manila envelope. "It was in there."

He picked it up, looking inside. "What else was in here?"

I shuffled through the papers, separating what I believed were the original contents.

To say Ryan was pissed was putting it mildly. "Where did that envelope even come from?"

"Remember the gorgeous redhead? The one with the painted-on skirt and legs that started here?" I pointed to my neck. "She gave it to me. She said it was for you."

Ryan suddenly slammed his fist into the dining table, stringing along a whole host of expletives.

"I think we should flush this down the toilet," Mike said, appearing less than happy with Ryan's outburst. "And then we are going to do a comprehensive check of all our luggage. Shirt pockets, pants, envelopes, everything gets checked. Marie, help Taryn. Go through everything and I mean *everything*."

Marie and I dumped out our suitcases.

"Make a fucking list of names," Ryan ordered. "There are only so many suspects here. When I find out who did this, I'm going to rip their throat out and bury them."

"We've all touched the envelope so prints are out. I don't think going to the authorities with it would be wise." Mike shook his head. "We can speculate all we want. Unless someone brags or confesses, I don't think we'll ever know."

Ryan stood, grabbed the little envelope thing with his fingers, and stormed off to the bathroom. I heard the toilet flush a few times.

The evidence was gone.

Ryan came back, staring at Mike as if he could magically come up with answers.

Mike was just as aggravated. "I don't know, man. Someone was trying to set you up. If one of us had been caught with that, we'd be looking at international jail time."

Ryan scoffed. "No shit."

Mike ran his hand over his head. "Well, the good news is you found it before we tried to leave the country. We came in on a commercial flight, so that means the drugs had to be purchased here. Unless we contact the authorities, we have no way of launching an investigation, and you just flushed the evidence."

"It was in my backpack," I uttered somberly, holding back tears while I searched Ryan's pockets for planted drugs. I turned his pocket inside out, feeling as if someone had just done the same thing to me. "I would have gone to jail." The thought cracked me. Tears blurred my vision while deep. burning sobs rolled up my throat. Visions of being handcuffed again, hauled away like some druggie to be locked away in some foreign women's prison for years—I couldn't deal with that.

I'd endured so much, knowing what it felt like to be placed under arrest, seeing Ryan being carted away from me in the back of a police car, the stress, the loss, the lies, the sacrifices.

It was finally too much. Too much.

Ryan fell to his knees next to me on the floor. "Hey, hey, baby. It will be okay. Shh."

I was shaking so hard, I couldn't breathe. How much more of this could I endure? "Cocaine, Ryan? I can't. I want to go home. Take me home."

Ryan wrapped me in his arms, pulling me between his thighs. "Shh. I'll take you home." He kissed my hair repeatedly, rocking me. "It's you and me, babe. You and me. Everything else is getting cut off. I promise. No more. I won't put you through this ever again." I heard his words but I couldn't believe them. What was to stop another Lauren or Nicole or even a disgruntled manager from repeating this nonsense?

Nothing.

WHEN RYAN said we needed some air to clear our heads, he wasn't kidding. He warmed my body as he leaned into me to share the view out of my side of the helicopter, after insisting that we follow through on our vacation instead of heading back to the States. He hadn't let go of my hand since we left the hotel in Rome. I think he was afraid I was going to end things with him.

This trip to Polignano a Mare was definitely a distraction.

Ryan was on edge, pacing around our room after we'd checked into the hotel. I opened the doors, finding some breathing space out on the balcony.

Ryan wrapped his arms around my stomach. "Nice view."

Staring out at the vast Mediterranean Sea, that was an understatement. "It's pretty spectacular. Thank you. It was a good idea to come here. Thank you for bringing me here."

He kissed my neck, lingering for a bit. "Don't leave me, Taryn."

I looked up into his eyes, shocked by his words, seeing the fear in his eyes. It gripped my heart.

"You've been so quiet. I'm scared to imagine what you're thinking."

"I'm not going anywhere, Ryan. I love you."

He sighed and met my lips for a kiss. "Thank God. I don't know what I'd do without you. You're my heart, Taryn. My heart. I don't know who did this to us, but I swear I will find out. There will be retribution."

I shook my head. "Nothing good ever comes from revenge. And any attempt at retaliation will surely bring more problems. No, our best bet is to just let it drop."

He rested his forehead on my shoulder. "I can't."

"Oh sweetheart, you have to. News like this gets out and your picture will be splattered all over the press again. No. No more. We've been humiliated enough and I'm sure something will happen to put us back in the news regardless. You'll sneeze, I'll have a jealous fit when you have to kiss another actress—it's always something."

"No. Not this time. I'm done, Taryn. All I ever wanted to do was make movies but all that brings is fucking pain. No more. When we return to the States, I'm announcing my retirement."

I looked into his eyes again, not sure if he was actually serious. "Ryan, you love being an actor. It's what you do."

He kissed my lips, then rested his forehead against mine. "Not anymore."

RYAN WASN'T kidding. After we'd returned to the States, he canceled all public appearances, turned down all requests for magazine cover shoots, interviews—everything. He was contractually bound to promote the final *Seaside* movie but that was it.

Trish and I had talked him out of making any formal public statements about being retired, arguing that it would only bring more attention. That was something Ryan definitely didn't want, especially since we had to settle out of court with the photographer he'd punched.

Instead, he devoted himself to building our house—to the point where we practically moved into my pappy's fishing cabin so we could closely monitor the progress on our adjoining land.

Marie had taken an assignment with Mike in L.A., working private security for a young actor who'd been plagued by an unwanted stalker. She was traveling so much, it was hard to keep up with her, and I missed my best friend. But I also knew she had a job to do; making chitchatty cell calls while protecting someone was frowned upon and could get you killed.

Ryan's entire celebrity life had ground down to a halt. After a few weeks of the media wondering where he'd disappeared to, other celebrities and their antics took over the front page and Ryan slipped off the radar.

Well, that was until he went grocery shopping with me and was recognized. He'd even grown a light goatee to disguise himself. It didn't work.

One evening, when I was finally able to talk about the white powder incident again, Ryan had built a nice fire in the fireplace and we curled up on the floor to make a list of suspects.

My money was on Nicole Devin. Lauren had brought her on the European press junket and both of them were always sniffing.

Kyle was also in Rome, but he wasn't on the top of my list. He'd pretty much ignored me while he hit on the leggy redhead who gave me the envelope and she seemed more than receptive to his charms. But he did have motive and opportunity.

Marla Sullivan was also a suspect to consider. But even though that nasally bitch would probably get her kicks seeing Ryan fall from grace, she didn't strike me as the type who'd solicit someone to get her cocaine.

And then there was David. Bitter, jaded, asshole David. Ryan had fired him officially in Rome, making sure the weasel knew in no uncertain terms that he'd been terminated. He'd flown off the handle when Ryan had called Aaron, his agent, to make sure the message was passed through the ranks. After that, David spent quite a bit of time scowling at us and bending Marla's ear, so imagining that those two got together and plotted against us wasn't too far-fetched.

There were quite a few others that had been on the press tour, but we'd quickly eliminated everyone who had no motive.

But we didn't make any progress, other than making a short list of people we wanted absolutely nothing to do with ever again. We also had the satisfaction of knowing that whoever did try to set us up had failed miserably.

DESPITE ALL the things keeping Ryan busy, I could tell he was unhappy. The sadness was always there, itching like a scab that just wouldn't heal. I was starting to feel guilty, as if he'd given up acting for me.

As much as I enjoyed being out of the spotlight, I knew in my heart that Ryan wouldn't be satisfied with life if he didn't act.

It was in his blood.

It was what he excelled at beyond all other things.

In front of the camera was where he belonged.

Ryan wasn't living; he was existing. He was doing everything possible to avoid admitting that he was miserable not working. He didn't need to say it; I could read him well enough to know exactly what plagued him.

We had set October 20 as our wedding date, taking Mike's advice and getting married in the Maldives. I didn't care where we got married; as long as we had a beachside villa to snuggle in, I'd be content.

But as much as I wanted to marry Ryan, I couldn't. Not like this.

I needed him whole before he committed to me and he was anything but whole right now.

That light that used to dance in his eyes was gone.

His spirit was broken and it tore me apart.

I HAD convinced Ryan to return to Seaport with me under the guise that I had business in the bar to attend to, but really I needed a strong

Wi-Fi connection, which was nonexistent at the cabin. I knew exactly what I wanted to get Ryan for a wedding gift, but I needed time to execute my plan.

Since the pub wasn't so busy, Ryan and I decided to have lunch downstairs. We were dying to sample some of the new entrees Tammy was serving up. Even the apartment smelled deliciously edible.

"Did you call your lawyer back?" I asked, trying not to burn my lips on the piping-hot French onion soup I was drooling over.

Ryan nodded, chomping down on his chicken club panini.

"So you told him no prenup? Are you sure?"

Ryan looked me square in the eyes. "Positive. You need a prenup? I've got one better." He grabbed a Mitchell's Pub napkin from the holder and borrowed a pen from one of the new waitresses. I watched him carefully write on the napkin, doing his best not to tear it. "After all, this love affair of ours really began when you gave me your phone number. Remember?"

I was dying to know what he was writing. I drifted my foot over his under the table. "Of course I remember. I wrote it on a Mitchell's napkin."

"Which I still have, by the way." He smiled fondly. As soon as he was done writing, he placed the napkin across the table in front of me.

I smiled and laughed when I read, "*I promise to never fight over the toaster.*" It meant a lot that he said that, knowing Marie and Gary had fought over such trivial things.

I motioned for the pen, grabbed another napkin, and wrote, "*I promise never to steal your toaster or your TV.*"

He laughed and tapped on the napkin. "That better include the remote when I'm watching hockey, hon. Just saying. Give me the pen. It's my turn." While he was busy writing, I went behind the bar to grab my own pen.

I came back to "*I promise to buy you your own TV so we never have to argue about what's on.*"

That made me laugh. "I draw the line at golf." I wrote on mine, "*I promise to never take your money.*"

He stared at me for a few moments and frowned. "That's a given, Tar." The note he passed back stated, "*I promise to never complain about you spending my money.*" "And when it comes to stuff for the house, I'm drawing the line at curtain shopping. If you love me, you'll never ask me what I think about that sort of stuff."

"Okay, no curtain shopping. Got it." I put his message on our growing pile and wrote, "*I promise to be a good wife.*"

His smile was mesmerizing. I got back, "*I promise to be a good husband.*"

I gazed at the warm, blue eyes that meant everything to me. "We keep this up and we won't have to write wedding vows."

"Well if that's the case." Ryan quickly scribbled another one. "*I promise to start every day and end every night telling you I love you.*"

I wanted to climb into his lap. I leaned over the table and kissed him. Trying to top that was difficult. I ended up writing, "*I promise to love only you until I take my last dying breath.*"

"Till death do us part," he whispered. His next message: "*I promise to love you forever.*"

"Well then . . ." I slapped "*I promise to always tend to your needs*" in front of him.

He tapped on my napkin vow and grinned. "I'm going to hold you to this one. You know how needy I am."

His next message said, "*I promise to only have eyes for you.*"

That one struck me right in the heart. I scribbled on the bottom of it: "*For as long as we both shall live?*"

He gave me a warm smile, a wink, and a nod.

I quickly followed up with "*I promise to give you a blow job on your birthday.*"

Ryan held the napkin up, looking like he'd won the lottery for a few seconds, and then asked. "Only on my birthday?" He sorted through the small pile and held up the one that said I'd always tend to his needs. "I'm thinking I'm *way* more needy than that, babe. My needs are constant."

I quickly scribbled, "*I promise no matter how needy you get, to never make you sleep on the couch.*"

Ryan held up a finger for me to wait while he wrote on his napkin, "*Do you promise to talk to me when something is bothering you?*"

I wrote on the bottom of it, "*Yes, and you?*" and passed it back to him.

Ryan wrote his "*Yes*" underneath mine and underlined it twice.

My next vow stated, "*I promise to find a way every day to make you happy.*"

He sorted through the sheets and held up the one with the BJ on it. "Can we edit the BJ vow to daily/hourly? That would make me really happy and tend to my needs all in one shot."

He looked so damn hopeful. How could I ever deny him anything? I sifted through the vows, finding the one that said he'd love me forever. "Since you promised, I'll see what I can do."

He reached across the table, took my hand in his, and pulled it to his mouth, placing a tender kiss next to my engagement ring.

CHAPTER 26

Marry Me

RYAN'S ESCAPE FROM celebrity life only lasted so long. He'd stopped looking at scripts and considering multimillion-dollar roles, which worried me more than he could have ever realized. I knew his career, his A-list status, could only take so much before it would be too late to revive. Fortunately, the premiere for the second *Seaside* film, *Day of Dawn*, sucked him right back into the spotlight.

It was almost as if he'd never left. I didn't realize how much I'd come to miss his hectic lifestyle until we didn't have it anymore. I missed Mike and Marie even more, and I was grateful that Ryan had another junket to get through so we could all be together again.

I was so glad that the premiere was in L.A. It made making secret deals that much easier. While Ryan was occupied with the press, I met with two influential producers and negotiated a two-hundred-thousand-dollar purchase. I had to sell all of my family's vested interests in the wineries to do it, but investing in Ryan's future was worth it.

Everything had gone off without a hitch.

Things continued to look up two weeks later when we were in Berlin. Mike had stormed into our room, Marie tight on his heels, a grin the size of Texas plastered on his face.

"You will never believe this shit," he announced, holding out his phone. "I just got a message from my buddy, Nix, who does security out in L.A. If this doesn't brighten your day, I don't know what will."

I'll never forget the smile on Ryan's face when he heard Nix say in his message that David Ardazzio, forty-five, was arrested today and charged with possession of 3.5 grams of cocaine.

Justice had been served. We were all able to put that horrible incident behind us.

BUT THAT was four weeks ago. I was now looking out at the breathtakingly beautiful blue water from the lanai of our gorgeous beachside villa in the Maldives, getting prepared to make my final walk as a single woman. My groom was off in his parents' villa, probably feeling just as nervous as I was.

"Your hair looks awesome," Marie said, spraying to hold it in place. She had twisted my hair into a loose ponytail, fluffing it out to make it look even thicker.

I lightly swatted at her. "Not too much spray. I want Ryan to be able to touch it without it breaking off or getting his fingers stuck."

Tammy had my sandals in her hands, smiling as if she had a secret. "Shoes or no shoes?"

"You've got to go barefoot, Taryn," Janelle answered. "It's the only way."

Tammy smirked. "Well, you may choose not to wear them, but you have to at least read them."

Read them? "What are you talking about?" She was really excited when she handed over my brand new Stuart Weitzman strappy bridal sandals. I turned them over, seeing a handwritten note penned on the bottom of one of the shoes.

You're my best friend,
You're my love,
You're my life.
I can't wait to
make you
my wife!
Love, Ryan

My breath hitched as his message sank in. I covered my mouth, holding back from sputtering. I had envisioned the man I would marry one day, and Ryan had transformed that image into an unbelievable dream. I wasn't nervous anymore. I knew with absolute certainty that my Ryan wanted me just as much as I wanted him. Tears dripped down my cheeks as I handed the shoe over to Ellen so she could see her son's sentiment. Tammy was already reduced to a pool of tears, spurring me to cry harder while I was reprimanded for ruining my makeup.

A few minutes later, Ryan's mom uncovered my dress. It was white silk and had a thin ribbon crisscrossed over the open back. I received four nods of approval when I first tried it on but my teeth chattered now as I shimmied into my dress.

Janelle unwrapped my three solitaire diamond necklace—my "something new" wedding gift from Ryan. I had my mother's beaded hair comb that she wore when she'd married my dad tucked into the top of my loose braid—my something old. As much as I wished my parents could have been alive to see me on this special day, I knew that they were looking down on me. They would be in the sunrays that cracked through the clouds and the warm breeze that tickled my skin.

Jill had a small box in her hand. "This is from Joe and me. Thank you for letting us be a part of your day, Taryn. It means the world to your father and to me that you've included us."

I hugged Jill, giving her a kiss on the cheek. "Thank you for being here."

She touched my face and smiled. "Go on. Open it."

My fingers fumbled opening the lid. I gasped when I saw the exquisite sapphire bracelet. "Oh my God! This is beautiful!"

"It's your something blue," she said happily.

"Thank you so much! Would you help me put it on?"

Leave it to Janelle to yank me back into reality with her humor.

"We have to go soon. This is the easy part. Not killing him when he ticks you off is the hard part."

I gaped at Ellen as she was nodding her head. "You're telling me there are times you want to kill Ryan's father?"

"Oh yes," she admitted. "It's not often —maybe three or four times a year—but it definitely happens."

I looked over at Tammy.

She agreed. "I threatened to kill Pete on the flight over here."

Marie was finishing trussing up my dress when I caught a sparkle on her hand. Her fingers were bare when she was putting on my makeup.

I spun so fast I almost fell over. I grabbed her hand. "Oh my God! What is this?"

Marie smiled coyly. "Mike proposed to me last night!"

I was so elated; it was hard to contain myself. *Could this day get any better?* I hugged her fiercely. "How? When?"

Marie giggled. "Last night. He took me for a walk on the beach and told me that he's never felt this way about anyone and he can't imagine living life without me."

I think I screamed. I definitely know I was tugging hard on her left hand, taking in the huge rock on her finger.

"He then said he didn't want to wait to ask; he didn't want me to think that he was motivated by your wedding or anything."

I hugged her again, whispering my words of congratulations. This was a big step, but I knew no matter what happened, I'd always have her in my life. After all, her three-bedroom house was physically attached to mine—separated only by a breezeway.

Marie gave me a smile. "What say we go get you married? Ryan Christensen is waiting."

There was a gentle knock on my door before I saw my birth father, Joe, peek around the corner. "Everyone dressed and ready?" he asked.

I smiled at his awkwardly innocent expression. Ryan had flown Joe and his family here for me as a surprise. They may not have been my parents growing up, but without Joe, I wouldn't have this moment, and that meant a lot to me.

THE SUN was just starting to set when I walked on shaky knees down the beach. I held Joe's arm as he steadied me.

I felt instant relief when I saw that Ryan was in fact standing next to the man who would be officiating our union.

As soon as I saw him there with his hands clasped in front of him, his hair gently tussled by the ocean breeze, that breathtaking smile he wore just for me—nothing else mattered. This man was my everything.

He'd been there for me through thick and thin, through the good, the bad, and the ugly. Our vows on silly napkins were framed and mounted above our bed for us to always remember and never take for granted.

As soon as Ryan took my hands in his, all of my nervous worry drifted off into the breeze.

I WOKE with a smile to tiny kisses peppering my shoulder. I think I actually fell asleep with this same smile on my face. I rubbed my hand over his arm so he'd know I was awake.

"Good morning, Mrs. Christensen," Ryan said while kissing my neck. It tickled.

"Good morning, husband." I glanced at the clock. "More like, good afternoon, husband." I rolled over and nuzzled into his chest. "Do you think they'll miss us if we skip out on dinner, too?"

Ryan laughed softly. "I have no desire to get out of bed. That's why they invented room service."

I drifted my fingertip around his new platinum wedding band;

my vow of "Yours Forever" engraved inside. I was hoping that this all wasn't just a dream. "I never gave you your wedding present."

Ryan smiled and kissed my forehead. "I think that thing you did last night when you were on top and riding me was a wonderful gift."

I nudged him. "Smart-ass. Hang on." I crawled out of bed.

"Gift number two—my wife completely naked."

I wrinkled my nose at him, retrieving the thin box I had wrapped in gold foil.

He flipped the box over, inspecting both sides. "What's this?"

I crawled back under the blankets. "A dream."

His eyes narrowed. "A dream?"

"Yep. Dreams only come true if you point yourself in their direction."

His fingers combed his hair back. God, that was so damn sexy. I hoped I'd never lose my appreciation for it.

He slid his leg over, tapping me in the foot. "Is that so?"

I fluffed the pillows under my head and nuzzled back into his side. "Yep."

"Well then, I guess we're tossing your birth control pills in the garbage."

He caught me off guard. "You ready for all of that?"

He shrugged. "I'm ready for whatever life throws our way."

"Good. Now open your gift already!"

Ryan slid his thumb under the edge of the paper, tearing it off. "Gold paper, eh?"

"Yep. That's what it is. Inside is your golden ticket, too."

He shook the box, separating the lid. A tinge of panic seeped through me when he frowned at my gift.

"A script? You bought this?"

"Yep. TLC Productions owns it."

He examined it again. "This is that script you were so adamant about me pushing. Tar, no one wanted to back it."

I shrugged. "That was then. We have a meeting with Jeff West-field at Universal whenever you're ready to put on pants again."

Ryan was astonished. "You got producers on board?"

I grinned proudly. "Yep. Anna Garrett's in on it, too. Word on the street is that *several* big-name directors are interested."

He grinned at me. "You were a busy girl."

"Yes, I was. Sneaky."

He pursed his lips. "You really want me to act again? After all we've been through?"

I rubbed my hand over his heart, noting the subtle change of pitch in his voice. "Yes, I do. It's who you are. It's what feeds your soul. The rest . . . the rest is just details."

EPILOGUE

Just Rewards

BREATHE—JUST BREATHE... *nope, holding my breath works better.*

Okay, okay ... I can do this. It's not so bad now. Breathe again, slowly. In and out, in and out. I hope this doesn't take too long. I don't know how much longer I have until it's officially too late.

My, those curtains are ornate. That sure is a lot of fabric hanging down from the ceiling. I wonder if all those lights make it hot up there?

I can't believe Johnny Depp is sitting right behind me. This place is packed with everyone who is anyone in this business. I wonder where Bill and Ellen are sitting? I'm glad they're here in the building somewhere. Save them another trip.

Oh damn, here comes another one. Hold on. Oh wow that freakin' hurts! Breathe through it, just breathe. One one thousand, two one thousand, three one thousand.

Why now? You couldn't wait one more day ... even a few more hours? Impatient little bugger—just like your father.

Breathe through your mouth, Taryn. No one will notice if you don't make it look obvious.

Should I tell him?

I probably should.

If I say something now, he's going to freak. He's already freaking out. No, don't say anything—not yet. I can make it. But will I be able to make it to the car?

Count. Need to count. Why didn't I wear a watch? Oh yeah, I have on this one-hundred-thousand-dollar diamond cuff bracelet on loan from Harry Winston. Count the value of diamonds I'm wearing ... bracelet—

one hundred thousand, necklace with drop pendant two one hundred thousand, heavy earrings pulling on my earlobes three one hundred thousand . . . just breathe.

Okay, they are getting closer together. Those last two were less than three minutes apart. Tell him.

"Ryan?" I squeaked. "Honey, um, how much longer, do you think?" I adjusted my sitting position.

He looked at his watch that I got him for Christmas. "Maybe ten more minutes. Why? Are you nervous?"

"No," I breathed out, feigning a smile. "Not nervous."

"Tar, you're sweating. Are you okay?" He turned his body to face me.

I breathed out through my clenched teeth. "Bad timing."

His eyes opened wide. "Timing?"

"Yep—a few days ahead of schedule."

"Are you saying it's time? Like now is right *now?*"

"I can make it. But after they make the announcement . . . Mmm." *Take quick shallow breaths. Oh shit, that hurts. I hope I don't stain this four-thousand-dollar custom gown.*

"When did they start?" he asked, trying to remain calm but not succeeding.

"Earlier," I replied.

"While we were out on the red carpet?"

"Before that," I whispered, trying not to moan from the pain. "When she was doing my hair and makeup."

"Taryn! That was almost five hours ago! We need to go now. Do you need to go now? Tell me if it's time to go now." Ryan started to panic. He was already lurching out of his seat.

"Calm down," I breathed between waves, grabbing a hold of his tuxedo jacket sleeve to pull him back into his seat. "We're okay. But I suggest we don't linger."

As soon as I spoke, another blast of excruciating pain shot through my abdomen. I held my breath and scrunched my eyes together. They were coming on faster and harder.

"Taryn, if we need to go, we go. I'm not going to get this anyway. It's not worth putting you two at risk."

"You don't know that." I hated that he was being so pessimistic. He was brilliant.

"We can go if you need to go," he said, already sounding defeated. "It's all right."

"No," I stated adamantly, gritting my teeth. "We're not going anywhere until we hear your name called and they open that envelope. This is your moment. A once-in-a-lifetime moment. I can stick it out."

I breathed through my pursed lips. "But I think it's safe to say that the little tiger and I are not going to make it to any after-parties tonight," I said, trying to add some levity to the situation.

"Honey," he started to argue.

"Stop. There is no way in hell we are going to miss this," I whispered. "We have time." I had to lie—he was freaking out enough for the both of us.

I grabbed his hand. We would go through this together, just like we'd done everything else . . . united as a team.

The enormous curtain dropped over the stage after the lifetime achievement award presentation ended.

"The camera is going to pan to us when they announce the names," he leaned over and whispered in my ear, inconspicuously wiping the bead of sweat trickling down my neck. "Just so you know."

"I know. The camera has panned to us before. I can see when the red light goes on. I'll be wearing this same smile, I promise." My smile was permanently glued in place. "But it will be bigger."

"Are you sure you want to wait?"

"Yes, just shut up already." I grinned at him. "I wouldn't miss this moment for anything in the world. Well, you know what I mean."

His shiny leather shoe slid across the floor and tapped gently into my low heels.

The music started.

"Please welcome two-time Best Actor Academy Award-winners

Daniel Day-Lewis, Tom Hanks, Sean Penn, Jack Nicholson, and Dustin Hoffman."

Ryan squeezed my hand and I could see he was holding his breath, too. He took my elbow in his hand and helped me stand up to applaud the actors walking out onto the stage. The five amazing and talented men each announced one of the five actors who were nominated for this year's Best Actor in a Leading Role.

I smiled so proudly as Ryan's name was announced. Jack then joked that he was willing to share the sex symbol status if he had to. We all laughed when he said that if you didn't know who Ryan Christensen was, just ask any female between the ages of six and ninety-six and they would surely tell you all about him.

Ryan, of course, rubbed his forehead while smiling.

I was so proud of him—it made enduring the pain worth it.

No matter what happened with his career from this moment forward, Ryan was now—officially—an Academy Award nominee.

He squeezed my hand tightly, holding our hands to his lips. We both stared off at the floor while each second seemed to last minutes.

"And the Oscar goes to . . ."

I held my breath while the excitement and contractions rippled through me.

Ryan was holding my hand so tightly my fingers were starting to tingle from lack of circulation.

"Ryan Christensen—*Isletin*."

I think I screamed.

Everyone stood up to applaud—everyone. Famous directors, famous celebrities, famous musicians—the entire audience rose to applaud for him.

Ryan looked like he'd been punched in the gut. He leaned over and kissed me. I couldn't stop smiling; I was giggling with excitement. He kissed me again, rubbing his hand over my stomach before heading toward the steps to the stage. Tears of happiness slipped from the corners of my eyes.

You could see in his priceless expression that he was shocked to have won. I hoped this overwhelming moment wouldn't render him speechless. He was visibly shaken; at least, visibly to me. His mouth hung open in disbelief and his hand nervously rubbed his forehead as he climbed the steps.

I stood and clapped for him, enduring each painful contraction bravely as my body readied itself to give birth to our child.

I watched in awe as five of the most iconic actors of our time each shook Ryan's hand and gave him congratulatory pats and hugs. His heroes, his mentors, the men he had admired and respected and strived to be like all welcomed him into their ranks.

Ryan stood at the podium with his beautiful gold statue clutched in his hands, still completely blown away that his dream had come true. He had finally achieved his greatest desire. His career as an artist had reached its highest peak.

"Thank you," Ryan said repeatedly into the microphone. His eyes were locked on mine.

Everyone sat down in anticipation of his acceptance speech.

He had been dragging his feet about preparing until finally last night I made him write down what he would say if this moment were his.

"Thank you," he said again. "I am so very humbled to be standing here in front of you all." He scratched his forehead. He was so nervous.

Breathe, honey, just breathe.

"I didn't think this goal would ever be obtainable, until someone convinced me otherwise and told me that dreams do come true if you point yourself in their direction." He winked at me.

"That person is my lovely wife, Taryn, to whom I owe everything for this moment. She said two years ago that this script was Oscar-worthy and I'm so glad I listened to her." He breathed out and chuckled nervously, shaking his award as proof.

I blew him a kiss from my hand and rubbed my stomach, pushing a tiny foot back down. Our child was anxious to have his birthday.

He reached for the little piece of paper that he had tucked away in the inside breast pocket of his jacket. Written on it were the names of people he wanted to thank. I was glad he wore the silver tie and white shirt with his black tuxedo. He looked absolutely dashing.

Another powerful contraction hit. I grasped the armrest of my seat and locked my arms to help me ride out the pain. This one was difficult to smile through.

He looked out over the crowd. "I promise to make this quick as my wife just informed me several minutes ago that she's been in labor for the last five hours, and I really don't want her to give birth to our first child down there in the front row."

The audience clapped and laughed.

He continued to fumble with the paper, nervously trying to unfold it. "Tell him to hang on, honey, I'll be done in a minute."

The audience laughed again.

He scratched his eyebrow. "I just let it slip," he muttered, mostly to himself, but everyone heard him. He shrugged, looking back at the five men still standing on the stage with him.

"Oh well, now the tabloids don't have to speculate any longer and the paparazzi can stop asking. It's a boy!" He looked out at the audience and grinned proudly.

The audience roared and applauded.

"I don't know which moment of my evening tonight will be bigger, receiving this award or the arrival of my son, but I am grateful that they are happening on the same day so I can truly say that *today* is the best day of my life." He took in a few quick breaths, trying to calm himself down.

"I'd like to thank my mom and dad, who are also here somewhere. Dad, yell so I know where you are."

I heard his father yell "here" from somewhere in the back right corner of the grand theater and couldn't help but smile.

Ryan continued his acceptance speech, thanking the amazing director, the crew, his co-stars, and expressing gratitude for being recognized among the other four nominees.

I was relieved when he finished, and I smiled when several of the superstars who flanked him patted him on the shoulders as he made his way to the side of the stage.

"Mrs. Christensen, are you in need of an ambulance?" a female stagehand asked, helping me as I tried to stand up.

"No," I breathed in between contractions. "Just my husband, his parents, and our limo."

FOUR HOURS later, on March 9, at 11:40 P.M., Mitchell Ryan Christensen made his debut. Seven pounds, ten ounces; twenty inches long— a perfect miniature version of his father, blue eyes and everything.

"OH IT'S good to be home," Ryan sighed when we walked through the front doors of our six-thousand-square-foot, completely pretentious log home. Our five-day-old son was bundled up in his cozy blue fleece outfit with little puppy dog appliqués on the toes. He was strapped securely in his car seat carrier and slept the whole way from the airport to his home.

I immediately started unbuckling him so I could hold him again.

"Call the crew, let 'em know we're back. I'm sure Pete and Tammy will rush right over to see him," he chuckled, dragging our suitcases into the entryway.

"I will in a bit. After we get settled."

Ryan took his Oscar out of the felt pouch that it was wrapped in. "I'm going to put this in the office."

"No!" I quickly yelled. "Put it on the fireplace mantel where we can appreciate it."

He smirked.

"No one ever goes in your office, honey. Put it up here." I moved a few of our wedding pictures, making a place for his statue.

I sat down on the couch with the baby, showing him the picture of all of us on our wedding day.

I smiled at the big grin Pete wore on his face when the picture was taken. The trip was a second honeymoon for Pete and Tammy, and sometime during that week, Tammy got pregnant. Their daughter, Madison, was six months old now.

We all joked that maybe our son and their daughter might get together one day. You never know which way the wind is going to blow. Anything is possible.

I had spent all that time worrying about what I would do with my life, only to have it all work out on its own. Wife, mother, partner, lover . . . it was all very fulfilling.

Ryan joined me and the baby in the sunroom that overlooked the lake. He propped his feet up on the coffee table and tossed the box he had in his hands onto the floor.

"Let me hold him now," Ryan whispered, slipping his hands around our tiny baby boy. "Come here, little guy. Come to Daddy," he crooned.

Seeing my husband so in love with his son filled me completely.

"What's in the box?" I asked, watching the sun set over the tops of the evergreens.

Ryan chuckled. "Scripts. More scripts."

"Well, you know, honey, you only have *one* Oscar. If you had two, we'd have matching bookends."

He grinned at me. "Nah, I already have one. Maybe *you* should work for the second one?"

I rolled my eyes. "I don't think so. Besides, I'm not an actress."

"But you could be, if you try. After all, you're the one who keeps saying that anything is possible if you point yourself in the right direction."

So he'd been paying attention.

I slid my leg down the table and kicked him in the foot.

Bonus Chapter

WHILE I WAS developing the story line for Love Unrehearsed, I had the following passage in the beginning as the original dream sequence. I chose to cut it because I didn't want to give too much away up front. I wanted Taryn's adoption to be a surprise.

While developing Taryn's character, I wondered what Taryn's last memory of Joe might be that caused her to have those recurring nightmares of the "boy with the black hair" and what caused the division on her mother's side of the family.

I have fond memories of being my father's "beer fetcher" while he and the other men in the family played horseshoes, so this scene partially comes from my childhood. We went to the same place to have a family picnic every year and the gray cinder-block garage on the property always seemed to be a few degrees cooler than the blistering heat outside.

The little blond-haired girl sneaking ice cubes with a Barbie in one hand? That was me.

Enjoy.

Grandfather's Fishing Shack

July 4, 1986

WHOA! CAREFUL THERE, sweetheart!"

Daddy's big hands latched tightly under my arms and he spun me up into his arms. The big metal U that Uncle Al threw tumbled right past Daddy's foot and fell softly like a whisper in the grass.

"Taryn, you know better. I don't want you to get hit with one of those horseshoes. It will hurt." His bottom lip stuck out like a big fat worm. It looked funny. I wanted to grab it and squeeze it.

I sat perched in my daddy's arms and watched Uncle Al make funny faces as he swung his arm, aiming for the rusty spike sticking straight up from the ground. The clanging noise was kind of frightening. I imagined that the horses that wore those big shoes had to be enormous. Like elephants. Or even bigger. Like houses. I wished I could ride one.

"Your cheeks are red, Daddy."

He placed a few kisses on my face. "So are yours, peanut. Mommy has to put more lotion on you. Who do you have here? Who's this bum?"

I waved my dolly's arm to say "Hi." "This is Ken. He's my boy-friend."

"Boyfriend, huh?" He raised his brow, giving me that one-eye look. "What happened to his pants?"

I pointed over to my tiny splash pool, where they were floating. Barbie was still in the water.

"Do I need to have a *talk* with him about showing his heinie in public?"

I giggled. "Can you take me in the big water now?"

"That's two points for us," Dad said proudly, shifting me on his hip to retrieve one of the metal U's.

I patted his cheek. "Daddy?"

He smiled his toothy grin at me and I knew I had him. "In a minute, sweetheart. Daddy and Uncle Al need to mop up Uncle Andy and Bean Man over there first. You don't go anywhere near that lake without Mommy or Daddy. Understand? You stay here where I can see you."

I watched Uncle Al drink from the brown glass bottle, tilting it far into the sky to get every last drop. "Hey, Taryn?" Uncle Al called. "Would you do me a big, big favor? Would you throw this away in the garbage and get me and your, um, daddy new bottles from the garage? You can be our special helper."

Happiness swirled inside me as I ran. I wanted to be the best special helper in the world.

It was cooler in the big gray garage than out in the hot sun. I dug my hands into the chilly coldness of the little squares of ice in the bucket, sneaking one into my mouth like Daddy does. It made my teeth hurt but it felt wonderful on my tongue. They were like special, secret candies that turned into water. And I had a whole pile of them to enjoy.

"Hey! What are you doing in there?"

The voice shook me hard and I immediately dropped the ice cube. I had been caught. I almost wanted to cry.

Joey. I recognized him right away, although he still frightened me when he yelled. His hair was the same color as my bedroom at night and it covered his eyes, but his teeth were really white. I wondered if he knew the monsters that lived under my bed.

"You are way too young to drink, young lady," he said sternly. Joey walked a little funny. Like one leg didn't work right. He took the brown bottle out of my hand and put it back in the ice. I wanted to ask him if his mommy painted his fingernails black like that. I thought boys didn't wear nail polish.

Crouching down in front of me, he pinched the wet strand of hair that hung over my eye and placed it behind my ear.

"You are so beautiful." He sighed. His eyes crinkled with happiness. "Just like your mommy." I beamed proudly. My mommy was beautiful.

"And look. You're already losing some teeth. How old are you now?"

I held out my hand and spread my fingers proudly, remembering to tuck in my thumb.

Joey sat down on the floor and crossed his legs. "Wow. Four. You are getting so big and so smart. God, I wish your mommy was here to see you. She'd be so happy. You have her hair and looks, you know."

I felt my eyes scrunch. My mommy's hair was brown, like the crayon I used to color dirt and trees. Not sunny buttercup yellow like mine.

He leaned in closer. "Can you keep a secret? Just between us?"

Maybe Special Secret Helpers had secrets, too.

"You and I have the same color eyes. See?" Joey's eyes were deep blue, like the color of the sky outside behind the puffy cotton clouds.

He looked sad, which made me sad. "I wish you had a chance to see your mommy again. But unfortunately, you can't."

I didn't like that. I wanted to run to her now. "Why not?"

"Because," he exhaled, rough and hard, "your real mommy lives in heaven with the angels."

Now I really wanted to cry. And get mad. "No she doesn't. My mommy is over there."

Joey was looking right in my eyes. "Listen to me. Your mommy's name is . . . was . . . Kelcie. And she loved you very much. But . . ."

I wondered which cloud in the sky was heaven.

"Damn, I wish I had more time. I wish . . . I don't know when I'll get to see you again," Joey said softly.

"Why?"

"Do you know what the army is?"

I nodded and scratched my nose. "Are they going to paint you green?" Green might be better for him than black. It's the color of grass.

Joey smiled and laughed. "No. But I'll have to wear special clothes and all of this will be cut off." He ran his hand through his dark hair. "Maybe you could write to me while I'm gone and draw me pretty pictures. Would you do that?"

I wished I had paper right now. He reminded me of a zebra. I could go get a crayon from my bag of toys if I ran fast enough.

"Taryn, sweetheart. Look at me. Remember, this is our secret. You can't tell anyone. Promise. Promise."

I nodded. He took both of my hands in his.

"God, I've made so many mista—" He sniffed a few times. "But I'm going to fix it." He nodded. "I want to be better for you." He looked me right in the eyes. "No matter what anyone ever tells you, no matter what you hear, know that I love you. I have *always* loved you. Remember. Da—Joey loves you. You'll always be my little girl."

A tear fell down his cheek. And then another. I wrapped my arms around his neck because big hugs always make the tears stop.

"My baby girl. I love you, so much."

"I love you, too," I whispered.

"Always keep your head up and be proud. Don't let *anyone* walk all over you. Ever. Be strong. Listen in school. And . . ."

Joey dropped his arms the second my daddy came into the garage.

"What? What's going on in here?"

Daddy sounded grumpy and he didn't look happy with Joey. I tugged on his shorts. "Daddy? Can you take me to see Kelcie?"

He looked down at me. "What?"

I really wanted another ice cube and to go bye-bye in the car with the cold air blasting in my face. Maybe there's a big swimming pool in the clouds. "Kelcie. In heaven. Can you take me?"

Daddy grabbed Joey by the shirt. "What did you say to her? Tell me right now!"

Joey yelped and tried to push my daddy. They danced into the big silver ladder that was on the wall and it scared me when it crashed down to the floor. Daddy hit Joey in the face and his white teeth turned red.

Daddy grunted. "You stupid, irresponsible moron. You're nothing but a piece-of-shit, good-for-nothing punk."

So many people came running and everyone started yelling. Mommy grabbed Daddy's arm and pulled. "Dan! Let him go!"

I covered my ears because it hurt. I wished Ken was with me.

We both needed someone to play with.

Acknowledgments

I'D LIKE TO thank the following people who've helped me turn this dream into a reality, listened to my lunacy, and guided me with a gentle hand:

First and foremost, a huge thank-you to my husband, Cory, and son, Ryan, for giving me the time, space, and freedom to drift off into imaginary worlds every day. You've allowed me to realize that dreams really do come true if you point yourself in their direction. Having the complete support of your family makes all the difference in the world.

This novel would not be what it is without the tireless help from my dear friend, Janeia Hill. She read, critiqued, listened to me cry, told me not to give up a thousand times, brainstormed, tweaked, kicked me in the butt, made long-distance calls, and gave her time and support generously. Thank you for holding my hand during this amazing journey.

To my best friend for the last twenty-five years, Marie S. You mean the world to me.

To my gals in the FP: Your friendships are invaluable and mean the world to me. Thank you for your support, your wisdom, and your unwavering love and acceptance. I am truly blessed to have each of you in my life. I cannot imagine having a better crew to make history with.

To all of my Facebook and Twitter friends—you make every day special.

To my ninja editor, Amy Tannenbaum, thank you for believing in me. You had me at "hungrily devoured," but then again, I think you know that.

A huge thank-you to the wonderful people at Atria Books. Judith Curr, you are an awesome woman and I thank you from the bottom of my heart for giving me a chance. And to your tireless team: Chris Lloreda, Kimberly Goldstein, Samantha Cohen, Alysha Bullock, Dana Sloan, Jeanne Lee, Paul Olsewski, Ariele Fredman, LeeAnna Woodcock, Julia Scribner—thank you for making this novel all it can be.

A special thank-you to my dynamo agent, Jane Dystel, and her equally fabulous cohort, Miriam Goderich, at Dystel and Goderich Literary Management. Thank you for giving me a shot and taking me under your beautiful wings.

To learn more about Tina Reber, visit her at:

Facebook
facebook.com/authortinareber

Twitter
@TinaReber

Atria Books/Simon & Schuster Author Page
http://authors.simonandschuster.com/Tina-Reber/409197896

Author Website
www.tinareber.com